*When Mary Rose married Gabe,
she never expected to share him.*

Enter the riveting world of the Brides of Gabriel.

Mary Rose is a young Mormon convert
of aristocratic English blood.

Bronwyn is a beautiful young widow with a baby.

And Enid, Gabe's first love,
holds a secret she's never revealed. . . .

THE SISTER WIFE

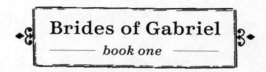

Brides of Gabriel
—— *book one* ——

DIANE NOBLE

AVON

INSPIRE

An Imprint of HarperCollinsPublishers

Published in association with the literary agency of Alive Communications, Inc., 7680 Goddard Street, Suite 200, Colorado Springs, CO 80920. www.alivecommunications .com

HarperCollins books may be purchased for educational, business, or sales promotional use. For information please write: Special Markets Department, HarperCollins Publishers, 10 East 53rd Street, New York, NY 10022.

FIRST EDITION

Library of Congress Cataloging-in-Publication Data is available upon request.

ISBN 978-0-06-196222-6

10 11 12 13 14 OV/RRD 10 9 8 7 6 5 4 3 2 1

I dedicate this series to the One who walks beside me
through life's valleys and leads me to the high places;
to the One who never fails to show me
the breadth and depth of His tender mercies;
to the One who fills my heart with an abundance of grace
and wraps me, flaws and all, in a love so strong
that nothing I do can ever change how He feels about me.

I also dedicate this series to those loved ones
who have given me the gift of better understanding
this story and its characters
because you are living examples of God's amazing
forgiveness, grace, and compassion.

I celebrate you and thank God that you are in my life!

Love is patient, love is kind.
It does not envy, it does not boast, it is not proud.
It is not rude, it is not self-seeking,
it is not easily angered, it keeps no record of wrongs.
Love does not delight in evil but rejoices with the truth.
It always protects, always trusts, always hopes, always perseveres.
Love never fails.

1 Corinthians 13:4–8 (New International Version)

PROLOGUE

June 28, 1842

Mary Rose refused to let the sting at the back of her throat turn to tears. Instead, she drew in a deep breath and reached over her swollen stomach to pluck weeds from between the rows of cabbage seedlings.

Distant wedding bells tolled, calling the Saints to the meeting-house for the ceremony sealing seven brides to fewer than half as many grooms.

As her knees sank into the loamy soil she gave little thought to the *peau de soie* gown she wore, one of the few stylish frocks that had survived the voyage and wagon journey to Nauvoo, and the only one with an Empire waist that could accommodate the child growing beneath her heart.

She plunged her hands into the wet soil and breathed in its soft fragrance, thinking of fertility, life, and growth. She would miss her garden; it had been a source of wonder since Bronwyn had helped her turn the first spade of soil. Throughout the winter and early spring they had talked about their plantings: radishes, beans, winter squash, corn, and herbs for cooking; and then they had convinced Gabe and Griffin of their need for an arbor, and amid laughter and loving conversation, all had worked together to build it. Neighbors had supplied them with healthy cuttings of grapevines and berries. With a sense of wonder, she had watched her early garden thrive and felt an almost motherly pride at the tender new growth.

Little more than a year earlier, back in England, the thought had never entered her pampered head that she might take such pleasure in the sun's warmth on her shoulders, or the burial of a seemingly dry and dead seed that days later pushed its tiny sprout-self through the soil, reaching for the same sunlight that gladdened her heart.

From the henhouse, several yards beyond the garden, the low clucks of hens and higher-pitched peeps of the fresh-hatched chicks brought another wave of sorrow. How could she leave this place she'd grown to love in such a short time? How could she leave the man she loved with every ounce of her being? Especially now that she carried his child?

The gentle breeze cooled her warm cheeks, and she drew in a deep breath, concentrating on the rhythmic music of the farm: the breeze rattling the oak leaves by the creek out back, the low murmurs of hens and chicks, the nickering of a newborn colt, and the answering neigh of his mother in the pasture.

Her eyes filled, and her heart ached with longing as if she'd already hitched the carriage and driven off.

She tried not to think about Gabe's decision as betrayal, but it crept into her mind anyway. Along with words from an Elizabeth Barrett Browning poem . . . *It was thy love proved false and frail.* She pictured her love's face, imagined him with Bronwyn, and for all her strength and determination to hold back her tears, this time she could not. She whispered the words to the last stanza of the poem. The words, as if driven deep with an ice pick, stabbed too close to the marrow of her bones.

> Ah, Sweet, be free to praise and go!
> For if my face is turned too pale,
> It was thine oath that first did fail,
> It was thy love proved false and frail,
> And why, since these be changed enow,
> Should I change less than thou.

She drew in a shuddering breath to regain control. She needed every ounce of strength to get through this day. She plunged her hands into the earth, drawing comfort from the cool soil and willing away the pain in her heart.

Gabe had taken his time, first with his toiletries, then with the new trousers and gleaming white shirt Mary Rose had laundered just the day before. As he prepared himself to look his Sunday best, she'd fled to the comfort of her garden. Now she heard his footsteps and pulled the brim of her fancy bonnet lower to shade her face from the unblinking sun. And to avoid her husband's eyes.

"Why are you out here? It's almost time to go," he said.

She kept her back to him. "You shaved twice."

He laughed. "I often do that. Why should this be any different?"

"You know why."

"I thought you'd decided to come with me," he said. "I know it's difficult for you, but you gave me your word." If he'd yelled or cursed, it would have hurt less. But as always, he was too much of a gentleman, a loving, kind man, to resort to such behavior.

"I changed my mind," she said as he helped her stand. She gave him a small half-smile. "A woman is entitled." In truth, she had dressed for the occasion, planning to make an appearance so none would be the wiser when she hitched the horse to the family buggy and rode off in the night. But when he preened in the mirror and then pulled out his straight razor a second time, she knew that no matter what she and Bronwyn had discussed, Gabe had plans of his own.

He drew her into his arms. "Mary Rose," he whispered, his breath tickling her ear. "It isn't right or proper that you stay away, today of all days. It is your duty to welcome Bronwyn into our family, standing by my side. I would not have done this without your consent."

She slipped out of his embrace and, pushing back her bonnet, looked up at him in rage. But when he swept his hair back in that way he had, raking it with his fingers, her heart overflowed with the same love she'd had for him since the day they'd said their own vows.

"My consent?" She almost laughed. "As if, after Brigham told me my options, I had any say in it. You do not have my consent, regardless of what the elders—and you—might tell others."

A fancy coach pulled by a single white horse slowed to a halt in front of the house. The groom tipped his hat toward Mary Rose and Gabe and smiled. He'd come to take Gabe to the marriage ceremony.

"Please, Mary Rose . . ." Gabe moved closer and lifted her chin, forcing her to look into his eyes. "I wouldn't do this if it had not been decreed by God."

Her grandfather had always said she inherited his ironclad spine. Today, her spine felt weaker than the stem of the milkweed that lay wilting in the sun at her feet.

She straightened, preferring the image of iron wrapped around her spine. "In your heart of hearts," she said softly, "can you really go through with this?" She started to touch his cheek, but instead first brushed off her hands. When she lifted her hand again, he caught it and covered it with his own. Turning it he kissed her palm. "We love each other," she said. "Our love has more to do with us than it does with the Saints. We fell in love before we even met the Prophet." She searched his eyes for the response she longed to see—a love for her that would be strong enough to say no to the Prophet's new edict. It wasn't there.

"Love has nothing to do with it. I've already explained—and really, Mary Rose, I shouldn't have to keep going over it." He let out an exasperated sigh. "I've not fallen in love with Bronwyn. I don't deny I care about her. Her husband was my friend. But every ounce of love in my heart is yours alone."

He touched her face, letting the backs of his fingers trace her jawline. The gesture was so familiar, so intimate, she could easily have wept. Except for the image that came to her: her husband touching Bronwyn's face with the same intimacy, perhaps as soon as this night.

She drew in a deep breath and then stepped back, crossing her arms. "Perhaps the Prophet has interpreted God's edict correctly—and I'm not the only first wife in Nauvoo to wonder—but tell me, Gabe, why did it have to be Bronwyn? And why does it have to be marriage? We could bring her into our home, take care of her and Little Grace for as long as they need us. Surely you recognize my feelings in this matter and can respect them. I would be happy to have her join our family under those conditions."

One didn't go against the Prophet's edicts, which came from God himself. But she also knew that the Prophet chose Gabe to care for an important martyr's widow because of his rising status within the hierarchy of the Church. If Mary Rose hadn't been so appalled over the whole thing, she would have laughed at the shading of the real truth: The strikingly beautiful Bronwyn, with her vivacious charm and hardy Welsh constitution, was a gift, perhaps a reward, for Gabe's loyalty and friendship.

"Bronwyn and her child are alone and in need," Gabe said. "She has no way to provide a home for herself or food for Little Grace. Bronwyn is a good woman. You are the dearest of friends, already as close as sisters." He shrugged. "It will be a happy household, just as Joseph has borne witness of his own. Brigham reports the same contentment among his wives. Initially jealousy and backbiting prevailed, but now his wives love each other like family. Sisters."

Mary Rose sighed. "The trial period has only been one month. That's hardly long enough to tell what the outcome will be once the, ah, sleeping arrangements are made, children are born, tasks divided up."

She hesitated, turning her gaze away from him. A butterfly landed on the dying milkweed then fluttered away. "We've talked about this, you know," Mary Rose said, her eyes following the insect as it landed on a clump of squash blossoms. "Bronwyn and I."

She didn't like the way the corner of his mouth quirked into a slight smile. "And what was your conclusion?"

"Should you decide to go through with the wedding, you will have no . . . rights. Conjugal rights."

"So you two have decided that for me." His eyes twinkled with amusement. "See, you're behaving like sisters already."

Mary Rose saw no humor in his words, but she had no time to voice her opinion before he continued, grabbing her hands again. "You know the Prophet speaks of anointing me as one of his chosen twelve soon. So, my dear, it is my honor and my responsibility as a priest, as an apostle of God, to carry out the revelations given by his representative on earth, our Prophet. I have no choice." He paused, then added, "If I did have a choice . . ."

"You would go through with it anyway," Mary Rose said softly. "But I have a choice. I can accept Bronwyn into our household or not."

She looked into Gabe's eyes without flinching, and when she spoke it was with quiet but desperate firmness. "If you go through with this, I won't be here when you return."

Silence fell between them as he stared at her. "Surely you can't mean that," he said. "You're . . . with child. Where would you go, what would you do?" She looked deeper into his eyes, trying to fathom the emotion she saw there. He paused and then swallowed hard. She had indeed taken him by surprise. "I love you. No matter what else happens, I swear to you I will always love you. You can't leave me, Mary Rose. Please say you won't."

"You leave me no choice, my love." She lifted her chin. "I don't wish to but I must."

"Exactly where would you go?"

"Back to England, of course."

For a long moment he didn't speak. In front of the farmhouse, one of the horses whinnied and the other danced sideways, sending up a cloud of dust. "You do not want to do that," he finally said.

His tone made her heart stop for an instant.

"What do you mean?"

"Have you forgotten?"

She frowned.

"Once sealed to me for eternity, you simply cannot leave. You would be accused of apostasy—"

"Which would bring harm to your reputation, to your authority as a priest and apostle?" She fought but failed to keep the bitterness from her tone.

He stepped closer, his eyes piercing hers. "That's of little regard compared to what would happen to you."

She tilted her head, still frowning. "What do you mean?"

"Apostasy is not condoned. Apostates, those who leave, are caught and returned." His voice dropped. "Punished." He stared into her eyes for a moment, and then turned to go.

Mary Rose stared after him, gaping. "I don't believe you," she said to his back. "I'm free to leave at any time."

"I thought you loved me," he tossed back, his voice thick with agony.

"I do. More than life itself," she whispered, her eyes brimming. She doubted that he heard her. "But not enough to share you with another."

She watched until he'd almost reached the carriage, and then she turned back to the garden. She knelt, and then gasped as a searing pang shot through her abdomen. She doubled over and attempted to shout to Gabe, but the sound wouldn't leave her throat.

He didn't break stride as he continued toward the waiting carriage. Seconds passed, then an even greater jabbing pain made her cry out.

A gush of water warmed her legs and soaked through the *peau de soie* into the garden soil around where she lay. She'd barely caught her breath when, too soon, another contraction came, pulling her into a dark velvet place: images of seedlings growing in the sunlight, of a blossoming milkweed torn from the ground and bleeding white blood, then, finally, of Gabe bending over her, his eyes filled with tears.

She heard him say to someone standing beside him, "The baby is coming. We need help." Then the velvet black darkness enveloped her again, and she surrendered to it.

PART I

The face of all the world is changed, I think,
Since first I heard the footsteps of thy soul . . .
—Elizabeth Barrett Browning

ONE

Liverpool, England
July 1, 1841

Lady Mary Rose Ashley sat at a forward angle on the plush velvet seat of the ornate carriage, gazing one minute out the window, wanting to jump, and the next minute, while swaying with the carriage, believing the long uncomfortable ride would never end. It didn't help that on either side of her sat a fidgety four-year-old twin and, across from her, their equally fidgety and considerably louder seven-year-old brother.

Grandfather had gone to great trouble to arrange for passage for them all, but she became more certain with each turn of the carriage wheel that he kept something from her. Two days ago when the team pulled the vehicle away from the portico and into the tree-lined lane, he had not turned for a last glimpse of the massive Salisbury manor house and manicured estate grounds that had belonged to the Ashley family for centuries. And it seemed his sadness grew with each mile as the groom urged the high-stepping grays on toward the harbor where the *Sea Hawk* anchored.

Mary Rose peered out the window, searching for her first glimpse of the tall ship in the distance. As the landau raced along the cobbled streets of Liverpool, Mary Rose studied her grandfather's lined face, wondering again what his stooped shoulders and downcast eyes hid from her. Whatever it was, in her heart she knew all was not right with her grandfather, the Earl of Salisbury.

"Lady," Pearl said, tapping Mary Rose's arm. "Am I going home?"

"Yes, Boston is your new home. You'll like it there."

"Will I like my new mama?" The catch in her young cousin's voice twisted Mary Rose's heart. She reached for the child's hand. Four-year-old Pearl and her twin, Ruby, sitting on her opposite side, asked the question at least a dozen times a day. She gave them each a confident smile. "Yes, dears, your new mama can't wait for your arrival."

Coal sniggered. "How is it you can know this? She's a relative so many times removed and so far away that I daresay—"

Grandfather held up a hand, palm out, and arched a bushy white brow in the boy's direction. "And *I daresay*, you should be aware of your elders and speak to them in a genteel manner, young man. You may have lived only seven years, but you are old enough to behave properly. You should also be aware of your sis-. ters' feelings. A positive outlook will pave the way to success in your new home."

"It didn't help in the last three," the boy muttered, turning to the window.

"That doesn't mean my words are false," Grandfather said. "It only means that all of you must try harder to fit in."

Ruby sniffled, her eyes wet with tears. She glared at Mary Rose's grandfather. "Don't talk to my brother tho mean." Her lisp was more pronounced when she was unduly stressed, and it seemed lately that the child's impediment was evident nearly every time she spoke.

The manor house had been nothing but mayhem since the children had blown in like small tornados in the company of Grandfather's brother and his wife, both looking white-faced and frazzled. The twins were identical, their only distinguishing mark a tiny heart-shaped beauty mark just below Pearl's right ear. And, of course, Ruby's speech impediment. It helped, when observing the two from a distance, that Pearl insisted on wearing her hair plaited so her beauty mark would show.

Still holding Pearl's hand, Mary Rose reached for Ruby's and gave them both a gentle squeeze. "Grandfather is merely trying to help your brother understand that you must adjust to your new circumstances."

Pearl looked up at Mary Rose with large eyes that seemed far too wise for one so young. She didn't speak, but Mary Rose wondered if the child was remembering all the times such an adjustment was called for since their parents sailed to the Sandwich Islands to evangelize the natives. She wondered how parents, no matter their fervency for serving God, could leave their children half a world away.

"I want to live with you," Ruby said, squeezing Mary Rose's hand. "I loved the manor houth, but a thip will be even better."

"Where you live is your mother and father's decision to make," Mary Rose said, "and she's very clear that Grandfather and I are to see you safely to her cousin Hermione's lovely home in Boston. We cannot go against her wishes."

"The thip!" Ruby stood up and pointed out the window.

Her twin scrambled to the window and reached for the handholds that hung above it. She'd discovered two days ago they were the perfect height for swinging.

Mary Rose sighed. "Pearl, child, you need to get down now.

Not only is it inappropriate comportment for a young lady, but you could fall and hurt yourself."

Pearl kept swinging.

Coal got to his knees and pulled the velvet window curtain back further. "I see it," he shouted. "The clipper. The *Sea Hawk*. She'll beat the record, I just know she will." In his excitement he bounced up and down on the bench seat.

The carriage rocked and swayed more violently than before, and Mary Rose felt more light-headed than ever. The sight of the crew hoisting sails on one of the taller masts did nothing to assuage her jitters.

Charles, the groom, did some fancy maneuvering in an attempt to crowd into the queue of waiting carriages but missed his first try. Then, racing along the cobbles, he tried the maneuver again, this time bypassing the queue and heading onto the wharf itself.

Mary Rose grabbed the edge of the seat, her knuckles white as they rumbled onto the wharf's rough wooden planks.

A wave of apprehension swept through her. She had gone along with her grandfather for all the wrong reasons. Her gaze darted to the *Sea Hawk* then back to her grandfather's face.

His smile broadened as he looked out over the harbor to the open waters beyond, and he exhaled a long sigh of contentment.

Mary Rose couldn't help but wonder if they had made a colossal mistake.

Even before he caught a glimpse of the passengers inside, Gabe MacKay knew the gleaming black landau, drawn by four high-stepping grays, meant trouble.

The rig clattered recklessly down the narrow cobbled street that ran parallel to the Liverpool wharf. Without so much as a nod to the other drivers, the white-haired groom cracked his whip above the team and bullied his way through the crowd to the front of the queue of waiting carriages. Gabe drew in his breath. It was only by God's good grace that someone had not been knocked down or run over by the vehicle.

The groom halted the grays precariously close to the edge of the wharf, just a few dozen carriage lengths from what would surely be a plunge into the brackish waters of the harbor. Gabe bit back an oath and stepped closer to the *Sea Hawk*'s rail to have a better look. One false move by that high-strung team and the fancy rig, along with its inhabitants, would be in grave peril.

Apparently oblivious to the danger, the groom set the brake and, in one slapdash move, wrapped the reins around the brake handle to keep it from slipping. Without a backward look, he stepped down from his driver's perch, rounded the carriage, and opened the glass side door with a flourish.

"Bannock's boucle!" Gabe muttered under his breath.

Just when he thought things couldn't get more perilous, a passel of children tumbled from the vehicle with shouts and giggles loud enough to carry across the wharf to the quarterdeck where he stood. A tow-haired lass of about five years exited by hoisting herself up like a small monkey to swing from the carriage door; another that looked to be the same size pushed around her then clambered up to the groom's bench; and an equally tow-haired lad sporting a stick-straight Dutch boy haircut, a sailor's suit, and striped stockings raced toward the horses, chose the one he wanted, then struggled to mount. *Ach!* But of course it would have to be the gray in the lead, the one that was already snorting and rolling its eyes.

The elderly groom may as well have been wearing blinders as he went about his business, unloading trunks and valises of varying sizes from a second landau that had pulled alongside the first. Neither the groom nor the stevedore now helping him noticed when the lass on the groom's bench clambered from her perch, unfastened the reins, then, struggling under the snarled weight of them, climbed back to the bench and pretended with great relish to drive the team.

Gabe heard a chuckle and turned as Captain Hosea Livingstone, master and commander of the *Sea Hawk*, strode toward him. His friend's expression said he was as worked up as Gabe about the clipper's maiden voyage and her challenge to break the world's speed record.

Gabe had overseen the building of the *Sea Hawk* for Messrs. R. Napier and Company on the River Clyde. Originally from Nova Scotia, Gabe had studied the architecture of shipbuilding in Boston, and then sailed to Scotland three years earlier to learn more about his trade from a company known to be the best in the world. He began as an apprentice to the head architect, but his skill quickly became apparent and he soon began working side by side with the aging but brilliant builder. The *Sea Hawk* had a curve and elegant beauty to her that, Gabe felt, was beyond compare. As the project was completed and the sale to Cunard neared, Gabe recommended his friend Captain Livingstone to Cunard, who as owner was in charge of hiring the captain and crew.

Now they were on the *Sea Hawk*'s maiden voyage to assess the ship's performance and endurance, in what they hoped would be the fastest Liverpool-to-Boston transatlantic crossing made to date.

He couldn't think of anyone he'd rather be with on this important voyage. Still watching the landau and its inhabitants, Hosea chuckled. "You are about to be introduced to the Earl of Salisbury and Lady Mary Rose Ashley—and from the look of things, perhaps it's better done at considerable distance." He laughed again.

"I have to admit their arrival has proven amusing." He smiled. "Though something tells me trouble's afoot, earl or not."

The fog blanketing the harbor during the predawn hours had rolled out to sea, leaving only a few ribbons of mist in its wake. The foghorn had stopped its mournful cry, and now, above the gusts of wind, Gabe heard snatches of conversation rising from the wharf where passengers and well-wishers had begun to gather.

The sounds mixed with a coarse seagoing ditty some stevedores were singing as they loaded cargo in the hold.

Just then a high-pitched *whoop-whoop-whoop!* carried toward Gabe. He turned to see that the little ruffian had indeed found a foothold and swung himself across the nervous gray's back. With another whoop and a holler, he bounced up and down as if riding across an imaginary prairie while shooting an imaginary bow and arrow at an imaginary target.

He extended his telescope and raised it to his eye. He had it in mind to stride to the landau himself, remove the lad from the gray, and then have a strong word with whoever was in charge of the little lad and lassies. Was there not a parent aboard that fancy carriage? Or perhaps a nanny? A nursemaid?

As if he'd summoned her with his words, a young woman appeared in the landau's doorway, and in the circle of his glass. She attempted to remove the giggling tow-headed monkey child from her swinging perch on the door, but the child took flight and landed on the ground in a tumble of skirts, petticoats, and pantaloons. Unhurt, she scampered toward the stack of varying-sized trunks the groom and stevedore had just unloaded and climbed them like stairs. Then she plumped down on top of them, her chin resting in her hands and elbows on knees in a highly unladylike pose.

Gabe couldn't help chuckling as he moved the lens back to the woman who, appearing dismayed, called something to the two children out of her reach—the boy still making Indian calls and bouncing on the nervous gray, the girl pretending to drive the rig by flicking the reins she'd unwound from the brake. A lethal combination, to be sure. Surely the woman could see that. He prayed the horses had grown used to such rowdy behavior and wouldn't bolt.

As if she felt his gaze, the woman glanced up just long enough for him to take in the unruly auburn ringlets beneath a straw bonnet, its froth of netting and ribbons framing a fair face, and the sparkling hue of her eyes, a shade of gold-green the Atlantic took on just before sunrise. She wasn't beautiful by the standards of the day, too thin and willowy, but something about the shape of her face, the fullness of her lips, and the dark fringe of eyelashes that framed her eyes captivated him.

Then she disappeared back inside the landau.

He kept the glass trained on the doorway. Seconds later she reappeared in the telescope's lens, this time to help a quite elderly man from the carriage.

Gabe turned to make a comment to Hosea, but his friend had left to talk to Mr. Thorpe, the chief mate. He returned the glass to his eye. It was indeed Langdon Ashley, the Earl of Salisbury. His manner, his dress, bespoke his position in life. Besides, Gabe had seen him caricatured in many a broadside sold by the hawkies in Glasgow's Saltmarket. His rotund midsection, his mustache with its magnificently waxed and spiraled ends, beaver-skin top hat, and waistcoat that strained its seams to fit his portly frame had long proved irresistible to political artists who penned his exaggerated image. He was well known for his relish for adventure, and had written extensively about his excursions in the Rocky Mountains with Sir William Drummond Stewart, a Scottish nobleman, the oddest of mountain men of the time.

The earl seemed to be searching for something . . . or someone. He stood near the landau, leaning on his cane. His gaze took in the *Sea Hawk*, and he scanned the knots of passengers and well-wishers on the wharf. After a moment, he stopped and seemed to recognize someone on the pier below Gabe.

He followed the earl's gaze to a man standing just yards from the dock, close enough for Gabe to see him well even without the telescope. He was a commanding presence: tall and slender with light brown hair that curled under just before reaching his shoulders, a curious style and not one often seen in England or

Scotland. More charismatic than handsome, he seemed to have a powerful hold on the small cluster of people who stood around him, appearing to hang on his every word.

Gabe caught snatches of his conversation before the winds whisked most of the words away. "Good of you to come, brothers and sisters . . . You'll be following soon, of course . . . You'll find America is a new world, your life with the Saints an exciting new . . ." He gave instructions that Gabe couldn't pick up, and then he gestured toward the earl and his party. "By all means, let them know you're here to see them off."

His accent was unmistakable. And his delivery bordered on oration. A preacher perhaps? If so, a preacher as American as Daniel Boone's coonskin hat or Jim Bowie's knife. But why would the Earl of Salisbury seek him out? And who were the people standing around him? They were mostly families, and rather impoverished in appearance at that. Crossing the Atlantic by clipper ship, especially this clipper, cost far beyond what most Englishmen could even dream of paying.

He was still pondering the connection between the earl and the preacher when a child's frightened shriek pierced the air.

For a moment, dead silence hung like a pall. Then another shriek, this time louder. The carriage—with the boy on the wildly rearing gray, the little girl in the groom's seat—had lurched forward, tilting precariously. As the horse reared again, Gabe's heart lodged in his throat. The earl fell to the ground and rolled toward the safety of the wharf. But the woman, frilly hat askew, had pulled up her skirts and petticoats and, holding on to the carriage with one hand, found her footing and catapulted herself into the groomsman's box to reach the now sobbing child.

Gabe kept the rig in sight as he took the quarterdeck stairs three at a time, raced to the outer rail, swung his legs over, and shimmied down a rope. It took all of three seconds to reach the bottom, where he dropped to the wharf.

As he ran toward the landau, he listened for the sounds that too easily could follow within seconds: the clatter of the wagon wheels on the rough wood of the wharf and the terrified screams of the horses just before they plunged into the deep waters of the harbor, dragging the carriage, two children, and their mother to certain deaths.

"Jump!" Mary Rose scrambled to get a foothold near the child as the carriage rocked first one way, then the other. "You must jump now—to the other side. Quickly. Do it now!"

Pearl, for the first time in the fortnight since Mary Rose had taken her under her wing, seemed as immovable as a chunk of granite. Nose running and cheeks glazed with tears, the little girl stared at Mary Rose. She held her hands around the tangle of reins in a seeming death grip. Not a strand of leather remained wrapped around the brake. Mary Rose prayed the apparatus would hold just long enough to get the children to safety.

"Jump to me, then, child, jump to me!" This time she didn't wait for Pearl to act. She flung herself toward the girl and pulled her from the seat. In one swift movement as the horses reared and the carriage rocked, she dropped her gently to the ground, cried after her to run to Grandfather, and then grabbed the reins. The team, following the lead of the gray that Coal clung to, reared and neighed.

With a screech, the brake slid from its shoe and the carriage lurched.

Mary Rose made a grab for the handle but didn't have the strength to jam it into place. In one swift movement, she tightened her grip on the reins and, holding her breath, pulled back. "Whoa, boys," she cried and then, swallowing hard, tried to use a calmer voice. "Settle yourselves. Come now, gentlemen, settle yourselves."

The cacophony rising from the gathering spectators made the team more skittish than before.

"Help uth!" yelled Ruby from somewhere behind Mary Rose. "Thombody, help uth."

"Jump, Coal," Pearl cried to her brother. "You can do it. Make believe you're Davy Crockett. Jump!"

"He'th not going to," Ruby sobbed. "He'th gonna get killed and we're not even to America yet."

The team reared and screamed again, wild eyes rolling. Even Prince, normally as calm as a feeble old cat, rolled his eyes right along with the others and neighed in protest.

And for good reason.

Coal had started screaming like a Comanche again, clinging to the mane of the wild gray in the lead.

Mary Rose's heart threatened to stop beating. "Jump!" she yelled. Until this moment she didn't realize how much she cared about the boy. He'd been merely a relative in her charge to see to his new home. And not a pleasant relative at that. Tears stuck in the back of her throat. If the team broke loose and he jumped, he'd surely be trampled; if he held on, the frightened horse would take him with the entire team straight into the deep harbor waters.

"He'th gonna die," sobbed Ruby from a few yards away. "Pleathe, Lady, don't let Brother die."

The lead horse reared again, and the team, sensing freedom, bolted forward and again Mary Rose yanked back on the reins. Her gloves split as the hard leather sliced into her flesh. Instantly, her palms became wet with blood.

Standing to gain better leverage, she repeatedly yanked. And cried out another command.

Still they ran wild.

"Jump, Coal," she shouted once more. But the boy, clinging to the gray's mane, seemed not to hear her.

The dark waters of the harbor lay dead ahead.

TWO

Mary Rose grabbed her skirts, intending to leap onto the back of the rear horse and make her way to Coal. Her brain—in less than a heartbeat—told her it was foolish to try. The child's screams told her she had to reach him—or die trying. A man seemed to appear out of thin air, racing like the wind toward the lead horse. He grabbed hold of the bridle near the bit ring, trotted with it a few feet, and then brought the team to a halt.

Knees as weak as melted butter, Mary Rose fell back against the upholstered seat of the groom's bench.

She swallowed hard, not daring to look at the team's proximity to the harbor waters. It was enough that she heard the lapping of wavelets against the pilings just beneath the wharf.

"Ho there, Brigham," her grandfather called out from behind the carriage. Holding the twins' hands, one on each side, he hurried toward Brigham and Coal.

Mary Rose took a closer look at the man who had saved them. Brigham Young himself. Saint, Apostle, and missionary to

England, successful in converting her grandfather, less so in his attempts to convert her.

She took a deep breath, wondering how long it would take her to settle the question of Mormonism in her heart and soul. It had taken her grandfather only minutes, it seemed, to embrace his new faith. She remained skeptical, which according to Brother Brigham, as all other converts called him, was perfectly all right. She would come around in God's good time, he assured her.

She watched as Brigham removed Coal from the gelding and placed his feet safely upon solid ground. The boy's face had turned a fiery red, but she could see no evidence of tears. Rather, he seemed to swagger a bit as he walked toward her grandfather. As if he alone had saved them all.

Her grandfather went to Brigham, shook his hand, and then heartily thumped the apostle on the back. "Saved the day, brother," he declared. "Or as they say in America, 'saved our bacon.'" He tweaked Coal's ear. "And you, young man, nearly caused a severe loss of life and limb—and I daresay, not just your own. I have it in mind to send you to live with the green boys during the crossing. Learn proper behavior as well as what happens to young men who do not follow orders. Forty lashes, that's what they get."

Her grandfather meant none of it, of course. The children likely didn't even comprehend that a green boy was merely an inexperienced seaman, usually relegated to the lowliest jobs aboard a ship. But the twins began to bawl anyway. Brigham bent down, said a few words, then patted each on the head and stood again.

Mary Rose stood to test her legs and found they seemed to have regained strength enough to hold her weight, shook the wrinkles from her skirt, looked around for her hat—which had sailed off to heaven knew where—and turned to step down from the landau.

She looked up in surprise to see Brigham standing by the groom's bench, his hand extended to help her.

"It's good to see you again," he said as if she'd simply been on a leisurely Sunday ride in the landau.

When she was securely on the wharf, she smiled up at him. "Thank you for coming to our rescue."

"No thanks necessary. Anyone would have done the same."

"But no one else attempted it." She winced as she lifted a hand to hook an errant curl behind one ear.

Brigham frowned in concern as he took her hands in his, turned the palms up, and peered at the slashes in her gloves and the raw flesh beneath. Then he moved his gaze from her hands to her eyes, his admiration clear. "You were ready to give your life to save the boy. I could see it in your every move."

"I needed to get to Coal." She gave him a wry smile as she repeated his words, "'Anyone would have done the same.'"

He smiled. "You'll make a good Saint, Lady Ashley."

She gazed at him evenly for a moment. "Perhaps."

He lifted her hands to examine them more closely. "These cuts need to be cleansed and treated." Before she could tell him about her honey solution, and that, yes, she had plenty, thank you, he rushed on. "In America we use a remedy developed by the fur trappers—sugar and soap made with beaver's oil and castoreum. I have some already mixed into a salve, if you would like to try it."

She imagined the stench and tried not to shudder. "Truly, it's not necessary." She pulled her hands away from his and smiled. "I have deepest gratitude for all you've done—not only today but during these past weeks, while seeing us through our relocation—and especially for the hope you've given my grandfather. Just the thought of stepping on the soil of the wild frontier again has made him happier than he's been in years."

His light eyes reflected his concern as his gaze moved from her face to her hands once again. "I will send the salve."

She fluttered her fingers. "Truly, you need not bother."

She glanced from Brigham to where the twins played around

her grandfather, the two grooms, and three stevedores continuing to load trunks onto a cart. Pearl, loud and bossy, directed the operation, and Ruby tried her best to be understood. She'd turned red in the face and planted her hands on her waist, elbows sticking out like triangular sails. Coal was nowhere in sight, which was a worry in itself. Her heart filled with affection for her grandfather, who looked as if he didn't know quite what to do next.

She laughed lightly and said to Brigham, "As you can see, I must get back to Grandfather. Thank you again for saving our team and carriage from disaster."

She turned to leave, but he fell in with her as she walked toward the earl. "Your grandfather asked me to employ a lady's maid for you, someone who can also serve as nanny for the children during the crossing. He also asked me to find him a butler."

"Yes, he told me," she said.

"I found the ideal couple, converts heading to Nauvoo. You will meet them soon after you are settled in your cabins."

"Thank you. I'll conduct an interview and let you know if I approve."

"Interview?" He threw back his head and laughed.

She felt her cheeks flush, and it was not from embarrassment. The man didn't know his place. She lifted her chin. "I'll meet the young couple you've hired on our behalf, give my approval if they are indeed suitable, and then let you know my decision."

He laughed again with genuine merriment. "Interview?" he repeated. "As if we had a line of applicants for the position. Lady Ashley, you have no choice." He was still laughing as he disappeared into the milling groups of passengers waiting to board.

Gabe couldn't have missed intercepting the runaway rig by more than a minute and a half. He was relieved the landau and its inhabitants were saved and, of course, thankful, but he balked at the idea that he'd arrived in second place. It didn't help that the crowd quickly and noisily crowned Brigham Young the hero of the day. The word spread quickly that he was one of the twelve apostles of the Latter-day Saints, the new American frontier religion.

Hearing that, he was even more intrigued by the interaction between Brigham and Lady Ashley. Delicate and feminine, every inch of her, but the way she jutted out her chin and cocked her lovely head while speaking with the revered leader of the so-called Saints told him she wasn't afraid to speak her mind. He liked that in a woman, and deemed her elderly husband a lucky man, though the poor old codger likely had his hands full with such a woman of spirit.

Gabe headed to the abandoned carriage. The elderly groom had taken charge of the team of grays as soon as Brigham rather miraculously stopped their forward charge. But now he appeared befuddled, holding the lead horse by the bit ring but obviously unable to leave him long enough to get to the groom's box. Gabe saw his dilemma. One false move by the team and the whole rig could topple into the harbor.

"Need assistance, old chap?" Gabe called out.

"Aye, that I do, sir." The groom looked relieved. "After all this foolery, they're ready to bolt again. If I let go, they may run for it."

Gabe climbed onto the driver's seat, where he found Lady Ashley's fancy bonnet squashed beneath a heap of gray pinstripe that appeared to have once been the driver's unsullied topcoat.

Gabe took hold of the reins, undid the tangle, and then held them as he'd seen other drivers do and attempted to look as if he was something close to an expert horseman.

Together they worked the team, inching forward then back, then forward again. The horses settled, but the gelding ridden by the child flicked its ears back with irritation as the driver manipulated him into position with a slap on the rump.

"I'd better stay beside 'em, mate," the groom said once they were in position to move. "You drive, if you don't mind. Slow and easy does it."

Gabe flicked the reins. But the team didn't move. One of the horses turned to look at him. One of the others snorted. Another danced sideways. Gabe counted his blessings that under most circumstances horses weren't seagoing animals and that his life was better spent behind a drawing board designing ships, or aboard testing their performance. He wasn't cut out to be a horseman.

He gave the team another gentle flick of the reins, and they remained as immovable as the image on a ha'penny.

By now the groom had started laughing, and just yards away, the earl's family had turned to watch. Somewhere in the vicinity of the *Sea Hawk*'s gathering queue of passengers, he heard a guffaw from a knot of grinning stevedores.

"Thank you, mate," the groom said. "I think I can take it from here."

Gabe stepped down from the groom's box but not before reaching for Lady Ashley's frilly straw hat. He dusted it off and tried to straighten the ribbons and fluff the froth of soiled netting as he walked over to her.

"M'lady," he said as she turned to him. "I believe you misplaced your hat."

Her face was as fair as fine porcelain, with the slightest hint of amber in her cheeks and a sprinkling of freckles on her nose. An easy smile played at the corners of her mouth, emphasizing the dimple in her chin that made him think it must have been placed there by an angel's kiss. The merriment in her eyes quickly ripped him from his uncharacteristically romantic thoughts. She'd obviously noticed that the horses in the earl's team responded to his commands to trot by remaining as still as statues.

Gabe was so taken by Lady Ashley—from her willowy figure and slender white neck to the soft color of her upturned lips and flecks of gold in her hazel eyes—that, for a moment, he couldn't speak. Or breathe.

Mary Rose gazed up into a ruggedly handsome face, bronzed by the wind and sun, and took in the touches of humor around his mouth and the corners of his eyes, the color of the ocean just before a storm. She had first noticed him minutes earlier when he hurried across the wharf to help Charles with the carriage and team: The way he carried himself told her that beneath his seagoing garb was a well-muscled and powerful body. Even so, he moved with easy grace that did nothing to diminish the sense of command evident in each stride. Except when it came to horses.

Even so, he seemed to have the ability to laugh at himself. She'd always thought that a critical skill in a man, and she'd seen his in action: no matter what command he gave the team, the geldings merely turned their heads and rolled their eyes in dumbfounded wonder. His grin and shrug as he stepped from the groom's bench, holding her crumpled hat like a prize, told her more about him than a thousand words ever could.

Now, as he stood in front of her, awkwardly turning the brim of her straw hat with strong tapered fingers, she pressed her lips together to keep from giggling. She still hadn't gotten over the look of him in the groom's seat, trying to get the stubborn team to move.

"I wondered where it had gotten off to," she managed as he handed the hat to her.

He gave her an irresistible and devastating grin. "Your actions as you tried to stop the team—pure courage."

Unexplainably, her fingers trembled as she set the crumpled bonnet atop her curls. "All for naught," she said, attempting to tie the ribbons into a bow at her neck. "'Twas Brigham who saved us from certain disaster."

"Aye, Brigham Young," he said. "I've heard much about him just in the past half hour."

She'd never before been drawn to a man in such a way, and in a mere half beat of her heart. She swallowed hard, blinked, and looked down as she tied the ribbons on her hat, taking great care to keep her palms from view.

When he said, "May I help you?" she didn't know whether he'd spotted her injuries and wanted to give her assistance, or if he just wanted to be in closer proximity to her.

Whichever it was, he didn't wait for an answer. He stepped nearer and she tilted her face toward his, about to forget every rule of proper comportment she'd ever been taught and nod her assent.

Then, as if on cue, Brigham Young stepped between them, his eyes bright with interest. "I don't believe we've been introduced."

"Gabriel MacKay." The man gave Brother Brigham a cool look of assessment and then stuck out his hand.

Brigham introduced himself, and then said, "May I introduce the Lady Mary Rose Ashley and her grandfather, the Earl of Salisbury. And please meet the children in their charge, Ruby and Pearl Ashley." The little girls curtsied. Brigham frowned. "Earlier their brother, Coal, was with them." He glanced around, looking a bit puzzled, and then shrugged. "A difficult one to keep track of, that boy."

Gabe barely acknowledged the children or the earl as he savored the word "grandfather." "So, Lady Ashley, you are not married," he said, then bowed his head slightly in greeting.

Before she could respond, the earl rushed forward and stuck out his hand in a friendly greeting. "Gabriel MacKay in the flesh, I do believe. I've read about your work on the *Sea Hawk*."

Brigham joined the conversation, looking toward the *Sea Hawk*, his admiration clear. "I was told by the captain himself that she's your design, bow to stern."

Gabe followed his gaze. Dozens of seamen now mustered on deck, listening to the chief mate's commands. Once at sea they would split into two watches, each under the command of an officer: the second mate and the third mate. As usual, even the cook and the carpenter had mustered right along with the others to receive their orders. The harbor pilot stood off to one side, waiting to take control until the *Sea Hawk* reached the high seas. Gabe took in the curve of the ship's bow, designed to bring her more speed, and he smiled. He would never tire of her elegant design, her solid strength. Now, if her speed would just live up to his expectations.

"My design? Not entirely," Gabriel said. "I just happened to be part of a larger company of builders."

"And you're along to see to her seaworthiness."

"And speed, yes."

The earl moved in closer, his face alight with interest. "To set a new record this trip, eh?"

"Yes, sir. That is our hope."

The earl exchanged a look with Brigham. "That alone makes this crossing worth it all."

Gabe noticed Mary Rose's alert expression, her gaze darting from one to the other as they spoke.

"Yes, indeed," Brigham said. "It does."

Just then Ruby came up to tug at her sleeve and pointed to one of the masts. "Look, Lady! Thereth Coal. Almotht to the top."

"Heaven help us," Mary Rose sighed.

Gabe looked up. "Blac Bullax!" he muttered and took off at a dead run.

THREE

M ary Rose was not one to swoon, but given what she'd been through with her cousins—and now, taking a good look at the quarters she and the twins would occupy for the duration of the voyage—she thought she surely might be given to the popular female malady.

She stood in the middle of the dark, dank cabin, her hands on her hips, and gave it a sweeping gaze. The only light came from some sort of trap door in the ceiling that opened to the deck. It was cracked only inches, just enough to let in a breath of fresh air and a rectangular bar of light. She'd known it would be compact, but she hadn't expected such a miserly space.

The bunk in one corner looked too narrow and short. It was flanked on either side by a small hammock barely fourteen inches wide. The twins spotted the hammocks at the same time, raced across the room and dove into them, squealing and whooping. They soon found they worked well as swings, devising a means to twist each other inside and then let go as the twin within giggled hysterically, then stumbled across the floor as if in her cups.

The only bright spot in the room was a small table and three chairs underneath the hatchlike ventilation window.

The trunks had been delivered and were piled one on top of the other in the center of the small room, and she had no means of opening them without help. The ship began to move out of the harbor, and even the slightest swell gave her stomach a feeling of disquiet. She caught a glimpse of herself in the mirror over a small stand that held a basin and pitcher of water. Her hair seemed to have exploded into a thicket of frizz from the sea air, her complexion had taken on the hue of dying forest moss, and her head ached with worry over her grandfather.

Someone knocked at the door, and she attempted to shush the children as she hurried across the room.

The children didn't shush, and when she pulled open the door, she stepped back in surprise. There, standing in the dark hallway, seemed to be the answer to her prayers—before she'd uttered a single word heavenward, or even thought to ask.

The woman attempted a curtsy but had a difficult time of it. She wore an ankle-length, long-sleeved gray dress that was covered from bosom to hem with a crisp white no-nonsense apron, high waisted, that seemed to accommodate the quite large stomach Mary Rose noticed as the woman straightened. Mary Rose smiled into her eyes. It seemed her new lady's maid was with child, and quite close to delivery, though she was no expert in such matters.

Her dark hair was pulled back into what seemed to be a loose plait, and in her hands were two items: a children's book of verse and a small corked pot. "My name is Bronwyn Carey, m'lady, and I've come to serve you and your children. But Brother Brigham said you wanted to look me over first, see if I'm suitable." Her cheeks colored as she spoke, and Mary Rose was sorry she'd spoken so obstinately to Brigham.

She smiled at Bronwyn. "I can't deny that I said such a thing, but it was because I didn't want Brigham telling me what to do."

"I would've done the same, m'lady."

"I'm glad you're here. My only concern is about your condition." She glanced at Bronwyn's stomach and then back to her face. "'Tis a delicate subject, but Brigham should have given me a hint. You shouldn't be waiting on me or anyone else."

"Me?" Her laughter seemed to float up from her throat. "I'm from hardy Welsh stock." Then she sobered. "Besides, Griffin and I needed to earn our way to America. Brother Brigham gave us this opportunity and we decided it was truly from God. If we hadn't come by clipper, we would have been relegated to steerage on the immigrant packet ship that left last month. Griffin wouldn't allow it, with me in such a condition." She laced her fingers together and rested her hands atop her stomach near her heart, then added, "I didn't want my wee babe to come into this lovely world in a not-so-lovely place. 'Tis a good thing actually that aboard this clipper there is no steerage. I would hate to think of the luxury of my quarters up here, while our brothers and sisters suffer in the stench below."

A mantle of shame settled over Mary Rose. It was such an unusual emotion that at first she didn't know what to make of it. Minutes earlier, she'd complained to herself about her small cabin, and now she wondered at her selfishness when, likely, Griffin and Bronwyn shared quarters half the size of hers, or smaller.

The twins had fallen quiet the moment the woman entered and now came toward Mary Rose and their guest, looking up into her face.

"Hello, little lambs," Bronwyn said and squatted down to their level. "I've been hearing a lot about two very pretty loves aboard this ship today."

Their eyes widened. "You have?" Pearl breathed.

"I didn't think anybody knew uth," Ruby said with just as much awe.

"I noticed you right off, I did," Bronwyn said. "I saw you, lamb, trying to drive that willful team of horses." She was looking at Pearl. "That must have been an exciting ride."

"I thought everybody would be mad at me once I jumped down. But even Brother Brigham patted me on the head."

"And you, love"—she drew Ruby in closer, wrapping her arm around the little girl's waist—"you climbed right up atop the trunks and protected your family's belongings while everything else was going on. Pretty brave actions by you both, I would say."

The twins were quieter than they'd ever been since their arrival at the manor. "I brought a book to read to you. Would you like that?"

They nodded in unison.

"Then I promise, that's the first thing we'll do—right after you take your naps."

Ruby started to protest, but with a smile still curving her lips, Bronwyn held her index finger to her lips. "I want you to make believe you're tiny little mice and tiptoe as quietly as you can to your hammocks. There will be no swinging and no talking or giggling. Understood?"

The little ruffians nodded in agreement and tiptoed across the room to their hammocks. Mary Rose was astonished. Bronwyn Carey had been in their quarters for less than five minutes and the children were completely under her control.

Bronwyn struggled to stand, and when Mary Rose realized she couldn't on her own, she extended her hand to help.

She laughed lightly and straightened her apron over her stomach. "I'm in my eighth month, and hoping to make it at least to Boston before our wee one's arrival."

Mary Rose was still calculating days at sea and over land, wondering what it must be like not to know when or where your child would be born, when Bronwyn interrupted her thoughts. "We must see to cots for the twins. Hammocks are for crew members, not children. I will speak to Brother Brigham about getting them better sleeping accommodations immediately." She walked toward Mary Rose's bed. "And this? Is it suitable for you?"

Mary Rose started to complain about its size, but thought better of it and clamped her mouth shut. Bronwyn, playing Pied Piper without even realizing it, seemed to have cast a spell on them all.

"'Tis suitable indeed," Mary Rose said and then, with closer scrutiny, noted the dark circles under the woman's eyes. "Will you sit with me?" She gestured to the small table beneath the hatch.

"It wouldn't be fitting, m'lady." Mary Rose felt a twinge of disappointment at the reminder of the class difference between them. Soon they would all be equals, at least that's what the missionaries preached, but she wondered how many of the immigrants, from all walks of life, would ever get beyond who they once were, the positions they once held, especially those born into titled families. Was friendship even possible?

"You brought a jar of ointment, which I'm assuming is from Brigham," she said. "Wouldn't it be better to sit while you cleanse my hands and treat them?"

"Yes, m'lady, 'tis true." Bronwyn's quick smile said she understood Mary Rose's sweet deviousness. She reached into her pocket and drew out the small corked pot, set it on the table, then retrieved the pitcher of water and basin from the stand beneath the mirror. With a clean cloth draped over her forearm, she returned to the table. Even in her condition, she moved with grace and kept her shoulders erect. Though she wore servant's clothing, she carried herself with confidence and even pride.

She sat down across from Mary Rose. They were in better light now because of the bar of sunshine streaming through the hatch; and as Bronwyn inspected the cuts, Mary Rose studied the young woman's face. Her bone structure could have been carved by a sculptor, it was so perfect—the delicate line of her jaw, the high cheekbones, and a smooth forehead emphasized full lips and animated eyes so blue they appeared almost violet. But it was Bronwyn's glorious mantle of dark hair plaited and tied with a ribbon that made Mary Rose envious: Not a single unruly curl bounced on the young woman's head. From what Mary Rose had observed in their short time together, it also seemed that Bronwyn was charmingly unconscious of her stunning beauty.

"I think it best to rinse your hands thoroughly before we open the ointment pot." A tiny smile played at one corner of Bronwyn's mouth. "In truth, I think it best to wait until the very last minute to open the ointment pot at all."

"'Tis the beaver oil, isn't it?" Mary Rose said. "You have opened it, then?"

"I didn't have to. Brother Brigham prepared this for you by taking it from a larger container. I could smell it from the hallway even before he opened his door." The crinkle at the edges of her eyes told Mary Rose she was fighting the urge to laugh.

"That bad?"

"And then some, m'lady."

"I've had a weak stomach since we set sail."

Bronwyn poured water over Mary Rose's hands and then patted them dry. "Terrible as it is, Brother Brigham made me promise, m'lady. He held my hand to the Book of Mormon."

"I am having supper at the captain's table tomorrow night. A few doses of this and I'll smell like the dank animals caught by trappers themselves."

Bronwyn smiled and a small laugh escaped her lips. "Let's just have a quick whiff up close and see exactly how bad it is." She popped open the cap, made a face, and quickly recapped the pot. "Oh, indeed, m'lady, 'tis worse than I recalled."

Mary Rose held her stomach, feeling green. "Worse than skunk spray." And across the table, Bronwyn, whose complexion now reflected Mary Rose's own nausea, held her nose.

"Worse than skunk spray mixed with rotten eggs."

They looked at each other and giggled.

"Worse than a barnyard full of cattle with noisy dyspepsia," Mary Rose said.

Bronwyn bent double with laughter, at least as close as she could get to double. She waved her hand in front of her nose. "Whatever was Brother Brigham thinking? He should have sent smelling salts with the potion." She gently patted Mary Rose's hand. "I noticed your honey potion on the stand. I'll be quite astonished if it doesn't work just as well. "

She had just finished swabbing the cuts on Mary Rose's palm when, from across the room, a sleepy little voice said, "Lady, why are you laughing? I never heard you laugh before."

"Liar, liar, panth on fire," another sleepy voice said. "Lady laughth all the time. I heard her."

"My little lambs are awake," Bronwyn said, effortlessly slipping into her role as their nanny. "And maybe now is as good a time as any to tell you why 'tis not a good and kind practice to call anyone a harmful name." Her voice was soft and loving as she spoke to the girls.

Pearl gave Bronwyn a wide-eyed stare. "Is 'liar' a harmful name?"

"'Tis indeed. The idea of such name-calling is taken from a poem written by a man named William Blake."

"Wath he a bad man?" Ruby's stare was equally wide.

"No. But the poem is not one that genteel young women should put in their minds." She walked across the room and helped each of the girls down from her hammock. "Little lamb," she said to Ruby, holding her close, "your mind is like a magic trunk full of treasures. You want to put only the finest and best and noblest thoughts into it."

"Liar, liar, panth on fire ithn't noble?"

"Not at all."

She reached for Pearl, gathering her in. "But I didn't say the bad words," Pearl said, rolling her eyes heavenward with an angelic look.

"And I am proud of you that you didn't," Bronwyn said as Pearl shot Ruby a look of chin-jutting superiority. "But 'tis not a good thing either to put puffed-up pride in your treasure chest."

The child's countenance fell and her chin trembled. "Can it ever get out again?"

"Of course, little love," Bronwyn said. "When you do something good, when you behave well, count it a blessing from God himself, not something you did because you're better than your sister or your brother. Soon you'll find that puffed-up pride will simply fly out of your treasure chest on its own." She placed a hand on the bodice of Pearl's frilly but soiled pinafore. "And that's where your treasure chest resides. Right in the middle of your heart."

She stood and led the children toward the door. "Now, my lambs," she said as they walked, "my guess is that before we read, you might need to go—"

"To the nethethary," Ruby shouted. "And then I want you to read Thimple Thimon met a pieman."

Bronwyn dropped her voice to a whisper. The children quieted immediately, trying to hear her. "When we return, we'll change from frilly frocks into playclothes."

"But we don't have any playclothes," Pearl whispered.

"Lady liketh uth drethed up," Ruby added.

Bronwyn winked at Mary Rose as if they were conspiring together to keep the children occupied and quiet. Then she said to the twins, "There are times for dress-up and times for play. And if you can keep your voices sweet and low as we walk down the hallway, I'll show you your new playclothes. I made them for you, little ones, as soon as I heard about you."

"You heard about us before you got on the boat?" Pearl breathed. "Truly?"

"Truly." Bronwyn pulled the door closed behind her.

Mary Rose wouldn't have believed the change in the girls if she hadn't seen it with her own eyes. Their soft voices trailed off down the hallway, and Mary Rose stared at the closed door. She didn't know whether to be thankful or envious.

It took her less than a heartbeat to choose the former. How could anyone not be completely charmed by Bronwyn Carey, whether Pearl, Ruby, or herself? She smiled thinking of their laughter together. She'd never had a friend; and just now, the thought swept through her heart: If she ever did find a friend, a soul mate, to laugh and share secrets with, Bronwyn Carey would be just the kind of friend she would want.

FOUR

Darkness had fallen when Gabe knocked on the door of the captain's quarters. The captain, sitting at his writing table with the logbook open, laid down his pen, closed the inkwell, and stood to greet Gabe. The two men shook hands, then Hosea gestured to a chair on the opposite side of the desk and Gabe sat down.

The captain, a muscular man with graying brown hair, looked every bit the master of the *Sea Hawk*.

Hosea leaned back, his hands behind his head. "I watched you climb the mast to retrieve the boy. Quite a feat. He looked determined to dangle a hundred and fifty feet in the air no matter what you did or said." He chuckled. "I had a talk with him earlier. He promised to behave himself the remainder of the trip."

"Or . . . ?" Gabe grinned.

"Or I'd send him up there to stay."

"Did he turn pale at the thought?"

"Strangely, he didn't."

Gabe chuckled. "Sir, the boy races full speed ahead no matter what the consequences. And I've only been observing him since this morning. I've never seen such energy or fearlessness in a boy his age."

They were close enough friends for Gabe to drop the "sir" when speaking in private, but he felt Hosea deserved the honor, despite his protests.

Hosea's eyebrow shot up. "And how many children his age—or any age, for that matter—have you been around?" He grinned, showing the uneven space between his upper and lower teeth where they clamped against his pipe. "I daresay, most seven-year-old boys have the same inclination toward mischief." He reached into a side drawer for his pipe and tobacco pouch.

Gabe laughed again, and then seeing a shadow briefly cross the captain's face, he remembered how desperately he and his wife wanted children.

The captain tamped the tobacco and passed the match over the charred surface, puffing softly. From Gabe's observation through the years, the ritual of attaining the perfect light seemed more important to Hosea than actually smoking the pipe.

When he'd finished, he sat back in his chair, partially covered the bowl with his thumb, and drew in a couple of deep puffs. He nodded in satisfaction.

"Mr. Thorpe is at the helm," he said. "Good night for him to take it. What are your preliminaries?"

"Eighteen knots, sir."

Hosea smiled. "Good. Very good. Any chance we'll make it to twenty?"

"That will be pushing it, but with favorable winds, we just might make it to nineteen."

The captain made a notation in the logbook. Then he turned up the lamp on his desk, checked the brass chronometer, and made another. Gabe gave him the details about the last sighting of land and the position of the sun as it set. "I'll report to you again after I take new calculations with the sextant tonight."

Hosea grinned and drew on his pipe. "I'll go with you. Can't let you take over my job completely," he said. "We'll hope for a cloudless night."

It was indeed the master commander's duty to see to all calculations, from the last point of visible land until they reached their destination, keeping the details of each reckoning in his logbook.

Gabe's being on board as observer and calculator for the speed record was new to them both. He grinned at his longtime friend. "I'll try to keep out of your way, sir."

Hosea leaned back and chuckled. "You recommended me as commander of the *Sea Hawk*. That gives you rights others might not have. "

"It didn't take much to convince Cunard, sir. Your reputation preceded you."

At the far end of the captain's quarters, through an open doorway that led to the captain's dining room, Gabe caught glimpses of Mr. Quigley, the ship's steward, preparing the table for supper, and heard clinks of china and glass as places were set.

"You're expected to join me for supper," Hosea said. "I arranged it with Mr. Quigley." He put down his pipe and stood. "Shall we go in?"

"Is anyone else joining us?" He knew it was the custom to invite dignitaries on the first night at sea.

"Knowing you as I do, I can say with full confidence the 'anyone else' of whom you speak will join us for supper tomorrow," the captain said as they entered the dining room. "Tonight is for private conversation, the topic I mentioned earlier."

Gabe chuckled. "Your powers of observation never cease to amaze me, even after all these years."

Hosea gave him a sly smile. "I've known you long enough to read your face like an open book. 'Tis no secret you're hoping to soon catch another glimpse of Lady Ashley."

Gabe laughed. "Now, what would make you think I have any interest in Lady Ashley?"

Mr. Quigley pulled out the captain's chair at the end of the table and Hosea sat down, and then the steward attended to seating Gabe.

Hosea's eyes crinkled as he unfolded his napkin and tucked it under his chin. "Could it possibly be the way you two looked at each other this morning? You looked as though you'd been struck by lightning."

Before Gabe could respond, Hosea added, "Let's ask the Lord's blessing on this food and on our voyage."

After the captain's prayer, the steward sliced pieces off a boiled beef shoulder flavored with garlic and black peppercorns, put them on each man's plate, and then scooped up potatoes from the same tureen and placed them near the beef, adding Yorkshire pudding and covering it all with beef broth. Goblets of Madeira had already been poured and caught the light of the single oil lamp, which swung over the table with each rise and fall of the ship's movement. Hosea lifted his glass to salute the voyage, and Gabe clinked his against the captain's.

"'Tis an honor, sir," Gabe said, raising his wine again toward Hosea's. Gabe was honored to eat with his friend this night. Traditionally, dignitaries were invited on the first night out because fresh food could only last so long in the galley hold. After a few days, the fare turned to only those things that had been pickled or salted and kept in airtight barrels.

The captain read his mind and chuckled. "I can dare to break etiquette with this group of passengers, but had Cunard's name been in the manifest, 'twould be he, not you, my friend, sitting beside me tonight."

"And he would have been had it not been for his daughter's illness."

"Yes," Hosea said, "and I understand it's serious."

"And unexpected, though he's hoping for a quick recovery. He plans to bring her aboard our sister ship for her maiden voyage next month, if the girl is well." He grinned. "Told me himself, though half in jest, that he plans not only to beat our record but that which was set last summer by the *Annie McKim*."

Hosea laughed. "I doubt there was an ounce of jest in his challenge—especially toward the *Sea Hawk*. That alone gives me reason to batten down the hatches and fly across the Atlantic." He glanced toward the steward, standing near the table. "Mr. Quigley, that will be all for tonight. Thank you."

Mr. Quigley inclined his head slightly toward the captain, and then took his leave.

The captain looked thoughtful as he took another bite of roast beef. After he'd finished chewing and lifted the Madeira to his lips, he leaned back in his chair. The glow from the overhead lantern made his face appear gaunt and lined with worry. "I am concerned about my wife, Gabe. I need your advice, your help."

"Anything, sir. You know how I feel about you both."

Gabe and the captain's wife, Enid, had been the dearest of friends since childhood. Both families had migrated from Scotland years before, along with most of the settlers who made up New Scotland, or Nova Scotia, as it was now called. Gabe and Enid became even closer when Gabe's mother, father, and younger sister died at sea. He'd watched them sail from the Halifax harbor not realizing it would be his last glimpse of the family he loved. He later learned that the packet ship proved unseaworthy and could not make it through the mildest of Atlantic storms. All on board had been lost at sea. When the news reached him, grief hit hard.

He'd stayed with Enid's family during the dark days of his grieving, and it was there, during long conversations with Enid, that his passion began to grow to design and build fast, unsinkable ships. Though she encouraged him to pursue his dream, her eyes spoke otherwise. He knew she wanted him to stay on the island so they could be together.

"In Enid's last letter," the captain said, "she spoke of notions that worry me."

"How so?"

"I've always known of her desire to help the helpless, whether human or animal. But lately she has convinced herself she has special abilities to heal animals, whether wild or domestic.

"She's begun correspondence with a man in the new field of veterinary medicine in Glasgow. He encourages her in this undertaking, perhaps too much in my opinion. He sent her materials to study, and has written a book on the subject that will soon be published." He sat back and steepled his fingers. "Gabe, this is no lady's profession. She has no need to tell me how she gets down in the muck and turns breech foals with her bare arm inside the mare. I can well imagine it without her words describing these procedures in detail."

Gabe remembered how, when Enid was a child, she found a fawn in the forest, lost and starving. She slipped it into her house without telling anyone in the family, fed it goat's milk, and cuddled it at night in her bed because the little thing was shivering with cold.

"I consulted with a doctor in London who told me Enid is likely suffering from a form of melancholia, probably because of her inability to conceive. It's his theory that she is trying to make up for the pain of deep loss she feels inside by taking care of an animal's pain. He referred me to another physician who treats barren women. I talked with him when I was in London and he's willing to examine Enid."

"Does Enid know you've done this?"

"I wrote to her last month. The letter went out on a schooner that sailed soon after with a stop in Halifax. She should receive it in time to meet us when we anchor there."

Gabe drew in a deep breath, again remembering Enid when she was a girl: skirts hiked above her knees, feet bare, flame-colored hair blowing wild in the wind as she rode her filly Foxfire bareback along the beach when the tide was out. Her laughter was like music, her shouts joyful as she let go of the horse's mane and reached to the skies, fingers splayed, urging the filly to go faster and faster as she dug into her flanks with her heels. It was no surprise that she cared for horses, or any other ailing or injured animals. The surprise was that Hosea didn't know this about her.

"I suspect you loved her once."

The comment brought Gabe out of his reverie. He hadn't realized Hosea was studying his face, or that his thoughts might be so transparent. "We were friends and schoolmates, confidants and explorers of the island's wild coasts and forests. Love, yes. But not romantic love, if that's what you mean." Though even as he spoke he remembered how, as they grew older, he began to notice how her dark eyes sparkled when she saw him, the wild strawberry hue of her lips, and the way her mouth curved up impishly at the corners just before she laughed. He thought her invincible: If she'd wanted to swing from the moon, she'd have found a way.

And then there was that night just after his parents died when his need seemed too great, and Enid's love for him too dear, her heart too willing to try to make his pain go away. One night in the forest on a bed of moss their emotions overtook their senses. It never happened again; they never spoke of it.

But that was long ago and far away, a time and feeling best forgotten.

The captain offered another helping of beef to Gabe, and then reached for another for himself. He cut his meat, seemingly lost in thoughts of his own.

After a moment he continued. "I want her to see this specialist. I'm losing her to other pursuits and worry that she no longer cares to be mother of our children as we'd always dreamed." He took a bite, chewed thoughtfully, and then wiped his mouth with his napkin. "This physician told me it's well documented that women who have outside interests, who are educated, have a more difficult time conceiving. I don't know if I believe him—or the experts who've documented such a connection between education and childbearing. Rubs against the grain somehow. But there are treatments for barrenness, and that's what holds promise for Enid. I know as a fact how she yearns for children. She's nearing thirty, and it won't be long until it's too late to reverse her barren state. I'm hoping she'll agree."

For a fleeting moment, the image of Enid came back to Gabe, the bareback ride across the still wet sand, the lapping of waves in the background, the shouts and laughter as she galloped. It always seemed to him that though her body tried to grow big enough to hold her wild spirit, and though her limbs grew long and lanky and she had a look of power and grace and raw-boned strength about her, her frame could never keep up with her spirit.

"I want you to convince her to come to London for treatment."

Gabe's eyes widened and he almost choked. He grabbed the goblet of Madeira and took a hefty swallow. "Me, sir?" He laughed lightly. "That will be about as easy as convincing the moon to change its orbit."

The captain chuckled. "Even so, my friend, promise me you'll try."

Gabe sat back, studying the captain. "You know I would do anything for you, either of you. But isn't this a private matter? Truly, I should not be involved, sir." Gabe sipped his Madeira again, this time more slowly. He was not one who took pleasure from drink, but aboard ship, water was a precious commodity and, after a few days out, could turn brackish and cause serious illness. "'Tis you, sir, who need to talk with her." He put his goblet on the table, watching the glittering reflection of lamplight in the deep red wine.

"Sometimes when I speak to her, she seems lost in another world. It's as if she doesn't want to listen to what I have to say, no matter its import. Enid looks up to you . . . you're like a brother to her. She'll listen to you."

"With all due respect, maybe you need to listen instead of speak, sir, let her pour out her heart to you."

The captain was silent for a moment, sighed deeply, then said, "I've tried to do that, but it's the one subject she keeps hidden." He smiled, suddenly, and lifted his glass. "Besides, you have no choice in the matter."

"Because it's a direct order, sir?"

The captain laughed. "Nothing like that. In my wife's letter, I wrote that you have something to ask and will meet her outside St. Paul's on the afternoon we drop anchor in Halifax."

"How did you know I would agree?"

The ship rose on a swell then dipped down violently. Both men instinctively grabbed their goblets. The lamp above them swung, dimmed, then brightened again.

"I've always known that you would do anything for your child-hood friend, even this." He lifted his goblet. "To my sweet Enid and to the two men who love her."

FIVE

When Mary Rose woke the next morning she was surprised to find the children gone. Their bedclothes were neatly pulled tight, small pillows on top and covered with brightly quilted counterpanes she hadn't seen before. Bronwyn had probably sewn them the same day she made the twins' knickers and brightly colored pinafore tops. It seemed there was nothing beyond this woman's capabilities. Surprisingly, the only stab of jealousy Mary Rose felt was one of wishful thinking: She wondered how it would be to think of others with such consideration.

She spotted a note on the stand near her water pitcher. Steadying herself against the movement of the ship, she made her way to it and unfolded the paper.

M'lady,

I have taken the children on a nautical adventure before breakfast, which is at seven bells. I have also spoken to

Mr. Quigley, the steward, about preparing your bath before breakfast bells, as you requested. I will return with the children to help you dress for the day.

The steward has asked if you prefer taking your morning meal in your cabin or with the officers. He also asked if you would prefer your morning tea before or after your bath.

Yours truly,
Bronwyn Carey

As Mary Rose slipped into her lacy dressing gown, she wondered why she was surprised at Bronwyn's obvious intelligence, literacy, and elegant penmanship. Just because she wasn't from the British aristocracy didn't mean she couldn't read or write or know details about poetry, such as the poem by Blake that Mary Rose had never learned.

A light tap at the door broke into her thoughts. She crossed the small room and drew it open. Mr. Quigley inclined his head slightly. "Lady Ashley, I have two seamen with me who will prepare your bath."

Mary Rose stepped aside, and let them enter. "Thank you." Never before had anyone brought a bathtub to her, but here it was, claw feet and all. The men set it in the corner of the square room, nodded to the steward, left for a few minutes, then returned with buckets of steaming water and a stack of Turkish towels.

"Will that be all, m'lady?" Mr. Quigley said when they had finished pouring the water into the tub. He wore a rather odd expression, she thought, as she indicated that it was a lovely bath and that she was grateful.

Then she said, "I would so appreciate a cup of tea, if you wouldn't mind. Cream and sugar with it also."

He bowed. "Yes, m'lady . . . before your bath?"

"Yes, please."

As he walked away she thought she heard him muttering about a scarcity of water aboard, but his back was to her and she couldn't be sure. Scarcity or not, a woman needed her bath. She might be willing to give up the manor house, cut back on the expenses needed for her wardrobe, but one thing she was unwilling to sacrifice was a bubbly soak after a dusty two-day carriage ride with squirming hot little bodies that smelled like wet puppy dogs.

She relished her soak in the fragrant water, congratulating herself that she'd remembered to bring a box of French-milled soap that smelled of lilies. She closed her eyes in pure pleasure and let her hair slip beneath the water, working it into a mass of suds then letting it fan out. Maybe life aboard ship wouldn't be so difficult after all.

It was with great reluctance she stepped out of the tub, wrapped herself with one Turkish towel, and dried her hair with another. She'd just finished pulling on her morning dress when another soft knock sounded at the door. Before she could open it, however, the twins raced in, all smiles, until they saw the bathtub. They were carrying a small wooden bucket between them.

"I don't need a bath," Pearl said, her eyes wide with vexation. "I had one last week."

Ruby let go of her side of the bucket and tried to hide behind Bronwyn. Mary Rose could see the merriment in Bronwyn's eyes as a strange odor filled the room, obliterating the fragrance of lilies. Fish. The children smelled like fish. And their playclothes were damp and smeared with something resembling spoiled spinach. Seaweed? Fish entrails? They looked more like ragamuffins than children related to the Earl of Salisbury.

Bronwyn laughed, acting as if they looked exactly as children should look. "Show Lady Ashley your treasure, lambs," she said.

Ruby reluctantly came out from hiding and took hold of her side of the bucket again. Together, they struggled to get it closer to the light that poured through the square trap in the ceiling. They set the bucket down and then sat on the wood plank floor to examine their treasure.

"Mithter Thorne thaid we could bring thith to show you," Ruby said, her eyes big. "We were on the poop deck when thome men were fithing for the people on our boat." She bent over her bucket and pulled out an orange creature the size of both Mary Rose's fists. It appeared to be a very large bug with feelers that waved in the air.

Mary Rose put her hand to her throat and took a step backward. "What is it?"

"It's a baby lobster," Pearl said, her voice filled with awe. "The fishermen said it's too little to keep so we have to throw it back in the water. We wanted to show it to you first." She took it from her sister's hand and held it out for Mary Rose to hold.

"And Mithter Thorpe thaid itth a miracle. Lobtherth live on the bottom, but we think thith one ran away from itth mommy."

"Or maybe its mommy didn't want it anymore," Pearl said, "so it just swam to the top of the ocean looking for another family."

The sting of tears at the back of Mary Rose's throat began even before she considered the smell, her still sore hands, or the eyes on the wiggling creature that seemed to be staring at her. Pearl's words still echoed in her heart as she took in their expectant faces.

Big orange bug or not, she wouldn't disappoint them. She knelt down between them and held her breath as she opened her hands.

"But Lady," Ruby whispered, "you have a hurt on your hand."

Pearl bent lower to see for herself. "Two big hurts," she said.

"It might make it hurt worth if you hold Othcar," Ruby said, her eyes large and fixed on Mary Rose's face.

"I'm quite certain this little lobster won't hurt my hands," Mary Rose said, swallowing hard. She met Bronwyn's gaze above the girls' head. Even in the dim light, her eyes appeared watery. Mary

Rose wondered if it was the shared experience, each seeming to know what the other thought, that made them exchange soft smiles.

She cupped her hands as Ruby carefully placed the baby lobster in her palms. She lifted the creature toward her face. "Hello, Oscar the Lobster," Mary Rose said in her best lobster voice.

Her words were met by gales of laughter, Bronwyn's giggle almost as loud as the twins'.

"Othcar the Lobthter," Ruby sang out and danced around the room. Her twin joined, and after Mary Rose gave the crustacean to Pearl, she gently danced poor Oscar along in both hands.

Mary Rose sat back, considering the scene. A half hour earlier, the sweet bouquet of lilies seemed to her the most precious in the world. Now? She took in the children's laughter, thought about Oscar running away from a mommy who didn't want him, and decided fishy lobster had just replaced lilies as the most beautiful aroma on earth.

The women and children proceeded through the cabin door single file, Ruby now holding Oscar and Pearl holding the bucket. They planned to switch turns as soon as they reached the deck because they had disagreed vehemently on who got to hold Oscar until he went for a swim to find his mommy—"who most certainly was swimming as fast as she could to keep up with the *Sea Hawk*," both Bronwyn and Mary Rose had repeatedly assured them. But when it came time to throw the little lobster overboard, Ruby started to cry. "But I love Othcar," she sobbed, clutching him gently to her heart.

"Me too," Pearl bawled inconsolably. She put her arm around her sister, though seeming more protective of Oscar than of Ruby.

Mary Rose looked to Bronwyn to see what magic nanny-spell she could cast on this event to get their smiles to return. But

Bronwyn looked as stricken about throwing the lobster overboard as the twins did.

Mary Rose pictured the bathtub that remained in their cabin and giggled, surprising herself as much as she obviously surprised the others.

The twins stopped their crying and gaped.

"I can think of no reason we can't keep Oscar."

"Keep Othcar?" Ruby whispered in awe. "Won't he die?"

"Not if we arrange for him to have a little water to live and play in."

Their eyes grew wide, and behind them, Bronwyn grinned at Mary Rose. "I suppose you'll be wanting Mr. Oscar the Lobster to live in our bathtub, then?"

The twins bounced up and down. "Can he, Lady? Can he?"

"The thought did cross my mind," she said, though her voice was nearly drowned out by the girls' shouts. "And I do say 'tis a grand idea for so grand a baby lobster, especially one named Oscar."

With great solemnity of purpose, the group marched along single file once more, across the deck and to their cabin.

"I daresay, m'lady, we need to get Mr. Thorpe to open the hatch entirely, not just a mere few inches," Bronwyn said as they traipsed into the cabin.

"Methinks this fragrance that greets us is not that much different than skunk spray," Mary Rose said.

"Or a barnyard full of cows with noisy dyspepsia," Bronwyn added, lacing her fingers together to rest her hands atop her abdomen.

"Or Brother Brigham's beaver-oil curative," Mary Rose added. "Tonight's our supper with the captain. Should I lather on the curative and give Oscar a good-night kiss when I give Ruby and Pearl theirs? I shall truly impress, and even perhaps make the captain and his guests swoon." She stood up, sniffed, and stuck her nose in the air. She lifted one hand dramatically. "'So good to meet you, Captain Livingstone,' I shall say. 'Would you care to kiss my hand?'"

Ruby's gaze darted back and forth between her sister and Mary Rose. Pearl's mouth fell open as Bronwyn jumped up to play the role of captain. She took Mary Rose's hand and with equal drama pretended to kiss it. Then she drew in a deep, audible breath. "'Tis eau de lobster, I believe, m'lady. Or is that the rare and beautiful eau de beaver oil, which I recognize from my fur trapping adventures in the Old West?"

"'Tis the latter, I am happy to declare," Mary Rose said, casting a mock glance at Bronwyn, who'd now stepped into the role of Brigham. "A healing ointment given to me by my dear Mormon brother, its fragrance sweeter than that of any other animal in God's kingdom."

"Sweeter than buffalo carrion, to be certain," Bronwyn said, raising an eyebrow.

"'Tis sweeter indeed," agreed Mary Rose, "than even owl *vomitare*."

"*Vomitare?*"

Mary Rose grinned. "Latin for 'vomit.'"

"Ah," Bronwyn said, frowning as if in deep concentration. She clasped her hands behind her and paced, head bowed, just as Mary Rose had seen Brigham do a dozen times. Her brow still furrowed, she then looked up and said in perfect imitation of his American drawl, "Ahh, yes, I have it. A word from the Lord . . ." She slapped a hand to her forehead. "I will use owl *vomitare* as the base for my next healing ointment . . ." Bronwyn started to giggle, no longer able to keep a straight face.

Mary Rose fell into a chair and doubled over as their laughter rang through the room. The sound was contagious and the twins joined in, though it was apparent they didn't know why Mary Rose and Bronwyn were carrying on so.

After a moment Bronwyn sobered. "Oh, dear," she whispered, sliding into a chair near Mary Rose. "What I've just said . . . do you think it blasphemy?" She looked stricken. "Please tell me I haven't committed some unpardonable sin by having a critical spirit toward God's great apostle."

Mary Rose reached for her hand and held it gently. "If you did, then I did also. But we meant no harm. I cannot believe our antics could be counted against us."

"There are rules, you know, m'lady." Bronwyn withdrew her hand. "Certain things we will need to learn as we travel. Brother Brigham has said that when the Prophet receives a word from God about anything, 'tis our God-given duty to obey without question. What if he's received a word from God that we aren't to poke fun at his apostles?" Her eyes were round with vexation.

At her words, tears filled Mary Rose's eyes, but they had nothing to do with fears of blasphemy. And everything to do with the fine line between mirth and sadness.

Bronwyn studied Mary Rose, her concern even more pronounced. "M'lady, what is it? Have I distressed you by speaking of worrisome things? I was speaking of my own sins, none others." She rose from her chair and knelt before Mary Rose, this time taking Mary Rose's hands in hers.

Mary Rose shook her head. "'Tis nothing you have said, but I wish you would stop calling me m'lady and simply be my friend."

Bronwyn studied her face for several moments, and then said, "'Twould not be proper, m'lady. Not as long as I am in your employ. But when we reach America, then perhaps we can be friends." She held on to Mary Rose's hands. "But that is not what troubles you, is it, m'lady? I sense there is more, perhaps much more."

Mary Rose studied the sweet uplifted face before her, sensing she could trust Bronwyn with anything she might tell her. Bronwyn's faith was strong, her view of the future full of hope and joyful expectation. Mary Rose didn't want to create the slightest doubt in Bronwyn's heart by voicing her own doubts about the future; her fears that Grandfather had made a terrible error in judgment in converting to a new religion that didn't seem to allow for independent thinking; her growing certainty that as soon as they reached Boston, presented their little charges to Hermione, she and her grandfather should book passage on the *Sea Hawk's* return voyage to Liverpool.

She gave Bronwyn a gentle smile. "I was lost in thought for a moment, considering everything from Grandfather's decision to embark on such a journey to the surprise of finding a kindred spirit onboard this ship. An accomplished kindred spirit." Her smile widened. "Is there nothing you cannot do?"

Bronwyn's cheeks turned pink. It seemed that she was so unused to such compliments that for a moment she didn't know how to answer.

"I've been fortunate. My father is the gamekeeper of the largest and grandest estate near Hanmer, Wales. My father's employer, Lord Kenyon, wanted his only child, Cara, to have a companion while being tutored in the classics. I was the logical choice." Her eyes brightened as she went on. "I soaked up everything our dear old tutor taught us as if I were a sea sponge. The education didn't stop in the classroom. I had full access to the estate library, day and night. I learned to ride the finest horses in the Kenyon stable, to shoot game, and to ride with Lord Kenyon on fox hunts—dear Cara Kenyon was fearless and her father adored her and seldom went against her wishes."

"That's why you knew the William Blake poem."

"'Tis," she said, "and hundreds of others."

"You said 'Cara *was* fearless,' as if something happened."

Bronwyn's expressive eyes filled with sorrow as she nodded. "She died after a fall from her father's prized stallion, a horse she was forbidden to ride. We slipped out one night to meet at the stables and took turns riding the stallion and a gentler gelding along the lakeshore in the moonlight. We were heading back to the stables when a rodent skittered across our path and both horses reared. I controlled mine, the gelding, but the stallion went wild.

"I blamed myself, and Lord Kenyon . . . though he said not . . . I am certain he placed some of the blame on me." She looked away from Mary Rose. "Cara loved an audience. If I hadn't gone along with her plan, she probably wouldn't have ridden the stallion."

"Cara was your friend."

"Yes. The dearest ever." She looked back to meet Mary Rose's gaze. "And you remind me of her. I spotted it the moment I saw you."

She glanced around the room at the wide-eyed twins who'd been silently taking in the conversation, and her demeanor changed. Once again, she was the nanny in charge.

"Girls," she said to the twins. "Let's help Lady Ashley choose what she will wear to the captain's fancy dinner tonight."

She smiled at Mary Rose. "I have the perfect style in mind for your hair, should you allow it."

The twins came to life, crowding in to help. Bronwyn worked her nanny magic once more and before the hour was up, Oscar relaxed temporarily in his bucket, the twins had been scrubbed clean in the lukewarm bathwater, dressed in clean clothes, and three seamen had removed the water from the tub with buckets.

Ruby explained to the tallest and most frightening in appearance that Oscar was going to live with them now, and that the tub was his new home. Therefore, it was important the tub remain in their cabin. The seaman, who wore a patch over one eye and called himself Fitzgibbons, soon returned with a large bucket of seawater. He gave each of the girls a large conch shell from the Sandwich Islands to place in the tub so Oscar would feel at home.

"The Thandwich Islandth." Ruby's eyes grew big.

"Aye, m'lady," he said kindly to the child.

"That's where our mommy and daddy live," Pearl said, hugging the large pink shell.

"They're mithionarieth," Ruby added.

The obvious question glinted in the seaman's uncovered eye. His scowl was so fierce Mary Rose wondered if he was planning to shanghai the parents to reunite them with their children. "'Tis a beauteous place indeed," he said. "And tomorry, if ye'll bring these conches upside whilst I'm on watch, I'll teach ye how to blow 'em like trumpets. Maybe just loud enough for yer ma'am and pap to hear ye."

The twins looked at each other then back to Fitzgibbons as if he was the handsomest, most bighearted man God could ever think of creating.

"Truly?" Pearl breathed.

"Truly," Fitzgibbons said.

"Croth your heart?"

He crossed his heart, then bowing to them all, he backed his way to the door.

SIX

Cavendish, Prince Edward Island
July 4, 1841

Enid urged Sadie to a trot along the white-sand beach, her senses alert as the filly obeyed the gentle pressing of her heels against its flanks. Bending low, she rubbed Sadie's neck, laying her cheek against the mare's mane and combing it with her fingers. "Good girl," she whispered. "The leg is healing, just as I told you." She slowed the mare with another gentle command, using her thighs and heels.

"Let's see how it feels." She drew the sorrel to canter, holding her breath to better hear the cadence of Sadie's hooves on the wet sand. As she feared, the rhythm was uneven. "Still favoring it a wee bit, now, aren't you?"

Enid drew Sadie to a halt. She'd been riding bareback and easily slipped from Sadie's back. She stooped to inspect the left fetlock, where weeks earlier Sadie's injury had gone bone deep.

It was healing, thanks to Enid's ministrations of bitter salts, though it seemed too swollen for Enid's liking. She kicked off her shoes, hiked up her skirts, and walked the filly to the water's edge.

She smiled into Sadie's warm and trusting eyes, and then led her into the shallows waves. Sadie nickered, and Enid glanced back. "Don't complain, dear, the salt water will do your leg good. Trust me."

She stopped when the water covered the injured fetlock and rubbed Sadie's velvet nose. The horse seemed to sense the need to remain still and, raising her head, shook her mane and softly snorted.

The surf seemed rougher than usual for a warm summer's day, almost as if a storm might be brewing. Shading her eyes, she looked west. No clouds building, but the sky had turned unnaturally dark where it met the horizon. And out a ways, a brisk wind created whitecaps.

They left the water's edge and stood for a moment in the warm sugar-soft sand. Enid dug in her toes, just as she had when she was a child. She closed her eyes and faced the sun, letting her face bask in its warmth.

As always, the thought of Hosea's ship getting caught in a storm stirred up troubled thoughts in her heart. He was an experienced sea captain, the commander of one of the finest ships—a clipper—ever designed. Besides, Gabe MacKay was with him on the voyage. If ever she could count on the sea to be wary of taking down another ship, 'twould be on this voyage— with such a fine commander and equally fine architect whose heart led him to build the safest and fastest ships ever to sail the seven seas.

But then, one could not count on the sea for much of anything. She knew that as God's absolute truth, as her husband knew, and especially as Gabe MacKay knew.

She looked out at the dark horizon again and shivered. How far was the *Sea Hawk* from that line between heaven and earth? Three days out, perhaps, maybe four, depending on when they set sail from Liverpool? And how far were they from the storm that seemed to stir itself into a brooding brew?

"Mrs. Livingstone!"

Enid turned, recognizing the boy's voice. It was Brodie Flynn, one of a half-dozen children from a neighboring farm—the old MacKay place, which Gabe had sold to the Flynns within a year after the shipwreck that carried his parents and sister to their graves. At the time, they'd been newly arrived from the Scottish highlands, and perhaps for that reason, their brogue seemed more pronounced than most of the islanders'.

"Mrs. Livingstone," the child called again, galloping like the wind on an old dun mare with a dark gray mane and tail. The boy's short flame-colored hair, almost as red as Enid's, stuck straight out as if uncombed for a month and perhaps last trimmed with his pa's hunting knife.

"Ma says ye need to get to the harbor right away. A ship's a-comin' and she thinks it might be a clipper—though it's still too far out to tell. Ma says I'm to trade ye horses. Ye'll take Miss Minnie to the harbor, and I'll walk Sadie back to the farm, because of her being lame." He peered down at Sadie's leg. "Looks good as ever to me, though. Is she healed?"

"Not entirely," Enid said.

"Folks around these parts think ye part angel, Mrs. Livingstone."

Enid laughed. "Now, why would anyone think such a thing as that?"

"Because of yer way with animals, that's why. Horses in particular, but there was that old sow out at the Montgomery farm—the one Mrs. Montgomery named Sweet Eliza Jane so the mister wouldn't slaughter it for supper. Take that fetlock there; no one's ever seen a horse mend from something so torn and ugly. Everybody says so. Ye could see clear to the bone inside 'er." He grinned up at Enid, showing two missing front teeth. "So ye'll take Miss Minnie, then? I'll be careful with Sadie. Put her in yer barn, rub her down for ye."

Enid laughed. "The *Sea Hawk* is trying for a speed record, child. The captain, much as he might like to, cannot be stopping here. They plan a stopover in Halifax, then they'll be on their way to Boston. Last I heard, it will be another few days before they anchor, and it will be only for a few hours."

"But Ma says it might be the clipper," Brodie insisted, "and ye'll need to be on your way, otherwise ye'll miss the captain."

"I'm quite certain the ship isn't the *Sea Hawk*." Though Enid spoke with confidence, she couldn't help the spark of hope the child's words kindled in her heart. Would her husband ever veer from his set course just to see her, to draw her into his arms? It was folly to entertain such a thought. She knew Hosea Livingstone well. Though she never doubted his love for a minute, he was the master and commander of a ship filled with some two hundred people whose lives depended on his wisdom and decisions. Those decisions could never include the whim of visiting his wife, no matter how deep his love might be. The thought made the back of her throat sting, which surprised her. She wasn't one to brood over Hosea's scarcity of visits.

Brodie Flynn slid off Miss Minnie's back. "I'll go with ye then, should ye just want to have a wee peek at her sails. Just in the rare event 'twould be the *Sea Hawk* comin' without ye knowin' it."

Enid ruffled the boy's hair. "I think someone's spotted a packet ship, likely bringing us mail from Halifax, sailing a different route to stop at other villages on the island. That's why the confusion. But now that I think about it, my dear Brodie Flynn, it may indeed be worth a trip to the harbor." With each schooner that arrived from Halifax, she expected mail from Scotland: a veterinary book from Dr. Fergus Duff in Glasgow, who'd written that as soon as it was published, he would send her a copy.

Brodie's eyes grew as large as teacups. "Yes, ma'am. Indeed it would."

"Go back home and tell your ma what we're up to, and then come by my farm in a half hour."

"Yes, ma'am." Barefoot, with trousers rolled above his ankles, he swung over the dun's bare back, waved to Enid, and rode off.

"And put on your shoes," Enid called after him.

"Yes, ma'am," he hollered back.

When they reached the Charlottetown harbor, the schooner *Flying Swan* had just dropped anchor, its sails gleaming as white as new-fallen snow in the sun. As she suspected, it was indeed a packet ship delivering passengers and mail from Halifax. She drove the buckboard alongside the wharf, just as the harbormaster met the ship's chief mate to exchange mail packets. Passengers milled, some waiting to board, a few making their way down the gangway, children and valises in tow. The harbormaster stood off to one side of the gangway, checking the list of passengers as they disembarked, and then asking information of those waiting to board.

Enid knew Angor Wallace, the harbormaster, well, as did everyone, young and old, on Prince Edward Island. He was known to read the mail and relate to his wife Maeve the contents, should they be of a curious nature. She would then spread the word about the island, telling each to dare not tell another, which of course they readily did.

Enid gave him a nod as she took her place in line with others awaiting Angor's distribution of posts and parcels. She was ready to turn away, disappointed, when he called out, "Mrs. Livingstone, I've something fer ye!"

Her heart lifted as she approached him. "'Tis terribly good news. Yer captain is on his way. This was sent by packet from Liverpool a full month before he sailed on the *Sea Hawk*." He handed her a letter with a broken seal. "Don't know how that happened," he said, just as always.

Enid accepted his curiosity as a fact of life, as did most other citizens of the island. Angor had been harbormaster for longer than she could remember. He meant no harm.

She thanked him and made her way back to the buckboard where Brodie Flynn waited.

"Did you hear good news, then, Mrs. Livingstone?" Brodie asked as she climbed back onto the seat beside him.

"The *Sea Hawk* will be in Halifax four days from now," she said. "And the captain wants me to meet him there. Also Mr. MacKay, so 'twill be a double blessing." Smiling, she looked up at the boy. "It's only for twelve hours," she said, "but even that is worth the voyage over."

"You'd best be leavin' soon, then," he said. "Takes three days by packet ship to get there."

"Aye," she said. "But I saw on a posting by the gangway that the *Liberty* will sail tomorrow."

Brodie grinned up at her. "And ye'll be on 'er."

"Indeed, I will." She chirped to Foxfire and the aging mare plodded forward as Enid unfolded the post once more.

"I'll take care of yer farm for ye," Brodie said.

Enid didn't answer. Holding the reins loosely with one hand, Enid held the unfolded letter in the other, her attention held fast on the first paragraphs.

Dearest Enid,

I have the best possible tidings. I have been in contact with an expert in the field of childbirth and related issues. I have arranged for you to accompany me on the return voyage from Boston. Once again, we will anchor in Halifax for twelve hours, then sail for Liverpool. I hope these good tidings bring you the same joy with which I have met them.

Of course I understand your reluctance to sail and your reasons, which run deep and fixed. But wouldn't it be worth it, should this physician get to the heart of your difficulties . . .

She scanned the rest of the letter, unable to concentrate on much of its content because of the shocking words in that first paragraph. Hosea mentioned something about the speed record, the joy of sailing with their friend Gabe again, and that Gabe needed to also speak to her.

Enid flushed as she thought of Angor reading the letter and then telling Maeve, who would spread it around the island. Perhaps Hosea didn't remember the old harbormaster's indiscretion. He had never liked the farm, had never liked being away from his ship, so it stood to reason that the insignificant matter of an old harbormaster's propensity to snoop would not have stayed with him.

She sighed deeply as she refolded the letter.

A trip to England to see an expert about her inability to conceive? Her heart thudded beneath her ribs. Her heart's deepest desire was to have a child.

She flicked the reins above Foxfire's back to pick up speed, her thoughts racing through her heart and mind as if they were a bird in flight with no place to land.

She had no right to worry about her husband's folly when she had committed greater sins of her own. A secret buried deep in her heart that meant she couldn't go to England with him, or anywhere else . . . unless she told him what she'd kept hidden all these years.

Only one other knew her secret, and he did not know the whole of it.

His name was Gabriel MacKay.

SEVEN

G abe was standing in the dining room with the captain, his chief mate, Mr. Thorpe, and Brigham when the earl, his Welsh manservant, Griffin Carey, and the earl's granddaughter, Lady Mary Rose Ashley, entered the room. The captain greeted them and then made introductions to the others, but Gabe couldn't keep his eyes off Lady Mary Rose. She was even lovelier this night than she had been the morning they met.

Her auburn curls had been tamed into an upsweep that showed off her lovely white neck. A few tendrils sprang loose here and there, but somehow the imperfections suited her. She wore an off-the-shoulder frock of a shimmering dark green that complimented the creamy hue of her skin, and a single strand of pearls encircled the base of her slender throat.

When she caught his gaze they shared a smile. For a moment, Gabe thought he couldn't breathe.

He walked over to her, and she turned away from the others to greet him. The earl's servant moved to one side of the serving board to stand with the steward, Mr. Quigley.

"Ah, 'tis the rescuer of errant hats," she said to Gabe as they moved away from the group, "and of mischievous little boys." Her smile widened, now showing only a hint of the dimple in her chin. "I didn't have a chance to thank you for the latter, but we are indeed indebted to you for your quick thinking—and for your obvious lack of vertigo." She laughed. "It seems as though from the moment we arrived to board, someone needed to rescue us from one mishap after another."

As she spoke, he found himself mesmerized by the sprinkle of freckles across the bridge of her nose. He tried to think of a quip to give himself time to regain his bearings. And to breathe again. But none came.

"Lady Ashley," he finally said with a slight nod, "it is good to see you again, and indeed, I would count it an honor to come to your rescue at any time day or night." The instant the word *night* left his mouth, he felt himself flush.

She assured him by her expression and musical laugh that he had not offended her in the least. "I truly thank you, good sir. I hope we won't need you again, but we appreciate the offer of your services. We now have a rather magical nanny watching over our little brood, and she seems to have brought them under control." She laughed again, lightly, and cast a bright look of appreciation toward Griffin Carey. "Or perhaps I should say she seems to have cast them under her spell."

"I didn't know Mormons believed in sorcery," he said.

The room became as still as a tomb.

He'd done it again. This time accused her of believing in witchcraft. He could have slapped himself on the head.

Surprisingly, it was Lady Ashley who came to his rescue. "I spoke in jest when I intimated our dear Bronwyn has magic powers. She simply has a way with children I've seen in no other." She looked again at Griffin, who was still standing by Mr. Quigley, and smiled. "You are indeed fortunate to have such a comely and gifted wife. There is no need for spells, with her innate ability to love and adore children. It is that love that causes them to behave. Nay, more than behave. They thrive in her presence."

Griffin inclined his head in acknowledgment.

"And I misspoke in accusing you or any of the Saints of sorcery," Gabe said to Lady Ashley, fully aware that everyone in the room was listening. And that Brigham's gaze was boring a hole through his back.

Lady Ashley didn't seem to care what anyone else thought. "Yet I understand," she said, "that those who use seer stones have powers of divination. 'Tis our own Prophet, I'm told, who in his past committed such foolery of his—"

The captain cleared his throat, interrupting the conversation. "I believe it's time to take our places at the table. Our galley cook will not be pleased if the fare he's provided goes cold." He gestured to the table. "Sit, please. Everyone. And I will ask a blessing upon our food and upon our voyage."

Gabe escorted Mary Rose to the table, pulled out her chair, and seated her. As soon as the others gathered, he sat down to her left. The captain took his place at the head of the table, though remained standing until everyone else had taken their places—Mr. Thorpe to the captain's left, directly across from Gabe. Next to him, and across from Mary Rose, sat Brigham. The earl took his place at the end of the table opposite the captain.

The captain opened his prayer book to the service of evening vespers, thumbed through a few pages, and began to read the ancient prayer of thanksgiving, his voice low and humble. Those who knew the words joined him, praying softly in unison. Though he kept his head bowed, Gabe glanced furtively around the table at the others as he intoned the words he'd known since childhood. Brigham met his questioning gaze with a steady one of his own. His lips did not move, and the angle of his head did not speak of reverence.

At the conclusion of the prayer, the captain, rather than murmuring the traditional *amen*, surprised Gabe by continuing:

"O Lord, we ask that a good measure of the blessings you might bestow upon us might instead be bountifully bestowed upon those in greater need. We also ask that your presence be with those we love who are away from us. We thank you for their safekeeping and ours, and for the knowledge we have that without your grace we would surely perish, and that without your love to sustain us, life would have no meaning."

When the captain looked up, his focus seemed to drill into Brigham's steady gaze. He then added, "May his grace sustain us, may his Spirit indwell us and give us peace. For we recognize that it is not our works that save us, O Lord. It is your grace alone that draws us to you. It is not our worthiness that enables us to come to you. We can do nothing to deserve your favor. Not one of us can provide a substitute for your sacrifice that will wrap us in your robe of righteousness."

He glanced around the table, his gaze again lingering on Brigham as if gauging his reaction, before adding:

"For all these gifts, and more, we thank you, O Lord. Amen."

In all the years he'd known Hosea, Gabe had never heard him offer a blessing over a supper table quite like the one he'd just uttered. It was more a homily than a prayer.

He was instantly aware of what seemed to be a silent conveyance of thoughts, not particularly pleasant, between the captain and Brigham. Gabe suspected that while he was caught up in conversation with Lady Ashley, he'd missed the meat of what surely had been a fascinating discussion about American frontier religions, perhaps the profusion of false prophets, or the age-old argument about faith versus works. He'd thrown something of all of these elements of Anglican faith into his prayers.

The captain reached for his goblet of Madeira and lifted it. "To continued safe passage," he said.

"To safe passage," the others murmured. Glasses clinked, and sips were taken.

"And to speed," Gabe added, lifting his glass higher. "To eighteen knots or higher."

"Hear, hear!" The captain touched his wineglass to Gabe's. There were cheers all around. "And as the Irish say, 'May the road rise up to meet you, may the wind be ever at your back.'"

"And may Cook's fare not have cooled after your most eloquent and ardent prayer, sir," said Mr. Thorpe with a crooked smile and a pointed glance toward the waiting steward. He lifted his glass to another round of "Hear, hear!"

The group chuckled and the tension dropped as Mr. Quigley, assisted by Griffin, served a hearty soup, followed by kidney and beef pie made with a suet pastry. The steward added more heavy bread rolls to the baskets, and then refilled the goblets.

Mary Rose took a bite of kidney pie, chewed thoughtfully, then turned to Gabe. "Eighteen knots. 'Tis a marvel." The ship rolled gently and the lamp swung, dimmed, and then settled.

"Possibly nineteen."

"And should we keep to that speed, how long until we reach Nova Scotia?"

After one look into her eyes, Gabe had a difficult time concentrating on anything as mundane as food. He had fancied himself in love only once before, many years ago. He'd thought his wounds had healed . . . until his talk with the captain the night before, when he was reminded that the captain was married to Gabe's first love. He surreptitiously chased a rather large and gristly piece of beef around his plate and then gave up before Lady Mary Rose might notice and think him a bumpkin. Instead, he picked up the Madeira and took a sip.

She was watching him with a quizzical look, and he realized

that he hadn't answered her question. "Seven days," he said. "After twelve hours in Halifax, taking on food supplies and water, we'll sail for Boston."

"And from Halifax to Boston?"

"Another seven days, eight hours, and we should sail into Boston Harbor"—he grinned at her—"with great fanfare of course." He attacked the hunk of beef when he thought she wasn't looking.

"That is certainly precise," she said, her gaze taking in his plate. "You have it down to the hour."

"That's why I'm on board. Precise calculations."

"Hear, hear!" rang out from the other end of the table. The earl lifted his glass and saluted Gabe.

Gabe inclined his head. "Thank you, but we haven't done it yet."

"I, for one, cannot wait to step foot on American soil. It's been years since I was last there." Twisting the end of his mustache, he smiled at the group and leaned in closer as if to tell a secret. "Nothing in this world can compare to setting eyes on land that seems to stretch out before you as if you're looking into eternity itself. I can't wait to see it again, to look up into God's heavens, brighter and bluer and sunnier than anything we have in England . . . and I'll thank my Heavenly Father for the Prophet, his vision, his status as the chosen one to usher us into this new era of church history." His eyes filled and he blinked rapidly, cleared his throat, and then continued: "To think that I will live to see the reestablishment of God's only Church on earth. For that alone, I will be eternally grateful—to the Prophet and to this great man who sits with us this night." He lifted his glass again in salute, this time toward Brigham.

After a moment of almost reverent silence, the captain reached for the bread basket, broke off a hunk of bread, passed the basket to Gabe, and then said to Brigham, "I hear you're taking a group overland to Commerce. That's on the Mississippi, isn't it?"

"You're partially right, though the Prophet has renamed it

Nauvoo, which means 'beautiful' in Hebrew." He smiled broadly. "We've drained swamplands and built homes and businesses. Our industry is booming, but we're still in need of workers—blacksmiths, shopkeepers, wheelwrights, harness makers—opportunities abound in Nauvoo." He played with the stem of his goblet, then turned to Gabe and said, "We're in special need of an architect. We could use someone with your skill."

Gabe sat back and chuckled. His life had to do with shipbuilding; nothing else interested him. He shook his head. "Sorry, I'm not interested, but thank you for the offer."

Brigham turned to the rest of the diners. "We built a magnificent temple in Kirtland, but unfortunately, we were forced to leave. We're building a new one that will surpass even the Kirtland temple in every way—especially because of its location overlooking the mighty Mississippi."

The captain settled against the back of his chair. "What exactly happened in Kirtland?"

"Unprovoked attacks," Brigham said, his expression changing. "In Kirtland, followed by more of the same in Far West. Persecution, worse than one can imagine, drove us out of both towns. Vigilante groups chased families, even little children, like we were animals, hunting us down to shoot for sport. They burned our homes, our farms, our businesses." His gaze took in everyone at the table as the lamp above them swung with the undulating movement of the sea. He kept the emotion in his eyes veiled, but his expression spoke of deep anger toward those who dared harm his people.

Lady Mary Rose leaned forward. "Unprovoked attacks? Why didn't you tell us of these before?"

"He did, my dear," the earl said quickly from across the table. "At least he told me."

"I should have been made aware of the danger we're heading into." Her voice was calm, her words precise, but they held an edge of anger. "Grandfather, you should have informed me of all these details before we made our decision."

Gabe noticed that Brigham and the earl exchanged glances. Lady Mary Rose noticed it too. She turned to Brigham with an unblinking stare. "You should have warned us that you were leading us into atrocities of this magnitude." She turned back to her grandfather. "I've a mind to—"

Brigham's voice was calmer when he interrupted. "I need to assure you, Lady Ashley, no one will ever again drive us from our homes and businesses. Not one child will be harmed—or forced to witness the deaths of his mother, father, sisters, or brothers."

"I just don't understand," Mary Rose continued. "What triggered the mob's response?" Her tone was accusatory, as if the Mormons had possibly brought it on themselves.

Gabe sat back, enjoying the interchange immensely. This woman knew her own might and was a fighter. He found himself enormously impressed . . . and attracted to her even more.

"They wouldn't simply attack a farmhouse, chase women and children for sport, would they?"

"The Saints were not the agitators," he said. "We are a peaceful people. At least we have been until now. As God is my witness and as Joseph Smith is his beloved Prophet," he said, "I tell you these attacks were unprovoked. I can also tell you that the Gentiles will never again come against us with force, because"—he drew in a deep breath and looked down as if praying—"because, my friends, we now are ready to fight back. Our militia has begun training in Nauvoo.

"We seek those who are young, bright, strong, and ready to serve the Prophet and their heavenly Father. And, I might add, our militia will not be hidden from those who are out to harm us. They will be well aware of righteous anger to be meted out against them, should they attempt to hurt us again." He smiled.

"And believe me, it will not take long for the word to spread that our militia is trained and ready."

Brigham moved his gaze to Griffin, who had been quietly watching the apostle from his station by the serving table. "This young man from Wales will be heading up a special platoon of this new militia. My son, the Prophet will bless you mightily for your service. Already, I have written to him of your leadership skills, and your arrival is greatly anticipated by all the Saints."

Griffin inclined his head. "Thank you," he said simply, but Gabe noticed a passion of purpose shone in the young man's eyes, which Gabe understood.

The captain leaned forward, his forearms on the table, his expression keen with interest. "Exactly who are these Gentiles you speak of? It's my understanding that the term means anyone who is not Jewish."

"Not according to the new revelations from God. A Gentile is anyone who doesn't adhere to our faith, is not a member of the one and true Church that God has reestablished on earth."

Gabe frowned, wondering at the statement. "There is only one true Church?"

Brigham surprised him by laughing. "I know what you're thinking—the same thing I did when I first heard Joseph make the claim. Every church thinks they're the only one true Church." He chuckled again. "But Joseph's story is one that he's looking forward to telling you himself. And I've dominated the conversation much too long anyway." He shot Gabe a disarming smile.

It took Gabe another few minutes to realize Brigham hadn't answered his question.

Persecution? Raids on farms? Chasing women and children to frighten or even kill seemingly for sport? A private militia? Gabe turned to the woman at his side. She and her grandfather, titled, wealthy, familiar only with a life where others saw to their needs, were heading into dangerous territory, perhaps to face the same fate that had befallen the Mormons in Kirtland and Far West. Smith had moved his followers to a place he thought was safe, but if Gabe understood Brigham Young's brief history lesson, the group had been run out—worse, burned and tortured and chased—from their two previous promised lands. What was to prevent it from happening again?

He had the urge to take her hand and lead her away from Brigham, convince her of the danger they would be in. He would lead her grandfather away from danger too, if he would go.

"As for me," the earl said from the end of the table, "I'm happy to count myself among the Saints." His round face stretched into a wide smile. "I believe in the frontier spirit, especially a fired-up frontier spirit, which I believe they—let me correct that—*we* have in abundance. And I believe in the witness of our Prophet, Joseph Smith. I felt the burning in my soul as I read the Book of Mormon." He lifted his goblet and sipped the Madeira before continuing. "I always wondered why there was no written record of the Americas in the Bible. And now, in my old age, I finally found out that Jesus Christ himself appeared there during the three days everyone thought he was in the grave. And to think of those gold plates . . . right there in America, waiting to be found."

He sat back and folded his hands over his rotund stomach. "Finding the truth about this in my old age pleases me immensely." His eyes glistened as he looked at each one seated around the table. "Not just finding the one true religion at last, one that resonates in my very soul, but also finding other followers of this truth, followers of the Prophet whom God chose to translate his word in these latter days."

He paused, his gaze resting on Lady Mary Rose. "And perhaps best of all, the Saints . . ." Gabe could see great love for his granddaughter in his expression. "The Saints take care of their own, come feast or famine, or, God forbid, worse. After what they've been through, they know the worst better than most. Among all churches of the world, it's that pioneer spirit that draws me."

"After all we've learned tonight, my spirit is telling me it might be wise to sail back to England and our home," Lady Mary Rose said. Her tone was dinner-party lighthearted, but Gabe sensed her grandfather hadn't heard the last of it.

"Dear, there is no going back once I've made up my mind. You know that."

She tilted her chin and gave him a little smile. "We'll see," she said and took a dainty sip of Madeira.

At once the conversation seemed to erupt into questions—all directed to Brigham—about the Saints' travels west, the gold plates, the lost tribe of Israel, or the angel Moroni's visit to the boy Joseph Smith.

Gabe sat back with relief. Maybe no one else cared, but at least one of the Ashleys seemed to be aware of the dangers ahead—and not just the romance of the Wild West and its wild religions. Maybe they would turn back. Though he wondered how much sway Lady Mary Rose had over the earl. It appeared to him that if the Earl of Salisbury wanted to start a new life with the Saints in America, there was nothing anyone could do to stop him.

As if sensing that she was in his thoughts, Lady Mary Rose turned to watch him with a concentration that could mine the ocean's depths, and, he wanted to believe, the depths of his soul too. And if her eyes didn't lie—and he could not conceive that someone with such purity and sweetness and lack of guile could allow them to veil the truth—he realized she was as great a skeptic as he. He couldn't help but smile.

Her eyes widened and she gave him an answering smile. It seemed she read his mind as well. And his skepticism.

Before Gabe took his first sip of coffee, Lady Mary Rose whispered behind her hand, "I don't know about you, but I believe I've had about enough of all this. I need some air. I'm going for a stroll on the deck." As she laced the strings of her reticule over her dainty wrist, Gabe stood to pull back her chair, and within seconds she had skirted her way to the captain and expressed her gratitude for the lovely supper.

She reached the captain's door, halted, and with that smile he was starting to enjoy immensely, cast a glance in Gabe's direction, then stepped from the captain's dining room.

Gabe shook hands with the captain, said he would see him on the quarterdeck later, and started for the door.

Just as he opened it, Brigham said to the earl, his voice loud enough for all to overhear, "It's time to tell your granddaughter the truth about why you can't return home."

EIGHT

Mary Rose drew in deep breaths of the crisp night air, thinking about the man who'd been seated next to her at supper. Something about his eyes—their unfathomable spirit and intelligence—had captured her attention from the first moment they met on the Liverpool wharf. And now those same gray-green eyes threatened to capture her heart.

She strolled along the deck near the rail to the ship's bow, looking out at the dark sea. She thought about the life she and her grandfather had left behind, the new world that awaited them.

A sudden north wind kicked up, ruffling her hair. She shivered, and returned to her cabin to fetch her cape. Even before she opened the door, she heard the murmuring of voices and the sound of soft laughter. She found that the twins were fast asleep, and the laughter came from Griffin and Coal, who sat at the table with Bronwyn. She was regaling them with a story the twins had made up about Oscar the Lobster.

A game of chess had been set out on the table, and from the

position of the board, it appeared that Griffin was about to teach Coal how to play.

Bronwyn and Griffin both stood as Mary Rose entered the room. "Is everything all right, m'lady?" Bronwyn peered anxiously into Mary Rose's face.

"Yes, of course, why do you ask?"

Though her question was directed to Bronwyn, it was her husband who answered. He glanced at Coal, now busily playing with the chess pieces, and dropped his voice. "Shortly after you'd left the captain's table, Brother Brigham stood rather abruptly and said he needed to speak with you. It sounded very important, almost dire."

Mary Rose frowned as she reached for her fur-trimmed cape, which Bronwyn had thoughtfully hooked over a coat tree near the door. Griffin stepped forward to help her place it around her shoulders.

"I've noticed that Brother Brigham often sounds dire," she said with a small laugh.

Bronwyn and Griffin exchanged a look and didn't laugh with her. "It was his tone," Bronwyn said, "and what Brother Brigham said to your grandfather after you left."

Griffin gave her a scolding look. "You're carrying tales, my love," he said, his voice still low enough not to be overheard. "When I told you what he'd said, my words were meant for your ears only."

"M'lady is my friend," Bronwyn said, casting a shy glance at Mary Rose.

"'Tis true," Mary Rose confirmed, shooting Bronwyn a conspiratorial smile. "We are indeed friends."

Bronwyn lifted her chin slightly and gave her husband a look that said, "I told you so." Then she turned again to Mary Rose. "He said it was time for you to know the truth."

Mary Rose felt the sting of tears at the back of her throat. "I knew it."

Bronwyn slipped into the chair on her other side.

"Did he say anything more?" she asked Griffin.

"I'm sorry," Griffin said. "That's all I know."

She stood, gathering her reticule and pulling her cape closer. "Is my grandfather in his quarters?"

"Yes, m'lady." Griffin inclined his head toward her. "He seemed overly tired from the dinner party. He may be asleep."

Mary Rose hesitated. "Then it's Brother Brigham I must find to get to the heart of his meaning. 'Tis not right to cause anxiety in any of us with such a statement." She met Bronwyn's gaze. "Do you mind watching the children a little longer?" She looked down at Coal's pleading expression and smiled. "Coal can return to Grandfather's cabin for bed when I return. It appears a game of chess is about to commence."

Coal grinned his thanks.

Bronwyn shook her head, though Mary Rose noticed her face looked unusually swollen, and lines around her eyes were more pronounced. "No, m'lady."

Mary Rose crossed the room to stand in front of her friend. She reached for her hand. "This is a direct order and I want you to promise me you will carry it out exactly as I say."

"Yes, m'lady." She would have curtsied if Mary Rose hadn't held tight to her hand.

Mary Rose looked to Griffin. "And after I walk from the room, if your dear wife has other ideas, you must remind her of my order."

He inclined his head. "Yes, m'lady."

"Bronwyn, you are to go immediately to your cabin and prepare yourself for a bath that I will order from the steward."

Bronwyn looked up in surprise, the hint of a smile curving the corners of her mouth. Mary Rose crossed the room to her bed, reached for a small case beneath it, pulled out an unopened packet of lily soap, and returned to place it in Bronwyn's hands.

"And then I want you to go directly to bed and sleep as long as you like tomorrow—" Bronwyn started to protest, but Mary Rose raised an eyebrow in mock warning and continued. "Remember, this is a direct order. You are not to come for the twins to allow me to sleep longer. You are the one who needs your rest."

Bronwyn again tried to protest. This time Mary Rose held up her hand. "I'm not through." She turned to Griffin. "You don't mind staying here to give your wife some quiet time alone, and to keep this little ruffian out of trouble"—she ruffled Coal's hair and he grinned—"until I return?"

"It's the best order I could hear or receive," Griffin said, his voice and expression reflecting his relief on behalf of his wife.

"Thank you, m'lady," Bronwyn said, this time finally managing a small curtsy.

Mary Rose let out an exasperated sigh. "I have one more order that you must obey, that I beg you to obey."

The young couple glanced at each other, their curiosity evident, then looked back to Mary Rose. "Please, I beg you, and utterly and completely and without reservation implore you, never to call me m'lady again. And please do not ever bow or curtsy or tilt your head or anything else indicating that I'm somehow your superior, because I am not."

This time when Bronwyn met her husband's gaze, she giggled, and Mary Rose saw loving merriment in his eyes as he took in his wife. He went over and wrapped his arms around her. "I told you so," Bronwyn said, looking up at him adoringly. "We're friends."

She left her husband's embrace and turned to Mary Rose. "I've needed a friend," she murmured.

"So have I," Mary Rose said, smiling into her eyes.

Though the hour was growing late, a few passengers remained on the deck, some strolling, other conversing in groups, their voices mostly lost in the wind, the snap of the billowing sails, and clinks of the rigging against the masts. Just as when she was on deck earlier, the watch seamen were at their stations, some inspecting the ropes, others manning the sails.

Mary Rose searched the length of the deck, both fore and aft, and then back again, keeping a watchful eye out for Brigham. When she reached the bow the second time, she stopped to consider where she might find him. It wouldn't be seemly to try his cabin, or even the gentlemen's smoking lounge, yet it was imperative she find out what he meant about telling her the truth.

She turned to face the bow. The wind ruffled her hair, and she felt the curls that Bronwyn had worked so hard to tame pull loose. She wrapped her cape tighter. Even so, she shivered in the chilly air.

She placed her hands on the rail and closed her eyes, letting her senses take over her worries about his "truth" statement: the scent of the sea air, the great speed and forward movement, the flaps and snaps of the multitude of billowing sails above her. Then she raised her eyes to the sky with its thousands of pinpoints of dazzling light and waited for a rush of emotion to fill her. Waited for the beauty of the night to become too great to contain, for the sweetness of the moment to soothe her heart.

It didn't happen. The sound of footsteps, unmistakably American boot-clad footsteps on the wooden deck, filled her senses instead.

Brigham came to stand beside her. "I've witnessed through your words and actions that you are not convinced your grandfather made the right decision to move to Nauvoo—and to bring you with him." The apostle seemed to be watching her with deep intensity, though it was difficult to tell in the pale starlight.

"Is that the truth you had to tell me?" she countered.

"No," he said without elaborating.

She let silence fall between them, and didn't hurry to fill it.

Finally, he continued. "It has to do with why your grandfather made the decision."

"That's no secret," she said. "He's been enamored with America's western frontier for years. Living in such a place, sharing a new, uniquely American frontier religion, appealed to him."

"You mention nothing about his decision to follow the revelations of the Prophet."

"I'm quite certain that if the same religion had been born in England, he wouldn't have given it a second look."

Brigham turned to look out to sea, the wind lifting his shoulder-length hair.

Without his asking the obvious, she went on: "I have to admit I don't feel as passionately as my grandfather does about going to Nauvoo, or about the Saints or God's role in this new church. Or mine, for that matter."

Above them the sails snapped and the ship rocked and swayed with the movement of the current. The breeze stung her face and made her eyes water.

"God is with you and your grandfather. There will be times of questioning, that's only natural, but you must trust God's chosen Prophet. Trust that what I and what others have witnessed is God's holy truth. That your grandfather has made the right decisions."

She narrowed her eyes as she looked up at him. "You said decisions?"

"Yes, decisions that weren't easy, any of them."

"Now you're finally getting to the truth you told the others that I need to know."

He studied her for several moments before speaking again. "You are an independent young woman, and that is commendable. But your grandfather made decisions about your future that you need to honor."

"We made the decision to sail to America together," Mary Rose said. "I knew how badly he wanted to see the Wild West one last time, and when he brought it up, I thought it seemed a grand adventure."

"A grand adventure? Has your commitment to the Saints, to our Prophet meant so little to you as that?"

"Perhaps I've been too frank, but I've made no secret about my doubts. I was put off by your announcement to the captain's guests after I left the dinner party—an announcement in which you said I needed to know the 'truth.'" She pressed her lips together and took a deep breath before continuing. "I am unused to the public airing of what is, I'm certain, a private matter, something that should remain between my grandfather and me."

"I've known from the beginning that for your grandfather this was a permanent move. I've also sensed that you thought you'd let him have his way for a while, look over our town, our Nauvoo, our way of life, and if it doesn't suit you, you'd merely tell your grandfather that it's time to go home. Just as you indicated tonight."

"I have held to that comfort. If Nauvoo doesn't work out for us, we'll make our way home."

"Now we're getting nearer to the truth you need to hear."

She lifted her chin and tilted her head, giving him a practiced patrician look she saved for suitable occasions. "I suppose you're about to tell me Grandfather signed away our lives to the Saints"—she laughed—"and that we'll not be allowed to leave Nauvoo for the rest of our days."

"No, no," he said, with a quite sober tone. "It's nothing like that. But the truth is, you can't return to Ashley Manor."

She stared at him wordlessly, her heart pounding. When she finally spoke she fought to keep her voice steady. "And why not?"

"Because the earl signed all of your holdings over to Joseph Smith before your departure."

She stared at him in utter silence. Finally, she said, "Would you repeat that?"

"Your grandfather gave the estate and everything on it to Joseph Smith."

Her mind refused to accept the significance of his words. "If you mean he made a gift of some of our vast acreage that makes sense. As to the other, I know my grandfather. He would never turn over our ancestral home to anyone, church, charity, the queen."

"Your home is with us. It's not a building of stone, no matter how ancient, no matter how many generations have lived there. Even the grounds, the gardens, are temporal. Your real home, that which is on earth, is building the kingdom of God, building up treasures in heaven by your work here . . ." His voice remained low and urgent, yet strangely quiet as if he were calming a troubled child.

"You've been toying with a new religion, not totally committed, yet not against it. The time will come when you need to stand either with us or against us, and that 'us' may very well include your grandfather."

"You are wrong," she said, "about my grandfather and me. But that is not what is important right now. Right now, I need to see if the wrong that has been done to him can be undone." She started to leave, but Brigham stepped in front of her.

"You need to hear me out."

"I've heard enough."

He spoke as if she hadn't uttered a word. "You will soon see," he continued, "that once you make the decision to give your all to the teachings of the Prophet and to obey to the uttermost his revelations from God, a strange and wondrous peace will fill your heart." He paused. "When that happens you will never look back. You will not want to look back. You will no longer yearn for your childhood home."

He stepped closer to her, the same sense of urgency in his voice. "Think of the angel that appeared to a simple, humble man, telling him God had a plan for his people . . . that after all these hundreds, yea, thousands of years, the God who spoke to Moses in the burning bush, the God who gave the Israelites the Ten Commandments, wasn't through with his people. His angels still appear, as the visitation of Moroni proves; he still draws those to himself who are worthy to be counted among his people."

She still glared at him. "Have you considered, sir, that right now I don't want to be counted among the worthy?"

Again he ignored her words. "I have wanted to tell you the truth from the beginning, to answer the unspoken questions I've seen in your eyes. Until tonight, you've held your tongue, a good and pleasant practice for a saintly woman," he said, "and I commend you for that. Because I believe that it was out of love and concern for your grandfather that you did not approach him with your questions."

"Tell me the rest," she said.

"Your grandfather contacted the Prophet by letter more than a year ago, asking to meet with one of the apostles when we arrived here. He wanted to speak to someone with authority, someone who was closer than anyone else to the Prophet. He had already met a number of times with his solicitor and understood every detail of what he was about to do. He wanted to make sure it was done legally and properly on the Church's end of the transaction."

Mary Rose frowned. "He said nothing of this to me."

"He'd heard of the Prophet's success in recruiting converts in Canada. He'd also heard that Joseph was planning to send his twelve apostles to England, Scotland, and Wales as missionaries. Your grandfather made inquiries about the new Church, and liked what he'd heard." Brigham smiled. "We're just rebel enough to appeal to that frontier spirit inside his soul. He'd also heard that the Prophet has an almost supernatural touch when it comes to making money. But as any good financier knows, it takes money to make money. All that was a consideration with the earl.

"He'd decided what he wanted to do long before I arrived, and he wrote of his plan in great detail in a letter to the Prophet, also his reasoning. He'd borrowed against the estate for years, plus the upkeep was getting beyond what he could manage. His solicitor drew up papers, and your estate was signed over to the Prophet the day before your departure. The Church took on the debt, and we'll pay it off. But the land, the home, now belongs to the Church and will help tremendously in upcoming missionary efforts in England."

She remembered how he never looked back that day. Sorrow mixed with anger settled into her heart. Why hadn't her grandfather told her? Did he think her incapable of helping him make such a decision? What if there had been another way? She drew in a deep breath, thoughts and questions flying into her brain, her heart, faster than she could capture them.

"The Church now owns the estate and everything on it. In return your grandfather will get a prime piece of farmland and the house of his choice built on it, a barn or two, livestock, a carriage or farm wagon, whichever he would like, even someone to help him on the property. Or if he'd prefer, a house in town near the Prophet's, which is located in a prime area near the new temple.

"Your grandfather also asked that the two of you sail by clipper ship, with first-class accommodations rather than steerage, which is how most converts travel, and he asked for a maid for you and a manservant for him—to experience, for the last time, the life of a country gentleman, a titled gentleman, playing the role of the wealthy."

Mary Rose turned to Brigham again. "Why this church? Why did he think it was the only one long before his conversion?"

"I think because the Saints embody that same wild spirit he grew to love on his previous travels there. And finally—and most importantly—that God had chosen this plainspoken young man from Palmyra, New York, as his Prophet to restore his Church—his only Church—on earth. He'd long believed other churches didn't offer a view of God he could believe in or dedicate his life to, yet the religious teachings of the young Prophet did."

"He had concluded all this before your arrival?"

Brigham shook his head. "The rest is as you yourself witnessed. Your grandfather read the Book of Mormon, which I brought to him, signed by the Prophet to your grandfather. He felt the burning in his heart, personally testified to its truth, and was baptized into the fellowship of the Saints, just as you witnessed.

"I have seen the longing in your eyes, a longing to go home. I feared even tonight at the captain's table when you spoke so boldly to your grandfather in front of the others that he would hesitate to tell you what he'd done."

"And you thought it should be a private matter?" Her voice was shrill, but she didn't care.

He didn't answer.

"You thought it so private that you waited until I left the room, and then you announced to my grandfather in front of everyone else that it was time to tell me the truth? You thought that private?"

"I knew it was time for you to know the truth. If others overheard, so be it. Your home is with the Saints now. You can't return to England."

He bade her good night, tipped his hat, then walked back toward the quarterdeck. She stared after him as he disappeared into the darkness.

You can't return to England.

She swallowed hard, started to cry, and then thought better of it. Brigham couldn't be right about this. Her grandfather had been duped. She'd heard of such things, especially when it came to a new religion led by a self-proclaimed savior. She felt it in her bones. Whatever had been done could be undone; whatever needed fixing could be fixed. Her iron-willed grandfather had taught her that much about life. And about herself. Her backbone was wrapped in iron, he'd always told her.

Never return to the manor? She almost laughed. Of course she could. It might take some planning, some sleuthing, but if ever she wanted to return, she would find a way.

She wouldn't cry, she willed herself not to. But the tears flowed anyway. She turned around to face the bow of the ship, closed her eyes, and let the wind dry her wet cheeks.

NINE

The *Sea Hawk* seemed to be running with a current or perhaps a sudden wind had caught her sails. Mary Rose felt the movement of the ship and an almost dizzying sense of speed—and vertigo. She caught the railing with her hands and waited until the sensation passed. Vaguely, she became aware of someone watching her. She glanced over to the curve of the deck, just beyond the bow. Gabe MacKay lolled against the railing, propped with his elbows, one ankle crossed over the other.

"My ancestral land," she said. "It's supposedly gone."

"Supposedly?" Gabe walked toward her and then turned to face the sea, just as she was, his hands on the railing.

"I'll get it back."

"What does your grandfather have to say about it?"

"I haven't talked with him, but Brigham made it clear. In exchange for his generous gift to the Saints, we'll have everything we'll need to get to Nauvoo—our passage on the *Sea Hawk*, wagons and horses for transport from Boston, lodging along the way—and when we arrive in Nauvoo, the means to build ourselves a house, and some livestock and crops to put on our new land."

"If I were a betting man, which I am not, I would bet that someone with your spirit and gumption and intelligence and heaven-knows-what-else that's inside that beautiful head of yours—I'd say that the sale or gift or whatever you want to call it of your ancestral home has little to do with who you are or how you'll make your way in life."

"I'm glad you think so." Her tone wasn't exactly without sarcasm.

He chuckled. "From the moment I saw you climbing over the groom's bench on the landau, I knew that nothing, absolutely nothing, would ever stand in your way to get at what you want."

"I'll keep that picture in mind when I visit the Prophet and demand my lands and ancestral home be returned to me." She couldn't help laughing at the image.

"I know without a doubt it is a picture I'll keep tucked away in my mind. If you could only have seen yourself . . ." He shook his head, his eyes bright with amusement, even in the starlight. He pointed to the North Star. "That, m'lady, is how brightly you burn—it is also a light you must pay attention to . . . and follow."

He quirked a brow. "Methinks, m'lady, you are a woman who very seldom does as she ought. In fact, my gut—if I may use such an indelicate word—tells me that until your talk with your dear apostle, you were about to convince your grandfather to get the captain to turn the ship around and return you to jolly old England."

"True, but 'tis not your gut, dear sir, 'tis your acute hearing. I so much as told my grandfather we should return home at supper."

He paused, again gazing into the deep night sky. "Look up at that star and tell me what is it you want in life, more than anything else? And I don't mean becoming a Saint."

The question took Mary Rose by surprise. He had guessed her ambivalence. "For weeks, even months, I've tried to think what life would be like, obeying the Prophet, laying everything that I am, or ever could hope to be, at his feet in the name of the heavenly Father. But it hasn't settled in my heart the way it should have, the way others have witnessed it has been for them."

"Commendable that you tried, and I can say honestly that I admire—even envy—such commitment in the apostle, in your grandfather, even in the Prophet himself. But what about you, Mary Rose Ashley, what do you wish for as you gaze at that star?"

She lifted her eyes to the dark heavens, aware that Gabe was watching her.

"That light," she said after a few minutes, "if such a light burns bright inside me, symbolizes love."

"Love?" he said, and she noticed a hint of gladness in his voice.

"Yes. Love for God, for others, for those things in life I hold dear—"

"And what would those things be?"

"Writing my thoughts in my journal . . ."

"Many people keep journals," he said, stepping closer as if to better see her in the starlight. "What brings the word 'love' to your mind when thinking of writing?"

She looked into his eyes, saw something deeper than mere curiosity, and felt instinctively that she could trust him with her heart's dream. "Poetry, sonnets, stories . . . the people who live in the worlds I create."

"You record people?"

She smiled, turning away from the North Star to see him more fully. "People who populate the stories I create in my mind."

"Characters," he said in wonder. "As in a novel."

"Yes. Characters." A comfortable silence fell between them, but he didn't take his eyes off her. "'Tis my heart's greatest desire to write such a book. I could never be a Jane Austen or Charles

Dickens, but . . . oh, how lovely it would be to attempt such a work."

"And your story," he said, "is it a love story?"

She smiled. "Aye, 'tis."

He laughed. "Next ye'll be sayin' 'bannock's boucle,'" he said in an exaggerated brogue. She laughed with him, then he said, "But back to your love story—it has a man and woman who meet and fall in love, does it?"

"I have yet to write that scene," she said, feeling her heart beat faster. "And truly, though love plays a part, the entirety of my story is broader and deeper than mere human love. There are other details to see to, other actions for the characters to carry out, puzzles to solve, troubles to get through, and of course triumphs in the—"

"Perhaps it plays so small a role because, Lady Mary Rose, you yourself have never experienced *mere* human love." A half-smile played at the corner of his mouth.

"'Tis true enough, I suppose," she said. "And you, Mr. MacKay? Have you experienced such a thing?"

He gazed at her for a long moment. Above them the sails billowed and snapped, the rigging clanked against the masts, and though the latest watch had just changed and the men were taking their posts, it seemed to Mary Rose that they were alone in the universe.

Taking her hand, Gabe turned her toward the North Star. She left her hand in his, enjoying the warmth and the gentle squeeze he gave her fingers. With this man at her side, she could almost forget the words of the apostle.

"I have not experienced such love, mere or otherwise," he said. "But tonight that star makes me believe such love might be possible."

"It would have to be a love that is willing to forsake all others," she breathed, keeping her eyes on the brilliant heavenly body.

"Perhaps giving up goals and aspirations . . . at least that's the kind of love the characters in my story have for each other. A love so strong it is nurtured and cared for above all other loves."

"Aye," he said, "a sacrificial kind of love."

"That is it exactly," she said, venturing a look at his moonlit silhouette.

"Where one is asked to give up, perhaps, a life's goal for the other," he said, "to win the abiding love of the one he or she adores."

"I must write your observations on love in my journal when I return to my cabin." She ventured another gaze in his direction. "How much would you be willing to sacrifice, should you find yourself in love . . . a love so strong it is nurtured and cared for above all other loves?"

He turned to study her, and for a moment he didn't speak. Then he lifted her hand and, turning it, kissed her fingertips. "At this moment, I can think of nothing I would not give up for the one I love."

Mary Rose smiled up at him and tilted her head. "Of course, you are speaking hypothetically," she said. "And I am exploring ideas for my novel."

He dropped her hand and bowed slightly. "Of course, Lady Mary Rose." He offered her his arm. "Now, may I escort you back to your cabin?"

"I would like that," she said, and when he offered his arm, she took it. "I'm curious," she said as they strolled along the deck, "about your beliefs."

"Do you mean about my church affiliation? I belong to the Church of England."

"No, I mean about God. What do you believe about him? Is he a personal God you can picture? Such as you can another human? Or is he distant and unapproachable?"

He laughed. "You do have a way with words. Sadly, I fear the second option is truer than the first. If I picture him at all, he's an old man with a white beard who gets easily distracted."

"Easily distracted?"

"Yes. It's been my experience that he doesn't necessarily watch out for his creation, for those he supposedly loves," he said, and she noticed his voice held none of the warmth of their earlier conversation.

They stopped near the railing before walking into the companionway between the cabins. She slipped her hand from the crook of Gabe's arm where he'd tucked it. "Something happened to you, then, to cause such a picture of God."

He smiled slightly. "Yes, and perhaps someday I'll tell you about it. Right now isn't the right time. But I don't believe my experience is much different than what other humans experience. Is the God of our universe a personal God, as you call him? Or is he a disinterested, distracted being that created the world on a whim and simply keeps things running and watches us all making a mess of things?" He paused. "We build cathedrals to him, we worship him with music and prayer, yet what does he do for us in return?"

She saw emptiness and pain in his eyes and wanted to cry because right now she almost agreed with him.

"Nothing," he said.

She turned to look up at him, studying his eyes, feeling she could easily get lost in their depths. For a moment she couldn't speak, then she said, "Would you do something for me?"

He gave her a half-smile and raised one eyebrow. "You're not trying to convert me, are you?"

"On the contrary," she said. "I'm trying to find out if I—and my grandfather—have been duped."

With this, Gabe threw his head back and laughed. "Is this a new method of reeling in new converts? Subversion?"

She did not laugh with him. "From the beginning, I have questioned this new faith. Though my grandfather has embraced it, I have not. But now I must make a decision." She looked down, studying her thoughts before continuing. "I suppose you could say I'm at a crossroads. I'm rather independent, and it has been difficult to me to think of submitting to a greater authority—to a fellow human being, I mean. To someone such as the Prophet.

"But what if he is God's chosen one for this time? What if he was visited by the angel Moroni and told where to find the golden plates and the translations are true, and what if when I turn my back on the Church and the Prophet, I am turning my back on God himself? I haven't wanted to believe . . ."

"Because of your unwillingness to submit to the authority of the Church and to the Prophet and his apostles?"

She walked a few feet away from him then turned back. "Can I have both? Can I follow my 'star' and write stories of love and follow my heart's desire"— she frowned—"and still bend to the authority of the Saints?"

"You're probably asking the wrong person," Gabe said, walking toward her. "I told you how I feel about God."

They started into the first-class companionway, lit by hanging oil lamps.

"That's why I'm asking your opinion," she said as they walked. "You are a learned man who is heading the opposite direction— from belief of any kind—because you don't believe in a supreme being who might dare to become involved in today's world, in your world. You will be honest." She looked up at him. "Brigham tells us that we bear witness to the message of the Book by feeling its truth in our souls."

"That burning inside one's soul I've been hearing about."

"Yes."

They reached her cabin. Gabe stepped closer, placed his hands on her shoulders, and searched her eyes with his own, dark with emotion. "'Tis the Book you want me to read, then?"

"My copy is inside, if you would be so kind—"

Gabe laughed again. "Right at this moment I would do anything in the world for you—as I said earlier. I must let you know that had this request been made by anyone else, it would receive a resounding *no*. You already know that I'm not searching for God. If anyone, whether it be Brigham Young, Joseph Smith, or Abraham himself, had tried to preach to me, I would run in the opposite direction. I'm quite happy with my view of a disinterested God. He's disinterested in me; therefore, I'm just as disinterested in him."

"But you will read the Book and tell me what you think."

"For you, I will read your Book."

She quickly opened her door and retrieved her copy of the Book of Mormon.

He gave her a gentle smile as the book passed between them and their fingers touched. "Had this been a true missionary effort, and had the object of your effort been anyone else but Gabriel MacKay, likely the object of your effort would feel the 'burning' inside that so many have described." He grinned at her. "And the object of your missionary effort would be baptized in the Atlantic before dawn."

She laughed as he bowed to kiss her fingertips. "'Tis me, dear Mr. MacKay, who needs the converting. That is why I asked."

Smiling, he straightened and, leaning in closer, kissed her cheek. "Good night, Lady Mary Rose."

"Good night, Mr. MacKay," she whispered.

He gave her a wink, and then was gone.

TEN

G abe's heart raced as he headed back to the deck, the Book tucked under his arm. He'd known Lady Mary Rose Ashley only two days, yet she was beginning to slip into his every thought, and he supposed she would be in his dreams this night.

He had to draw a halt to feelings for her that already filled his heart to the spilling point, creating havoc with his sensibilities. He'd been correct when he said he'd do just about anything in the world for her—making it clear to himself and to her that if it had been anyone else asking, he wouldn't crack open the Book of Mormon—supposedly translated from ancient Egyptian . . . from the missing golden plates . . . by a fourteen-year-old boy . . . shown by an angel where to find them. Only no one could verify their existence because the plates were missing. Or stolen. Or hidden. Or never existed in the first place. He chuckled. What a pile of *firlot mell*.

The whole thing was preposterous. But here he was, holding the Book in his hands because he was falling in love with a woman he would never see again once she and her grandfather stepped off the ship in Boston, less than two weeks from now.

He shook his head at his own foolishness. No, worse than that, his own madness.

It was growing late. The passengers rested in their cabins and only the night-watch seamen remained on duty. Even with seas turning rough, late watch provided time and space to mend sails and tend to the riggings. Several hailed greetings as he strode toward the quarterdeck, where he knew he'd find the captain.

Hosea called out to him. Gabe looked up to the railing where he stood, pale in the starlit night, and gave him a mock salute. Then he bounded up the stairs three at a time.

The chief mate stood at the wheel and acknowledged Gabe with a nod as he approached. "Storm's approaching," Mr. Thorpe said, keeping his gaze on the dark horizon.

The swells had been rising over the past hour, and now white-caps were visible as far as the eye could see, their peaks of white froth luminescent in the starlight. The *Sea Hawk* rose and fell and shuddered. "How far out?"

"I say by morning we'll hit the worst of it, but that doesn't mean it won't be a rough night," Mr. Thorpe said. "Signs have been apparent all day, especially before sundown."

"This ship can take anything nature throws at it," Gabe said.

The captain laughed. "Would you tell us otherwise?"

"My only wish is that Cunard had seen fit to outfit us with a barometer."

The captain laughed again. "Those small enough to transport are still not accurate enough to bother with, especially considering the cost."

"I've heard good things about a new barometer made in Italy," Gabe said. "Talked to Cunard about it, but he's in a wait-and-see state of mind."

"Wait till we become the fastest ship to ever cross the Atlantic," Mr. Thorpe said, tossing a grin in Gabe's direction. "Then you can ask for a dozen barometers of any size, and he'll deliver them to your cabin himself."

Gabe chuckled. "Unless it's his clipper we beat for the record."

"I'd take two eyes and a good nose over a barometer any day," Mr. Thorpe said. "I can smell storms brewing. I smelled one this morning, and sure enough, the other signs were apparent by dusk."

"Fish?" Gabe said as the ship rose on the crest of a wave.

The captain nodded. "The passengers should be warned."

The captain bade good evening to the chief mate and told him to give him a report at the end of his watch. Then he led the way down the steps to the main deck, Gabe following.

"It will be a long night," he said to Gabe. "I'll get the steward to bring coffee while we record your latest findings in the log." He gave the sextant Gabe was holding a pointed look, and then grinned. "Unless, of course, you were too busy to take readings." Then he frowned. "What's the book?"

"The Book of Mormon, sir."

Hosea halted. "Tell me I didn't hear you right, Gabe."

"You did, sir. Lady Mary Rose asked me to have a look, tell her what I think."

"I would think she'd already know her own mind on the subject."

"Apparently not, sir. She's unsure of the leadership and bristles that she may be told what to do, when, and how."

The captain chuckled. "What's so unusual about that? I thought most women had that character quirk." Then he sobered. "Truly, Gabe, there's something about this new religion that doesn't sit well with me." He looked into his friend's eyes, his concern evident. "I've always thought that when a man sets himself up as equal to God, and tells his followers that his revelations are from God, there's something to be concerned about."

They made their way to the captain's quarters. They had just reached the door when a child shouted from several feet away.

Gabe frowned. It was the little ruffian traveling with the earl and Lady Mary Rose.

Even before he reached them, Gabe saw his tears and frantic expression. "Hurry, sirs," Coal cried to Gabe and the captain. "You gotta do something."

"Son, what's happened?" Gabe stooped to look the child in the face.

"'Tis Mrs. Carey, sir. I think she's a-dyin'. She's screaming and hollering something terrible." He rubbed his wet eyes with his fists, his gaze darting from Gabe to the captain, and then back again. "I'm sure of it. She's dying. Lady told Mr. Carey to fetch you or the captain or just about anybody, a midwife if there's one aboard, or a surgeon—but I took off running 'cause it didn't seem he could bear to leave Mrs. Carey, with her a-dyin' and all." He sniffled then wiped his nose on his sleeve. "Somebody's gotta come. Please hurry!"

ELEVEN

Mary Rose sat at Bronwyn's bedside, holding her hand, as the *Sea Hawk* sailed deeper into the night skies and into the storm.

The twins were with her grandfather, and Coal was who knew where, having panicked at Bronwyn's crying out when the birth pangs began, mistaking Mary Rose's requests to Griffin as his own.

She swallowed hard. Truly, all she knew about childbirth was that her own mother had died giving birth to her baby brother who died within minutes of their mother. Mary Rose had been just six years of age at the time.

She had to do something. Anything. She couldn't just sit there, waiting for someone to come to her rescue.

She might be the only one to help Bronwyn. The thought terrified her, but she pushed back her shoulders and stepped outside the door. In an authoritative voice, purposely loud enough for Bronwyn to hear, she ordered the first cabin boy who walked toward her cabin to bring two bowls, one of boiling water, the other tepid, rags, blankets, and a sharp clean-cutting instrument—though with the latter, she wouldn't know what to do. She added tweezers and a large, flat stirring spoon for good measure.

With quaking knees, she made her way over to the basin on the stand, poured cool water on a cloth, and then went back to sit by Bronwyn's side. She brushed wisps of her friend's hair from her face, and then folded the cloth and placed it on her forehead.

Bronwyn's eyes fluttered open and she gazed up at Mary Rose. "'Twill be a long night." She winced as another birth pang shot through her body. She grabbed Mary Rose's hands and held them so tight Mary Rose thought surely her bones might break.

She gave Bronwyn a courageous and calm smile. "Just try to breathe easy and let your muscles go slack," she said. "Babies do most of the work on their own; you just need to try to relax and let the wee one do the rest."

Bronwyn shook her head. "Not this one," she whispered, which worried Mary Rose further. She'd known Bronwyn to expect the best outcome no matter the signs to the contrary . . . until now. Her face seemed to grow paler in the dim light.

The ship rocked and swayed worse than before. Besides Mary Rose's knees feeling made of fresh-dripped candle wax, now her stomach was beginning to complain as well. She looked around for an empty basin should she need it even as she continued a soft, calming conversation about the twins, Coal, Griffin, and the adventures ahead in America. Bronwyn still clutched Mary Rose's hands as if they provided her a lifeline, but she relaxed her grip somewhat.

A quick rap sounded at the Careys' cabin door. Mary Rose crossed the room and peered out. It was the boy she'd spoken to earlier. It seemed he'd brought a small battalion of green boys with him, some carrying tubs and buckets of steaming water, some carrying the other items she'd called for. She asked a couple with empty hands to move the table nearer the bed, showed them where to set the tubs, stacks of rags, and extra blankets.

The army of cabin boys left the room, looking somber and scared. She thought it probable that they might be as frightened as she was over the mystery of this childbirth, but as they left, they were speaking of the great squall ahead, bad enough that the captain himself was on watch with the chief mate on the quarterdeck.

At that news, her stomach lurched. She took several deep breaths, and went again to stand by Bronwyn's bedside to keep vigil and decide what to do next. If the captain was busy on watch, that likely meant he hadn't found a midwife, or had been too busy to send for one.

Another pain caused Bronwyn to cry out in agony. Tears in her eyes, Mary Rose reached for her hands and held them tight until it passed.

Bronwyn closed her eyes and Mary Rose paced, twisting her hands behind her back, searching her mind for any snatches of conversation she might have overheard during the years about what one does when assisting in childbirth. She'd not even had the experience of watching a mare foal, or even a barn cat or rabbit for that matter. She chastised herself for not paying closer attention, but who would ever have thought she would need such a skill?

She'd acted quickly and without thought when she attempted to save Coal, the team of horses, and the carriage from flying off the wharf. Surely such a thing as catching a child couldn't be much more difficult.

Unless there were complications.

The word had been repeated through the years when relatives talked about the passing of Mary Rose's mother in childbirth. To Mary Rose, childbirth and complications equaled death.

She looked down at Bronwyn with affection, her eyes filling again. What if there were complications? She could not stand by and do nothing. It wasn't her nature.

She measured time by her heartbeats; a minute passed, and then two. And then another. Outside, the wind blasted and moaned and soon the patter of rain hitting the overhead ventilation door turned into a downpour. Bronwyn endured another contraction, sobbing as she cried out in pain.

Mary Rose had had quite enough. She bent close to Bronwyn and whispered, "I'll be right back, dear one. I promise. Nothing is happening right now, so I'm going to the captain to ask the whereabouts of the midwife I ordered him to find."

Bronwyn managed a small, lopsided smile. "You gave an order to the captain?"

She grinned. "In a manner of speaking, though I'm not certain anyone delivered it. Poor Griffin is frightened out of his wits, and Grandfather is trying to keep him calm, and who knows if the captain or anyone else paid attention to a scared little boy carrying a message such as I sent. I'm going to march right up to the quarterdeck, look the captain in the eye, and demand that he find a midwife for us right now."

Bronwyn nodded, a hint of a smile still on her face. "Hurry," she said.

She grabbed her cloak and slipped through the doorway, surprised to find one of the cabin boys standing outside her door. "Mr. MacKay told me to stay," he explained, "and let him know if you be needin' anything."

For an instant, she considered sending him for the captain but realized he would not be allowed on the quarterdeck, so she said, "Just stay here, and if Mr. MacKay comes by, please ask him to wait here with you. I need to have a word with him. "

"Aye," the boy said.

Mary Rose pulled her cloak closer and, head down, made her

way toward the quarterdeck. The wind whipped her clothing as the ship dipped and swayed, the deck waves now crashing high enough to send foam racing across the slick surface. She lost her footing twice, regaining it each time. Above the sounds of the wind and rain she heard the chief mate calling out orders to the starboard watch. Ropes flew every which way, rigging clanked, some sails were hoisted down and others shot up to the tops of masts.

It wasn't safe to continue on to the quarterdeck. Neither could she return to Bronwyn without help. She took one more step and slipped again, sliding toward the rail.

A strong arm came from behind and caught her around the waist, holding her fast until she regained her footing. Before she could turn around to see who it was, she was back to the safety of the lower deck.

Soaking wet, she whirled from the man's hold.

Gabriel MacKay stood in front of her. "It's getting tiresome, these rescues of the Ashleys," he said. Though his words were half in jest, his eyes flashed with anger. "What did you think you could accomplish by going on deck in such a storm?"

She gave him what she hoped was an equally withering look. "I sent for a midwife at least an hour ago for Bronwyn Car—"

Taking her elbow, he propelled her toward her cabin, growling between clenched teeth, "You could have been killed out there. Besides, no one is allowed on the quarterdeck, fair weather or foul. Don't you know that?"

She glared at him. "You can make me walk the plank tomorrow, but for now, you—or someone, anyone—must find a surgeon or a midwife. Someone who knows how to deliver a baby."

"The boy Coal told the captain earlier. He gave the second mate the order to go over the manifest. That's been done, and indeed, there is a midwife on board."

Mary Rose let out a long sigh. "Has she been contacted?"

"Yes, she's gathering her things and should be at the cabin now."

He kept his hand cupped beneath her elbow longer than she thought necessary. But she didn't pull away from him; instead, she relished the warm strength of him striding next to her. And she didn't want to think what might have happened had he not been there to catch her when she slipped.

When they reached her door, she looked up at Gabe. The anger in his eyes had dissipated, and in its place was something akin to tenderness.

She turned and stepped inside just as she heard Bronwyn's cry turn into a long wail. Mary Rose rushed over.

"There's something . . . wrong," Bronwyn breathed once the contraction was over. "The baby is blocked somehow from passing through the birth canal. I can feel it . . . in my . . . bones." She started to cry. "Help me, Mary Rose . . ."

The pure agony of the sound brought tears to Mary Rose's eyes. *Complications.*

A light tapping sounded at the door. Without waiting to be invited in, a tall, slender woman entered and strode over to Bronwyn.

She walked with grace, carrying herself in a way that seemed ageless, and Mary Rose thought of something she'd read many years ago. The Anglo-Saxon word for midwife was *med-wyf*, which meant "wisewoman." This woman's wide intelligent eyes and hair the color of lightning in a black sky made her seem as though she was of some medieval line of wisewomen.

She carried a leather valise, which she opened, removing several instruments. "My name is Grace Carolyn Brumby," she said. "I'm a midwife, and I've come to help in any way I can." Without waiting for a comment or answer, she turned her attention to Bronwyn, probed the sides of Bronwyn's face, felt for her pulse in her neck and then her wrist. She lifted Bronwyn's right foot and pressed her fingers around the ankle. She did the same with the left. "Very swollen," she said, mostly to herself.

"Let's have a look now, shall we?" She pulled back the blanket at Bronwyn's feet.

Mary Rose had already propped Bronwyn's back and head with extra blankets and pillows and now she helped the midwife lift Bronwyn's legs into position. "Our little one is not cooperating, that's the trouble," Grace Carolyn said after the examination. "We have a wee behind where the head should be." She looked up at Mary Rose. "And she's not yet sufficiently dilated for me to turn the baby."

Bronwyn cried out as another strong contraction hit, this time sobbing hysterically as the midwife laid out her tools on the table. Mary Rose held the lamp steady as she took at least a dozen small pots of dried herbs from the valise and lined them up on the table. Each was labeled: Squaw Vine, Beth Root, Goldenseal, Blue Cohosh, Chamomile, and St. John's Wort. Next she brought out some oils: lavender, rose, almond, and jasmine. The last item was a sturdy but shallow clay dish. In it she spilled some juniper twigs and berries and the seeds from another pot labeled Ashenkeys.

She asked Mary Rose to lower the lamp and reached for a juniper twig, igniting the short slender wood. Then she dropped the enflamed twig into the clay dish. Immediately, the fragrance of juniper filled the room.

"For cleansing," the midwife said.

She mixed the oils together, and their fragrance wafted throughout the room, mingling with the scent of juniper.

Mary Rose was surprised when she poured some of the liquid into her palms, and then instructed her to massage it into Bronwyn's hands, wrists, arms, neck, and shoulders.

While Mary Rose was doing as asked, Grace Carolyn poured small measurements of the dried herbs into a shallow ceramic dish and crushed them with a pestle. As they worked, Bronwyn would cry out, though Mary Rose noticed her cries becoming weaker and, when sobbing, no tears came to her eyes.

The midwife stirred the mixture into a cup of water. The fragrant earthy scent reminded Mary Rose of the ancient woods near Ashley Manor.

"You'll need to hold her head," Grace Carolyn said. "Careful now . . ." She drizzled spoonfuls of the medicine on the inside of Bronwyn's cheek until the glass was empty. Bronwyn lay back against her pillow, her breathing shallow.

"First we relax the muscles," she said, "so I can turn the baby. I'd rather not use forceps, but if I must I will."

The *Sea Hawk* hit a large swell, and as it crested, she slammed down, the table shifted, and the pots of medicine tipped. The rain was as loud as any thunder Mary Rose had ever heard, and the wind wailed and moaned. With every move of the ship, Mary Rose imagined it breaking to pieces and wondered how the vessel could withstand such punishment. Her knees threatened to buckle beneath her, and then she turned to Grace Carolyn, expecting to see the same fear Mary Rose felt in her eyes. But the midwife seemed unconcerned: The storm could rage, the ship creak and groan, but it seemed she possessed an unshakable tranquillity.

"Now we pray," Grace Carolyn said. She knelt beside Bronwyn's bed, and Mary Rose knelt beside her.

The midwife held Bronwyn's hand with her left and Mary Rose's with her right.

"Almighty God and Father of all mercies, we give you thanks for your child Bronwyn," she prayed. "We bless you for her creation, and for the creation of the child she carries, we bless you most of all for your immeasurable love for them and for her friend Mary Rose, and for me. I lay this mother and child at the feet of the risen Christ: though we hold them dear and beg that you might turn this child so he may be born and so the mother will live, we know your love for them is far greater than ours and that your will for them goes far beyond what we can imagine is best. So we ask that your will be done, trusting in your immeasurable love that you showed in the redemption of this world through your Son, our Lord and Savior Jesus Christ."

The midwife placed her hand above where the baby lay unable to move. "Father Almighty, keep this child in your loving care—give my hands the strength and skill to turn him, and give Bronwyn the strength to bear it."

She reached into a pocket in her apron and retrieved a tiny vial of oil. As she opened it, Mary Rose breathed in the soft fragrance of almond oil. The midwife poured a few drops in her hand, touched them with her fingers, and then made the sign of the cross on Bronwyn's forehead, also on her own.

Out of habit, Mary Rose crossed herself as they both stood. The midwife went to the foot of the bed and prepared Bronwyn for turning the baby; Mary Rose bent over the bed and kissed her friend's forehead. Bronwyn's eye didn't flutter as before, and her color seemed almost gray.

Mary Rose held the lamp over the midwife's right shoulder as she began to force her hands into the birth canal. Her hands were delicate and nimble, her fingers strong for their small size. She gave few orders as she worked to turn the baby. There was a slight movement . . . and then another. . .

Bronwyn groaned and her breathing became shallow. Then it stopped completely. The sounds of the storm rushed into the room, the pounding of the rain and rumble of distant thunder. Mary Rose held her own breath, waiting . . . Finally Bronwyn gasped for another breath.

Instinctively, Mary Rose reached for Bronwyn's wrist and felt for a pulse. "It's weaker than before," she said, tears filling her eyes. She waited for the next breath to come.

A light knock at the door sounded, and when Mary Rose cracked it open, she saw it was Griffin. "How is she?"

"The baby is in breech position. The midwife is working with her right now."

"Is it bad?"

Mary Rose couldn't lie. "Aye," she whispered. "Bronwyn and your baby both need our prayers."

TWELVE

Minutes later the cabin door burst open. Brigham strode in with Griffin following.

Mary Rose stood. "This is woman's work. You'll need to leave."

Brigham ignored her and returned to the doorway. "Gabriel, Coal, you need to come in here. We're going to pray."

"But we already—"

Griffin rushed to the bed, and reached for Bronwyn's hand. "It's icy cold," he said. "Oh, my darling Bronwyn—wake up, dearest heart. Wake up." He fell to his knees, holding her hands to his face. Gabe came over to stand next to Mary Rose. He looked uncomfortable and ready to bolt. The midwife had quickly covered Bronwyn with a light blanket, and now retired to the table with the water tubs and clean towels to wash her hands. She remained standing there with head bowed reverently as everyone else knelt around Bronwyn's bed.

Brigham moved to the center, laid his hand on Bronwyn's stomach, and said, "Heavenly Father, we ask that you would heal this child and its mother." He waited, then cried out again, "Heavenly Father, heal this child, heal this mother, move this infant into its rightful position for coming into this world."

A third time he repeated the words, and breathless, all waited to see what would happen. Bronwyn took a deep breath, the first in several long moments; stunned, Mary Rose held the lamp closer, unable to believe what she was witnessing.

There was a movement beneath the light blanket, then another, and another. The baby was turned.

Hot tears came to her eyes and Mary Rose watched the faces of the others in the room, as tears filled theirs as well, even Brigham's She looked back to the still moving infant. The baby was alive. It was well. Murmurs of awe and wonder filled the dark room. The midwife stepped closer, her expression puzzled as she watched Brigham.

The contractions began again, and Bronwyn cried out.

"We praise you, O God, for this miracle," Brigham intoned. "What you have accomplished this day, we will never forget. We will be forever grateful, for your works are marvelous beyond compare. We delight in them and thank you for the lives of our Sister Bronwyn, our Brother Griffin, and this miracle child who is about to come into this world, fresh-sent from heaven."

Gabe's eyes met Mary Rose's, and in their depths was something new. She was stunned.

Faith.

Pure and simple and wondrous faith. She smiled at him and he grinned back, seeming as surprised as she was.

Bronwyn cried out as another intense pain took control of her body, drawing Mary Rose's attention back to the task at hand.

"This time I insist you leave for reasons of Bronwyn's privacy," Mary Rose said with joy. "Go now, and hurry."

Grace Carolyn moved to the foot of the bed and peered beneath the blanket, her face almost glowing with joy. "Mary

Rose," she said, "I want you to have the honor of catching this baby."

Mary Rose thought she might never breathe again as she took her place at the end of the bed. "It's called the crowning," Grace Carolyn said with awe. "I never get over the miracle of birth."

Another swell caught the ship, tipping it to the starboard side. The table slid across the room. Thunder rumbled, but Mary Rose was so caught up in the moment, she almost didn't notice.

"A tiny miracle," Mary Rose whispered. She looked up to see that Bronwyn, her eyes filled with tears, was watching her face. She squeezed her eyes closed as another contraction hit. She cried out and pushed hard, pushed again.

A soft tearing sound made Mary Rose cringe, and then moving closer, she held out her hands.

Seconds later, she held the infant.

She met Bronwyn's eyes and they shared a smiled. "'Tis a girl," she said. "A perfectly formed tiny girl."

The child let out a healthy cry.

Grace Carolyn took care of the umbilical cord, and gently wrapped the infant in a soft, clean cloth. Mary Rose laid the child in Bronwyn's arms.

THIRTEEN

Mary Rose slept in a chair beside Bronwyn's bed. The midwife stopped by frequently to check on mother and child, who both slept peacefully. She mixed herbal drinks to give Bronwyn strength and applied a poultice to stanch the bleeding. She showed Mary Rose how to measure the proper amount of chamomile for the hot water that the cabin boy had been told to bring on the hour. This would help her milk come in, she explained.

By sunrise, the *Sea Hawk* had passed through the storm. At eight bells, Grace Carolyn appeared at the cabin door. Her eyes were full of sympathy for Mary Rose.

"I've had a cat nap or two during the night, but you've had not a wink of sleep," she said, giving Mary Rose a quick hug. "We've taken care of your friend, and now you need some taking care of yourself. Get some fresh air while I order something to eat for you both."

"I can think of nothing that sounds better," she said. "Unless it would be that you join us."

Grace Carolyn looked pleased as she went about the business of checking the tie in the baby's umbilical cord, changing the soft blanket, then rewrapping her.

Mary Rose gave her face a quick splash of water, ran her fingers through her hair and headed to the main deck for fresh air. The *Sea Hawk* was moving into calmer waters, and now that Bronwyn and the baby were safe and well, she felt like singing.

Words from Elizabeth Barrett Browning's "A Child Asleep" came to her . . .

> 'Tis the child-heart draws them, singing
> In the silent-seeming clay . . .

She went to the bow, closed her eyes, and stretched her arms out to catch the wind, letting it lift her hair. At a time like this, she didn't care that her thicket of curls had kinked from her venture into the rain the night before, or that her clothes were wrinkled and limp.

All she cared about was the miracle of the baby and Bronwyn and how it had changed her life.

She drew the fresh sea air deep into her lungs and relived the moment the child had moved during Brigham's prayer. And the first moment she held the warm, moist body of Bronwyn's tiny miracle baby and recognized God's creative power. How could she not believe?

Someone stepped up beside her. She turned. It was Gabriel MacKay. He held the Book of Mormon as if it were more precious than gold. He caught her hand and held it with his against the soft leather binding. Then he threw back his head and laughed. It was a sound of utter joy. "I believe," he said. "I needed a miracle, and God provided it last night."

For a moment neither of them spoke. Mary Rose felt her wrinkled skirts billowing in the wind and her curls flying everywhere.

It seemed like a long time ago since she cared about such things. Right now all she cared about was the man standing in front of her, his declaration of faith, and what it might mean to them both.

"And I as well," she said. "I've been as much a Doubting Thomas as you have been. It took the movement of that infant for me to believe, to truly believe. I've played around the edges, not knowing for certain about the Prophet, about his missionaries, his apostle Brigham. But after last night"—she blinked back her tears—"after seeing Bronwyn almost die . . . Her pulse was so weak I couldn't find it. There were moments when I thought she had left us, she struggled so to draw in a single breath toward the end." She looked out to sea again, still unable to believe what she'd witnessed. "And now she is alive and well, her wee babe at her breast."

Gabe stepped closer and put his arm around her, and she laid her head against his shoulder. The Book lay against his side in the crook of his other arm. The rigging clanked against the masts, the starboard-watch seamen spoke in hushed voices from their stations, and from the quarterdeck, the chief mate called out tacking orders. Mary Rose wanted to linger there forever.

He turned her gently and looked deep into her eyes. "It is my belief that God planned for us to be on this voyage, to find our new faith, to go with Brigham and the others to a new promised land"—he hesitated for a heartbeat, and then smiled—"together. Lady Mary Rose . . ."

She laughed lightly, still looking up into his eyes. "I believe, Mr. MacKay, that it's time to call me Mary Rose."

Chuckling, he drew her close, holding her tight against his chest, resting his cheek on top of her head. When he spoke, she heard the resonance of his voice through his chest. "Mary Rose, what I'm trying to say is that I've fallen in love with you." He took a step back and gave her a smile that quickened her pulse. She started to speak, but he touched her lips with his fingers. "If I

don't get this all out now," he said, "I may never work up the courage to attempt it again."

Her heart pounded madly as she waited.

He cleared his throat, then reached for her hand, drew it to
his lips, and kissed her fingertips. "What I'm trying to say . . . to
ask . . . is, will you marry me? I know it's sudden, and if you need
time to think about it, I certainly understand. We've only known
each other days, been together maybe just a few hours . . ."

She reached up and shushed him with a fingertip. "I will, Mr.
MacKay," she said.

His laughter was tender and joyous and filled with wonder as
he drew her close once more. "How I love you," he whispered
into her hair. "I will cherish you till the day I die." He pulled
back slightly and, with that half-crooked smile at the corner of his
mouth, his dark eyebrows arched mischievously, he added, "But
please, I think it's time to call me Gabe."

She was never one to follow another's direct bidding. Even now.
She raised her own brows just as mischievously as he had. "I love
you, Gabriel," she said, looking deep into his eyes. "You are Gabe,
yes, and I will likely call you that most of the time, but when I
say Gabriel I can almost hear the brush of an angel's wings. Right
now I hear a legion of them." She reached up to touch his cheek,
running her fingers lightly along his strong jawline.

He drew her closer and, bending his head, captured her surprised little gasp with his lips. Enjoying the sensation even more
than she thought she would, she put her arms around his neck
and clung to him.

The whistles and hoots of laughter from the seamen on starboard watch, obviously enjoying the spectacle, did nothing to
deter her. They stood kissing as the sails billowed and snapped,
the wind ruffled their hair and clothes, and the seamen continued their hoots.

Mary Rose leaned back, breathless, and felt herself blush.

Grinning, Gabe gave an impatient order to the men, and they hastened back to their stations. Then he turned Mary Rose so that they were both looking out at the sea once more, and spoke of plans for the future. Gabe said he had decided during the night that he would post Cunard a letter of resignation the minute they reached Boston; and if she agreed, he would speak to the captain about marrying them on board ship even before then.

"I want to be married before we begin our journey," he said. "Though I admit it will be quite an adjustment going from one to a family of six."

Her countenance fell. "The children won't be with us," she said. "We are simply acting as their guardians until we reach Boston and hand them over to an elderly cousin of my grandfather's."

"An elderly cousin? As in old? As in doddering? Dour?"

She shook her head. "I've never met her, or even corresponded with her. She might be spry, apple-faced, and lovable. But she's my grandfather's cousin, so we know that she's . . . well, old."

"This will not do at all. Can you imagine the little ruffians, sprightly and vigorous as they are, living with an old woman?"

"I truly don't know how capable she is of handling them; I only know that she is expecting them, that their parents wrote to say it's all arranged."

He raked back his hair with his fingers and turned to gaze out at the ocean again. "How long have they been with you and your grandfather?"

"A fortnight before we left."

He gave her a glance and chuckled. "No wonder you didn't know what to do with them on the carriage."

Her voice softened when she said, "I freely admit I did not know the first thing about children, and still don't know as much as I need to. It was Bronwyn who showed me how well they responded to her once she filled their hearts with all the love she could."

"They were probably starved for it," he said, still staring at the horizon. "Do you think a distant cousin will give them the love they need?"

"I believe it's possible. Maybe that's exactly what she—and they—need. The one thing I do know is that Hermione is their mother and father's choice for their next guardian, and I must abide by their wishes."

"Coal told me his parents live in the Sandwich Islands."

"Yes."

"It might as well be Mars." He raked back his hair again and furrowed his brow. "I think we should take them with us. Count them as ours."

"I promised their mother I would follow her wishes to the letter," she said. "We'll need to pay Hermione a visit. As hard as it would be to let them go, maybe Richard and Sarah were right when they chose her." She paused. "Besides, what if Richard and Sarah are on their way to Boston right now? They wouldn't know where to begin looking for the children should we just cart them off to Illinois. And what about the danger we face?"

"True," he said, narrowing his eyes. "That's a consideration. But I might want to add a postscript to your letter about their parental responsibilities." He fell quiet for a moment. "What is it they do there, and why can't their children be with them?"

"They are missionaries. Richard is a surgeon," Mary Rose said. "He and Sarah live on an island set aside as a leper colony."

"It's understandable that they don't want their children exposed to the disease." He turned to her. "But I can't imagine anyone choosing to serve their church, or their God, over the good of their family, of their children." He shook his head slowly.

"Sarah's letters tell of God's call to bring healing to the suffering souls and bodies of those in the leper colony. She also says that she knows God is watching over their children—he loves them more than she and Richard do."

He was still fuming when he turned to her again. "Coal, Ruby, and Pearl need a real family," he said.

"I agree, but they know they have parents. They write them letters and speak of them often. Their dearest hope is that their parents will return for them soon. But I've always felt it would take a miracle for that to happen." Her eyes filled. "I never knew I would grow so attached to them. Even if Cousin Hermione is the perfect guardian, I will leave a large portion of my heart with the children."

He took her hands in his. "We know something today about miracles that we didn't know yesterday."

She couldn't help smiling. "We have seen one with our own eyes."

"Then we will pray for another, that the children will be reunited with their rightful parents, as they so earnestly pray. But until that day, they deserve to be properly cared for." Gabe stood there, gazing down at her, his eyes so full of warmth they made her soul want to take wing, or dance, or both. "The greatest miracle of all, my love, is finding you"—he smiled—"and loving you."

He drew her closer. This time she felt his lips touch hers like a whisper.

FOURTEEN

Halifax, Nova Scotia

It was a sunny day, and the sun warmed Enid's shoulders, though it did little to thaw her troubled thoughts. For nearly four days she'd been worrying about what she would tell Hosea about London. It was only this morning as the packet ship from Charlottetown dropped anchor in Halifax that she had concluded what she must do.

Gabe wanted to speak with her, and for that she was grateful. Though she had kept the dark secret close to her heart for so many years, it seemed inconceivable that she would now speak of it. And to Gabe. No one knew of it except Earie Lundie, the old woman in the woods, and she had died years before. Her house burned to the ground not long after and, if she kept records, they were but ashes now.

Sitting in the memorial garden of St. Paul's Church, Enid heard a gate open and close, and then the sound of footsteps on gravel. She looked up.

Gabe MacKay rushed to her and grabbed her around the waist, lifted her off her feet and twirled her around.

They both laughed as he set her upon the solid ground again. His crooked smile was the same, his ready laugh, the beloved gesture of raking his hair with his fingers . . . all the same. But as she studied his eyes, she could see that something was different behind the twinkle of gladness to see her; they veiled another emotion that for now remained a mystery. She could feel it in her bones. Whatever it was, his ready laughter told her he was happier than he'd been in years.

"Just look at you," he said, lifting his hand to touch her hair. "You haven't changed."

She laughed, and her cheeks turned pink. "I was surprised when Hosea said you wanted to talk with me," she said. "Though I can't imagine why the three of us can't have the same conversation at the same time. I suppose he thinks you can talk me into doing his bidding about this visit to London."

When he didn't answer she knew she was right. "What is it that you can say that my husband can't say for himself?"

When he spoke his voice was tender. "Hosea desperately wants you to go back to London with him for the reasons he told you in the letter."

Enid drew in a deep breath, held it, and then let it out slowly. She walked over to a small stand of hemlocks and stood beneath them, somehow feeling more secure in their dappled shadows.

"I have a letter I want you to give him," she said, pulling it from the deep pocket in her skirt.

"He'll be here in just a few minutes. You'll have nearly twelve hours together. Can you not give the letter to him yourself?" Frowning, he walked over to her. "And why a letter at all?"

"'Tis better if you're not so close to me," she said. He looked completely confused, almost boyish, which made what she planned to say all the more difficult. "Please, sit down or I'll never get this out. Please, Gabe. It's important."

He walked back to the bench and sat down, still facing her. "So this involves me too."

"It has everything to do with you," she said, "and everything to do with Hosea, and with the reason I cannot conceive."

She knew his beloved face so well, and could see his mind racing to keep up with her, but at the same time dragging the past that connected them.

"That night so long ago," she said, her voice a hoarse whisper, "in the woods."

"You don't need to describe where we were," he said. "I remember every detail, from the loamy scent of the soil, and the earthy perfume of the moss . . ."

She held up one hand. "Don't," she said. "Please. This is painful enough without hearing the details."

"We never spoke of what happened after that night," he said.

"I didn't because you didn't."

He seemed to let that sink in for a moment, then he said, "I loved you. I loved what happened between us. It may've been young love, but I thought it was real. But you never said anything about love that night."

"I thought you were trying to forget what happened . . . your family, their deaths. That your pain was so deep and so great that all you felt was sorrow. That there was no room for love."

"There was that, but surely you know I'd loved you since childhood."

She gave him a small smile. "Maybe you should have told me."

He looked down at the ground. She wanted to go to him and take him into her arms, just as she had that night. But after he heard what she had to say, it wouldn't matter anyway. It struck her that she might lose both men she loved so well, all because of her choice.

"You left for Boston too soon after," she said, "sooner than you had planned. I thought it was because of me; that your guilt was too great. That you couldn't bear to tell me there was no love in the act, no commitment to any future for us."

He stood and came over to her, gathered her into his arms, and she rested her cheek against the rough fabric of his jacket. She knew it was an embrace meant to comfort, not anything else. She understood that, but she took a few steps backward anyway.

"I became . . . with child . . . that night."

Standing in the dappled shadows of the ancient hemlocks, he stared at her dumbfounded. A simple birdsong suddenly sounded, so sweet it made her heart hurt. When he spoke, it seemed he could get out only one word: "Enid." It spilled from his lip, jagged, husky, choked.

He sat down on the bench again, dropping his head into his hands. Without looking up, he said, "We have a child?"

She blinked back her tears. "Our child didn't live. He came too early. He was fully formed and beautiful, but his lungs and heart were not yet strong enough for this world. He died in my arms three hours later."

"A son," he whispered. Several seconds passed and then he looked up at her, his face crumpled with emotion. "Why didn't you tell me?"

"You were in Boston. I didn't want you to marry me for all the wrong reasons; I didn't want you to give up your dreams."

He groaned, his shoulders slumping.

Enid's eyes filled. "I wanted to tell you. I wrote you letters . . ."

"I never received them."

"I never posted them." She came over to him and knelt before him, then took his hands in hers. "I had hidden my condition well beneath my skirts, not knowing how to tell my mother and father. When the pains started I visited Earie Lundie." She didn't have to explain who the woman was. Everyone on the island knew about the midwife and her herbal medicines and potions.

"I should have been with you," he said, unable to look her in the eyes.

"Even then I was strong, Gabe. You had left me to pursue other dreams. You hadn't spoken of love, only of need. I didn't want to be just someone you needed to heal your own pain. I wanted to be loved. Cherished. Though all these years later, I look back with a different perspective. I think had Gabriel lived, I would have told you. I would have wanted him to know his father."

"You named him Gabriel?"

"Gabriel MacKay the Second," she said. "And Earie helped me bury him in a garden behind her cabin. I stayed with her for several days. She rocked me when I cried and helped me heal with her medicines. My parents knew of my interest in healing animals and thought I was staying with her to learn about her medicines."

Gabe watched her with an inscrutable expression.

"I had hoped you would forgive me," she whispered. "That's one reason I've kept this secret to myself all these years. I thought I might die if, when I told you, I saw bitter accusation in your eyes where once I hoped and prayed I would see love."

He reached for her and drew her from her knees to sit beside him—and holding her in his arms, he sobbed. She could no longer hold back her own tears, and while holding him, she cried too.

After a moment, he said, "If ever there was forgiveness to be given, I would have given it the moment you asked. But there is none needed. " He placed gentle, strong hands on either side of her face and, looking into her eyes, he said, "I'm the one in need of forgiveness—for not thinking through the consequences of our act, for not telling you I loved you when—with all my heart, soul, and spirit—it was only you whom I cherished for all those years."

She was still weeping when she said, "You loved me?"

"I would have moved heaven and earth to come back to you. I would have married you, shouting from the very rooftops how much I loved and adored you, and always had. If Hosea hadn't come along and captured your heart, I would have told you then of my deep feelings."

She gave him a tremulous smile and reached into her sleeve for a handkerchief. "We were little more than children, growing up the way we did, best friends running wild all over the island, playing make-believe, building castles of sand on the beaches, then discovering that our friendship had turned into something else." She dabbed at her watery eyes. "'Tis time to tell Hosea, but I cannot tell him face-to-face. I wrote it all, every bit of it, in a letter, and I want you to give it to him after you anchor in Boston."

"Are you certain that is wise?"

"I have to take the risk. I want children of my own; I want children with the man I love. The specialist will see that I have born a child. It is the only way. Hosea must know. But I kept your name out of the letter. He will not know it was you. It would destroy your friendship. "

"He is a bighearted man, filled with God's mercy and grace, more so than any other man I've known." His gaze followed another trill of birdsong in the hemlocks. "But I am responsible for what happened. He needs to know that."

Enid stood, walked a few feet away, and then turned back to him. "I've kept these things in my heart all these years. Earie is dead, her cabin nothing more than ashes. Even our baby sleeps beneath the ashes. If she kept records of people she treated with her medicines and why, those records were destroyed. I could easily decline the visit to London and let everything go on as before, my secrets intact."

She lifted her gaze into the slender hemlock branches, watching the flutter of the leaves as the breeze caught them. "But when I received Hosea's letter, I realized I wanted more than anything to bear another child, Hosea's child. And that this might be the only chance we have to see that happen."

Gabe came over to stand in front of her. "You bore our child alone. But you're no longer alone in this. I will support you in any way possible. All you need to do is ask. I will deliver the letter and do my best to try to explain to Hosea what happened. And I will tell him it was me that night."

She nodded, feeling she might cry again at any moment.

"I will deliver your letter, and then write to you myself from Boston after I have spoken to Hosea." He gave her a gentle smile. "Though he and the letter will probably arrive at the same time on the return of the *Sea Hawk*."

She kissed the letter and whispered, "Godspeed," and handed it to him.

He tucked it in his inside breast pocket. "This may change everything," he said. "When I give it to him, I mean, and tell him my part in it, our friendship may be destroyed. And your marriage may never be the same."

"It's a risk I need to take," she said. "I love Hosea and have from the moment I saw the two of you, bedraggled and looking half starved, practically crawling onto our farm."

"Ah, yes, the aftermath of the *Thunderer*." He broke the tension with a chuckle.

"Your ordeal was talked about for years in Charlottetown."

"I'm glad the townsfolk thought it humorous. We didn't. At least, we didn't at the time. It's one thing to have actual pirates take over your ship; it's quite another for a couple of green boys like us to hear rumors of piracy and jump overboard and swim to shore, thinking what we'd heard was true." He chuckled. "I doubt that we will ever live that prank down."

"Gabe," she said solemnly, "when you give this to Hosea, tell him that there's never been anything between us since that one night." Her sorrow had twisted into a huge, painful knot inside as she imagined Hosea reading the letter. Especially now that she knew Gabe planned to tell him he was the baby's father.

"I will."

"And tell my husband how very much I love him, and that the last thing I would ever want to do is hurt him."

"I'll tell him that as well." Another bird trilled from the top of the hemlocks, and an answering call drifted down from the steeple, the bird then flapping away as the bell struck one o'clock. "Hosea said he would be here at one. What shall I tell him of your decision?"

"That I will go with him to London. And truly I will—if he forgives me after reading my letter. I wrote that I will be waiting, trunk packed, when the *Sea Hawk* sails into the Halifax harbor."

"You'll be all right?" Gabe asked as a breeze kicked up, picking up locks of Enid's hair.

"Yes, especially now."

He tilted his head. "Why now?"

"Because of you." She didn't elaborate.

"Me, why?"

"Because you love us both, and if anyone can help Hosea understand what happened between us in the past, it would be you. Knowing that you will be with him when he reads the letter calms my heart."

He studied her face for a moment, looking as if he had more to say on the subject. But instead of commenting on her words, he swallowed hard. "I didn't have a chance to tell you," he said. "I'm resigning my position with Cunard. I won't see you again on the return trip."

She tilted her head, too surprised to speak for a few heartbeats. "Designing ships is your life's passion, Gabe. It's all you've ever wanted to do."

"I've had something rather unusual happen to me," he said, his half-smile returning. "I suppose you could say I found religion."

Again, Enid was too startled to say anything at first. Her eyes widened as she recovered. "What kind of religion?"

"They're called Saints—Mormons. Led by a modern-day prophet, Joseph Smith."

She looked at him incredulously. "I didn't think such things interested you."

"They haven't until now. I'll write and tell you more about my adventures once I have arrived in America."

She stared at him. "But your designs and building of ships," she finally managed, "your passion for the open seas, so much like Hosea's." Then she frowned. "Does he know?"

"Yes, though he's being unusually silent about it. I think he's disappointed in me for leaving."

"I don't blame him. Shipbuilding has been your life." She took a few steps closer, looking up at him, wondering if a new contentment had settled into his heart, if that was what she noticed when she first saw him.

He looked down at her, still grinning. The sparkle in his eye had returned and she knew that had to be the reason for his new-found happiness.

"Where will you be . . . in America?"

"Nauvoo, Illinois." He took her hand as if to steady her for yet another revelation. "I have something else important to tell you," he said.

"The only thing that would surprise me more would be news that you're marrying one of these . . . what did you call them?"

"Saints."

"That it's, isn't it?"

He threw back his head and laughed. But she couldn't tell if it was laughter because of the absurdity of such a statement—or if it was because she'd guessed the truth.

Before she could inquire, a nearby gate opened and closed and the crunch of footsteps on gravel reached them.

Gabe moved closer and gave her a tight hug. "If you ever need me," he said, "remember where I said I'll be—with the Mormons in Nauvoo. No matter what happens, I will be there for you."

She nodded. "I'll remember . . . but, Gabe, you didn't answer my question."

Hosea strode into the garden just then, his smile wide, eyes only for his wife. They ran to each other and Hosea wrapped his arms around Enid and she slipped her arms around his neck.

Gabe watched as their eyes met, and even before Hosea covered her mouth with his, he saw a deep and abiding love in their expressions.

He turned for the gate, the letter in his pocket weighing heavy against his heart. As he walked away, he wondered why he had found it difficult to tell Enid that he was getting married. At this moment, she was likely quizzing Hosea about it. But even the captain hadn't yet been told.

Enid had enough on her mind, he told himself. Adding the news of his coming nuptials might only make things more difficult between Hosea and Enid . . . if there was any love left in her heart for Gabe.

And he suspected a tiny spot remained untouched by any other love. He knew because it was the same for him.

FIFTEEN

Holding a lacy parasol in one hand and the strings of a matching reticule in the other, Mary Rose strolled with her grandfather along the wooden walkway that wound along Halifax harbor. Coal and the twins tumbled alongside, sometimes running ahead, other times falling behind as they inspected candy shop windows and street corners where fiddlers played, or puppets danced with the help of their puppeteers, or silent mimes entertained gathering crowds.

"Lady," Ruby said over and over again, "thith ith the moth beautiful thity I ever thaw."

To one side, the aquamarine water sparkled in the summer sun; to the other, brightly painted wood-framed buildings—shops, businesses, and homes—dotted the green hills above, reminding Mary Rose of a toy village that, as a child, she played with on her quilted counterpane. The steeples of two churches near the harbor and one in the distance—which she thought was the Anglican church, St. Paul's, that Gabe had pointed out as they anchored—spiraled into the sky, and cobbled streets laced in and out of the village bearing their carriages, buckboards, and high-stepping teams. Besides the *Sea Hawk*, at least a half-dozen sailing ships had anchored in the harbor, with at least as many more either heading out to sea or piloting in. A steady stream of travelers and seaman spilled off the ships and onto the harbor walkways and streets, creating a cacophony of noise—from both visitors and hawkers, who vied for the travelers' business, selling everything from dried jerky to smoked fish to teas from China.

The children seemed to have a hundred questions about each hawker they passed, and Mary Rose quickly gave up trying to answer each one. Instead, she talked to the children, and Grandfather, about the beauty of the village, and the joy of being on solid ground once more.

At the top of a hill, when they had almost reached a gleaming white church, she realized that her grandfather had fallen quite silent, even glum, as they walked.

A lovely green spread across a gently rolling hillside to the south, with sugar maples and yellow birch trees spreading their leaves above shaded iron benches. At the entrance to the green, a hawkie dressed like a clown stood at the back of a small brightly painted wagon, selling girds and cleeks.

To squeals of delight from the children, Grandfather bargained with him for three. Once they had the hoops and sticks in hand, the children took off at full speed, tumbling and laughing and skipping as they ran.

She stopped underneath a sugar maple, furled her parasol, and turned to her grandfather. "I thought you would be pleased with the turn of events," she said quietly, so the children wouldn't overhear. She sat down and looked up at him. "The miracle that brought both Gabe and me to belief. But something tells me you're not."

"You've known Gabriel MacKay for less than a week," he said and sat down beside her. He looked across the green as the children played, and then released a great sigh. "He's professed faith in the Prophet's teachings—though without so much as cracking open the Book of Mormon. 'Tis my opinion, dearest, that he fancies himself in love with you and that in order to take you as his wife, he must profess to believe."

Mary Rose smiled. "You are saying, dear Grandfather, that 'tis possible he could simply have fallen in love with me and would do anything on Queen Victoria's seas and lands to make me his?"

Her grandfather twirled his mustache as a grin took over his face. "Perhaps that is what I am saying—though 'fancy' was the word I used instead of love."

"'Fancy,' generally speaking, means high emotion not meant to last. Foolish infatuation is another way of putting it."

"Foolish, no." Her grandfather reached for her hand. "No man who finds you the object of his ardor—whether it be a fancy or lasting love—could ever be considered foolish. The fool would be he who overlooks your loveliness altogether."

Mary Rose threw back her head and laughed. "Methinks my dear grandfather is attempting to dig himself out of a hole."

He squeezed her hand. "With your leave, then, let me start over." He turned to her, his countenance somber once more. "I fear you are rushing into this . . . romance. It worries me, Mary Rose. I think you should give it time, determine if he's sincere about his conversion. Let him ask questions of the missionaries, study the Book of Mormon, and question them, just as I did"—he smiled—"and as we tried to get you to do. Let him find out if this is truly what he's searching for."

Mary Rose stood, playing with the parasol handle as she watched Ruby race down a hillside next to her wobbly hoop, her blond plaits flying, her cheeks pink with exertion. Pearl tumbled along beside, squealing and laughing as she tried to keep up

Ruby's pace. Some creature at the edge of a duck pond caught Coal's attention, and he squatted to poke at it with a twig.

She turned again to her grandfather. "I can't explain it, but the moment I looked into Gabe's eyes it was impossible to look away. We touched each other's souls with a sense of knowing. For me, it was as if I'd been waiting all my life to have someone touch my soul—to recognize me—in such a way."

Her grandfather came up to stand beside her. "So much exists ahead of us that is new: a new country, new people—friends and foes—and a new faith. You're adding another dimension to all that. Are you certain you want to?"

She smiled and touched his cheek. "I'm certain."

"We don't know much about his background." He smiled. "His pedigree, as one might say."

"He is our captain's dearest friend, which speaks of his good character."

"'Tis true," her grandfather agreed. "But with your permission, I'll make inquiries into his background, perhaps ask the captain how long he's known him."

Mary Rose laughed. "If you insist, but I'm a good judge of character, and Gabe is all I could ever want in a husband. I know he's a good man." She paused, thinking of Gabe, the light in his eyes when he gazed into hers, the low timbre of his voice when he spoke her name, making it sound like a caress.

"Will you wait until I ask some questions of the captain?"

"I cannot promise you that, because in my heart I know 'twill be only the best report."

"Marriage should last a lifetime, the commitment of one man to one woman, for as long as you both live. Surely you could at least wait until I've made inquires of the captain."

Mary Rose didn't answer, her attention held fast by a man who stepped from behind a gate at St. Paul's across the green.

"Grandfather, is that Gabe?"

Squinting, he followed her gaze. "'Tis difficult to tell from this distance, but I believe it may be."

"Will you watch the children? See that they get back to the ship in time for their naps?"

"Yes, of course, but . . ."

She reached up on tiptoe to kiss his cheek, gave him a quick embrace, then turned and hurried to the exit of the park.

Gabe glanced back to the church, then started for the harbor area, his head bent, seemingly deep in thought.

She had just stepped into the street to go to him when another figure appeared at the gate: a strikingly handsome woman with dark red hair. She was taller by a head than Mary Rose and carried herself like a queen, her bosom ample, her waist tiny, her legs appearing lean and long underneath a simple woolen skirt. The woman stepped out onto the walkway, her gaze riveted to Gabe's back as he strode toward the harbor.

Mary Rose hesitated at the side of the street, baffled. Before she could decide what to do, Captain Livingstone stepped through the gate and joined the woman. She turned to him then and they exchanged a loving look. He slipped his arm around her waist and they too walked toward the harbor half a block behind Gabe.

Something about the woman's expression and the way she kept her eyes trained on Gabe's back even as she conversed with the captain puzzled Mary Rose.

Her grandfather appeared at her side. "You changed your mind?"

She gave a little wave of her fingers. "With a stride like his, I doubt I could have caught him." She laughed, turning back to the green, taking her grandfather's arm. "Besides, how would such a thing appear? Lady Mary Rose Ashley of Salisbury, England, seen chasing after a man along the streets of Halifax."

Her grandfather watched the captain and his companion and, farther along, Gabe MacKay as they made their way to the harbor.

"Promise me," he said softly, "that you will follow your head, rather than your heart, as you make your decision."

"It's already made, Grandfather. I will marry him because when I look into his eyes I see a love that I know will last forever." Observing his disgruntled expression, she softened her words with a smile. "Though I promise I'll listen after you've asked the captain to vouch for his friend."

"Good." He gave her a pleased, decisive nod.

She laughed again. "I can say with full confidence that the captain will sing his friend's praises."

"I hope so," her grandfather said and then turned away from her. "I think it's time to call the children."

SIXTEEN

Just hours outside Boston Harbor, Mary Rose and Gabe stood in front of the captain of the *Sea Hawk* on the main deck, near the bow. Bronwyn and Griffin stood slightly to one side, Bronwyn looking beautiful in a gown and bonnet that Mary Rose had given her. Slightly behind Bronwyn, Grace Carolyn cuddled the infant. And flanking the couple were the twins on Mary Rose's side and Coal on Gabe's.

Brother Brigham came up to stand next to the captain to give his blessing after the captain led them through their wedding vows. Several of the officers stood nearby, and about half the seamen on watch.

Coal eyed some green boys who'd hoisted themselves to the shrouds and climbed up the ratlines. They had settled comfortably in the crosstrees, legs dangling, firmly wedged despite the wild gyrations of the ship, to get a better view of the ceremony. Mary Rose elbowed Gabe and pointed out Coal's readiness to join the boys.

Gabe put a gentle hand on Coal's shoulder. "We need you here, sailor. Later maybe I'll climb the mast with you."

The boy's eyes shone, and he nodded as Gabe turned back to Mary Rose. But Pearl had wiggled between them and held out her hands for Gabe and Mary Rose to hold. Ruby, not to be outdone, took Mary Rose's opposite hand. At her feet sat Oscar, whom she'd insisted not be left out, in his bucket.

Gabe winked. "I told you we make quite a family," he whispered.

"Mary Rose Ashley and Gabriel MacKay," the captain began, "you have come here today to ask the blessings of God and his Church upon your marriage. I require, therefore, that you promise, with the help of God, to fulfill the obligations that Christian marriage demands."

He turned to Gabe. "You have taken Mary Rose to be your wife. Do you promise to love her, comfort her, honor and keep her, in sickness and in health; and forsaking all others, to be faithful to her as long as you both shall live?"

Gabe gave out a booming "I do!" to the delight of the seamen who whooped and hollered and whistled.

The captain turned to Mary Rose and asked the same question.

She gave him a wide smile and said, "I do." All her hopes and dreams for the future rested in those two little words. Oh, how she cherished this man! Her heart danced with joy when the captain then asked them to turn and face each other and she looked up into his eyes.

Ruby, her mouth agape at being part of such a ceremony, stepped back slightly but remained close enough to cling to Mary Rose's hand as she and Gabe exchanged their vows.

In turn, they pledged their vows to have and to hold each other from that day forward, for better for worse, for richer for poorer, in sickness and in health, to love and to cherish until death would part them.

"This is my solemn vow," Gabe said, his voice ragged and hoarse with emotion as he finished.

"This is my solemn vow," Mary Rose said, looking deep into Gabe's eyes as she finished saying her vow to him and to God.

He slipped a ring onto her finger, and then bent to kiss her.

Ruby gasped. "I didn't know Lady could kith," she said.

"Yuck, I hate all this mushy stuff," Coal said.

But Mary Rose and Gabe were the only two who heard the children as an outcry from the seaman began anew. Mary Rose thought her knees might give out, so thoroughly did Gabe's kiss move her. Her heart was still pounding, her face flushed, as he slipped his arm around her.

"I now pronounce you husband and wife," the captain said, eyes dancing merrily. "Ladies and gentlemen, may I present Mr. and Mrs. Gabriel MacKay."

Cheers went up again, this time the more genteel joining the rougher fracas of the seamen and green boys.

When the noise subsided, Brother Brigham stepped forward. "Let us bow our heads in prayer," he said. "Heavenly Father, we ask thy blessing on this union today, for we know it is pleasing in thy sight. We ask that you would keep your hand upon these your children Gabriel and Mary Rose as they set forth to become vital members and to serve you in the glorious Church you have restored upon this earth.

"Bless them and make them fruitful, Heavenly Father, that they and their progeny might someday enter your gates with thanksgiving, having left a legacy of service to you through which others might come to know the true way."

Gabe watched the twins and Little Grace, and then his eyes found Mary Rose and she turned almost as if she felt his gaze. He thought his heart would surely burst with love and joy and every good thing about her, about their marriage. The Heavenly

Father had truly brought them together. He'd had many talks with Brigham since sailing from Halifax, and was beginning to understand a different concept of God. Now he wondered how he could ever have thought him disinterested in the lives of those he created.

He strode across the distance between them, rejoicing in the new life they were about to begin, their coming together in a joyful union, creating a family—perhaps even a readymade family. Three weeks ago he wouldn't have believed such a change in him possible.

But Brigham had told him that with God everything was possible. His change of heart and change of direction were as much a miracle as the baby moving into position in Bronwyn's womb. They both had changed direction because of Brigham's prayer. He smiled at the whimsical thought.

Even the turning of the infant seemed somehow related to a turning of his own faith in God, a faith that meant he didn't need to understand why sorrowful, painful things happened in life—such as the deaths of his family. Faith meant that through sorrowful times or joyful times God was with you—and with those you loved. Besides, with his new faith he'd discovered a new family, not only a new wife and possibly three ready-made children, but a family of Saints that cared for each other, according to Brigham, like blood relatives.

One of the green boys still atop the mast called out, "Land ahoy!"

The passengers crowded to the starboard side of the ship. With the horizon a good eleven miles out from the top of the mast, it would be some time before those on deck could spot Boston.

"Ships ahoy!" another boy cried, pointing to the bow.

Gabe's heart leapt. Twelve days, eight hours. They had done it. Beat the record, with hours to spare.

He hurried to Mary Rose, found a place at the railing, and

wrapped his arm around her. The children crowded in close. Everyone wanted to be the first to spy the parade of boats that met other record-setting ships. They peered out at the empty seas, sparkling in the sunlight. Minutes passed. Then a half hour. Soon the first brightly decorated fishing boat appeared, several small sailboats rocking along in the wakes behind, followed by the pilot boats and dozens of others with flags flying, bands playing, and banners whipping in the wind.

He looked up to the quarterdeck. Hosea met his eyes and nodded, looking proud.

The crew shouted, sending up still more whoops and hollers and whistles as the parade of boats reached them, then turned to escort the *Sea Hawk* into harbor.

He looked back to the quarterdeck to give the captain a victory salute but Hosea had left, likely for his cabin.

Gabe patted his jacket pocket, where he'd tucked Enid's letter. Even the thought of it weighed heavy on him. He wished there was another way. But he had given Enid his word.

He gave Mary Rose's hand a squeeze, and said, "I have business with the captain. I'm not sure how long it will take. But I'll return as soon as I can."

She stood on her tiptoes and gave him a kiss. "I'm not going anywhere," she said.

"Lady did it again," Ruby whispered in a loud voice. "She'th going to be kithing Mithter MacKay all the time now."

Gabe entered the captain's quarters, and Hosea stood to greet him. "We did it, sir," he said, shaking his friend's hand. "Cunard will be ecstatic when he finds out."

"And more competitive than ever." Hosea grinned. "Your leaving Cunard, the ship, overshadows the triumph, Gabe. It won't be the same."

Gabe looked down, studying his hands. "I know I've made the

right choice for a lot of reasons." He was thinking about Enid as he spoke. After Hosea read the letter, it would be difficult, if not impossible, to work with him on the return voyage.

"You look troubled, Gabe. Certainly not like a man who's just married the woman of his dreams."

Gabe looked up, trying to find the words to soften Enid's disclosure.

Hosea leaned forward. "What is it, man? You look like you'd rather be anywhere but here right now. What's going on?"

Gabe reached into his coat pocket and drew out the letter.

"Your letter of resignation to Cunard." Hosea chuckled as he reached for it. "Don't tell me you changed your mind . . ." He looked at the handwriting on the envelope and frowned. "Enid . . . ?"

Gabe sat back in his chair and closed his eyes, unable to bear taking in Hosea's expression as he read.

A cold silence dominated the room.

He heard Hosea put the pages down, and looked up.

"She had a baby out of wedlock." He dropped his head into his hands and held it there, his fingers splayed in his hair. "Did you know this?"

"Not until I saw her in Halifax, sir." Gabe's heart pounded, knowing the confession he needed to make and how it would change everything.

When he lifted his eyes the captain's gaze was boring in on him. "Why did she need to tell you? She says in her letter she was sixteen. You knew her then; you would have been aware . . ." An unnatural light came from someplace behind the captain's eyes and he leaned forward. "I can think of only one reason she told you—and I would imagine it was not in Halifax. I would imagine it was on the island. Do you know why I think this?" His voice was low, but filled with anger, disappointment, and brokenness, a tone that Gabe had never heard in it before.

"You are wrong, sir. I didn't know until Halifax, until that day we spoke. She gave me the letter to deliver to you and told me its contents."

"Because you were the father of that child." His words were clipped.

"I didn't know about the child, sir. Enid told me he died in her arms just hours after his birth."

"You didn't answer my question."

Gabe drew in a deep breath and released it as if it were his soul spilling out in front of his friend. "Yes, he was my son."

"You had a son with my wife, and as close as our friendship has been all these years, you never uttered a word about it. You never told me you bedded her. You said you were friends. I knew you loved her, but I never imagined . . ."

"Sir, I swear to you I didn't know about the child. What happened all those years ago never happened again. We never even spoke of it."

Hosea stared at Gabe as if he were a stranger. His eyes had turned to ice. He stood formally as if to dismiss a crew member.

Gabe tried to regain his emotional bearings. "Sir, how could I have told you? It's not something I could just drop into one of our conversations. You're my friend as no other has been. What we've been through together should count for something."

The silence was unbearable.

"Please forgive me," he said with a heavy sigh, dropping his head into his hands. "Forgive us both. It happened long before she met you . . ."

"Did you love her?"

He was damned if he said yes, damned if he said no. He'd feel more like a sniveling eijit if he tried to explain that it happened soon after his parents' death. On her part it was meant to comfort; on his, to be comforted. It was wrong, so wrong to have given into their love for each other for those reasons. But how could he explain that to Hosea? So he didn't answer the question.

"We have nothing more to talk about." The captain turned his back on Gabe.

Gabe tried once more to get through to him. "I've always looked up to you and your sense of mercy and forgiveness. You're a just man, whether as master and commander, or in dealing with other relationships.

"Doesn't a friend deserve such consideration? When I ask for forgiveness, or for that matter, when Enid does—as I'm sure she did in the letter—is your heart not big enough to extend to us the same mercies that you extend to others?"

Gabe's voice rose as he continued. "You've been my family—both of you—since my own died. The only crack in the wall I put up around myself when I thought that God was distant and disinterested in his people, when I shut him out of my life . . ." He strode around the captain's desk and stood in front of him, unable to take the sight of his back a moment longer. "The only crack in that wall was you, Hosea. You showed me God's unconditional mercy and compassion. I saw it in you. I wanted to be like you. I clung to the compassion for others I saw in you—it was the only reflection of God I could live with."

He was breathing hard, his emotions charged, not realizing until this moment how unjust Hosea's actions toward him seemed. "Has it all been an act?"

Hosea didn't answer, just stared at him with those cold eyes.

"The reading of Scripture, the talk of God's mercy and grace? Don't you realize that your faith was my lifeline all these years?"

Hosea almost roared, "Then why did you forsake that God for another?"

Gabe stepped back in surprise. So the anger wasn't just about Enid. It was about Brigham Young, Joseph Smith, the Saints, his new faith. A different kind of betrayal that compounded the other.

"He is the same God."

Hosea stepped closer to him, and for a moment Gabe thought he might grab him by the collar. His face was red, and he too was breathing hard. "The Mormons believe in a false God. They say all the right words, they pray and, yes, they somehow perform miracles, but who is the entity behind those prayers?"

"Why haven't you said anything about this before?"

"I've only known since Halifax. While you and my wife were talking over old times in the St. Paul's memorial garden, I spent an hour with the rector, a friend, and asked if he knew anything about the Mormons. He knew plenty. And he warned about their teachings. They believe man can become a god. They believe our God was once human, just as we are. He is not eternal, in their thinking, but he progressed to the godhead through good works on earth. It's a false religion, Mr. MacKay."

Gabe backed away from the captain. "That is not true. How could the infant move into the right position in the birth canal if not for a miracle? It had to be of God."

"A different god, Mr. MacKay."

"There's only one."

"That's what I'm trying to tell you. And he is eternal, as we find in Isaiah. He calls himself by the name I AM, not I WAS or I WILL BE."

"The great eternal God I thought I knew," Gabe said, "didn't save the ship that capsized with my parents and sister on board."

"You knew that ship was ready for the boneyard before it pulled anchor. You warned them. You can't blame God for everything that goes wrong in the world. He gave man the gift of free will, and sometimes man abuses it."

Gabe winced. Hosea might as well have hit him in the stomach. "You feel I betrayed you because of my new faith that doesn't match yours, not because of Enid. You think I betrayed our friendship because I have now turned to those who believe as I do. Perhaps, my captain, this has as much to do with these things as it does with your wife."

"You obviously have it figured out and don't need me to help you. Go to Brigham, let him advise you."

"What about Enid? Can you find it in your heart to forgive her? She loves you, she told me—"

Hosea's laugh was bitter. "You obviously know my wife better than I do."

Gabe lowered his voice. "Forgive her, I beg of you, Hosea. Forgive her. She was only sixteen when this happened, and she's been burdened with this terrible secret for all these years. She didn't have to tell you now. Or tell me. She could have kept it to herself and never told anyone. She did it at great cost."

Hosea's eyes blazed. "I am the master and commander of this ship. I can damn well do as I please. Do not tell me, sir, to forgive or not forgive, to extend mercy and justice, or not to extend either. And as master of this ship, I command you, Mr. MacKay, to take your family as far away from me as you can get as soon as we drop anchor. Be on your way to your promised land with your Saints."

"Hosea . . ."

But the captain had turned his back once more.

SEVENTEEN

Halifax, Nova Scotia

On the afternoon the *Sea Hawk* was scheduled to drop anchor in Halifax, Enid waited at the harbor, her trunks packed and ready for the voyage to England with Hosea. A light rain had been falling since midnight and at first those passengers milling about the harbor supposed it was the inclement weather that had put the *Sea Hawk* behind. But as dusk settled in, Enid's worries increased. The rain now began falling in earnest. In the distance, lightning split open the sky, and the thunder grew closer.

Though her parents' town house was only a short distance away, she remained at the harbor, keeping vigil for her husband's ship, her buggy and Firefox in the livery across from the wharf, where she stood in the doorway, which provided an expansive view of ships entering and leaving the harbor.

When darkness fell and the storm moved onshore, she walked over to the small customs building across the street. It housed the harbormaster's office, which she had already visited several times that day.

The harbormaster recognized her and nodded as she came in again. "G'evenin', Mrs. Livingstone," he said. "Still no word. I'm sorry." He pulled out a piece of paper and handed it to her. "If you'll write down where you're staying, when the ship drops anchor, I'll get word to you right away. I'd say they've likely laid anchor in some safe harbor on the coast, waiting till the squall passes. We probably won't hear anything till morning, so you might as well go home."

Her heart heavy, Enid crossed the street to the livery and, minutes later, driving the buggy, returned to her parents' home to wait. She spent a restless night, unable to sleep, worried about the ship, Hosea's safety, and his reaction to the letter.

She finally dozed off just before dawn only to be awakened by pounding at the door. The murmur of voices carried up the stairs to her bedroom and she heard the words "*Sea Hawk*."

Just as she pulled on her duster her father called for her to come downstairs. His voice was solemn, and her heart quickened. Something was wrong.

As she reached the bottom stair she recognized Hosea's chief mate, Mr. Thorpe. His face was etched with sorrow. Enid's parents moved close to her, one on either side. Her mother took her hand, and her father encircled her shoulders with his arm.

She stiffened, prepared for the worst. Why else would Mr. Thorpe be paying her a visit?

"Mrs. Livingstone, I fear I bear the worst news possible," he said.

Enid backed away. "No," she said. "It can't be true."

"We came upon a sudden squall. The captain had gone aft to check on something he thought was amiss when a rogue wave crashed over the deck. No one noticed at first that he was missing, so we lost valuable time starting the search." He shook his head. "Once the call was given, we turned back. The seas were so rough it was an impossible task from the beginning, but we spent nearly six hours looking."

Enid's eyes filled. "No," she whispered again. "It can't be."

"I'm so sorry," Mr. Thorpe said. "The entire cadre of officers and crew send their condolences. I'm sure you will also hear from Cunard as well, but it will take some time to get the news of the captain's death to him." His gaze met hers. "He was a good man, a good captain, Mrs. Livingstone. Admired by all who knew him. We will send one of the seamen with your husband's things later this afternoon."

"Thank you," Enid said.

He again expressed his condolences and took his leave.

Enid fell into the nearest chair, while her mother went into the kitchen to make her some tea. She covered her face with her hands and rocked back and forth, her agony so great the tears would not come. She tried to get the picture out of her head of what it must have been like for Hosea in the crashing waves, the frantic search for something to hang on to, watching his ship sail away from him—and her heart twisted so hard and ached so deeply, she thought the blood had surely stopped its flow.

Looking up at her father, she said, "The commander of a vessel never leaves the quarterdeck unless it's for his cabin. The chief mate said that Hosea had gone aft to check on something."

"Aye, that he did, child."

"Mr. Thorpe knows that too, and perhaps that's why he was vague about what Hosea was doing. The commander of a ship gives the order to the chief mate, who would then send a seaman to fix whatever it was that needed fixing. The commander of the ship is just that—the commander. He makes decisions, critical decisions, but he does not put himself in unnecessary danger, because the lives of all on board are in his hands." She watched her father's face, and saw his agreement. "Yet Hosea broke all the rules and went aft during a raging storm."

"What are you saying?" Her father leaned forward.

Her mother came into the room, and stood in the doorway, holding the cup of tea. She apparently had heard Enid's last statement and exchanged a worried glance with her father.

"He purposely put himself in danger," Enid said. "The question is why?"

By late afternoon, a seaman by the name of Fitzgibbons delivered Hosea's personal effects: three large trunks and a smaller one that Enid recognized as that which he kept under lock and key on the table in his quarters.

The sun was fading into a red sky when she placed the small trunk on her lap in her parents' parlor. She unlocked the box and opened it. Her letter, sent with Gabe, lay on the top. Underneath it lay another, addressed to her. Her fingers trembling, she unfolded it and began to read:

Dear Enid,

It was with great dismay that I read your letter. I wish you had told me in person, not in Halifax, but years ago. You have asked my forgiveness, and because of my love for you, I extend it. Forgetting your transgressions and your secret relationship with Mr. MacKay is another matter. This news is of course disquieting, to say the least, and I am uncertain what steps to take next. I will need time to sort out my feelings. I think it best that we do not see each other when the Sea Hawk *drops anchor in Halifax, which of course means that I do not wish you to accompany me to London.*

I must tell you that I am considering legal proceedings to dissolve our marriage; however, I need time to search my heart regarding this matter. Betrayal is not something easily forgotten. . . .

The letter was unfinished and unsigned. Enid refolded it and returned it to the small chest. She locked the chest, carried it upstairs, placed it under the bed, and then dropped the tiny brass key in her shoe. She refused to cry; she would save her tears for later. If she did start to cry, she would never stop.

She kept her thoughts on her animals, those that were injured and needed her. She wanted to be with them, to hold on to a newborn colt, or look into the eyes of a beloved horse, or watch a child's face after she'd healed a sick puppy or kitten. She let the images of her farm flood into her mind as she tried to crowd out the sorrow.

It didn't help. Almost frantic to return to Charlottetown, she dressed in the same clothes she had arrived in, asked her parents to keep Hosea's trunks if they would, and with her head held high she strode down the street to the livery. Minutes later, she flicked the reins above Foxfire's back and drove her buggy to the wharf to catch the next packet ship home.

As she came over the rise above the Halifax harbor, the sunlight caught the gleaming sails of the *Sea Hawk*, being piloted from the harbor. She was magnificent, her sails billowing, her movement both graceful and powerful.

It was then, watching her disappear into the horizon that Enid finally cried.

EIGHTEEN

It took nearly three weeks to make the necessary purchases for the long journey, join up with the immigrants who arrived by packet ship one week after the *Sea Hawk*, and organize the leaders to oversee the company that now numbered nearly three hundred men, women, and children. The group first made their way to Baltimore, then mustered again, preparing for the trek straight west on the Cumberland Road.

Gabe insisted on purchasing a Conestoga with a team of oxen. The big freight wagons were notoriously clumsy and had difficulty on the trails west of the Mississippi, but the roads east of the Mississippi accommodated wagons of all sizes: carriages, farm wagons, and large freight wagons. When the company finally gathered the last week in July, the rigs were split into three divisions with a captain over each, chosen by Brigham.

The morning the first division rolled out, Gabe, Mary Rose, and the children stood on a cliff watching the line of thirty-some carriages and farm wagons. They would leave the following morning, with Gabe as captain of another twenty-seven wagons, those that were the largest in the group. The third company was readying to leave the morning after that.

Mary Rose looked up at her husband, whose eyes were on the wagon company spread out on the road below them. Brigham rode with the first group, and he could be seen riding horseback out front with some of the other apostles newly returned from England.

She worried as she studied Gabe's face. He had not seemed the same since the day they were wed, and he hadn't told her why. She didn't probe but hoped that as their love grew, he would open up to her. When she questioned him about it, he said only that he and the captain had had a falling-out over what the captain called the "false gods of the Saints." He would say no more, but the deep hurt in his eyes was acute and didn't fade with the passing of days.

Before they left Boston for Baltimore, she encouraged Gabe to go see the captain and patch things up between them; she knew how much the friendship meant to both men. But Gabe refused.

Now as they stood on the rise, watching the train of wagons and carriages snake out before them, she reached for Gabe's hand. His expression was tender as he met her gaze.

"Tomorrow I'll feel like we've actually begun," he said. "Everything until now has seemed like preparation."

She nodded and gave him a small smile. "'Twas likely because we were heading more to the south than straight west. As Grandfather asked a dozen times, 'If it's the Wild West that we're headed for, why take a road south?'"

He chuckled. "I thought it was because of the supplies and people we kept picking up along the way. It never felt like we were truly headed for our promised land."

"And don't forget uth," Ruby said. "You picked uth up along the way too."

Mary Rose laughed. "There was really never a choice. We'd

decided long before we met Cousin Hermione that we wanted you in our family."

"I wanted Oscar to come too, though," Pearl said.

Ruby agreed. "Othcar wath part of our family too."

Coal kicked a rock over the cliff, watching it tumble into the valley below. He sniggered at his sisters' words. "Oscar needed salt water. He would've died before the first wagon rolled out of Boston."

"I'm glad Mr. Fitthgibbonth promithed to take good care of Othcar," Ruby said.

Mary Rose reached for Ruby's hand. "And he will, that's for certain. And don't forget, he said to listen for the ocean in the big shell he gave you."

"I already did, and I heard it," Pearl said, coming closer. Mary Rose circled her arm around the little girl, thinking what a mistake it would have been to leave them with Hermione. The elderly woman seemed loving and kind, and Mary Rose and Gabe had exchanged a glance or two, each thinking—they discovered later—that they had perhaps misjudged her. Then Hermione had said with a big smile that the children had arrived just in time. She'd been planning to hire new girls to help her in the house and a barn boy to clean the stalls.

"What about schooling?" Gabe had asked, and the woman had looked surprised. "The children need book learning, and work with figures; they need to read poetry and biographies and fairy tales," he said.

Mary Rose added, "They love to sing and dance and recite nursery rhymes. They love to have someone read to them. They love to act out their stories. Their imaginations have no boundaries."

As soon as Hermione gave any thought of education a dismissive wave, Gabe and Mary Rose stood and told her that they'd decided to keep the children. Mary Rose said she would write to Richard and Sarah and let them know.

"But what about my barn boy?" had been Hermione's parting words.

Coal was still kicking dirt and rocks over the cliff when Gabe bent down to talk with him. "You want to ride with me tomorrow, or in the wagon?"

Coal's eyes grew big. "You mean it?"

"You know the little pinto you helped me pick out?"

His eyes grew bigger as he nodded. "Yes, sir."

"I let you pick her out because she's yours. You can ride along with me, if you'd like." The boy threw back his shoulders and nodded solemnly. "We'll let the womenfolk ride in the wagon," Gabe continued. "And . . . I have a secret to tell you."

Mary Rose looked away, ready to giggle. She knew what was coming.

"I don't know much about riding horses. They don't seem to know what I want them to do," Gabe said.

Coal grinned. "I've got a secret for you too. I don't know much about 'em either."

Gabe ruffled his hair.

"Grandpa Earl told me he'th goin' a-courting thith morning," Ruby said. "A widow lady named Thithter Cordelia Jewel whoth wagon ith juth behind hith."

Mary Rose glanced at Gabe, who looked ready to laugh. "The earl doesn't let any grass grow under his feet."

"He dothn't?" Ruby frowned and studied the barren ground. "Why not?"

"Sister Beulah has a buckboard and a mule," Pearl said. "The mule's name is Gulliver, and he sometime kicks. Sister Cordelia says to not walk up from behind, because it scares him. And Sister Cordelia used to be a riverboat dancer and she's from a long ways away. New Orleans, she said."

"She'th pretty too," Ruby said. "Her hair ith thiny black. And thee hath an acthent that Grandpa Earl thath ith French."

Before Mary Rose could take in the news, Bronwyn and Griffin with the baby walked toward them from their wagon.

Mary Rose stepped forward to take the baby. She couldn't get enough of Little Grace.

The sun's morning slant hit the river that ran alongside the Cumberland Road, giving it a golden hue. The tail end of the first wagon company disappeared into the horizon.

"That'th where we'll be tomorrow," Ruby announced, "riding our ponieth and driving our teamth."

"You won't be riding ponies or driving teams," Coal pointed out.

"Yeth I will," she said.

"Me too," Pearl said. "We're gonna be wild women of the West. Lady told me so."

"Tho did Thithter Cordelia Jewel," Ruby added.

Bronwyn met Mary Rose's eyes and quirked a brow. "I believe all us womenfolk are," she said in her best imitation of a Southern drawl. She came over to stand beside Mary Rose, circling her arm around Mary Rose and Little Grace.

"I'm glad we're all going together," Mary Rose said, smiling at Bronwyn. "It wouldn't be the same if we hadn't met."

Grandfather came up to stand beside her. "The Wild West," he said with a wide grin. "I always knew I'd get here again. And here it is, by cracky. Tomorrow we move out, following my dream."

Mary Rose looked at him and laughed. "By cracky?"

His bushy eyebrows shot up. "Heard it in one of the inns. Time for us all to sound more like Americans, by cracky."

Bronwyn leaned around Mary Rose and shot him a wide smile and winked. "We'll learn the lingo in a flash."

"Yes, ma'am," he said in an exaggerated drawl.

He'd cut the waxed curls from the ends of his mustache, let his beard grow full and curly, his hair grow longer. He now wore galluses to hold up his pants and had taken to wearing a white stovepipe hat, a blue swallowtail coat with brass buttons, and fine calfskin boots he'd purchased in Boston. He'd also trimmed down somewhat, and Mary Rose suspected it had something to do with Sister Cordelia.

She smiled up at him. "I hear you're courting Sister Cordelia."

He nodded slowly. "But we're not rushing into anything. She's a fine woman, and I'm considering marriage. But as I once counseled you, sometimes things are best taken at a slow pace."

Mary Rose touched his arm. "I wish you all the happiness you deserve." She laughed, and then she teased, "But perhaps I should check into her background, ask someone to vouch for her." Too late, she realized Cordelia's past was exactly what *didn't* need looking into. She felt herself blush. "I'm sorry," she said to her grandfather. "That was uncalled for. I meant it as a joke because of your intention to talk to the captain about Gabe."

"Cordelia would be the first to say no offense taken. Her past is colorful, to say the least. But it's behind her and she says she's not ever looking back. I believe her." He gazed to the horizon with a wide smile. "She told me that she long hungered for something that her soul was missing. She said she hungered for God. Once she tried to attend church and slipped into the back pew. People turned around, upset to see a dance hall girl among them. They whispered and pointed, and afterward snubbed her.

"One day in St. Louis, years before, she heard about a young man who was baptizing down by the river. She'd just left the riverboat where she'd worked all night and looked every bit the dance hall girl who'd seen too many dances with too many men. But the preacher, who turned out to be Joseph Smith, gestured for her to come and join the group.

"He spoke of God's love, not his condemnation, and told the story of the golden plates. She couldn't get enough of the warmth and acceptance she felt—from our Prophet and from the people who'd gathered with him. She came back three times, and finally Joseph said to her, 'Sister Cordelia, don't you think it's about time you heeded God's call in your life?'

"Well, as far as she knew, no one had told him her name. She said she just about fell over on the spot. It was as if God himself was calling her into his bosom.

"She almost ran to Joseph to be baptized. She stayed on the riverboat a few more years, thinking dancing was all she knew. Then one day she met another missionary who told her about the trek to Nauvoo. It didn't take her long to decide to come along.

"She's a lively one, this Sister Cordelia," her grandfather said with a wide grin. "She makes me smile just listening to her."

Mary Rose squeezed his hand. "I'm happy for you, Grandfather. And for her."

Behind them someone began to play the fiddle. A harmonica joined in, and soon voices were lifted in song and the sound of shuffling feet carried toward them as people began to dance.

Mary Rose hooked her arm through her grandfather's as they turned back to camp. "I never did ask if you talked to the captain about Gabe. I assumed you did and all was well or you would have told me otherwise."

"I spoke with him before your wedding. He said that he holds our Gabe in the highest regard." He studied her face. "Everything is going well between the two of you?"

"Oh, yes," she assured him as she tried to push from her mind the haunting expression that sometimes shadowed his face.

NINETEEN

The aging fisherman rose early on a morning in late July, and groaned as he folded back the bedclothes, put his feet on the floor, and sat on the edge of the bed.

"Giovanni," his wife said softly, "why are you awake so early?" She turned on the oil lamp beside the bed. "It's too dark to go out."

"Something stirred my heart just now," he said. "Perhaps it was just the dream of an old fisherman, but this was so real. I was drowning in violent waters and arguing with God, but he wouldn't let me have my way. I wanted to give up fighting to stay afloat and let myself sink downward into the darkest of the waters. I was still floating suspended between the lighter waters above me and the black waters below when I woke."

Cara reached for his hand as he continued. "When God nudged me from my slumber . . . I felt he had something for me to do.

Down by the shore. I can picture it in my mind, and I know I must go there. "

She sat up. "I'll go with you. Two lanterns are better than one."

"That's why I love you so," he said.

"Because I have my own lantern?" She gave him a smile that lit up her aging face. Her white hair shone like an aura in the lamplight.

"Because you are so willing to come along with me no matter how harebrained the idea might seem."

She squeezed his hand. "Very few of your dreams have turned out to be harebrained, my love. More times than not, it is the Spirit speaking to your heart. I've learned to pay attention."

"Some people think I'm crazy," he said with a grin.

"People who preach to trout in a stream are generally not thought of as stable."

His grin widened. "They are God's creatures too." He stood, yawned and stretched, and then went to the window. "I don't know where to begin looking—or even what it is I'm to find."

"We'll start by the ocean," she said. "Since that was in your dream."

Minutes later, they walked north along a rocky spit of land, wearing their knee-high fishing boots and heavy oilskin coats. Though it was summer, the predawn air chilled them and the wind off the ocean brought a fine spray with it. Each held a lantern high and walked slowly, several feet between them.

"There," Giovanni shouted as the pale dawn sky began to lighten over the ocean. "Cara, I think I see something, an injured animal perhaps . . . ?" He ran toward the object, dodging rocks and boulders.

He set the lantern on a flat rock and knelt beside the pile of clothing and flesh. Cara came up behind him—and gasped.

Giovanni bent over the barely recognizable human and touched his cold, battered face.

"Is he dead?"

"It appears so. He's battered and broken. I don't see how anyone could have survived what he's apparently been through."

Cara reached for a tattered piece of cloth. It had a captain's insignia on it. "He's a sea captain," she said. "Have you heard news of any shipwrecks? Perhaps we should look around. There may be more. And they might have made it."

But Giovanni didn't move. "This is the one I was sent to find."

"But he's dead."

Giovanni lifted the man's hand and felt for a pulse. He gazed into the man's face and wondered what kind of ordeal he had been through. He'd noticed there were two breaks in his left leg, another in his right. His face was covered with cuts and abrasions. He was as pale as death, and just as cold. Giovanni gently touched the man's neck, and then let out a sigh as he met his wife's worried eyes.

"His heart still beats. He's alive."

Her face glowed in the light of the lantern. "He was the man in your dream."

Cara knelt beside Giovanni and, with her gaze, watched as he examined each limb, his torso, and his neck. "We need to get him into the house," Giovanni said after a few minutes. "He will die if we don't hurry."

"He's a big man. I don't see how the two of us can lift him."

"We have no choice," Giovanni said. He bent over to pick him up, and then struggled to his feet. Cara took the broken and mangled legs into her arms, and slowly they made their way back to the house.

The sun was rising as if from out of the ocean when they reached their small home. Minutes later they had him on the bed in their second bedroom. Cara went into the kitchen, pumped water into a large iron Dutch oven, and set it on the stove. She stoked the fire beneath, then returned to the bedroom.

Giovanni had removed the man's tattered uniform and replaced it with a nightshirt of his own.

Cara carefully looked through the pile of torn, waterlogged clothing. "Is there anything that tells us his name?" she asked.

"No," Giovanni said. "All we know is that he came from the sea so violently it seems to me the water spewed him out of its mouth."

PART II

It was thine oath that first did fail,
It was thy love proved false and frail . . .
                    —Elizabeth Barrett Browning

TWENTY

Nauvoo, Illinois
October 24, 1841

From across the meetinghouse aisle where he sat with Grandfather and Coal, Gabe turned and caught Mary Rose's eye
as the Prophet began to speak. Her husband winked, and she
grinned at him before turning forward again to continue her assessment of the Prophet.

He was taller than Mary Rose expected. He loomed well over
six feet tall, and weighed more than two hundred pounds. In
total, he carried himself as though he were the general of some
great conquering army. He reminded her of likenesses she'd seen
of General George Washington, with his mane of light brown,
almost blond, hair and vivid blue-gray eyes. His head was excep-
tionally large and his face was comely, which she had expected.
After all, who could command the attention of even a single fol-
lower had he been as ugly as a warthog?

A warthog? Joseph Smith? She almost giggled, wishing she could share her thoughts with Bronwyn, who sat on her left. But Bronwyn was giving their Prophet her undivided attention. Not even the sleeping Little Grace, held fast in her arms, received the kisses and caresses Bronwyn usually bestowed.

They'd arrived in Nauvoo just days before. Today was their first Sunday since, and they were required to go to the meetinghouse as the Saints did each Sunday. It hadn't occurred to Mary Rose until that morning that though the Church as a whole was known as the Church of Jesus Christ of Latter-day Saints, the buildings where they held their meetings were simply that—meetinghouses. And in one such meetinghouse, as Brother Brigham had informed her, she and Gabe would go through another marriage ceremony, one that would join them throughout all eternity. Once the temple was completed, endowment ceremonies, celestial marriage ceremonies, and baptisms for the dead would all be held in that sacred place—first for men only; later, it was rumored, women would be allowed to also participate.

She had complete faith in her husband who, when answering her questions, tried to be as open as possible without betraying Brother Brigham's trust. It was understood by the women in the wagon party that their menfolk were privy to information not given to their wives, and it was delivered in such a way, Gabe told her, that it was as if decreed by God himself. Irked as she was over such an audacious practice, she loved her husband enough to believe he would tell her every detail as soon as he could.

During the long wagon trek, Gabe would meet with Brother Brigham when the company stopped for their midday meal. Sometimes they met alone, other times with the other men, to receive instruction from the Book of Mormon and learn the doctrines of the Church. Then men, in turn, were instructed to teach their wives from the Book of Mormon, even read to them should they be unable to read it themselves. It was odd, she thought, even now as she watched the Prophet at the podium in front of the meeting, that the men were seated on one side of the room, the women on the other, with a wide aisle separating them.

From the first turn of the wagon wheel on the Cumberland Road, her anticipation never wavered, for reaching Nauvoo, for giving her heart and soul to a new church and her new way of life. She'd never known such contentment, in spite of the discomfort and radical changes she underwent along the way: She shed her jewels, her fancy frocks, her frothy bonnets—the whole of Lady Mary Rose Ashley. With each mile the Conestoga rolled, she dressed more like the others, brought about at Gabe's request after one of his meetings with Brother Brigham. She loved him, so she didn't mind.

By the time the company rolled wagons and livestock onto barges to float down the Ohio, she had become Mary Rose MacKay, and by the time they reached Nauvoo, just three months after leaving the *Sea Hawk*, she let it be known, again at Gabe's request, that from this day forward she was Sister Mary Rose.

Just months before, she would have refused any title but Lady, but being called Sister somehow filled a place in her heart that she hadn't realized was empty. It meant that she belonged. That she was part of a larger family, unique in a way she had never imagined.

"I'm thirthty," Ruby whispered loudly. "And I have to uth the nethethary."

"You should have gone earlier when you had the chance," Mary Rose whispered in her softest voice. "Now you'll have to wait."

The child squirmed in her seat and then settled back with a huff.

Pearl gave her sister a superior look and sighed as if she was above such behavior.

Mary Rose turned her attention back to the platform. The

Prophet had finished his welcome speech, and she realized, feeling her cheeks warm, her mind had wandered and she hadn't paid close attention to what he'd said. Now he was introducing his adopted son, obviously a leader in high standing, an apostle named Fenton Webb.

Tall, broad-shouldered, with flint black hair and ice blue eyes, Fenton Webb was an imposing figure, in some ways even more so than either Joseph Smith or Brigham Young.

Mary Rose sat forward, intrigued.

When the apostle began to speak, all other thoughts, of the long journey west, of her husband and the three little ones she now counted as her own, fell away.

He smiled at the crowd in front of him. "Welcome to America," he said. "And even better than that, welcome to Nauvoo, the beautiful city of God and his Saints."

He paused, his ice blue eyes seeming to gaze through to the souls of every individual in the room. "Whoever would have thought," he said, "that a plain and ordinary farmer's son would be chosen by God to be his prophet?

"But Joseph was an ordinary boy, of no higher intelligence than most, but with perhaps more curiosity than most. Even as a boy he had many questions, the most important being which was the right church? Should I become a Baptist, he wondered, and if a Baptist, which Baptist? Or should I become an Episcopalian, or a Shaker, or a Methodist? What about the Catholics?

"He knew enough, even as a young man, that if he asked preachers from any of these churches if they were the only right and true way to God, their answer would have been . . ." Webb grinned as he looked out over the congregation of Saints. "Of course, each would've said it was his own church that was the only church, the only true way to reach God. Isn't that right, Saints?"

Murmurs of agreement passed among the congregants.

"Our Prophet took these questions to God, fell on his knees in the woods one day to plead with God to tell him which church was right. To his great astonishment—and this, dear Saints, is where the story gets interesting—a glorious light flooded the woods and poured over him. It was midday, and unable to believe his eyes, Joseph at first thought the light was surely sunlight washing through the leaves of the trees."

Webb paused, dropped his head as if in prayer, and when he looked up, Mary Rose thought his eyes were filled with tears. "Dear Saints, it was not the sunlight. It was as if the light emanated from a single point so bright Joseph had to shield his eyes. When he finally lifted his gaze, there before him, as if standing in a shell, were two people—as human in appearance as you and me. The Father and the Son, God and Christ, descended from heaven to bring him a message."

No one spoke until Ruby looked up and said, "I really have to go to the nethethary, Lady."

A few people close by chuckled, and Mary Rose cringed, expecting Webb to scowl at the interruption. But instead, he gave her a smile and a nod. "The necessary is sometimes . . . necessary for a little one. Though we try to make children aware of the solemnity of our meetings, you are newcomers, and our practices may take some getting used to. Please"—he gestured to the side door—"take the little one to the 'necessary.'"

Mary Rose took the twins by the hand, aware that every eye was upon her as she led them to the door.

"Can girlth become propheth?" Ruby said as soon as they stepped outside. "If he wath juth an ordinary boy, couldn't an ordinary girl be one too?"

"That's silly," Pearl said, and then ran into the outhouse first and closed the door. "Everybody knows there aren't any girl prophets," she called out.

"I want to thee the light in the woodth," Ruby said thoughtfully, turning to look at the woodsy shallow hills around them, afire with the changing color of the leaves. She focused on a glimmering maple, its leaves the color of molten gold. "That lookth like a plathe God could come. Look at the pretty light."

"I want to see too," Pearl said, flying back out of the outhouse again.

"Over yonder," Ruby said, then went into the necessary. "It thinkth in here," she said. "Maketh me feel thick."

"Just hurry," Mary Rose said, now impatient to get back to the story of the Prophet.

A few minutes later, Mary Rose led them back into the meetinghouse. This time the apostle didn't stop his oration or even seem to notice their return. She settled the girls and sat back, eager to hear more.

"The Father and Son said to him, 'Joseph, do not join any church, for all are abominations before God. Since the time of Christ, those who have claimed to be his rightful interpreters—the apostles, the priests, the popes, the ministers, the reverends, the fathers, everyone, brothers and sisters—have led astray God's people from the true words and deeds of Jesus Christ.'"

Webb stepped from behind the podium, his expression solemn. Mary Rose noticed that he did not preach with bulging eyes or shouted words about damnation and hell. Instead, his message, his delivery, was done with love, much the way she'd heard Joseph preached. She found her own eyes watering as she watched him.

"'Joseph,' they said to him, 'you are living in an era of great apostasy. My people have wandered from the Truth.' Then all fell quiet in the woods. Even the birds stopped their singing. Not a leaf fell from a tree. Not a whisper of wind.

"He remained on his knees, his head bent in worship. For how long? To this day, he cannot say. But the next words spoken to him struck his heart: 'The time has come for the Church's restoration, and you are to be my messenger.'

"I ask you, if this had happened to any one of you, what would you have done? Would you have run away, thinking God surely was mistaken, that he had chosen the wrong young man?"

Webb chuckled. "That's what Joseph did, dear Saints. He ran away and tried to forget the entire time spent with God the Father and his Son Jesus. He even went so far as to become full of disbelief." He smiled again and winked at Coal. "I would have done the same at that age, had I been there. Joseph was just a boy; he had some growing up to do.

"When he was seventeen something else extraordinary happened to him. One night as he lay sleeping, an angel by the name of Moroni appeared by his bedside. He told Joseph that buried in a hillside near Palmyra was a set of golden plates, on which was written an ancient language. The angel of the Lord told him to go and find these plates and deliver them to man. Those were his words, 'deliver them to man.' Brothers and sisters, Joseph was stubborn—just as stubborn as I'm sure I would have been, or perhaps many of us would have been." He smiled at the congregation. "Moroni appeared to Joseph three times before he would listen."

"Ith an angel gonna come bethide my bed?" Ruby whispered.

"Shhhh," Pearl said equally loud.

Coal turned around from his seat across the aisle and made a face, causing the twins to giggle. Gabe put his arm around the boy and gently turned him forward again.

The apostle stopped in the middle of his message and let that engaging smile beam across the congregation.

"Now that, sisters and brothers, is how God handled Joseph when he wouldn't listen. Did you all just see what our Brother Gabriel did? He put his arm around his errant son and turned him gently around.

"That's love, pure and simple. And that's how God turned Joseph around, got him to rethink all he'd revealed to him . . ."

Mary Rose watched Gabe's reaction. There was an emotion,

an expression she hadn't seen in him before. Adoration for the Prophet and his teachings as told through this charming apostle? A sense of pride in his actions being used as an example of God's actions? She waited for him to turn around again and make eye contact, but he seemed so enthralled with the story about the golden plates, the thought must not have occurred to him.

She tried not to let it bother her, but she couldn't help it. She turned to Bronwyn to see if she noticed. But she seemed as enthralled as Gabe did.

Her heart twisted in a way it hadn't before when she moved her gaze once more to Gabe.

The expression remained.

The apostle stood behind the podium, his voice clear and pleasant, his expression loving. "Our great Prophet finally did as he was told, and he found the plates. He took them home and translated them." Apostle Webb held up the Book of Mormon. "And this, dear Saints, is named such because it was brought to you and to me by Mormon's son, the angel Moroni."

He placed the book on the podium and, pulling out his handkerchief, mopped his forehead. "There is much more to the story of our beginnings, and we will spend weeks, yea, years studying these words, learning what God has to say to his restored Church. And we will learn from it how to share the love God has placed in our hearts."

Mary Rose again waited for her husband to glance back with a smile or a wink . . . any acknowledgment that she was in the same room with him. But his gaze was firmly fixed on the Prophet's adopted son.

TWENTY-ONE

Fenton Webb stepped down from the platform and, looking out over the men on his left, said, "Because you are all newcomers, you may not understand our order of service. Each Sunday it will be the same. After I speak to you about what God has put in my heart for you to hear, our sisters will be excused to retire to the ladies' meeting, and the children to their classes. And I, or one of the other elders or apostles, will remain with you men to continue preparing you for the priesthood.

"Today, the Prophet himself has a revelation of the utmost importance to tell you, and because it is a revelation for those in the priesthood only, I'm going to ask boys under the age of twelve to leave, please, with their mothers."

Coal scurried toward Mary Rose looking disappointed. Something didn't sit right about all this. What could he reveal from God that a boy could not hear? For that matter, that wives couldn't hear?

She was still considering what the revelation could mean when she looked up to meet the Prophet's intense blue-gray eyes. It was as if he knew she wasn't happy about being excluded from the revelation. She stared at him for a long moment, wondering about the priesthood of the men and why the messages she'd received from God came through Gabe and no other.

Even as she turned with the children to make her way down the aisle toward the door, she had that prickly feeling that the Prophet still had his eyes on her.

The Prophet waited while the women and children filed through the door. Mary Rose was among the last to leave, and Gabe knew she did so reluctantly. He caught her eye just before she turned to step outside the building and gave her another wink and slight nod. She treated him to that tiny smile he loved. This was so new to them both, but he was certain they would all adjust. After all, they'd been in Nauvoo less than one week. As soon as she disappeared outside, one of the elders closed the door.

The Prophet again returned to the podium. "I received the following word from the Lord," he said. "And until the time is right, word of it cannot leave this room. You are not to speak of it to your wives, for God needs to prepare their hearts to hear his words."

He unfolded a written document, and began to read:

"'Verily, thus saith the Lord unto you my servant Joseph, that inasmuch as you have inquired of my hand to know and understand wherein I, the Lord, justified my servants Abraham, Isaac, and Jacob, as also Moses, David, and Solomon, my servants, as touching the principle and doctrine of their having many wives—

"'Behold, and lo, I am the Lord thy God, and will answer thee as touching this matter.

"'Therefore, prepare thy heart to receive and obey the instructions which I am about to give unto you; for all those who have this law revealed unto them must obey the same.'"

Gabe sat forward, his heart pounding. There had been rumors

of plural marriages among the Church leaders, but this was the first concrete evidence it existed. He'd dismissed the reports, just as most other Saints had, rumors spread by the Gentiles to fire up the populace against them. Surely he wasn't hearing correctly. How could this be?

The Prophet continued: "'For behold, I reveal unto you a new and an everlasting covenant; and if ye abide not that covenant, then are ye damned; for no one can reject this covenant and be permitted to enter into my glory . . .'"

Damned? Gabe's eyes widened. The revelation wasn't just giving permission; it was an order. From God. Griffin was sitting two rows up, and Gabe would have given anything to know his thoughts right then. He'd been in the Church longer, maybe he had greater wisdom about the revelations than Gabe did.

"'And again, verily I say unto you, if a man marry a wife by my word, which is my law, and by the new and everlasting covenant, they shall pass by the angels, and the gods, which are set there, to their exaltation . . .

"'Then shall they be gods, because they have no end . . .'"

Gabe sat in stunned silence as the Prophet stepped from behind the podium and walked over to stand in front of the group. "I know this may be difficult to understand right now. It is for me, and I have been on my knees pleading with God to make certain I heard him correctly.

"Brothers, the answer is yes, I did receive this revelation without error. As you can imagine, it will be a difficult revelation for our wives to hear, for they will balk at sharing you with another. But let me be clear. This is not about simply taking more wives for the sake of variety. God forbid!

He took a few steps closer, and his voice dropped. "God himself was once as we are now, and is an exalted man. It is the same for each of us, brothers. Our glory in the next world will be determined by the knowledge we gain in this world and the excellence of our works upon the earth. If you enter heaven with ten wives you will have tenfold the glory of a man with one, and your advance toward progress, toward godhood, would be ten times as rapid as that of the man who's been blind to the truth upon the earth.

"Think on these things, brothers, and keep them to yourselves until the time is right.

"Now let's close in prayer."

Gabe's heart pounded against his chest, and he thought he might not be able to draw in another breath.

His first thought was not about himself but about Mary Rose. How could he do this to her?

His second thought was about godhood. Did he hear the Prophet correctly? Man could become a god? Could that be true?

Mary Rose offered a smile to the woman seated next to her at the women's meeting. She was young, round-faced, holding a baby maybe ten months old in her arms, and she was expecting another. For a moment, Bronwyn, who was seated on the opposite side of Mary Rose, and the young mother traded stories about childbirth and raising babies. "I should have said so earlier," the young woman said, "but my name is Polly McGuire, and this is Maevie."

Mary Rose relished the time to get to know some of the Saints better. The twins discovered friends their age as soon as the earlier meeting adjourned, and had gone with them to find their classroom. Coal had raced along with some boys he'd spotted, and Mary Rose could hear their wild whoops and hollers. She whispered a prayer for their teacher, hoping he had imminent patience.

As they waited for the other women to be seated, Polly looked around as if to be sure they weren't overheard and then, behind her hand, whispered, "You know what the revelation is all about, don't you?"

Mary Rose and Bronwyn exchanged glances, then Mary Rose turned back to Polly.

"I have no idea," she said. "Do you?"

"Well, I don't exactly, but I've heard rumors . . . about, well, you know . . ."

Mary Rose frowned and looking puzzled; Bronwyn leaned forward to better see Polly. "We don't know," she said.

"I'm not one to pass along tales, believe me," Polly said, lifting her brows. "But this one, well, it ultimately has to do with us all."

"What do you mean?" Mary Rose whispered as two older women in the row ahead turned around.

"Plural marriage," one of the older women said. Her companion looked distressed.

Polly turned pink. "Certain men, and I won't mention names, have taken more than one wife."

"That can't be," Mary Rose said. "I don't believe such a thing could be true."

"Oh, but it's true, all right," the older woman said. "I have it on good authority that the Prophet himself has at least three, maybe four other wives besides poor Emma."

"It's just a rumor," Mary Rose said. "A good and godly man like our Prophet would do no such thing."

"I agree," Bronwyn said, though her voice held a slight tremor. "Rumors such as these are meant to discredit the Mormons. We heard them as far away as England before we left."

"Brigham Young too," Polly said. "I heard he's got more wives than Joseph does."

"Untrue," Mary Rose said, more adamantly than before.

"That's what the revelation meeting is about, that's what the Prophet is revealing to our menfolk this minute," the older woman said. "Mark my words." She turned around to face the front of the room as a smiling middle-aged woman came up to stand before them.

"I'll clear this up with Gabe the minute the meeting is over," Mary Rose whispered to Bronwyn.

"As will I with Griffin," Bronwyn said.

"Where there's smoke there's fire." Polly lifted her infant to her shoulder and patted her back. A small burp ended the conversation as several women around them laughed.

Gabe smiled and waved as the children ran to him after the meeting. He knew without asking that Mary Rose was puzzled about something, and he hoped it had nothing to do with the revelation. There had been rumors all along, but he'd dismissed them. Now, faced with this new reality, what could he say to calm her anxious fear?

His smile widened as she approached, and his heart beat madly, just as it always did, when he looked into her face.

"I heard something this morning," she whispered. "But we'll talk about it later."

The twins pulled on his hands, chattering like magpies, and Coal shouted for him to watch as the boy swung by his knees from the branch of a willow tree.

"Yes, later," he said to Mary Rose, and prayed for wisdom. How could he tell her only what she needed to hear without lying? How could he tell her the rumors were false when he now knew as a certainty they weren't? How could he follow the Prophet's dictates yet remain true to his vows to love and cherish Mary Rose?

He had come to a crossroads, and he had to wonder which road he would take.

TWENTY-TWO

The day was autumn crisp, the deciduous trees as bright as liquid gold and claret wine, beneath a sky so blue it looked violet. Mary Rose and her family—how she loved the word "family"—and Bronwyn, Griffin, and the baby strolled beneath the canopy of trees from the meetinghouse to Eliza Hale's large home in town. The twins kicked the piles of dead leaves, skipped and tumbled and twirled; Coal threw himself into them, then turned over and lay there, staring up at the sky as if he was happier than he'd ever known possible.

Mary Rose walked next to Sister Eliza, a pretty woman of about forty-some years, who had generously opened her three-story house to the immigrants. There they would stay until their own homes were built—beginning straightaway, according to Church leadership.

The Hale residence was nearly as large as the Prophet's mansion and just a few houses down on the same street. Sister Eliza's husband, Liam, was in England on mission work and wouldn't return for another year.

On their second day upon arriving in Nauvoo, Gabe and Griffin chose their acreage, and the families celebrated when the husbands revealed that they had purchased adjoining farmland. When the homes were completed, the MacKays and Careys would be neighbors. Grandfather hadn't yet decided if he would prefer being in town or in the country. He'd taken a liking to Sister Eliza's town home and said he thought he might like one just like it.

Mary Rose almost laughed. So much for equality. Already she'd noticed that the poor were still poor and the wealthy still wealthy. And she'd picked up the notion, mostly set forth by Brother Brigham during the trek west, that gaining knowledge and making money were considered virtues. The more one could invest wisely, and reap rewards from that investment, the better. It seemed not simply to be a virtue to be admired, but a godly virtue.

Bronwyn bustled around the kitchen with Sister Eliza while Griffin and Gabe entertained the children. The kitchen was fragrant with a chicken stew bubbling in an iron pot on a fancy stove larger than that at the manor house.

Mary Rose never felt more helpless than when watching a competent cook in the kitchen. Or two, as in this case. Was there anything Bronwyn Carey could not do? With a sigh, she watched as, without a bit of instruction, Bronwyn mixed together the ingredients for dumplings—without measuring a single thing—then began to drop them by spoonfuls into the bubbling stew.

At her second loud sigh, Bronwyn turned and laughed. "If you'd like, m'lady," she teased, "you could come closer and watch the proceedings."

Mary Rose walked closer, and Bronwyn lifted her hand and put a long-handled spoon in it. "There now, put the spoon end in the pot and stir while I show you how to do the rest."

Mary Rose watched Bronwyn's technique until she felt confident to try her hand at dropping dumplings. She dropped the first too high above the pot, splattering gravy, which sizzled and spit on the stove. Mary Rose jumped back in alarm. Bronwyn held both her friend's hands and giggled as she tried to show Mary Rose exactly the twist of the wrist it took to let the spoonfuls drop at precisely the correct angle and height.

Eliza stood back laughing with the women. "With an upbringing like yours, Sister Mary Rose, this new life must be quite a shock."

Mary Rose laughed. "I've never known so much enjoyment could be gotten out of life. A year ago I would never have thought it possible." She reached for Bronwyn's hand and lifted it slightly, giving it a gentle squeeze. "And much of it is due to our friendship. I don't know what I would have done without Bronwyn."

She walked to the sink, pumped a handful of water to wash off the gravy, dried her hands on her apron, and then sat down at the small kitchen table opposite their hostess. "And then there's my Gabe," she said, getting misty eyed. "Once we fell in love, there was no turning back. I knew life would not only be different, but it would also be difficult—though I had no idea how difficult." She sobered, thinking of the long dusty, unbearably hot, dirty, cold, rainy days on the road to Nauvoo. "My friend and my husband saw me through."

"I beg to differ." Bronwyn came over to Mary Rose, stooped to give her a hug, and then slid into the chair beside her. "This woman saved my life and the life of my baby the night she was born aboard the *Sea Hawk*."

Mary Rose looked down, embarrassed. "Many things happened that night and many people helped. The biggest miracle of all was Brother Brigham's prayer."

"'Twas you who thought to fetch him, Mary Rose."

She smiled. "Actually, it was Griffin who did that. But I would have if I'd thought of it."

Bronwyn laughed. "Can I not get you to take credit for anything?" Her face softened. "And 'twas before you believed in the Prophet's testimony."

Mary Rose nodded. "We were running out of choices—even Grace Carolyn was worried."

"Sometimes it takes reaching the end of our human resources to cause us to reach out to God," Sister Eliza said. "I'll amend that. Perhaps it *always* takes reaching the end of our rope, as they say here in America, before we reach out to our Heavenly Father for help."

From the parlor came the strains of a song wheezing from a pump organ. "'God Save the Queen,'" Sister Eliza said, looking at Mary Rose. "Is that your Gabriel?"

"No, it's our grandfather," Gabe said.

Mary Rose looked up in surprise. Her husband had walked into the kitchen so silently, she hadn't heard a single footstep. And, as if in on the surprise, Bronwyn had kept her beautiful face completely blank, as if she didn't know he was there, though she sat facing the door.

At her look of surprise, Gabe and Bronwyn laughed together. Mary Rose watched their faces and the obvious delight they took in conspiring together, even in a small jape.

Mary Rose stood, and he pulled her into his arms. "I need to tell you, Mrs. MacKay, that you've got a ravenous family on your hands. The twins say they will perish within the minute if not fed some of that scrumptious stew. Coal says it's the dumplings he craves, and yea, everyone in the parlor has a stomach growling louder than the pump organ."

Laughing, Sister Eliza picked up a small glass dinner bell and gave it to Gabe. "If you'll be so kind as to call the others, we'll meet you all in the dining room. The Prophet told me of his plans to take you all to the temple site this afternoon, and you will not want to keep him waiting."

*   *   *

Precisely at three o'clock, Fenton Webb came to fetch the group at Sister Eliza's door. The twins were taking a nap in their bedroom on the first floor and Grandfather was playing a game of chess with Coal in the parlor.

Mary Rose didn't know why it surprised her that the Prophet's adopted son had invited Bronwyn and Griffin to ride with him and Porter Rockwell, the Prophet's bodyguard, in his barouche, drawn by a two-horse team. It had originally been arranged for Gabe and Mary Rose to ride out to the temple site so that Gabe, who was taking over as lead architect, could review it. But now they rode alone in a smaller curricle, drawn by a single horse.

Gabe shot her that crooked half-smile she adored and flicked the reins over the back of the horse. She saw her husband's lips move as if praying the gelding wouldn't embarrass him by standing still as a statue.

He sighed when the horse pulled into the lane behind the barouche, and then he reached for her hand and gave it a soft squeeze. He smiled into her eyes; she didn't think she'd ever seen him look so completely content.

"It's the temple," he said, practically reading her mind. "It's as if all my life, God has been preparing me for this single task." He looked back to the road. "Think of it. We're working with the Prophet God has appointed for our day and age. And as Solomon was commanded to build the temple in his day, our Prophet has been commanded to build another in our day." He shot her another quick grin. "And because I just happened to be an architect on the ship that the Apostle Brigham was traveling on to accompany you and your grandfather, and because I fell in love with you—and only then agreed to open my heart to God's word in the Book of Mormon—"

"Though you didn't read it," she chided with a light laugh, remembering that night.

"True enough. But I witnessed the miracle of Little Grace's birth. The miracle that Brigham wrought by his faithfulness to God's healing power. I saw it with my own eyes." He fell quiet for a moment, and the only sounds were those of horse hooves clopping on the pavement, rustling leaves from trees hanging low over the road, and here and there a trill of birdsong.

The walkways of the town were dotted with families out for Sunday-afternoon strolls, the women plainly dressed, sleeves and hems long, most wearing poke bonnets and knitted shawls. Even their hairstyles were subdued: older women wore their plaited hair wrapped into tight little buns; younger women, even those with bounteous hair, wore it covered or plaited in a single braid that rested on their backs. Snatches of laughter and conversation carried toward Mary Rose. Beauty radiated from their faces like lanterns from within. With awe, she watched as they strolled, talking with attentive husbands or sisters or friends, animated, laughing . . . happy.

She turned back to Gabe when he spoke again.

"God knew I would believe what I saw with my own eyes," Gabe said. "Like Doubting Thomas who needed to touch the nail prints in the palms of our brother Jesus Christ, I needed the same physical proof."

They followed the barouche as the driver turned his team onto another street. They had gone only a quarter mile or so when the incline steepened. Gabe flicked the reins and the horse actually trotted a bit faster. He grinned, looking proud enough to pat himself on the back.

Mary Rose chuckled. "You're getting much better at this," she said.

He was still grinning as they rounded the next curve, and the temple site came into view.

Mary Rose gasped and leaned forward. The view was stunning. Ahead of them, Fenton Webb's driver pulled the carriage to a halt, and Gabe did the same with another sigh of relief as the horse actually halted.

The group toured the building site. The foundation had been laid, but little else had been completed. The Apostle Webb, who, it turned out, had a working knowledge of architecture, mentioned some of the mistakes the previous designer had made. "Possibly on purpose," he added. "He became an apostate and left us for reasons I won't go into."

He turned to Gabe. "Can you work with what's been done, or do we need to start over?"

Gabe smiled. "I've thought of little else since we started for Nauvoo. I already have some preliminary drawings if you'd like to see them. And, no, there's no need to start over."

The group walked to the edge of the bank overlooking the Mississippi. The city of Nauvoo lay in the foreground, farmland dotted with cattle and other livestock farther out. "This is God's kingdom," Webb said with a sweeping gesture. "The Prophet has a growing conviction that we are a state within a state, that the federal and state governments have no jurisdiction over us. He wanted that for us in Kirtland, and he wants it to come to pass here. And as soon as possible."

He turned to Griffin. "You're a great asset to us. Brigham has high regard for you, and I hear you've already pledged to join our militia. The Church leadership wants it to grow to be four thousand, yea, ten thousand strong, so that no army can stand against us. Not from Washington, neither from this state.

"In the spring a man named Boggs came against us. He's a candidate for state office, and spread lies about us in his campaign. Got the people in a neighboring town riled up to the point I thought we might be under mob attack again."

Mary Rose and Bronwyn exchanged worried looks, but the men seemed mesmerized by his words.

"Joseph made a prediction then, and I repeat it now: 'Boggs will die a violent death within the year. And as for Governor Carlin of Missouri, he will also die, and in a ditch, that scoundrel.'"

Porter Rockwell, who was standing nearby, threw back his head and laughed bitterly. "I also have put a price on his head: five hundred dollars to any Destroying Angel who will kill Boggs."

He studied Griffin's face, and then did the same with Gabe's.

Mary Rose blinked in disbelief. Was this the same man who, only this morning, she thought of as delivering a message filled with love?

Webb stepped toward him almost protectively and, lowering his voice, said, "Porter, you need to take greater care when you say such things, even in jest. Should anything truly happen to either of these men, you could be arrested as an accessory to murder."

Porter laughed. "I should worry? It's you who has the ear of Joseph. I would say you'd be the accessory." He chuckled as if it all were a joke. "God's hand is on us all, brother. We have nothing to worry about."

Mary Rose and Bronwyn went back to stand near the foundation of the temple and looked out at the brilliant crimson sunset, the silver snaking river, and the town below them, fading in the evening light.

Mary Rose shivered, and Bronwyn reached for her hand. "'Tis not exactly what I expected," she whispered.

"Nor I," Mary Rose said. "Yet look how mesmerized our husbands seem to be by the words of violence."

"I suppose it's because of the Church's history, what's been done to them."

"I thought the Prophet was a man of peace," Mary Rose said as the sun sank deeper into the horizon.

"Maybe he is," Bronwyn said, turning to look at Mary Rose. "Maybe it's just those men around him who seem to want nothing to do with peace."

*   *   *

A wind kicked up near midnight, coming from the river, rattling the shutters and ripping leaves and twigs from trees, buffeting and dropping and swirling them until they sounded like dried bones. Mary Rose woke with a start, shivered and moved closer to Gabe. He drew the bedclothes over them, wrapped his arm around her and then kissed her temple. "Scared?"

"A little," she admitted. "But it's not the wind or the sounds outside that frighten me."

"What is it, love?"

"Our safety. We've given everything—our all—to the Prophet, to his Church—yet the rumors . . ."

"What rumors are those?"

"Today, in the ladies' meeting I met a woman named Polly."

"And . . . ?"

"She said that Brigham and Joseph have taken more than one wife."

"Does she know this as a fact?"

Mary Rose shivered again, wondering why the reality of plural marriage seemed more believable now than when Polly had first spoken of it. "No, she said it as if it were a fact, but she'd heard it from someone else."

Her husband sighed as if relieved. "There are always going to be rumors," he said gently, turning toward her. "We've talked about that before."

"What was your meeting about this morning? The revelation that the Prophet mentioned . . ."

For a long moment, Gabe didn't speak. The wind brushed a branch against the window, and dappled shadows danced eerily across the bedroom walls. "The Prophet said that the revelation must be kept in our hearts until the right time, that we are to tell no one."

"Not even your wife?"

"I'm sorry."

Her heart felt like it was about to twist into two pieces. "Gabe, we can't have secrets from each other. We're beginning a lifetime together. How can our love grow if I can't tell you my heart's innermost longings, fears, or joys? Or if you can't tell me yours?"

"Those things I can tell you, just not the Prophet's revelation. At least, not yet."

She wasn't about to let the dismissal go. "You must have had some feeling about the revelation. If it had to do with paving the street in front of the meetinghouse with cobblestones, you would feel something. Maybe boredom? If the Prophet's revelation had to do with moving to a new town, you would feel something. Maybe irritation because we just arrived here."

He chuckled and reached for her hand.

"Every revelation must lead to a reaction, a feeling, and those are the things we can't keep secret."

"I agree."

"Then you must also agree that if the Prophet's revelation had to do with plural marriage, you would have a resulting feeling about the revelation."

"Yes." He withdrew his hand and turned his face to the ceiling.

Her voice was almost a whisper as she continued. "You wouldn't necessarily have to tell me the revelation. You could just tell me the resulting feeling."

For a heartbeat he didn't answer, then he said, "The Prophet has asked that we keep in confidence all he has said on the subject." He turned toward her and drew her closer. "That, my love, includes feelings. I'm sorry." He kissed her temple and she cuddled closer, trying to draw warmth from him and shut out her fears.

"Those things that were said tonight at the temple site . . . I've tried hard to put the Church history behind me, to think that it's all in the past—all the hatred of the Saints, the persecution"— she rose up on one elbow to look at him in the dim light—"but as both Porter and Fenton talked about it, it was as if all that ugliness is still nipping at the Saints' heels."

"True," Gabe said. "I worry about our little ones, and Grandfather, and our friends . . . should anything happen to any of them"—he pulled her close—"to you, Mary Rose, I don't know what I'd do."

She rested her cheek against his chest, listening to the steady rhythm of his heartbeat, drawing comfort from it. "Did you know about the latest political turmoil?"

"No, Brother Brigham said nothing about it."

"But he surely must have known."

"We need to remember that he was in England doing mission work during that same time."

Another gust of wind rattled the windows.

"Sometimes . . ." Mary Rose began, "sometimes I feel this God is unreachable. You once told me God was disinterested and you didn't mind because you were disinterested in him."

"Aye, that I did."

"That's not how I feel—that God is disinterested. Not that exactly."

He chuckled lightly, then bent down and kissed her nose. "Then how exactly?"

She thought for a moment. "I don't know how to pray to him." She adjusted her head so she could see Gabe's profile. "Do you?"

"I'm learning that he was once a man like me, so I feel that I understand him better, and that he better understands me."

"If he was once a man, how can he be supernatural? How can he answer prayers? Or does he progress beyond being human at all? And if he does, then how can you understand him?" She paused, staring at the play of swirling leaf shadows on the ceiling. "When I was a child, before my mother died, she spent hours teaching me Scriptures. I was only six years old, but I remember some of them to this day." She searched her mind until one came to her. "This one was a favorite of hers: 'The lord hath appeared of old unto me, saying, yea, I have loved thee with an everlasting love: therefore with loving-kindness have I drawn thee.'

"It seems to me," Mary Rose continued, "that if the Lord was once a man, he did not exist in eternity. And if he did not, then how can he have loved me with everlasting love?"

"You yourself have heard Brother Brigham say that there are things in the Bible that are written in error. Anything that doesn't agree with the Book of Mormon, or with his revelation, is an error."

She let the disturbing thought settle into her heart. "I suppose there are many questions I'll need to have answered. But those few little words my mother taught me, I'm not willing to give up as if they were written in error. I choose to believe them, because that is the only Lord I can give my heart to."

A thoughtful silence fell between them. "Even the Bible says we cannot know God."

"It also says he is unchangeable," she responded. "Think about it. If I'm right about God's everlasting love for me that means our God is unchangeable. He cannot have once been a man. I remember distinctly that somewhere it says that. I AM, he calls himself, not I WAS or I WILL BE, but I AM."

"It's in the Book of Isaiah," he said, surprising her.

When her stunned silence met him, he laughed. "Hosea told me the same thing when he tried to talk me out of marrying you—and of being baptized into the Church."

"I didn't know he didn't want us to marry."

"It wasn't because of you. It was because I was becoming a Saint. My love for you, he said, had colored my decision."

"I need to tell you something," she said quietly. "We both saw the miracle of Brigham's prayer for Bronwyn and her infant . . ."

"Yes."

"What you didn't see, but I did, was the prayer of Grace Carolyn before Brigham entered the room. And she gave her an herbal drink to relax the muscles so the baby could turn."

"I still believe it was Brigham," he said. "All that other was a deception from the enemy to confuse you."

She thought about what he'd said. Surely he didn't think of Grace Carolyn as the enemy. "So it doesn't change your mind about our new . . . beliefs?"

"Not a bit." He chuckled. "But enough of all that for one night. I have a question to ask that will certainly take your mind off Church doctrine. And I think it's a question you will like."

"What is it?" She sat up to get a better look at him and could see his crooked half-smile in the pale light.

"Will you marry me again?"

"Again?"

"This time it will be a spiritual marriage, which means we will be married throughout all eternity."

"Spiritual marriage," she whispered in wonder. She liked the sound of it. Perhaps that's what the revelation was about. Not plural marriage at all. But a new perspective on the union of one man and one woman. She smiled in the dark, pushing her earlier doubts away, remembering it was the same that Brother Brigham had told her about earlier.

"You didn't give me an answer."

Mary Rose giggled. "I would marry you a thousand times, Mr. MacKay; all you have to do is ask." She turned to look at him, her heart flooding with emotion. "'Tis true, my love. I would do anything for you."

He reached for her again and gathered her close. She waited

for him to say something in return, but only the wind rattling the trees and the blowing of bone-dry leaves met her ears.

He squeezed her tight as if he were afraid she might pull away. She reached up to caress his face, and when she drew her hand away, her fingertips were wet with his tears.

TWENTY-THREE

Gabe kissed Mary Rose's cheek as she stepped down from their new buckboard in front of the meetinghouse.

"We'll be together throughout eternity," he whispered, his breath tickling her ear. "This sealing of our marriage is far more significant than the civil ceremony aboard the *Sea Hawk*."

"Though I thought that day dearer than any others in my life," she said, trying to imagine heaven, its everlasting joys, and being sealed to this man she would adore forever. She scarce could take it all in.

"Mary Rose—" Gabe took her hands in his. "You complete my life. I never knew I could be so content, so happy, until you came into my life. When I think of being with you through—"

His words were interrupted by Brigham, walking toward them dressed in a dashing cutaway coat, a Valencia waistcoat, and woolen trousers. He swept off his top hat and gave her a little bow. She'd already begun to notice that he liked the finer things in life, and she knew enough about fashion to guess its cost.

"Sister Mary Rose, you are looking lovelier than usual this morning."

"Thank you, Brother Brigham."

He shook hands with Gabe. "Son, may I steal you away from your wife for a few minutes?"

When Gabe glanced at her, as if for approval, she wondered what would happen if she said she preferred that Gabe remain with her. Lately, her husband seemed too ready to be at the beck and call of Brigham and the Prophet. She decided the day of their spiritual marriage wasn't the day to do battle with the leaders of the Saints. So she merely smiled and tipped her head.

Bronwyn waited in the outer room that had been set aside for brides to ready themselves. Several other brides milled about, primping in the mirror and adjusting their dresses. As soon as Bronwyn spotted Mary Rose, she headed across the room.

She glowed with happiness as she took Mary Rose's hands. "You look beautiful." Then she quirked a dainty eyebrow. "Though, beneath that smile, methinks you might be perturbed over something?"

Mary Rose rolled her eyes. "Brigham stole away my husband again. It seems that just about the time we're lost in each other's eyes, telling each other something significant, he barges in."

At once, the room fell quiet, and Mary Rose felt the disapproving looks of the other brides focused on her.

Bronwyn laughed merrily. "Men!" she said, more to turn the attention from Mary Rose than as a true expression of sentiment.

The other women went back to their conversations, but Mary Rose felt she was at the receiving end of several suspicious glances. One did not, apparently, make negative remarks about Brigham where others could overhear.

She bit back the lecture she'd like to give the women and

tried, instead, to focus on the joy of the day. Bronwyn seemed to understand and grabbed her hand, propelling her to a mirror at the end of the room.

As two other brides stepped away, Bronwyn pulled Mary Rose into place beside her and assessed their reflections. "We look enough alike to be sisters."

Mary Rose's demeanor lifted, at least temporarily. "It's the hair," she said. "Though yours is behaving much better than mine." Bronwyn had taught Mary Rose how to plait her hair, though Mary Rose remained all thumbs with each attempt.

Today, they were dressed in white, the products of a sewing project that took weeks to complete, with Bronwyn helping Mary Rose learn the art of needlework. When Mary Rose made no secret about it being tedious and tiresome, Bronwyn suggested they take turns reading aloud as the other one stitched. It took all of Jane Austen's *Pride and Prejudice* for Mary Rose to finish her gown, but only a few chapters of *Sense and Sensibility* for Bronwyn to complete hers, lace trim and all.

"I only wish the children could be with us," Mary Rose said as they moved to a group of chairs near the door. "Ruby got it in her mind that she wanted to carry a basket of posies and throw petals—" She frowned as snatches of conversation drifted toward them.

Two words stood out: "plural marriage."

She exchanged glances with Bronwyn, Mary Rose holding her breath so she could better hear the woman who spoke. Bronwyn gave Mary Rose an almost imperceptible nod toward the speaker and they made their way to the empty chairs nearby.

Apparently, the older bride next to them didn't realize she spoke loud enough for the Saints in downtown Nauvoo to hear.

The white-hair woman sniffed. "This is just the preliminary, you know."

"Now, now, Abigail," a second woman said. "You don't know that to be true."

"My George is not one to keep secrets from me," Abigail said. "And he does not speak with a forked tongue, if you know what I mean."

"This is not the time and place," the second woman said, lowering her voice.

"What did you say?" Abigail cupped her hand behind her ear. Then she shrugged. "It's called spiritual marriage now, but George says that it won't be long before it becomes a ceremony in which our grooms will be encouraged to seal themselves to more than one wife."

Mary Rose's eyes widened. Surely this couldn't be true. Spiritual marriage had nothing to do with plural marriage—at least that was what she understood from Gabe's explanation of it.

"It's just a rumor," the woman from across the room said. "Set upon us by Gentiles and their wicked printing presses that've spread the lies throughout the country."

Abigail examined her fingernails. "My George doesn't lie. You mark my words, these ceremonies pledge that we belong to our husbands throughout all eternity, but you soon will be given a secret name"—she drew a dramatic breath—"and your husband will have the power, the authority, given him by God, to call you into heaven by that secret name."

Mary Rose sat back, stunned.

Bronwyn took her hand. "Mary Rose, can it be true? Is that what this ceremony is all about? Will it give our husbands permission to take other wives?" She shuddered.

Mary Rose stood. "I must find Gabe. I will ask him."

Bronwyn stood. "And I must find Griffin." She looked ready to cry. "I won't go through the ceremony if that woman is right."

"I'll check the rooms inside, if you want to take the entrance," Mary Rose said. The words had barely left her lips when Bronwyn pushed through the door leading outside.

Mary Rose entered the room where they held their Sunday meetings. Brigham was speaking to the grooms, and beside him stood some of the other apostles, Joseph Smith, and Porter Rockwell. Gabe sat and listened raptly to his words, until Brigham spotted Mary Rose.

"I'm sorry," he called to her, "but this is a meeting of the priesthood. You will need to wait with the other brides. We will begin soon."

"I need to talk with my husband," Mary Rose said, walking closer. "It can't wait."

Darts of light seemed to flash in Brigham's eyes. "Whatever it is, Sister Mary Rose, that you think is so important will have to wait. This—and the wedding sealing that follows—cannot be disturbed."

Mary Rose tilted her chin high and thrust her shoulders back, feeling every ounce of her patrician upbringing take over the movement of her body as she moved down the aisle toward the men. "I will speak to my husband now, thank you," she said. Her eyes searched the group and finally focused on Gabe.

She expected him to give her a wink and perhaps an understanding smile, but he simply watched her make her way toward him. He didn't stand to greet her.

When she tore her gaze away from Gabe, Brigham's bodyguard stood before her. She tried three times to get past him; he blocked her each time. "I need to talk to my husband," she said. "It's important."

Brigham laughed, though the sound wasn't entirely pleasant. "I believe Lady Mary Rose is still with us," he said, giving her a pointed stare, "and that Sister Mary Rose sometimes forgets her place among us." He shrugged. "I was about to adjourn the meeting anyway, brothers. Gabriel, I suggest you calm your bride's obvious jitters."

Gabe looked displeased as he walked toward her. "What can be this important?"

She felt her cheeks flame. "You think I would interrupt your meeting if it weren't important?"

He let out a noisy sigh. "You're right, and I apologize. It was just, well, somewhat embarrassing—as if I can't control my own wife."

Her eyes widened. "Did you say 'control'?" Though men commonly used the term in reference to their wives, even back in England it had annoyed her. She'd told Gabe so the first time he used it. He hadn't let the word, or any like it, leave his lips in her presence . . . until now.

"I misspoke," he said, grinning, which completely disarmed her. "You are one not to be told what to do, and that's what I love about you. Please forgive me." They walked toward the exit, and Gabe held the door open for her. She stepped through to the foyer. Other brides and grooms milled about.

"'Tis private," she said

"All right." He led her outside and they took a few steps away from the meetinghouse.

"In the brides' room, I heard that this ceremony is preliminary to the very thing we were discussing the other night."

Gabe looked nervous, as if he knew what was coming.

"Plural wives."

He looked down as if embarrassed, and when he again lifted his gaze, his eyes were watery, his expression troubled. "Yes, plural marriage is being taught to a chosen few in the priesthood. I've already let my feelings be known, believe me. But when you think of the Old Testament patriarchs and kings . . ."

Her face grew warm. "I'm not Bathsheba and you're not King David," she said. "We're us, we're in love, and we're vowing to love only each other for the rest of our lives, and through all eternity. And I think every woman in the bridal room feels the same way." She stepped away from him. "What if this new doctrine requires you to take another wife?"

He surprised her by giving her an irresistibly devastating grin, the kind that always made her heart pound. "I love you, Mary Rose, and you alone. There will never be anyone else."

Porter Rockwell came up just then and told him the Prophet needed to see him about an important matter. As they walked away, Mary Rose heard snippets of their conversation about new attacks against the outlying farms in the settlement. Her heart continued to sink.

A few minutes later, the couples lined up at the rear of the meetinghouse and then slowly walked down the aisle to stand in front of the Prophet. The vows were taken separately, the words similar to the civil ceremony aboard the *Sea Hawk*, though each also took an additional vow to be sealed to each other throughout all eternity.

Afterward Mary Rose and Gabe, Bronwyn and Griffin, were ushered into a separate room where a luncheon had been prepared.

"I love you, my eternal bride," Gabe whispered, and kissed the top of her ear.

"And I love you, Mr. MacKay." But pain squeezed her heart even as she said the words.

He smiled and pulled her into an embrace.

On the other side of the buffet table, the hard-of-hearing Abigail had caught the ear of another bride. "Just you wait," she said, "within just a few months—a year tops—all of us womenfolk will have sister wives in our families."

"Sister wives?" She looked up at Gabe, desperate for him to tell her the old woman was wrong.

"That's what I've heard they call each other."

Her heart stopped. "Has it already begun?"

He gave her a reassuring smile. "Some say it has, but I have not witnessed it." He bent low and whispered, "I would tell you if I had."

She leaned against him as an odd heaviness weighed down her heart, replacing the love and trust she should have felt on this day. She dropped her lashes to hide her tears.

TWENTY-FOUR

An Island off Jonesport, Maine
December 24, 1841

Hosea Livingstone woke to endure another day of pain. It was just before dawn and he heard Cara, the fisherman's wife, at the old metal stove in the kitchen, positioning the damper with two loud clinks, dropping in chunks of wood with several loud thuds, then closing the metal door with a loud clank. He hadn't told her the comfort the sounds brought him, together with smells that would follow, of woodsmoke and baking bread.

Early mornings had become the only part of the day he looked forward to since coming to the cottage of the fisherman and his wife. One day slipped into another, one dark night into another, when he could close his eyes and attempt to sleep, attempt to forget what brought him here.

At first, a small window above his bed gave him sunlight by day and moonlight by night, depending on its phase. The starlit nights were most difficult to endure because with them came memories of navigation, of the ship he once commanded, of the seafaring years that had been his life. Of his last voyage with Gabe, the two of them on the quarterdeck under the stars, telling tall tales, exchanging japes, and sometimes laughing so hard they cried.

But now, day or night, he saw only snow.

The betrayal filled his mind. How could Gabe and Enid not understand the lie they'd lived all those years would dig into his gut and grab hold to stay, its poison accurate and deadly?

The good fisherman and his wife had been kind from the moment he woke and discovered the sea hadn't taken him after all.

Giovanni told Hosea he'd been unconscious when they found him and remained in that state for several days after—a good thing, the fisherman told him, because setting the broken bones and tending to his wounds would have been unbearable.

As if the pain he felt now—both interior and exterior—was bearable.

Each day Cara asked Hosea if he remembered his name and how he'd come to land on their beach. Each day he told them the same answer: He couldn't remember.

As the sky turned pearl gray in the small square of window over his bed, Giovanni came into the cabin, greeted his wife with loving Italian words as he sat in a chair near the door, and removed his snowshoes and then his boots.

Hosea's bed, though in a separate room, faced the doorway, so he saw their comings and goings. He figured they would wait until spring to take him by fishing boat to the nearest town, which Giovanni told him was Jonesport.

He turned his face to the wall as he heard Giovanni's approach.

"How are you faring this day?" The fisherman lifted the heavy woolen blanket to check his legs, which made it difficult for Hosea to ignore him. "Any feeling yet?" He pushed and probed along Hosea's calf, knee, and thigh.

Hosea shook his head.

"How about this?" He lifted the opposite leg.

Hosea winced. "Yes, that side has feeling."

"The injuries aren't as severe. A cleaner break, this one. I know it's painful, but it's a good sign." He frowned, probing Hosea's left leg again. "Several breaks on this side and some crushing of bone near your hip, and your kneecap took a beating." He covered Hosea's legs with the blanket again. "But you will heal. You will walk again."

He walked over to a small table with salves and bottles of herbs on the top shelf, a round bedpan on the second. "Need the pan?"

Hosea shook his head. "Not yet. I'll let you know."

"Good. How about coffee? Cara's just put some on to boil."

"Yes, please. That would be nice." They had the same conversation every morning, and every morning Cara's coffee appeared, carried by Giovanni in a chipped, speckled porcelain-covered iron mug. The sameness of it touched him, but he couldn't fathom why.

The coffee always contained a spoonful of brown sugar and a bit of warm goat's milk. They never thought to ask if he might like it plain; he supposed it had something to do with how little they had materially. What they shared was a gift not to be picked over.

Giovanni stood next to the bed with the coffee as Hosea struggled to prop himself up against the pillows at the headboard. He'd noticed that Giovanni helped him less every day.

The fisherman pulled up a chair beside Hosea. "I thought we'd get you up again to try a few steps today."

Hosea shook his head as he sipped the coffee. "It hasn't worked before, I see no reason to try again."

"Your muscles will seize up if we don't get them moving."

He shook his head again.

"It's Christmas Eve, a good day to take your first steps. Think of it as a gift."

Hosea let out a bitter laugh. That was it. As soon as he could walk, they could be rid of him. His gift to them.

"Cara is making a lovely Christmas dinner, and we would like to have you join us at the table. It would do you good to get out of bed."

"One leg is numb, the other too painful to even touch," Hosea said. "I can only imagine the pain if I tried to put my weight on it. How can I walk on such limbs?" He turned his head away from the fisherman's searching gaze.

But that didn't stop Giovanni from speaking his mind. "You've told us nothing of your past; you say you can't remember. You are well spoken, an educated man, and I venture to guess, educated in the ways of the seas, therefore a seafaring man. How do I know this? When I speak of taking my boat out to fish, or mention the beauty of the sea, a light appears in your eyes that a blind man couldn't miss.

"You, sir, know exactly who you are and how you got tossed by the waves upon our beach."

Hosea turned back to the fisherman, at first indignant and then chagrined. He tried to smile, but it seemed his muscles forgot how. "I'm not a good liar. Maybe I don't want to remember."

"You've been with us five months now; your wounds, though serious, are healing. What isn't healing is that which is eating you up inside."

"And while we're on the subject of identities," Hosea said, "you don't sound like any fisherman I've ever known. And believe me, I've known many."

Giovanni threw back his head and laughed. "Hear that, Cara? Our guest does not think I'm a fisherman."

She came to the bedroom doorway, wiping her hands on her apron. "We wondered how long it would take for you to figure it out."

"Actually, I didn't say you weren't a fisherman. I said you don't sound like one. There's a difference."

"I fish only for what we need to eat," Giovanni said. "Our needs are simple. I don't take my boat out to bring back bulging nets of haddock or perch to take to market for profit. Most of the year I don't fish for more than what we can eat in a day. Though before winter sets in, I catch enough to salt or pickle to see us through the weeks our island is icebound."

"Our growing season is short," Cara said, "but my garden gives us an abundance of good bounty. Some we eat the day it's fresh-picked; some we set up as preserves for winter."

"What about the woods behind your place? I've heard you talk about it—the abundance of wildlife you see even now in the dead of winter. I would think the deer and rabbits alone would keep meat on your table."

Cara laughed. "Oh, we couldn't eat any of the animals that come to visit us. We feed them." She headed back toward the kitchen, tossing over her shoulder, "Giovanni even preaches to them. Lands no, we couldn't eat them."

"So you're a preacher," Hosea said to Giovanni. He couldn't keep the bitter tone from creeping into his voice.

"No, not a preacher." Giovanni's eyes flickered slightly in recognition of the bitterness in Hosea's tone.

"What are you, then?"

"Do I have to be something?"

Hosea wanted to laugh for the first time since his arrival, but again he noticed that one side of his face didn't seem to remember which muscles to use, which puzzled him. "No, I guess you don't."

Giovanni sat back, crossed his legs, and then clasped his hands over his knee. "I do a lot of things; but none of them for income."

"Such as?"

"Woodwork."

"You're a carpenter, then?"

Chuckling, Giovanni called in to Cara, "Now the man thinks I'm a carpenter."

"If you call whittling a walking stick carpentry," she called back, "then I guess you are, love."

"I have a gift for you," Giovanni said to Hosea, "a Christmas Eve gift."

"I have nothing to give you . . ."

"Ah, but you do." He smiled mischievously. "You must use my gift."

"The walking stick."

"That's for later. You aren't yet ready."

"You said that I need to walk today."

"And you will, but only to move into the chair I made for you."

"We tried chairs before. I don't have the strength to sit upright."

"You will in this one." He leaned forward. "But you've gotten rather nicely around the question I asked earlier. Now that we've established that you know your identity, who are you?"

"I can't go back," Hosea said.

Giovanni studied his face. "This isn't about going back. It's about the here and now, who you are now, not who you were or what you did five months ago."

Hosea looked up at the window, the bleak gray sky. How could he admit even to himself that all he had worked for, had ever wanted in life, he'd let go of in less than an instant? He had betrayed himself.

He turned back to Giovanni, studying the man's kind face, wanting to tell someone what he'd done, wanting to ask for help to untangle the brokenness inside and out. He took a deep breath.

"I can't go back because when the wave washed over the deck, I could have clung to the rail. I saw the rogue coming. I should have been in my quarters, but I went out on the deck. Not the quarterdeck, but aft, where no seamen would see me. And when the wave hit, I simply let go."

Silence fell between them. Hosea searched Giovanni's face for condemnation. None appeared.

"You're a captain, then."

Hosea studied Giovanni's face. Not everyone knew the ways of the seas, the protocol of naval officers, where they were to be and when. His curiosity was piqued.

"You said that who I am now is different than who I was five months ago."

"And it is."

"I was master and commander of the *Sea Hawk*, a clipper that had just set a speed record for crossing the Atlantic. My name is Hosea Livingstone."

Giovanni didn't look impressed. "And you are now?"

"A broken man, in spirit and in body."

"But it was because of the broken spirit that you did not try to save yourself."

"True."

"So that part is the same now as then. What happened to make you give up on life, on living?"

Hosea leaned back uncomfortably, the pain in his tailbone and spine too hard to bear. He needed to lie flat again. "I've told you my name. But I have nothing else to tell."

"It isn't necessary," Giovanni said, surprising Hosea.

The pain and the talk had worn Hosea out. The hand that grasped the now-empty coffee mug was too weak to hold it any longer. Giovanni reached for the cup just before Hosea's fingers let go.

"I will bring your chair later," Giovanni said, helping him settle more deeply into the bed. He turned Hosea on his side, a painful process because of the bedsore at the base of his spine. "Rest, and then Cara's bread will be ready and we'll have breakfast."

Hosea now faced the window. It was snowing again: large, fat flakes, floating down against a dull gray sky.

His thoughts drifted to another time, another place. Summer, when the skies were violet and the hillsides green, when he and Enid laughed and talked and wondered about the future, which both believed held only good things. He was strong then, and life knew no boundaries. He had reached his life's goal: master and commander of the world's fastest clipper ship. He'd had the world in the palm of his hand.

He thought he knew his God. He read the prayers in his Psalter daily, he could argue with the best of them about world religions, especially when he found something evil in them.

Pure arrogance.

What did it matter now? Who cared about him? Certainly Gabe didn't; Hosea had seen to that when he practically threw him off his ship and out of his life. And Enid? Who knew if she cared or not? She obviously hadn't cared enough to be truthful.

How ironic for Gabe to say he'd always held Hosea up as an example of someone filled with God's grace and mercy, that he had been a lifeline. Gabe had thought God indifferent toward him, and he had openly said he was indifferent toward God.

Strange, how things had turned. Now Gabe had found religion with the Saints, and Hosea was indifferent toward God. Indifferent wasn't the half of it. In truth, he had lost all belief.

The snowflakes were smaller now and falling more rapidly. A wind kicked up and whorled them, taking them from their downward course. He heard the wind's moaning and the sounds of it took him back to that night . . .

Hosea closed his eyes and the image of white foam at the wave's crests replaced the image of the snow outside his window. The crashing waves with their white-capped ridges, the frigid waters, his suspension between two places came back to him: above, the lighter hues of the surface beckoning, below, pulling harder, the black depths.

How long he hung suspended, he didn't know. It seemed like

an eternity, his lungs ready to burst, his body unwilling to swim to the surface for a life-giving gasp of air, unwilling to choose life. And then, as if by some unseen hand, he'd been lifted out of the water and thrown onto the rocky shore near the house of this man who said he wasn't a fisherman.

If he still believed in God, he would have thought it was the hand of God. But Hosea's broken body and spirit only reinforced his refusal to think any supreme being would bring such suffering to one he supposedly loved.

He fell into a deep sleep and when he woke, it was as if he existed in a different place, and none of the pain and terror and heartache of recent months had yet happened. The scent of buttery chowder and fresh-baked bread, a violin, simply played, and two voices singing carols so sweet they made his heart hurt drew him to a place where all else was forgotten, at least for a moment.

> Whilst shepherds watched their flocks by night,
> All seated on the ground,
> The Angel of the Lord came down,
> And glory shone around.
> "Fear not," said he, for mighty dread
> Had seized their troubled mind.
> "Glad tidings of great joy I bring
> To you and all mankind."

"'Fear not,' said he, for mighty dread had seized their troubled mind . . ." Hosea whispered the words as Giovanni and Cara sang. Tears trailed from the corners of his eyes down his cheeks and dripped onto his pillow.

TWENTY-FIVE

Cavendish, Prince Edward Island
January 18, 1842

Alight snow dusted the landscape during the night, following a short, noisy hailstorm that rattled across the island and quickly moved offshore. Knowing the horse would remember the terror brought by thunder and lightning, Enid spent the night in the barn, lying near the iron stove on a cot.

Now, as dawn produced her first look at the overcast day, Enid tried to approach Miss Minnie, Brodie Flynn's dun mare, with a handful of oats. But the mare rolled her eyes and backed away from Enid's extended hand. Enid had stabled the mare in her own barn since summer, when the horse had endured injuries that by all rights should have taken her life. Short of that, should have caused one of the Flynns to put her out of her misery. Enid wondered, if she'd been the one to decide, what she would have done. But she was on the packet ship returning from Halifax, her heart heavy with the news of Hosea's death, having sobbed until her shoulders ached.

"Come on now, girl," she said, attempting once more to approach the frightened horse.

The dun nickered and rolled her eyes, expelling white steam from her nostrils that rose into the cold air. Enid slowly stretched her arm toward the horse, her hand cupped and filled with oats.

"I won't hurt you," she whispered. "And I'm not giving up on you."

Behind her, from the barn's entrance, Brodie Flynn called out to her. At the sound of the boy's voice, the big mare nickered and flicked her ears forward.

"I'm back here," Enid called to the boy. "With Miss Minnie."

He raced toward her without stopping to warm himself by the stove.

"You're here early today," she said, giving him a glance.

"The storm last night," he said in a worried voice as he rubbed his hands against the cold. " 'Twas so much the same as . . ." His voice dropped off and a moment passed before he could continue. "The sounds and all. I thought Miss Minnie might need me. But Ma said I couldn't come till first light."

"I'm glad you came. Her ears flicked forward when you spoke."

The boy's eyes brightened. "Ye think I might touch her today? Maybe just her neck? I'll be careful."

Enid cracked open the stall door and slipped inside. The big horse didn't rear, but snorted and tried to disappear into the dark corner. "Come with me," she said softly to Brodie. "But don't make any sudden move toward her. Just let her sense your presence. Think about how much you love her, and maybe she'll see it in your eyes."

" 'Tis a wonder to even be this near her," the boy whispered. He moved his gaze from her eyes, then, and fixed his gaze first on her scars, the flap that had been torn open on her neck when lightning hit the tree under which the boy and his horse had taken shelter.

The boy had told her the story a dozen times, at first sobbing as he described what happened. A branch fell, the tree caught fire, and the horse screamed in terror, bolting under a smoldering, jagged, broken branch that knocked the boy off her back and cut deep into the horse's neck. Brodie never knew a horse had so much blood. The jagged branch split from the tree and hit the ground and in Miss Minnie's panic, she caught her hoof in a V-shaped limb attached to the larger branch and dragged the whole thing with her until she disappeared from sight, the child running after her, crying out for her to stop, crying out that he would fix it. Hours later the boy and his pa found Miss Minnie trembling by the ocean's shoreline, wet with blood and sweat, frothing at the mouth, so fearful she seemed to have lost any recognition of the boy who loved her.

When she first saw the horse, Enid knew she should be put down, but she couldn't do it. The horse needed healing and so did she. Over those first few weeks and months, Miss Minnie became her obsession; getting her to trust again became Enid's life's work. She thought of little else, even as she treated other animals at neighboring farms.

Miss Minnie nickered again, her fearful gaze now fixed on Brodie. Enid moved in front of the boy to protect him if the horse suddenly reared and kicked. The mare associated the boy with the lightning storm, her injuries, her terrifying flight, just as she associated Enid with the ministrations meant to heal but that brought greater pain, distrust, and fear.

The boy slipped out from behind Enid. "Miss Minnie," he whispered, adopting the same soothing tone as Enid. "'Tis me. Yer best friend Brodie. Do ye remember?"

The mare nickered, keeping her eyes fixed on the boy's. Enid held her breath. They had connected, even if for just a heartbeat; they had connected for the first time since the accident. It had nothing to do with actions or movement by the horse or the boy. It had to do with what she saw in both their eyes.

Enid whispered for Brodie to slowly lift his hand and cup his fingers together. She dropped her handful of oats onto his palm. "Lift it slowly," she murmured. "Let Miss Minnie see what you have for her."

The boy did as Enid suggested, and Miss Minnie eyed his hand warily. "I used to bring ye carrots and apples, and I will again, if ye'll eat the oats. But ye must eat the oats first, Miss Minnie." He held out his hand, and Enid held her breath in worry. At the slightest disturbance the injured mare would kick at the stall, rear, and scream.

"Perhaps this is enough for one day," she said. "Miss Minnie is making good progress." She turned to lead the child out the stall door.

"Look at 'er now, Mrs. Livingstone." He couldn't keep the excitement from his whisper.

Enid heard the telltale sounds of the horse nuzzling Brodie's hand for food, and turned. As she nibbled at the oats, the horse remained wary and attentive, her gaze locked on the boy's.

Brodie stepped closer and patted the dun's neck. Again, she didn't shy away. His eyes filled as he laid his cheek just below the worst of the scars. When Miss Minnie didn't move, Brodie buried his face in the mare's mane. Enid saw his shoulders tremble and knew that he cried. The mare arched her neck, looked down at the boy, and nuzzled him.

By late morning, Enid had finished her chores around the ranch and rode back with Brodie to the Flynns' farm for Sunday dinner.

The dusting of snow melted, and though the thin winter sun

was out with a buttermilk sky backdrop, dark clouds billowed in the north. She told Brodie she would need to leave early because of it.

"Can ye not just stay the night?"

Enid laughed. "Then who would take care of all my animals? No, I need to get back after supper."

She slowed Sadie to a walk, and Brodie did the same with his horse. He turned to look at her solemnly. "I'm glad ye'll be with us tonight, at least for supper." He thought for a minute, looking at the ground. "I'm glad yer back for good."

"Well, thank you, Brodie," she said. "Though I wasn't gone for long."

"We all thought it was going to be forever, sailing off to London and all, like ye planned."

"I thought so too, but everything changed the night Captain Livingstone died."

"Do ye miss him?"

"Terribly."

"Ma says she's worried ye'll run off to find that fellow we bought our house from. What is his name . . . Mr. MacKay?"

Enid laughed. "Yes, Gabriel MacKay. He invited me to look him up in a faraway place called Nauvoo. But I'm quite content to stay here and do what I love most. Practice veterinary medicine."

"That's what I want to do when I grow up," the boy said. "Help animals heal."

"You'd be very good at it."

"Can I ask ye something?" Their horses clomped along the road. Puddles held ice and were as slick as glass. Enid nudged her horse to take the lead, concentrating on guiding them around the slippery obstacles.

"Anything," Enid said.

"Are ye planning to marry Mr. MacKay?"

She laughed. "Goodness, no."

"Don't tell Ma I said so, but she and Pa are saying that ye will. She says ye'll work on animals no matter where ye go."

Enid chuckled. "You can tell them I have no intentions of leaving the island again for a very long time."

"Ma said it will be in the spring, when the wildflowers bloom again and when Miss Minnie is healed. And when you're healed too from feeling so bad about the captain." In truth, Enid didn't think she would ever heal from her wounds. She had too many, most of them brought on by her own doing, and then, digging deeper into her heart as with a knife, there were the last words Hosea had written about forgiving but not forgetting.

They reached the highest point of land between the two properties, a place where she and Gabe often came to watch the ships on their way to the harbor, or at night to watch the stars and pick out constellations.

She halted Sadie as a magnificent sailing ship passed by below. In full sail, it sped along as if on glass. It brought back memories of both Hosea and Gabe.

Gabe had written her from Boston, just as he'd promised. He reported Hosea's reaction in a short letter, only three sentences long. Hosea had taken the news harder than expected. Gabe hoped that with time her husband would realize how much they both loved him, and Hosea would forgive them. He ended the missive by letting her know again that should she need him, he would come to her, or welcome her with open arms, should her desire be to come west.

"When the flowers bloom? That's when your ma thinks I leave?"

"Aye, she said herself. Ye'll leave when the primroses and marigolds bloom. 'Twill make yer heart think of love again—and she's long thought ye once loved Mr. MacKay . . . Can I ask ye one other thing?"

"Of course."

" 'Twas a bad thing that the captain died the way he did, but it was a good thing that ye came back to save my Miss Minnie. And ye wouldn't have done it if the captain hadn't died." He scrunched up his face in thought. The sunlight briefly left its cloud cover and touched his tufts of red hair. Two big front teeth had replaced the empty places where the baby teeth had fallen out last summer.

"How can something bad make something good happen?" He blinked back tears. "It doesn't feel right somehow." A breeze came off the ocean, and from a stand of willows a great blue heron took flight. "It doesn't feel right to be glad the bad thing happened," he whispered, so low Enid almost didn't hear him. "But I can't help it."

TWENTY-SIX

Nauvoo, Illinois
March 17, 1842

Mary Rose sat at her writing desk near an open window in her bedroom. She chose this room as the one she would share with Gabe because of the view of the sunset on the river, that moment in time when the river turned from silver to gold to bronze and then black. And now, sitting at her desk beneath the window, she could see the sky changing from the vivid blues of midafternoon to a paler wash of scarlet and yellow hues as the sun began sinking into the horizon.

The farmhouse had been completed the week before, thanks to the efforts of the industrious Saints who, working together in barn-raising style, built town homes and farms almost as fast as new converts arrived. Many of their friends had contributed furniture, and the rest she and Gabe had shopped for in St. Louis and had delivered.

Bronwyn's laughter, mixed with that of Coal, Ruby, and Pearl, floated toward Mary Rose through the window. Next week, Bronwyn, Griffin, and Little Grace would move to their new farm on the neighboring property. Mary Rose's heart twisted when she considered how much she would miss them. They'd become part of the family while living with the MacKays during the building of their new home.

She looked out at the patch of land where she and Bronwyn had started a garden, thought of the seedlings just beginning to sprout, the growth she would oversee in the coming months . . . and mostly, how much she would miss her friend who showed her how to plant a garden.

She opened her journal and began to write:

This day I am profoundly blessed: by love I would not have known had I not met Gabriel MacKay—my heart, my all—on the voyage from England to this new land; by friendship I would not have known were it not for Grandfather's insistence that we throw in our lot with the Prophet; by the delight of children I would not have known, yet whose presence bewildered me until I found love in my heart for them. Now I know not what I would do should their real parents come for them. I selfishly pray that day never comes, though the sweet little ones pray each night that their mama and papa would soon come to fetch them.

I thought my longing to keep them might be lessened by the coming of my own child, but the closer we draw to his—or her!—birth, the more I realize that not even my own will take the place of our Ruby, Pearl, and Coal.

I long for them to call me "Mama" and call Gabe "Papa" but I am still "Lady," and Gabriel is still "Mr.

MacKay." If ever I hear the music of any word relating to motherhood from them, I will weep with joy.

Grandfather has found a true love in his beloved Cordelia Jewel. They were married last month and sealed for eternity. They are now trying to decide if they will have a farm built or continue living in town. 'Tis a wonder that the Earl of Salisbury would marry a dance hall girl from New Orleans, but I suppose conversion comes in all shapes and sizes and backgrounds.

Sometimes I have to remind myself that when the self-righteous men brought before Jesus the adulteress caught in sin and asked that she be stoned to death according to the law, he said, "He who is without sin, cast the first stone." Of course, they all turned away.

Though Scripture doesn't say, 'tis my belief that it was the woman's heart that changed that day, not the self-righteous "holy" ones who thought they knew God's law.

Forgiveness is not a subject I think about often. But today, as I sit here, with my life the happiest I've ever known it to be, I wonder if something more terrible than I can imagine were done to my family, my children (and I count Coal, Ruby, and Pearl my own), my friends, would I find forgiveness in my heart?

I feel the little one beneath my heart wiggling and kicking and sometimes even tumbling. What greater joy can anyone know but that? I think often of the words that seem to flow from somewhere in my heart's depths . . . "Thou hast covered me in my mother's womb . . . I will praise thee; for I am fearfully and wonderfully made: marvelous are thy works; and that my soul knoweth right well."

To think such a miracle is happening in my own womb even now brings me joy beyond all measure.

That night, Grandfather and his new bride stopped by for a visit, though what appeared to be a social call revealed itself as something more when the earl helped Cordelia from the buckboard, then headed straight for Gabe and Griffin, who were saddling up in the barn.

Mary Rose, curious about what was going on, decided to leave the social niceties to Bronwyn who, understanding what she was up to, gave her a wink. Bouncing Little Grace on her shoulder, Bronwyn greeted Cordelia warmly and led her inside the house for tea, the twins trailing behind asking endless questions about the riverboat and if she would teach them how to dance.

"I've alwayth wanted to learn how to danth," Ruby said. "Will you thow uth?"

"Me too," Pearl said. "I want to know how to waltz."

Coal's gaze darted from the house to the barn where the men were talking, likely trying to decide if he would rather ask questions about riverboat gambling or hear about the secret meeting of Porter Rockwell's militia.

Mary Rose ruffled his hair. "You're dying of curiosity and so am I. We can ask Sister Cordelia about life on the riverboat later."

He grinned up at her. "If I didn't already have a mother, I'd want you to be her."

Mary Rose stopped and looked down at him, her heart aching with love. "I believe that's the nicest thing anybody ever said to me." She rested her hand on his shoulder as they continued to the barn.

Her grandfather was talking as she entered the dark barn. "Word in town is that there've been new threats against us, especially against the outlying farms. You sure it's a good idea to leave tonight?"

"There's only one road in to reach our farm," Gabe said. "And we'll be guarding it." He gave the earl directions: the river road to the intersection of the main road into town. He described the meeting place: outside an abandoned farmhouse that had been recently burned, the family driven out—just behind a stand of pines.

Griffin gave the earl a reassuring pat on the shoulder. "We know about the renewed threats. That's what the meeting's about—the escalating violence and what we will do about it."

"If it's Porter Rockwell who's heading it up, you must be meeting with the Destroying Angels, not the militia." The earl looked worried. "Anyone else of importance going to be there?"

Mary Rose knew the difference between the two armies very well. The militia was meant to show outsiders that the Mormons were ready to protect themselves from invaders. The secret army, sometimes called the Destroying Angels or Avenging Angels, was dispatched to attack their enemies, create fear and trembling among the neighboring communities. They carried out their secret raids in the dead of night, faces covered, identities unknown even among the other Mormons. Mary Rose abhorred the idea of Gabe carrying out such violence.

"The Prophet and Brigham, a few of the apostles," Gabe said.

Mary Rose stepped out of the shadows, unable to be quiet any longer. "If the Gentiles get wind of such a meeting with our leaders, they might choose the place as a target to get all our leaders at once."

Gabe smiled and came over to embrace her. "You're thinking like a soldier, love. We're actually hoping they do get wind of it." Then he sobered and looked at the earl. "I'm glad you're here. You know where the firearms are, should you need them."

"I do."

"So do I." Coal stuck out his chest. "And I know how to shoot."

Mary Rose shuddered at the thought of the little boy picking up a gun of any kind.

Gabe squatted beside the boy. "You need to let the earl handle the firearms—unless it's an absolute emergency."

The boy nodded.

"We'll go out shooting again soon, so you can get even better." He stood and turned to the earl again. "We chose the grove just beyond the turnoff to the river so we can catch the thugs either way they come—by road or by water."

"It's a trap, then," the earl said.

Griffin's horse snorted and danced sideways as he prepared to mount. "We're hoping it will be."

"We're determined to catch them red-handed," Gabe said, swinging his leg over his horse.

She went over to the bay and looked up at him. "Be careful, Gabe. This Destroying Angels business isn't what we're all about. The Prophet has said in the past that we're a peaceable people."

"That was then; this is now," Gabe said. "The Prophet and every last apostle agree, the Destroying Angels are as necessary as the militia."

She fell silent for a moment. One of the horses nickered, pawing the ground, and the other shook its mane as if impatient to be on its way. "Are we stooping to their level by attacking their farms and outlying settlements? Isn't the militia and an impressive show of arms just as effective?"

"We can go on thinking that," Griffin said, "until it happens to one of our farms, or if one of our family members is injured or worse."

The two men rode out of the barn, but Bronwyn, standing on the porch, called out to Griffin. He halted and she ran toward him.

"This doesn't feel right to me," she said. "You shouldn't go."

Griffin dismounted and stood in front of her. "I'm doing it so we can all rest easier. It has to be done."

"Let the militia take care of it, I beg you. Don't go to the meeting tonight."

Her husband looked into her eyes and then, reaching for her, drew her and the baby into his arms, holding them as if he never wanted to let go.

Bronwyn drew back and looked up into his face. "I love you," she said, "and I just don't want anything to happen to you."

He kissed her cheek and then the top of Little Grace's head. "I'll be back before you know it." He mounted again, and with a nod to Gabe, the two started down the road.

The earl, Coal, Bronwyn, and Mary Rose walked back to the house. Darkness had fallen completely, and only a sliver of a moon was out to light their way.

Mary Rose let the others enter the house first, then she sat down on a porch chair, squinting into the dark night, feeling as unsettled as Bronwyn did. She thought she heard voices, listened carefully but heard only a symphony of frog song near the river.

After a few minutes she went into the house and, stepping onto a chair, unlatched Gabe's new Mississippi percussion rifle from where it hung above the bedroom door. She made sure it was loaded, just as Gabe had once shown her, and then she attempted to hide it in her skirts as she walked toward the front door.

The girls were drawing pictures of dolls, planning to make paper dolls in the morning, chattering happily about the dresses they planned to make. The baby slept peacefully in a crib in the corner, and Coal sat by Cordelia, looking up at her almost worshipfully. Mary Rose gave him a wink and a quick smile.

"Go ahead," she said, "ask her."

"Ask me what?" Cordelia turned to the boy and smiled. "About the riverboat?"

He nodded. "Did it have gamblers?"

"Oh, yes, a lot of them."

"Did they win lots of money?"

Cordelia laughed. "Not the one I was married to. Oh, they bragged that they did, but most were as poor as church mice."

Ruby looked up from her drawing. "I'd like to have a church mouth."

"Where are you going, Lady?" Pearl's eyes grew round as saucers.

"Watth that you're hiding?" Ruby said, her eyes equally wide.

Mary Rose smiled at her family. "Just to be on the safe side, I thought I'd sit outside for a while." She drew out the long Mississippi rifle from the folds of her skirts to sounds of awe. "I don't know how to shoot the thing, but I figure it will scare off anyone we don't want on our property."

"Sure would me," Cordelia said, chuckling. She didn't sound, or look, as worried as the rest of the family. Mary Rose figured she'd probably seen her share of gunfights in her day.

"Do you know how to shoot?"

Cordelia grinned. "I've been known to shoot the eyelash off a gnat if I have to. I'd rather not, but if worse comes to worst, I can always help."

Bronwyn looked worried, but she turned her attention to the twins and told them to put away their drawings and get on their nightclothes; she would come upstairs to hear their prayers shortly.

"I'll sit with you," the earl said to Mary Rose. He rummaged around in the armoire near the front door and found a pistol. He lifted it toward the lamplight, examining it. "Looks new," he said.

Cordelia came over and took the pistol from her husband, sighted down it, and nodded. "Nice piece," she said. "French. Flintlock converted to percussion. Just be careful of the bite. It'll throw you across the room.

"I'll stay in here with the baby," she said. Then she grinned. "You two just holler if you need me."

Mary Rose went out to the porch, pulled up a chair, and leaned back, the rifle lying crosswise on her lap.

Her grandfather followed her out and sat down beside her. From the river, the sounds of crickets and frogs raised a ruckus, making it hard for Mary Rose to hear voices or hoofbeats.

She strained to sort out the sounds: the children upstairs saying their prayers, Coal asking Cordelia how she learned to shoot the eyelash off a gnat, and finally Bronwyn's clear, sweet voice singing a lullaby to Ruby and Pearl.

A snap of a twig made her sit up, alert.

The earl heard it too. He stood, the pistol in his hand.

The crunch of footsteps followed, the sniggering of two rough voices talking about ridding Illinois of vermin.

"What about the brats?" one asked the other.

"Nits make lice, don't they?" the second said, and let out a coarse laugh.

Several more voices joined the first and shadowy figures began to gather, their torches lighting up the night.

TWENTY-SEVEN

The torches blinded Mary Rose and her grandfather, yet kept the bearers in the shadows.

"Get out of here," the earl said, walking toward the mob. "We're peace-loving people and have never hurt anyone."

"Whooeee," someone guffawed as soon as Mary Rose's grandfather spoke. "Fee-fi-fo-fum! I smell the blood of an Englishman. Be he live, or be he dead, I'll grind his bones to make my bread."

"Upper-crust English, methinks," mocked someone toward the back of the mob. "Perhaps titled? Or royalty, might it be?"

"We think English royalty a few steps beneath the so-called Saints," hollered someone else.

Mary Rose's heart pounded.

"I say, let's see if he can do the minuet." Coarse cheers rose. "Come on, old man, put down your gun, and get over here or we shoot the pretty lady by your side." The distinctive sound of metal on metal told Mary Rose the first gun had been cocked. Others would follow.

She raised her rife to her shoulder and growled. "Leave him alone or I shoot."

Laughter met her threat.

One of the shadowy figures started toward her. She aimed the rifle, got the man in her sights, pulled the trigger, but nothing happened. Still laughing he climbed the steps and ripped the rifle from her with one strong hand; with the other, he held the torch near her face.

"A pretty one we got here," he said.

She smelled the whiskey on his breath.

He stepped closer as if to reach for her, and she shoved him. He fell backward, stumbling down the porch steps. She didn't care what happened to her, she just knew she had to keep the men out of the house.

Catcalls and whistles rose from the mob. "Ah, we've got a spunky one, now. Most Saints do what we want once we let it be known," Whiskey Breath said. "I've got a feeling you're a fighter." He laughed as he climbed the porch to get to her again.

The earl's pistol went off and the man roared in pain, grabbed his knee, fell backward, and rolled on the ground.

"Who wants to be next?" her grandfather said. "Next one to step toward this woman gets it between the eyes."

"You forgot our bargain, old man," someone in the front of the mob called out. "We don't kill your woman if you lay down your gun, nice and easy. You don't do that for us, we shoot 'er where she stands. You got nothing to bargain with, old man."

"Fee-fi-fo-fum," someone sang out and the others guffawed again.

"I wanta see ifn he can dance," a whiny young man's voice called out. "You let me do it last time. I wanna do it again."

"Hector wants to see the old man dance, shall we let 'im?"

The mob yelled its approval.

"Maybe if you dance the minuet for us, Redcoat, and dance

fast enough, we'll do nothing more than burn your farm. You'll get off easy."

"Burn it and everyone in it," the whiner said and let out a high-pitched laugh.

"Come on down here now, where we all can help you with the minuet."

"Don't go," Mary Rose said between clenched teeth. "Stay right here."

"I'll dance," the earl said without looking at her. "Just leave the woman alone. I'll do whatever you want."

As he walked toward the mob, Mary Rose sidled to the door. If she could only reach Cordelia, get her to help. Heart pounding, she reached for the latch.

"Wait just a minute, missy," a coarse voice called out. "You gonna miss out on the fun of seeing an old man dance. You move back where you were or we'll have you dancin' right alongside 'im."

Trembling, Mary Rose moved away from the door.

The first shot rang out at his feet, and the earl hopped. Another came too soon. Then another, and another, and her grandfather's arthritic legs moved as fast as they could. The mob laughed, and more joined in. Her grandfather fell, and someone shot his right hand. "The other'll go ifn you don't stand up and dance."

He stood again, blood dripping from the wound in his hand. Another volley of shots rang out again, and dust rose around his feet. He stumbled, caught himself, then fell.

Another single shot rang out, this time hitting his left hand. He didn't utter a word or cry out.

"Well, shoot, we plumb ran out of hands." Someone laughed. "We'll do the knees next. Get 'em both and you'll never walk again, Redcoat."

Her grandfather struggled to his feet once more but couldn't make it.

Mary Rose screamed before the next shot was fired. "Stop it, all of you. Stop it. Just let us go. Let us have our lives, and you can take what you want."

The mob quieted. "What did you say?" the whiner asked, his voice pitched high with excitement. "We can take what we want?" He laughed as he came up the stairs and leered at her hungrily.

The sound of shattering glass split the silence. First one window upstairs. Then a second from a different room.

Downstairs to her left, another sound of breaking glass shattered the air. It took her an instant to realize what was happening. She dropped and snaked her way to her grandfather as the shots from inside the house began. Volley after volley zinged through the air, some hitting their targets, others missing. It didn't matter— the men who'd been hit screamed and the others retreated. Some crawled; others ran hollering into the night, dragging along the injured. As a parting shot, nearly every one tossed his torch into the barn. Then all was quiet . . . except for the crackling fire that quickly turned into an inferno.

The front door opened slightly, and Cordelia looked out. "Pity they had to leave so soon. I was just starting to have fun."

Mary Rose was shaking so hard that for a moment she couldn't speak. She nodded and moistened her lips. "You're pretty good with that rifle," she finally said to Cordelia.

"I had help. Bronwyn and Coal were shooting from upstairs." She grinned. "Why, I had no idea that little gal Bronwyn could shoot like that."

Mary Rose bent over her grandfather, relieved when he gave her a weak smile. "Always did want to learn to dance," he said. As soon as she knew he was all right, she rushed to the barn. Only one animal was inside, Coal's pinto.

Covering her face with her sleeve, she ran inside. The barn's interior was engulfed in flames, the smoke so thick she couldn't see more than a few feet in front of her. She heard the pinto screaming from the end stall and made her way to it.

Coal was in the doorway, crying for the horse. "Go back," she shouted to him. "Stay out. It's not safe."

"I'll help," he cried, ignoring her pleas. "I've got to get to him."

"I'm almost there. I don't want to stop and rescue you too. Get back now!"

She reached the pinto's stall and glanced back. Barely visible through the smoke, Coal was still making his way toward her.

"I've got him," she yelled to the boy. "Go back. I'll bring him to you."

A roof timber crashed down, blocking her way to the door and igniting the hayloft. The pinto reared, bucked, and kicked in terror. Mary Rose frantically searched for a way around, or under, or over the timber. There was none.

She was trapped.

She tried to pull in breaths, but they came in short, painful spurts, bringing no oxygen to her lungs. She thought of the baby she carried, the twins, and Coal, wondering if he'd made it out alive.

As she was losing consciousness a voice called to her. Was it Gabe?

She lifted her head and tried to answer, but no strength remained.

TWENTY-EIGHT

Mary Rose woke outside the barn in Gabe's arms. He was sitting on the ground, holding her as if she were a child, tears streaming down his face. She coughed, tried to catch her breath, and then coughed again. Her lungs burned more intensely with each cough.

"We need to get her inside," he said. "In her condition . . ." He lifted her and gently carried her to the house. She leaned against his shoulder, willing him to hold her there forever.

He placed her on their bed. "Don't try to breathe deeply yet," he said.

"Don't leave me . . ." She reached for him.

"I'm here."

"Tonight, the mob . . ." She choked and started to cry.

Sitting beside her on the bed, he bent low and wrapped his arms around her. "I know what happened," he said. "We saw them too."

"The same ones?"

"Probably."

Her eyes stung from the smoke, but as they watered, the stinging subsided. "Did you come in the barn to save me?"

He nodded.

She reached for his hand. "I thought I heard your voice." She closed her eyes. "What about Coal's pinto?"

"You got him out."

"And Coal?"

"He made it too."

"How about Grandfather? Will he be all right?"

The room smelled of smoke, Gabe's hair smelled of it, her clothing smelled of it. She wondered if the blur of her eyes was caused from the heat, or if the room was filled with smoke.

He gave her a slight smile. "He's being well taken care of by Sister Cordelia. She told me how brave you were tonight . . . I'm so sorry I left you and the family alone. I shouldn't have."

"We made it through alive and with no irreparable harm, Gabe, that's what matters. God was with us."

He didn't answer.

She turned to better see him. "Something's wrong. I can see it in your eyes." He stood and walked a few feet away from her, turned his back, and dropped his head into his hands.

When he turned back, he said, "Griffin's dead."

Mary Rose gasped. "Griffin?" She tried to sit up but couldn't. "Not Griffin. That can't be."

"The mob was after the Prophet." His voice choked. "Everything happened at once. We saw the fire, which momentarily distracted us, that's when they attacked. If it hadn't been for Griffin's quick actions, it would have been Joseph they killed, not Griffin. He gave his life to save that of our Prophet."

She tried to let the words soak in. "Does Bronwyn know?"

He nodded. "Brigham is talking to her now."

"Oh, Gabe . . ." She wept, thinking of her friend, and the tears burned her aching eyes. "I need to go to her."

Gabe shook his head. "You need to think of our baby. You've been through a lot tonight and need to rest. I'll tell Bronwyn you'd like to see her." He leaned over to kiss her cheek and gave her a gentle smile.

"Thank you."

Mary Rose lay back against her pillow, her heart aching for Bronwyn. Griffin was such a good man, lighthearted, boyish at times, but completely in love with his wife. A fierce warrior, from what she'd been told, though he was never one to speak with pride about his past accomplishments in war.

Her thoughts turned to Bronwyn. What would she do? Surely she wouldn't return to Wales. Mary Rose couldn't bear it if she moved away.

A light tap sounded at the door.

"Bronwyn?"

"'Tis me," she said, peering around the door. Her eyes were swollen and red, her clothing wrinkled. She too reeked of smoke. "Are you all right?"

Mary Rose patted the edge of the bed. "I just need a little rest to recover." She took Bronwyn's hands in hers. "It's you I'm worried about."

"Gabe told you what happened?"

She nodded. "I still can't take it in. I'm so sorry. So very sorry."

Bronwyn's eyes filled. "He's my whole life. What will I do without him?" She buried her head in her hands and sobbed.

Mary Rose swung her legs over the side of the bed and sat upright. She wrapped an arm around Bronwyn and cried with her. "You'll get through this. We don't know the answers yet, but we'll find them."

Bronwyn reached for a handkerchief and dabbed at her eyes

and nose. "Brigham is a great comfort. He said my Griffin died a hero, a martyr. There will be a proper funeral in just a few days, with much celebration of his life among the Saints, because if it hadn't been for Griffin's quick actions the Prophet wouldn't be alive tonight."

She started to weep again. "I'm sorry for saying it, Mary Rose, but I wish it had been the Prophet who died, not my Griffin."

"Don't be sorry," Mary Rose said softly. "It's only natural to feel that way."

She gave Mary Rose a tremulous smile. "And think about our spirit marriage. How happy I am that the Prophet insisted we go through the second ceremony. His death is almost bearable when I think that I will someday join him in heaven and we will be there together through all eternity."

She dabbed at her eyes. "But, oh, how I will miss him until then. I don't know if I can bear the loneliness."

"You have Little Grace," Mary Rose said. "She will be a great comfort."

"And you," she said to Mary Rose. "My dearest friend, what would I do without you?" She fell into Mary Rose's arms and sobbed as though her heart might twist in two.

After the funeral three days later, Brigham pulled Gabe aside and asked him to walk with him to the temple site.

"You have heard the Prophet's revelation about taking multiple wives," he said as they walked.

"Yes." Gabe wasn't surprised. As soon as Griffin died, he suspected that either Brigham or Joseph would come to him.

"You also know that we take care of our widows and orphans," Brigham said. "And in this case, because of Griffin's special status, what he did to save the Prophet's life, we need to take special care of his widow and child."

"I thought that would be the case," Gabe said. His heart felt like the lifeblood was being squeezed out of it.

"She is a beautiful woman, one that any man would love to take as his wife."

They reached the temple, now partially built, and looked down on Nauvoo, the river, the hills beyond. "You have been a good and faithful servant. You are like a son to me, and I believe you know that we are grooming you for leadership."

Gabe nodded.

"Leadership has to do with adhering to the Prophet's revelations. Celestial marriage is necessary for your salvation." He looked down at the silver snake of a river, watched it for a while, then moved his gaze back to Gabe. "You do remember the revelation?"

Gabe nodded but could only think of Mary Rose, her love, her trust, her utter faith in him. All that could be destroyed. "Yes."

Brigham walked closer again. "I probably shouldn't be telling you all this today, of all days. But I wanted to prepare you."

"Prepare me for what?"

"For taking Bronwyn as your second wife. I know of your friendship with Griffin, and the friendship that your wife and Bronwyn enjoy. Believe me when I tell you that your union with Bronwyn Carey is God-ordained. I daresay, looking back on how you met aboard the *Sea Hawk*, how you've become closer than blood relatives, God's intent from the beginning is now clear. You need to talk to your wife and Bronwyn Carey as soon as possible."

He smiled as Gabe stood before him, speechless. "Of course, I'm sure you realize that you really have no choice in the decision, and that by speaking to your wife, I'm not indicating that you're asking her permission. This directive comes from the Prophet."

"I have no choice." Gabe drew in a deep breath and let it out slowly, feeling he might suffocate.

"Not if you want to proceed into celestial godhood—if you're thinking of the union's eternal value. And if you're thinking of its temporal value, I remind you again that you're being groomed for leadership—perhaps as an apostle. If you disobey, there will be consequences on both fronts."

Gabe looked out over the terrain. His heart pounded, in dismay for what the news would do to Mary Rose, and surprisingly in anticipation of taking the beautiful Bronwyn as his own.

Brigham turned and walked away from Gabe, the sounds of his footsteps heavy on the gravel path, followed by snapping limbs as he cut through the brush.

The following week, Mary Rose drove the buckboard up to the temple site, the children laughing and chattering in the back.

"We're going on a picnic," Ruby sang out as they rounded the corner to the temple.

"I'm gonna find the best fishing hole ever and bring fishes home for us all to have for supper," Coal said, wielding his fishing pole. "Sister Cordelia said if I catch a catfish, she'd fix it a special way. She says it's the Cajun way, spicy and hot." He rubbed his stomach.

"Catfith? Thath the thillieth thing I ever heard." Ruby giggled. "Doth it purr?"

"No, but it has whiskers," Coal said. "Sister Cordelia told me so."

"Does it meow?" Pearl said, dissolving in gales of laughter.

"I mith Othcar the Lobthter."

"Me too," Pearl chimed in.

"And Little Grathe."

"Auntie Bronwyn needs time for her heart to heal," Mary Rose said. "She loved her husband very much."

"But he'th in heaven now," Ruby said.

"But not the high heaven," Coal said, sticking out his chin in a posture of superiority. "Because he had only one wife."

Mary Rose frowned and halted the mare at the top of the hill. She turned in the seat to look back at Coal. "Where did you hear that?"

"Cornelius and Elroy told me they heard it at the meeting-house."

She gave him a stern look. "Don't ever repeat that again, do you understand me?"

His eyes grew wide and he blinked. "Why not?"

"I don't believe it's true."

"The Prophet says it's true," Coal said. "My friend at the meet-inghouse says he knows lots of our friends who have more than one mother."

"I would like to have more than one mama," Pearl said. "That way Lady could be our mama and our real mama could also be our mama."

Mary Rose had to smile at the logic. "And I would like to be your mama," she said. She turned back to Coal. "Come to Mr. MacKay or me first whenever you hear such rumors. We'll talk them over and decide what's true and what isn't."

She slipped off the wagon, retrieved the picnic basket from the back of the buckboard, and gave it to Coal to carry. Spotting Gabe, she waved and helped the twins down so they could rush to him.

He saw them coming and waved back. Reaching for the twins and picking them up together, he spun them in circles. They squealed and giggled. "I brought my fishing pole," Coal said. "To catch us some catfish."

"I know where to find them," Gabe said, ruffling the boy's hair. "I also know a special place to have a picnic—by the river. Turns out the catfish hole isn't far."

Ruby went to the edge of the ridge and looked down. "Ith far down there."

Gabe grinned. "I have a secret path I take to the river."

The children were wide-eyed as they followed Gabe along a path that wound through willows and cattails.

Mary Rose relished the warmth of the sun on her shoulders, and drew in a deep breath. Her grief for Bronwyn's loss was still acute, but the sound of the rolling river, the birdsong, the children's voices did much to assuage it. She felt the baby move, a little foot or elbow rippling across her stomach, and laughed at the joy of life within her.

They came into an opening in the foliage. Gabe stepped through and held some willow branches so the others could enter. A few feet away, a brook cascaded down some stones, clumps of fern on either side. Beside the brook stood a flat piece of granite, the perfect height for a table.

Mary Rose clasped her hands together in delight. "It's beautiful, Gabe. How did you find it?"

"It's where I come daily to read the Book of Mormon."

"It would be perfect for that."

Gabe laughed. "I thought you'd ask me why I'm suddenly interested in the Book of Mormon." The children ran off to catch frogs and pollywogs, so they could speak plainly.

"I've had a lot to think through," he said, moving his gaze to the river. The sun caught a scattering of ripples, turning them to a thousand sparkling diamonds. He turned back to Mary Rose. "I'm hoping to find the answers to my many questions."

She raised a questioning brow. "And?"

"So far, I haven't found them. I just end up with more questions than before." He gave her that half-smile she loved.

"You still believe? In the Prophet and his revelations?"

"Oh, yes. I have no doubts that his testimony is true."

She unfolded the quilt, shook it out, and then laid it on the ground next to the slab of granite. Gabe put the basket in its center. "Hmm, smells good," he said, rubbing his hands together.

"Fried chicken." Mary Rose hesitated for a moment and then added, "I've sensed that you're pondering something that is so important it's almost taken you away from me."

"Taken me away?"

"'Tis true, though I haven't said much about it. Sometimes your body is there, but your mind is absent."

"You speak in riddles."

She laughed. "It does sound like a riddle." She looked out over the river, focusing on the other side. "Sometimes I wonder if you don't want to be near me anymore," she said quietly. "Your thoughts travel far away. I can see it in your eyes."

"I'm trying to be the best husband I can be."

"I'm not denying that you are. I think back to those days when we fell in love aboard the *Sea Hawk*. Your spirit seemed lighter somehow; now it seems as though you carry a heavy weight on your shoulders. You can't lay it down, but it's too heavy to continue on. Gabe, something's wrong between us. I've felt it for some time. Can you not trust me with it?"

Silence settled between them for a moment as Gabe traced a finger idly along the lid of the picnic basket, apparently gathering his thoughts—and perhaps his courage—to speak.

"Brigham approached me the day of Griffin's funeral. It's been eating away at me." He sighed deeply, looking away from her. "I haven't known what to say or how to say it, so I just kept busy doing other things."

Mary Rose leaned back, her arms straight, supporting her weight. She sensed what he had to tell her was not good news. "Tell me, please, Gabe, so I can help you."

"Brigham wants me to marry Bronwyn."

Mary Rose gasped, too startled for several moments to say anything. "Bronwyn? A second wife?"

He stood and walked closer to her, kneeling almost as if in

supplication before her. His eyes were filled with an emotion she couldn't read.

"You disagreed, of course." Her words were a statement, not a question. "You told him no, that we would not live that way under any circumstances. That's what you said, wasn't it?"

"We aren't being given a choice, Mary Rose."

Mary Rose reached up and held his face between her hands. "Gabe, you can't . . . we can't." Her heart ached just knowing he considered it.

Her heart was beating so hard she was certain Gabe could hear it. "We've already taken her in, Gabe. She and Griffin have been practically living with us from the day we sailed out of Liverpool a year ago." As she continued, her words contained more bitterness than she intended. "Leave things the way they are. You don't need to marry Bronwyn to care for her."

"According to the Prophet's revelation, I must." He looked at her steadily, searching her eyes. "I beg of you to calm yourself. Think this through."

"You said we have no choice. I disagree. We can say no." She stood. "There's nothing else to think about; I've made my decision." She turned her back to him.

Mary Rose was breathing hard, her heart still pounding. "We should take the children and leave," she said. "Just get out of here. None of this is right. The Prophet makes up his rules as he goes and calls them revelations. Can't you see it, Gabe? Until now, it didn't seem important. Now it's more important than life itself. He is a charlatan."

"That's blasphemous," he said, slapping his forehead in disbelief.

She stared at Gabe, wondering if she knew him at all.

His tone held the utmost patience when he next spoke. "Speak to Bronwyn, ask what she would prefer to do. If I don't marry her, someone else will. It's better that she be with us, a family who loves her."

Mary Rose shook her head. "I can't do that. It would be a slap in the face after all she's been through. She will not agree to a plural marriage no matter who the groom is."

She looked around for the twins and Coal, suddenly aware they might have overheard the argument. But moments later, when the children raced back into the picnic area, they apparently hadn't heard a word of disagreement. Pearl had three frogs in her pocket, and Ruby had captured two pollywogs because she liked their "tailth."

Coal grabbed the fried chicken from the basket and passed it around. The children's tales filled the space between them.

Then Ruby looked from Gabe to Mary Rose and back again. "Lady, are you mad at Mithter MacKay? Whatth wrong?"

Mary Rose reached for the child and hugged her close. Gabe did the same with the other two. "We're just talking about something serious that will affect us all," Gabe said.

Coal's eyes grew big. "You're not sending us to Cousin Hermione's, are you?"

"Or the Thandwich Islandth," Ruby said. "I don't want to go there anymore. I like it here with you."

"We want you to stay with us forever," Mary Rose said. She looked across the picnic blanket at Gabe, hoping for a wink or a smile. He let his gaze drift over her shoulder.

The following day, Bronwyn wept when Mary Rose told her what the Prophet, Brigham, and even Gabe had planned for her.

"Am I mere chattel?" she cried, and then buried her head in her hands. Tears were streaming down her cheeks when she looked up. "Am I to have no voice in the matter? My husband's body is not even cold, my grief still too terrible to bear, yet Brigham and Joseph are already deciding my future." They were sitting on a quilt near the garden while the twins played by the creek and Little Grace napped nearby. Mary Rose moved closer to her friend and circled her arm around her shoulders.

Mary Rose was surprised that she found herself defending the Church leaders. "They have your best interests at heart," she said gently. "You are not chattel. Don't consider yourself as such, no matter what happens."

"I can't," Bronwyn wept. "I—I—I can't even think of being with another m-m-man. Not now. Not ever. I—I just want Griffin . . ."

"What will you do to take care of yourself and Little Grace?"

Wiping her tears, Bronwyn looked up. "I—I d-don't kn-know. I have the farm. Maybe I can sell vegetables or eggs or something." She blew her nose. "I can grow enough food for the two of us. I can make it."

"Did Griffin take out a loan from Joseph to build it?"

Fresh tears filled her eyes. "Yes. I'd forgotten. But, yes, he did. It will have to be paid back."

Silence fell between them. They both knew without saying that Bronwyn had no means, no way, of repaying such a loan. The farm would have to be sold.

Mary Rose swallowed hard. "I've thought about this a lot . . . about our choices. I've tried to convince Gabe that you and Little Grace can stay here. That we could keep our household just as it is now. You would be cared for. We're already as close as sisters and you and the baby are part of the family."

Bronwyn gave her a trembling smile. "We wouldn't have to change anything. I would pull my weight, do what I could to contribute to the household . . ."

Mary Rose patted her hand. "You always have. You don't need to worry about such a thing. Your being here is a blessing."

"What if . . ." Bronwyn began, fear clouding her eyes once again. "What if Gabe and the others insist it be official, insist I become the second wife? What if we truly have no choice?"

"I'll keep trying to convince my husband that he must say no." Mary Rose sighed, feeling her own tears well. "Otherwise, we have two choices."

Bronwyn looked up at her quizzically.

"Leave with the children. Go anywhere away from Nauvoo . . ."

Her friend looked skeptical. "With all the children?"

Mary Rose bit her lip. "And the other choice—"

Bronwyn interrupted, lifting her chin. "—is one that we can control." She smiled slightly. "If you're thinking what I'm thinking, we might just be able to see this thing through, keep our dignity and chastity. "

Mary Rose stood as Bronwyn did the same. The friends embraced as Gabe came out of the barn.

"It will remain our solemn vow to each other . . ." Mary Rose said.

Before Bronwyn could answer, Gabe joined them, stooped to pick up Little Grace, and gave her a hug and a kiss.

When he looked up, Mary Rose was surprised that instead of meeting her eyes, he had fixed his gaze on Bronwyn.

Down by the creek a mockingbird's trill joined the laughter of the twins and Coal, and closer in a breeze rattled the maple leaves and lifted an errant tendril from Mary Rose's flushed forehead. Still, her husband's gaze did not move from her friend's face.

TWENTY-NINE

June 28, 1842

Mary Rose refused to let the sting at the back of her throat turn to tears. Instead, she drew in a deep breath and reached over her swollen stomach to pluck weeds from between the rows of cabbage seedlings.

Distant wedding bells tolled, calling the Saints to the meeting-house for the ceremony sealing seven brides to fewer than half as many grooms.

As her knees sank into the loamy soil she gave little thought to the *peau de soie* gown she wore, one of the few stylish frocks that had survived the voyage and wagon journey to Nauvoo, and the only one with an Empire waist that could accommodate the child growing beneath her heart.

She plunged her hands into the wet soil and breathed in its soft fragrance, thinking of fertility, life, and growth. She would miss her garden; it had been a source of wonder since Bronwyn had helped her turn the first spade of soil. Throughout the winter and early spring they had talked about their plantings: radishes, beans, winter squash, corn, and herbs for cooking; and then they had convinced Gabe and Griffin of their need for an arbor, and amid laughter and loving conversation, all had worked together to build it. Neighbors had supplied them with healthy cuttings of grapevines and berries. With a sense of wonder, she had watched her early garden thrive and felt an almost motherly pride at the tender new growth.

Little more than a year earlier, back in England, the thought had never entered her pampered head that she might take such pleasure in the sun's warmth on her shoulders, or the burial of a seemingly dry and dead seed that days later pushed its tiny sprout-self through the soil, reaching for the same sunlight that gladdened her heart.

From the henhouse, several yards beyond the garden, the low clucks of hens and higher-pitched peeps of the fresh-hatched chicks brought another wave of sorrow. How could she leave this place she'd grown to love in such a short time? How could she leave the man she loved with every ounce of her being? Especially now that she carried his child?

The gentle breeze cooled her warm cheeks, and she drew in a deep breath, concentrating on the rhythmic music of the farm: the breeze rattling the oak leaves by the creek out back, the low murmurs of hens and chicks, the nickering of a newborn colt, and the answering neigh of his mother in the pasture.

Her eyes filled, and her heart ached with longing as if she'd already hitched the carriage and driven off.

She tried not to think about Gabe's decision as betrayal, but it crept into her mind anyway. Along with words from an Elizabeth Barrett Browning poem . . . *It was thy love proved false and frail.* She pictured her love's face, imagined him with Bronwyn, and for all her strength and determination to hold back her tears, this time she could not. She whispered the words to the last stanza of the poem. The words, as if driven deep with an ice pick, stabbed too close to the marrow of her bones.

> Ah, Sweet, be free to praise and go!
> For if my face is turned too pale,
> It was thine oath that first did fail,
> It was thy love proved false and frail,
> And why, since these be changed enow,
> Should I change less than thou.

She drew in a shuddering breath to regain control. She needed every ounce of strength to get through this day. She plunged her hands into the earth, drawing comfort from the cool soil and willing away the pain in her heart.

Gabe had taken his time, first with his toiletries, then with the new trousers and gleaming white shirt Mary Rose had laundered just the day before. As he prepared himself to look his Sunday best, she'd fled to the comfort of her garden. Now she heard his footsteps and pulled the brim of her fancy bonnet lower to shade her face from the unblinking sun. And to avoid her husband's eyes.

"Why are you out here? It's almost time to go," he said.

She kept her back to him. "You shaved twice."

He laughed. "I often do that. Why should this be any different?"

"You know why."

"I thought you'd decided to come with me," he said. "I know it's difficult for you, but you gave me your word." If he'd yelled or cursed, it would have hurt less. But as always, he was too much of a gentleman, a loving, kind man, to resort to such behavior.

"I changed my mind," she said as he helped her stand. She gave him a small half-smile. "A woman is entitled." In truth, she had dressed for the occasion, planning to make an appearance so none would be the wiser when she hitched the horse to the family buggy and rode off in the night. But when he preened in the mirror and then pulled out his straight razor a second time, she knew that no matter what she and Bronwyn had discussed, Gabe had plans of his own.

He drew her into his arms. "Mary Rose," he whispered, his breath tickling her ear. "It isn't right or proper that you stay away, today of all days. It is your duty to welcome Bronwyn into our family, standing by my side. I would not have done this without your consent."

She slipped out of his embrace and, pushing back her bonnet, looked up at him in rage. But when he swept his hair back in that way he had, raking it with his fingers, her heart overflowed with the same love she'd had for him since the day they'd said their own vows.

"My consent?" She almost laughed. "As if, after Brigham told me my options, I had any say in it. You do not have my consent, regardless of what the elders—and you—might tell others."

A fancy coach pulled by a single white horse slowed to a halt in front of the house. The groom tipped his hat toward Mary Rose and Gabe and smiled. He'd come to take Gabe to the marriage ceremony.

"Please, Mary Rose . . ." Gabe moved closer and lifted her chin, forcing her to look into his eyes. "I wouldn't do this if it had not been decreed by God."

Her grandfather had always said she inherited his ironclad spine. Today, her spine felt weaker than the stem of the milkweed that lay wilting in the sun at her feet.

She straightened, preferring the image of iron wrapped around her spine. "In your heart of hearts," she said softly, "can you really go through with this?" She started to touch his cheek, but instead first brushed off her hands. When she lifted her hand again, he caught it and covered it with his own. Turning it he kissed her palm. "We love each other," she said. "Our love has more to do with us than it does with the Saints. We fell in love before we even met the Prophet." She searched his eyes for the response she longed to see—a love for her that would be strong enough to say no to the Prophet's new edict. It wasn't there.

"Love has nothing to do with it. I've already explained—and really, Mary Rose, I shouldn't have to keep going over it." He let out an exasperated sigh. "I've not fallen in love with Bronwyn. I don't deny I care about her. Her husband was my friend. But every ounce of love in my heart is yours alone."

He touched her face, letting the backs of his fingers trace her jawline. The gesture was so familiar, so intimate, she could easily have wept. Except for the image that came to her: her husband touching Bronwyn's face with the same intimacy, perhaps as soon as this night.

She drew in a deep breath and then stepped back, crossing her arms. "Perhaps the Prophet has interpreted God's edict correctly—and I'm not the only first wife in Nauvoo to wonder—but tell me, Gabe, why did it have to be Bronwyn? And why does it have to be marriage? We could bring her into our home, take care of her and Little Grace for as long as they need us. Surely you recognize my feelings in this matter and can respect them. I would be happy to have her join our family under those conditions."

One didn't go against the Prophet's edicts, which came from God himself. But she also knew that the Prophet chose Gabe to care for an important martyr's widow because of his rising status within the hierarchy of the Church. If Mary Rose hadn't been so appalled over the whole thing, she would have laughed at the shading of the real truth: The strikingly beautiful Bronwyn, with her vivacious charm and hardy Welsh constitution, was a gift, perhaps a reward, for Gabe's loyalty and friendship.

"Bronwyn and her child are alone and in need," Gabe said. "She has no way to provide a home for herself or food for Little

Grace. Bronwyn is a good woman. You are the dearest of friends, already as close as sisters." He shrugged. "It will be a happy household, just as Joseph has borne witness of his own. Brigham reports the same contentment among his wives. Initially jealousy and backbiting prevailed, but now his wives love each other like family. Sisters."

Mary Rose sighed. "The trial period has only been one month. That's hardly long enough to tell what the outcome will be once the, ah, sleeping arrangements are made, children are born, tasks divided up."

She hesitated, turning her gaze away from him. A butter-fly landed on the dying milkweed then fluttered away. "We've talked about this, you know," Mary Rose said, her eyes following the insect as it landed on a clump of squash blossoms. "Bronwyn and I."

She didn't like the way the corner of his mouth quirked into a slight smile. "And what was your conclusion?"

"Should you decide to go through with the wedding, you will have no . . . rights. Conjugal rights."

"So you two have decided that for me." His eyes twinkled with amusement. "See, you're behaving like sisters already."

Mary Rose saw no humor in his words, but she had no time to voice her opinion before he continued, grabbing her hands again. "You know the Prophet speaks of anointing me as one of his chosen twelve soon. So, my dear, it is my honor and my respon-sibility as a priest, as an apostle of God, to carry out the revela-tions given by his representative on earth, our Prophet. I have no choice." He paused, then added, "If I did have a choice . . ."

"You would go through with it anyway," Mary Rose said softly. "But I have a choice. I can accept Bronwyn into our household or not."

She looked into Gabe's eyes without flinching, and when she spoke it was with quiet but desperate firmness. "If you go through with this, I won't be here when you return."

Silence fell between them as he stared at her. "Surely you can't mean that," he said. "You're . . . with child. Where would you go, what would you do?" She looked deeper into his eyes, trying to fathom the emotion she saw there. He paused and then swallowed hard. She had indeed taken him by surprise. "I love you. No matter what else happens, I swear to you I will always love you. You can't leave me, Mary Rose. Please say you won't."

"You leave me no choice, my love." She lifted her chin. "I don't wish to but I must."

"Exactly where would you go?"

"Back to England, of course."

For a long moment he didn't speak. In front of the farmhouse, one of the horses whinnied and the other danced sideways, sending up a cloud of dust. "You do not want to do that," he finally said.

His tone made her heart stop for an instant.

"What do you mean?"

"Have you forgotten?"

She frowned.

"Once sealed to me for eternity, you simply cannot leave. You would be accused of apostasy—"

"Which would bring harm to your reputation, to your authority as a priest and apostle?" She fought but failed to keep the bitterness from her tone.

He stepped closer, his eyes piercing hers. "That's of little regard compared to what would happen to you."

She tilted her head, still frowning. "What do you mean?"

"Apostasy is not condoned. Apostates, those who leave, are caught and returned." His voice dropped. "Punished." He stared into her eyes for a moment, and then turned to go.

Mary Rose stared after him, gaping. "I don't believe you," she said to his back. "I'm free to leave at any time."

"I thought you loved me," he tossed back, his voice thick with agony.

"I do. More than life itself," she whispered, her eyes brimming. She doubted that he heard her. "But not enough to share you with another."

She watched until he'd almost reached the carriage, and then she turned back to the garden. She knelt, and then gasped as a searing pang shot through her abdomen. She doubled over and attempted to shout to Gabe, but the sound wouldn't leave her throat.

He didn't break stride as he continued toward the waiting carriage. Seconds passed, then an even greater jabbing pain made her cry out.

A gush of water warmed her legs and soaked through the *peau de soie* into the garden soil around where she lay. She'd barely caught her breath when, too soon, another contraction came, pulling her into a dark velvet place: images of seedlings growing in the sunlight, of a blossoming milkweed torn from the ground and bleeding white blood, then, finally, of Gabe bending over her, his eyes filled with tears.

She heard him say to someone standing beside him, "The baby is coming. We need help." Then the velvet black darkness enveloped her again, and she surrendered to it.

Mary Rose's eyes fluttered open. She lay in her bed, on her side, facing the window. A soft breeze fluttered the gingham curtains, and a mockingbird trilled from somewhere near the apple orchard out back.

"Gabriel, let me take over for a while. You're needed downstairs," a soft voice said behind Mary Rose.

Her husband murmured something Mary Rose couldn't make out, and then she heard the creak of the wood-plank floor as he moved across the room. A moment later the door closed with a click.

Bronwyn came around the bed. Her eyes swollen and red, she looked weary, as if she'd gone days without sleep. Or had endured something tragic.

Mary Rose searched her friend's face. "The wedding . . . ?" she breathed.

Bronwyn smiled gently and touched Mary Rose's forehead. "You are improving," she said. "You have had us very worried. You had a difficult time of it, but you're healing now." She turned to a small lace-covered table beside the bed, picked up a pitcher, and poured water into a glass. She slipped her arm beneath Mary Rose's pillows to support her head, and then held the rim of the glass to her lips. "For now, you must continue to rest," she said as Mary Rose gratefully took a drink. She returned the glass to the table.

Mary Rose settled back into her pillows and closed her eyes. She expected her friend to stay with her for a time, sit in the rocker by the bed, but instead Bronwyn's light, quick footsteps crossed the floor, the door opened then closed, and all was silent.

Silence?

Shouldn't she hear the sound of a fussing infant? Or his soft breathing in a cradle near her bed?

Where was her baby?

THIRTY

Brodie Flynn flew across the spit of sand on Miss Minnie's back. He held his hands in the air, fingers splayed, laughing as he rode. His tufts of red hair shone brilliant in the sun, and the golden coat of the dun mare gleamed, her mane and tail almost silver as she seemed to soar weightlessly with the boy on her back. Behind them the sea was as vivid a blue-green as Enid had ever seen it. A great blue heron flapped into the sky, lifting ever upward until she soared on giant wings. Two others remained on their nests in the foliage. A ship passed by, its sails full and billowing.

Enid climbed a small sand hill and, shading her eyes, looked out to the horizon, that place where the sky met the sea. Brodie came riding up, his face flushed. "Did ye see us?"

"I did. 'Twas a sight to behold. You can be proud of what you've done for Miss Minnie."

"Ye said I needed to show 'er love with my eyes, so that's what I did." He bent low to lay his cheek on the back of the horse's neck.

"Love heals," Enid said. "That, and time."

"The marigolds are out," the boy said. "Ye remember what me ma said last winter?"

Enid laughed. "Yes, I remember."

"She said ye'll be heading to the States to find that Gabriel MacKay who lived in our house."

"She did say that."

The dun danced sideways and lifted her head, her warm eyes fixed on Enid. Smiling, Enid climbed from her perch on the sand hill and made her way down to the horse and the boy. She stroked Miss Minnie's neck, examining the barely visible scars.

"She's different somehow," Brodie said. "It's like she knows me better."

"She does know you better. She knows you love her no matter what. You showed her love even when she was rearing and kicking and screaming and too frightened to let you get close. That's why she trusts you now. No matter what you do, that love is imprinted in her brain and heart."

"Watch us again," Brodie cried. He nudged the big horse with his small bare heels, and the dun responded. They raced farther along the beach, this time nearly out of sight, and when they returned, it seemed to Enid the horse took as much delirious joy in the run as the boy did.

She sat down on a smooth boulder and looked out to sea again. In the year since Hosea died, she had come a long way too. Someday maybe she could forgive herself. Until then she'd decided not to wallow in it, but to leave it where it belonged: in the past.

Her parents planned to return to the island to care for the farm, and she'd already purchased passage to Boston. She had packed her books on veterinary medicine, her spinning wheel for making wool, and her notes on all the animals she had treated. Unable to leave the aging Foxfire behind, she would take the mare with her. Sadie too, for hitching to the buggy.

Her heart quickened at the thought of her journey.

It was time to see Gabe.

THIRTY-ONE

Weeping, Mary Rose sat at her writing desk, her journal spread open before her. For a long moment, she hesitated to put pen to paper. How could she begin to capture the tangle of emotion within? She turned to her book of sonnets and, nearly blinded by her tears, read:

'God lent him and takes him,' you sigh;
—Nay, there let me break with your pain:
God's generous in giving, say I, —
And the thing which He gives, I deny
That He ever can take back again.

He gives what He gives. I appeal
To all who bear babes—in the hour
When the veil of the body we feel
Rent round us,—while torments reveal
The motherhood's advent in power,

And the babe cries!—has each of us known
By apocalypse (God being there

Full in nature) the child is our own,
Life of life, love of love, moan of moan,
Through all changes, all times, everywhere.
                                    —Elizabeth Barrett Browning

The tangle of emotion eased as she read, and her own words came to her then, and dipping her pen in the inkwell, she wrote furiously, letting her feelings fly from her heart.

Oh, dear Lord, are you listening when I cry out to you? Can you hear me? I've cried so many tears that I believe none are left inside, yet all I get in return is silence. My heart is torn asunder by grief. I can find no comfort in you, but maybe 'tis because I don't know which God you are.

If you are listening, dear God of my childhood, I pray thee, come to me and cover my heart with your healing balm. Fill me to overflowing with your peace and comfort.

I cannot forget my child. My arms ache to hold him, my eyes ache to see him—oh, that I could have beheld him just once! I remember learning at my mother's knee words she said spoke of your deep love for me, a little child: "Can a woman forget her sucking child, that she should not have compassion on the son of her womb? Yea, they may forget, yet will I not forget thee."

I know now the strength of such love. I will never forget my son, never forget how he moved and turned and jumped inside my womb. He was alive! He was part of me!

Dear Lord of my childhood, is this the God you are . . . one that would not forget me because of a bond as strong as that of mother and child? Is your love for all your people?

Sweet heavenly balm, come to me! Come, wash away my pain! May I in peace sleep again, to awake and find my loved one, my friend, as they once were to me, to awake and find my child at my breast, sweet breath, sweet cry.

Lord God, did you cast your heart, your help, your sweet balm to others while I lay sleeping?

Did you forget I too am your child?

A soft knock sounded at her door. It was Bronwyn, for at least the third time this morning.

As she did the previous times, Mary Rose remained silent. And waited for the footsteps to recede. This time they didn't. Instead, the door creaked open. Mary Rose held her breath and kept her back to the door.

"Mary Rose, please. Can we talk?" Bronwyn's hoarse and broken voice did not move her. She heard her friend move toward her and kneel beside her chair. "Mary Rose," she whispered. "Please, we must talk."

Mary Rose turned then, and when she looked into Bronwyn's eyes, red-rimmed and swollen with tears, she remained unmoved. "What is it you want?" Her voice was cold, but it didn't begin to compare to her frozen heart.

Bronwyn touched her arm. "Remember what we talked about . . . before . . . ?" She blushed. "About the marriage bed?"

Mary Rose stared at her. "Has he bedded you, then?"

Bronwyn's face flamed. "That's what I wanted to tell you. I have kept my promise. He has not asked me to sleep with him, and I cannot fathom that he ever would, Mary Rose. 'Tis you he loves, not me. He—we—only did what we had to do."

"You didn't have to do anything, either one of you," Mary Rose said. "He knows, and so do you, how I feel about plural marriage."

She stood and went to the window that overlooked the river. "I was going to leave the day you married."

"Gabe told me what you said."

"And I would have, had I not"— she looked down at her stomach, feeling an almost sickening stab of loneliness and emptiness—"lost the baby. If you and Gabe went through with it, I felt I had no other choice."

Bronwyn came to stand beside her, facing the river with her own thoughts. She slipped her arm around Mary Rose's waist and laid her head gently on her shoulder. "It's in name only."

Mary Rose's feelings battled within her. "I didn't know if he could resist you," she said. "I knew that you would try to keep your promise. I trusted you to try. But when I woke and found I'd lost the baby, you both were in my room. I heard the way he said your name, and I feared my marriage to Gabe was over."

Bronwyn's eyes filled. "Oh, my dear, nothing has changed between us. We are friends, just like when Griffin was alive. I promise you I will do everything I can to protect your marriage."

"What about the vows you took?"

Outside the children played. The sounds of giggles and chatter, punctuated by Ruby's lisp, floated upward. The ordinary sounds brought comfort.

"Gabe has details to discuss with you, but he hasn't made me privy to them." She rushed on, smiling down at the children. "But he assures me things will go on the same as always. Except for those we lost and grieve for."

Fresh tears stung Mary Rose's throat. "I've been so caught up in my own grief, I almost forgot yours." She reached for Bronwyn's hands. "You're still grieving."

"And you must too," she said. She led Mary Rose back to her chair at the desk, and then pulled up another for herself. After they were seated, she leaned forward. "If you'd like I'll tell you about the baby. I'll tell you everything that happened that day."

Mary Rose nodded. "I want to know about the baby. Only my baby. I don't want to hear about your . . . marriage . . . to my husband."

"The baby came too early, but he could have survived if there hadn't been complications. He was perfectly formed and beautiful. When you fell in the garden . . ." Bronwyn looked down as if ashamed. "The wee babe's umbilical cord was wrapped around his neck." She started to cry. "I was waiting for you at the meetinghouse. By the time I realized something was wrong, it was too late. I got here as fast as I could . . . but still"—she blinked back her tears—"it was too late." Her voice dropped. "Gabe didn't know what to do. I should have been here." She dropped her head into her hands.

Mary Rose didn't think her heart could beat with such pain. Her arms even ached with the loss. "A little boy," she whispered. "I wish I could have seen him."

Bronwyn pulled her chair closer and reached for Mary Rose's hands. "He had a dimpled chin, just like yours, the tiniest bit of curly hair, and little pink ears that looked like seashells." She pulled out a dainty handkerchief. "I kissed him for you," she whispered. "And I made the sign of the cross on his forehead, just like Grace Carolyn did for Little Grace."

Mary Rose buried her head in her hands and sobbed.

Bronwyn squeezed her hands. "You slept for days, waking for sips of water or broth, and then sleeping again. We couldn't wait any longer to bury him."

She looked up. "Where is he buried?"

"Near the garden. There is a headstone, if you'd like to see it."

"Did you name him?"

"Not I," Bronwyn said. "Gabe did. His name is Ashley MacKay." She squeezed Mary Rose's hand. "I read from your Psalter, Psalm 139, the same that Grace Carolyn used in her blessing."

"Thank you. 'Tis what I would have done."

"You should rest now. Later, Gabe wants to talk with you." She stood and started for the door. "He suffered a terrible loss that day too," she said. "Nearly every day, I find him kneeling at the gravesite. He weeps when he thinks no one is looking, so hard that his shoulders tremble."

"I can't see him. Not now. Perhaps not for a long time."

"One more thing . . ." Bronwyn drew in a deep breath. "About the celestial marriage ceremony . . . ?"

Mary Rose held up a hand to stop Bronwyn's words.

"You must hear me," Bronwyn said. "You need to know that we did not marry on the day your baby died. We would not have done that. Gabe called it off altogether. He told Brigham things would go on just as they always had. That I could stay here and be part of the family without a ceremony."

Mary Rose's heart lifted. "Gabe said that?"

Bronwyn's smile lit up her face. "Aye, 'tis true. That he did." Then her expression changed. "The other brides and grooms were married that day, as planned. We did not attend." She lifted the corner of her apron to dust the edge of a chest of drawers by the door. "But two days later, a Sunday, Brigham surprised us by announcing a special ceremony after the meetings and a grand party to follow, prepared by the ladies of the church. He said the Prophet himself would officiate . . ." She looked away from Mary Rose.

"At your wedding."

"Aye," she whispered, "at our wedding." Silence fell again between them, a silence so empty that Mary Rose could hear the ticking of the mantel clock downstairs. "We felt we had no choice but to go through with it."

It wasn't until Bronwyn closed the door behind her that Mary Rose wept.

THIRTY-TWO

As the days passed, Mary Rose spent hours in her garden, tending to the seedlings as though they were her children, letting the sun's heat seep through her flesh until it reached her bones. As she thinned the rows and plucked weeds, her heart began to thaw—toward Bronwyn and finally toward Gabe.

Even so, she could not give up her vigilance. She watched for any sign of a new intimacy between them: shared smiles, gazes held too long, a new lightness of step. But the only shared emotion seemed to be a genuine, mutual concern for her.

One night Mary Rose woke, the light from a full moon streaming through her window to bathe her bedroom in a silvery glow. An ache deep inside, too strong to ignore, drew her to her baby's gravesite. Wildflower seeds, a gift from Cordelia, who'd gathered most of them herself, lay in a small container near the cross that marked the infant's resting place.

In the light of the moon, with her bare hands, she dug into the soil, breathing in its heavy, earthy scent. With quick, determined movements, she scooped out small holes and dropped the dried seeds into each space. She pictured bachelor's buttons, dandelions, lupines, and black-eyed Susans popping up in a few weeks' time. And sweet alyssum, which she hoped would cover the grave in frothy abundance, as pure and delicate as a baby's breath. Though the latter wasn't native to Illinois, Cordelia told Mary Rose she had been given the seeds while on board the riverboat by a gentleman from Europe.

It wasn't the season for wildflowers to bloom, but she prayed God would make special compensation for just the tiny gravesite, letting the blossoms cover her child's body and bring peace to her tortured soul.

Hot tears came then, followed by wracking sobs, almost violent in their silence. She covered her face, not caring that tears streamed down her face and dripped from her chin into the soil above the grave.

She caught a shaky breath when she felt a warm hand on each of her shoulders.

"Dearest, dearest Mary Rose," Gabe whispered behind her. "Oh, my darling . . ." His voice broke off as he choked on his own tears. "Our little one . . ."

She turned to him, and in the moonlight studied his face, a portrait of grief. Behind them, frog song rose from the creek behind the newly rebuilt barn, and from the pasture beyond drifted the lowing of their few head of cattle.

"I need you, Mary Rose," Gabe said. "I can't live without you . . . I can't go on this way . . ."

She let him gather her in his arms. But she was too empty inside to force her arms to wrap around him. After a moment, he pulled back. "Will you ever love me again?"

"'Tis not a matter of love," she whispered. "I love you still. I love you with my whole being."

"The marriage to Bronwyn is on paper only. I swear to you with all my heart's blood that we both intend for it to remain that way unless . . ."

"Unless . . . ?"

"Unless you give your permission."

"Permission?" She laughed as she stood, walked a few feet away from the garden, and, keeping her back to him, stared up into what should have been starry skies. But a mist had risen off the river, laced among the trees, and crept up the low hills. Now the moon seemed more shadowed than bright, and the stars slowly disappeared. "We've been over this before," she said. "You know how I feel."

"How long," Gabe said, walking toward her. "How long will you let this go on? Even the children have noticed that you barely speak to me."

She spun to face him. "How long?" She let another bitter laugh fall from her lips. "I suppose what I'm waiting for is another revelation from God that will turn our lives upside down again."

"What do you mean?"

She stared at him. "Tell me again about celestial marriage and why it is important to the priesthood."

"Priests in good standing must take multiple wives. Not all Mormons, only a chosen few."

"And you're one of the chosen?"

He nodded. "I am a priest, just as all good Mormon men are, but I'm also a man working to become more godlike here on earth, and preparing for my own godhood in eternity. The more wives a man takes, the greater his place in eternity, the greater his blessings here on earth."

"Because you are working to become like God?" She'd tried to understand the Prophet's teaching on this, but the sense of it still escaped her. Yes, she believed that Joseph Smith was God's modern Prophet sent to restore the only rightful Church, the only way to salvation. He taught that those who called themselves Christians had corrupted Christ's teachings. Even the original disciples and apostles had gotten it wrong.

But to become like God? She didn't remember much of what she'd learned at her mother's knee, but something deep in her memory brought up an image of the serpent in the Garden who taunted Eve. "Just eat of this fruit, and you shall become like God . . ." She couldn't remember the exact words, only that it was the serpent, not God, who invited Eve to become divine.

Or was this one of the Bible stories the Prophet claimed was full of errors?

Gabe seemed to study her with more interest than before. Had he guessed her blasphemous thoughts? "Not just me, Mary Rose. The Prophet's teachings have to do with women's roles. You will be a goddess." He took her face between his hands and looked lovingly into her eyes. "One of the most beautiful revelations of our faith has to do with family." His eyes were bright with passion, shining even in the moonlight. "Can you imagine, Mary Rose, that we are sealed throughout all eternity—not only the two of us and our children, but our children's children and all of those to come?"

He blinked back his tears. "Mary Rose," he said softly. "Even our baby is sealed to us in heaven. He is not lost to us. When we die, he will be there waiting for his family to join him. He is alive. We will recognize him." Silence fell again, and the frogs kicked up their singing and somewhere a mockingbird sang, answered by another farther away.

"Don't you see? Spiritual marriage has to do with family. Keeping us all together. Forever."

"And if a man has many wives, is he sealed to them all?"

He nodded, his expression utterly sincere. "And to the children of that union," he said, keeping his gaze on her.

"And if a first wife disagrees?"

He turned toward the river. "She can be tried as an apostate and excommunicated—which means she's lost to us through all eternity. She's lost to her family." He stared into her eyes. "Should that happen to you, Mary Rose, you will never see our child. He will go to another mother."

Her heart throbbed at the thought. "Another of your wives."

"If you want to put it that way. Yes."

"Besides Bronwyn, then, you plan to take another?"

"We don't need to think about that now. We only need to consider our family as it is right now, including Bronwyn and Little Grace."

Mary Rose couldn't get the image of her infant out of her mind. Her empty arms ached for him. When she weighed spending an eternity with or without him, she had to agree that her family meant everything to her, enough to make choices she might not otherwise consider.

"You said that you and Bronwyn had agreed not to physically consummate the marriage."

"Unless you agree."

He walked over to her again and pulled her into his arms. "All I know is that I love you with all my heart, and the last thing I want to do is to hurt you. But so much is at stake here—not just for me, but for our whole family, the children under our care now, and those to come. And Bronwyn has now been sealed to us for eternity, as has been her daughter, Little Grace. We are all part of the same family.

"So if you say no to our consummating our union, you are saying no to eternity—you are in essence breaking up the celestial family." He placed his hands on either side of her face and lifted it so that she was forced to look into his eyes, now pale in the moonlight. "I love you more than you can ever know. But it is your decision. And whatever you decide, I will abide by it."

She swallowed hard as hot tears stung her eyes. How could she say yes to such a thing? How could this God she thought she knew require it of her? Could he be so cruel? Was it really his way to bring such heartache? She dropped her head into her hands and felt Gabe come up to stand behind her. Gently, he pulled her into his embrace and turned her so she faced him. His voice was gruff with emotion when he spoke.

"I will not love you less if you agree to this," he said. "I will love you more."

"How can that be, if it is Bronwyn who lies in your arms?" Her voice trembled and again the tears flowed. "How can you make love to her and still say you love me?"

"Only by God's strength am I able to do this. Think of the children that will come from my union with Bronwyn. They will be as much yours as hers. Sister wives share everything, including their husband's love, the children they bear, and the home they create for their loved ones. Your blessings will increase, dearest, not decrease, if you say yes to my request . . . to our request."

"You are certain that Bronwyn wants this too?"

"We have spoken of it, and yes, she agrees."

Mary Rose moved out of his arms and turned her back. How could she utter the words? Even her lips seemed unable to move to tell Gabe what he wanted to hear.

Drawing in a deep, shuddering breath, she finally spoke: "If this truly is the Prophet's revelation—and though I don't like it, I trust that it is a true revelation from God . . ." She thought of her baby. Her sacrifice now on earth would allow her to spend eternity with him. That was truly all that mattered.

When she spoke again her voice was soft and ragged. "I give my permission."

Her eyes watered again and she turned away from Gabe, almost gasping for breath. This was too hard, the sacrifice too great.

But it was for her child. An eternity spent with her baby.

He gathered her close once again. "You don't know how happy this makes me, Mary Rose," he whispered into her hair. "We'll all be together throughout eternity. We'll know greater happiness here . . . and there . . . than we can possibly imagine."

He left her then and strode across the yard to the back door of the house.

Minutes later, Bronwyn came to stand by her side beneath the starlit sky. "Are you sure, Mary Rose?"

Mary Rose couldn't look at her friend. She nodded and whispered, "Yes."

Bronwyn reached for her hand, but Mary Rose withdrew it. After a moment, she turned to look at Bronwyn.

Her face was more beautiful than ever in the starlight. She wore a sweeping duster, delicate and feminine, apparently new, but Mary Rose didn't want to ask how she came by it.

She wept as she tried to give Mary Rose a quick embrace. But Mary Rose dropped her head and turned away. She heard the padding of soft footsteps move toward the back door.

After the door closed, she turned and imagined Bronwyn climbing the stairs, imagined how fast Gabe's heart beat as he waited for her. It didn't surprise her when a lamp went on in his bedroom.

Long minutes later, soft sounds of their lovemaking drifted downward from the still-open window to the garden.

Tears streamed down Mary Rose's face and she turned once more to the baby's grave and bowed her head. "God of my childhood," she wept. "I don't know what to do with my heartache. I don't even know how to pray. I don't know what is right and what is wrong. How can this be love? How can this be your will when it hurts so deeply?"

I have loved you with an everlasting love . . . She thought she heard spoken words. But no one was there.

"I can't abide this, I cannot!" she wept. "How can I be the one who has the power to break up families in heaven? How can a mere human being—a man—whether he is part of the priesthood or not, have the power to call me into heaven to be with him through eternity?"

I have called you by name, you are mine . . .

Drifting from the window came the lilt of Bronwyn's delighted giggles followed by the resonance of Gabe's voice, both sounds she had loved until now.

She stood, holding her hands over her ears. "I must leave this place. I cannot bear it a moment longer. But where can I go? What can I do?"

Come unto me, child, and I will give you rest . . .

"Which God is true . . . the God of my childhood . . . or the one who has restored his true Church through the Prophet? The one who says all men can become like him, become gods of their own worlds, their blessings increasing with each new wife he takes? Or the one who remains so shadowy from my mother's teachings that I can't remember him?"

I am the First and I am the Last; besides Me there is no God.

Mary Rose moved as if through a dreamscape toward the back door, thinking about the iron strength that encased her backbone. It had seen her through before, and she trusted it to do so again.

She hurried up the stairs and moved down the hallway to her bedroom. Just as she passed Gabe's room, the door opened. Bronwyn, looking ravishingly beautiful in a new silk chemise that emphasized her shapely body, stepped into the hallway, saw Mary Rose, and stopped.

For a long moment they stared at each other.

Mary Rose imagined she could smell Gabe's scent on Bronwyn's skin. Her mouth looked swollen and almost bruised with the passion of his kisses, and her long, thick eyelashes emphasized her dreamy, half-closed eyes.

Bronwyn reached out to touch Mary Rose's hand, but Mary Rose stepped away from her and shook her head.

"I'm sorry," Bronwyn whispered as Mary Rose rushed by. This time there was no mistaking the scent.

She rushed to her bedroom, closed the door, locked it, and threw herself on the bed, this time her pain too great for tears.

THIRTY-THREE

After a fitful few hours of sleep, Mary Rose welcomed the coming dawn. She poured cool water over a cloth from a pitcher at her dressing table, held it against her swollen eyes, and then as clumsily as ever, braided her flyaway curls into a long plait. After slipping into a plain gingham morning dress and white apron, she stepped into the hallway, her heart still heavy. She drew in a deep breath, determined to be finished with her weeping.

She hesitated in front of the twins' door, her heart overtaken by a sudden need to wrap her arms around the children. She stepped into the room and opened the shade. The sun was still well below the horizon, but the scattering of clouds that dotted the sky had already begun their transformation from pearl gray to pink.

The twins, in a trundle, rubbed their eyes and yawned when they saw her. Mary Rose gave them each a good-morning kiss, and then sat on the edge of the lower trundle next to Ruby. "Lady," Ruby said, "Pearl and me dethided thomething."

"Pearl and I," Mary Rose corrected, ruffling her hair, though she hated to draw attention to anything additional now that Ruby was working so hard to correct her lisp.

Ruby crawled from beneath her bedclothes and snuggled close to Mary Rose. "What did you decide?" Mary Rose wrapped her arm around the little girl.

"We want to call you Mommy." Pearl slid from the upper part of the trundle to cuddle on Mary Rose's other side.

Mary Rose smiled for the first time in days. "Mommy? I like that, but your real mommy might not be so glad to hear it when she gets here."

"She'll never come for us," Pearl said. "If she was, she'd be here by now. We don't think she likes us very much."

"Papa too," Ruby said. "Bethideth . . . be-*sides*, we don't ever want to leave. We like it here this much." She held out her arms as far as they could stretch.

"How would you like to go back to England with me?" Mary Rose ventured. "Coal too, of course."

"On the big thailing thip?" She let out an exasperated sigh. "Sailing th . . . ship."

Mary Rose could see by their expressions that her idea wasn't going over well. "Aye, yes, the big ship. The same way we came over, only in reverse."

"Auntie Bronwyn and Little Grace and Papa?" Pearl asked. "Will they come too?"

It didn't take Mary Rose much thought to realize Gabe had now become Papa. "I thought it might be a nice holiday for just the four of us to go—just you girls, Coal, and me."

"What about Grandpa Earl and Grandma Cordelia?" Ruby's bottom lip trembled and her eyes filled.

Mary Rose bit her lip. She hadn't expected the children to hold such fierce love for their family. "Just us."

Pearl looked up at her. "Don't you love Papa anymore?"

"Yes, I do," Mary Rose said. "And he loves me." She pushed from her mind the images and sounds of the night before.

"How come you don't ever look like you love him?" Pearl said.

"Sometimes you just thit . . . sit and stare without thmiling . . . smiling . . . or talking or laughing," Ruby added.

"I've had many things on my mind," she said quietly.

"The baby that went up to heaven. That made me very sad." Pearl flopped back on the bed. "I cried and cried 'cause I loved that baby."

"Me too," Ruby said. "I was tho thad." She sighed again. "So th . . . sad."

Coal tumbled through the doorway and jumped up onto the upper trundle. Mary Rose gave him a warning look and he sat, grinning and swinging his legs over the side.

"Mommy wants us to go to England," Pearl said.

He tossed his sisters a look of superiority. "Mommy's in the Sandwich Islands. How could she want us to go to England?"

"Thith mommy, thilly," Ruby said and gave his bare foot a poke.

"What's going on in here?" Gabe stuck his head in the door, smiled at Mary Rose, and strode across the room. He ruffled the twins' hair and gave Coal a quick hug.

He bent to kiss Mary Rose's cheek and whispered, "I love you." But when she raised her eyes to look deep into his, a new emotion seemed to have crowded in. A glow? A spark that hadn't been there before last night? She had no doubt that it had to do with love. But it wasn't love for her.

"Mommy wants uth to go to England," Ruby announced.

Gabe didn't miss a beat; he went on as if Ruby had mentioned they were having potatoes for dinner. "It's pretty this time of year," he said. "Not so cold and foggy."

"I don't wanna go," Pearl said. "I like it here better."

"Me too. Papa, don't make us go, pleathe . . . please."

Gabe quirked a brow and grinned at them. "Papa? What's this Papa business all about?"

They explained, and Gabe gave them a big grin and gathered them into a hug. Bronwyn came to the door and peeked in, smiling as though nothing unusual had happened the night before. She held Little Grace, who smiled and patty-caked her hands when she saw Mary Rose and then reached for her.

Mary Rose took the baby into her arms, unable to keep her heart from lifting when she gazed into the baby's sweet face. It was for the children, she reminded herself, that she had made her decision. Not just the babe who lay in the ground by the garden but for Little Grace too.

She kissed the baby's fingers, vowing that she would allow nothing to break the celestial bond: not jealousy, or pride, or her strong inclination toward having her own way.

She'd determined sometime in the early predawn hours that she didn't need to stay in the same home, or even the same country, to remain true to those vows.

"I'm hungry," Coal announced, leaping from the top trundle and landing with a thud on the wooden floor.

Mary Rose laughed. "'Tis no wonder. You are a growing boy and need your sustenance." The child stuck out his chest. "But not one mouth in our growing family can have even the smallest taste of my fresh blueberry pancakes until that person is fully washed, dressed, has combed their hair, and set the table for us all."

"Blueberry pancaketh?" Ruby's eyes grew big. "Did they get ripe?"

Gabe exchanged a smile with Mary Rose, though deep inside his eyes she could see his puzzlement. He looked back to the children. "Indeed they did, and I know as a fact that the mockingbirds will eat every one if we don't get outside to pick them."

Still holding Little Grace, Mary Rose stepped toward the door-way where Bronwyn leaned against the doorjamb. As she gently handed Little Grace back to her friend, their eyes met.

Mary Rose couldn't imagine a more difficult act to carry out at this moment, but she smiled into Bronwyn's eyes and gave her a nod as if the nightmare of the previous night never happened. Then she circled her arm around Bronwyn's waist and led her out to the hall.

"Would you like to help with the pancakes?" she whispered.

Bronwyn looked confused for a moment, and then laughed. "Have you never made them before?"

Mary Rose shook her head. "Have you?"

"Aye, and 'twill be my honor and pleasure to show you how." Her eyes filled, and grabbing Mary Rose's hand, she held it tight. "I'm so very sorry . . . about last . . ."

Mary Rose stepped back and forced her smile to stay in place. "We will never speak of it again."

Early that afternoon, Mary Rose hitched one of their horses, a white mare she'd secretly named Angel Moroni, to the buck-board. She'd told no one where she was headed; she merely asked Bronwyn to watch the children.

The sun was high, so she opened her parasol for shade as Angel Moroni trotted toward Nauvoo. Soon, she could see the temple up on the hillside, and though Gabe had ridden there earlier to meet with the carpenters, she bypassed the road leading to the site and continued her journey to the center of town.

The Prophet's newly completed home, which he and Emma called the Mansion House, stood taller than the other homes around it.

Mary Rose halted Angel Moroni in front of the mansion and furled her parasol, then secured the mare to a hitching post. She gazed up at the two-story house with its gleaming white exterior, deep green shutters, and twin brick chimneys, one at each end. A wide elegant doorway seemed designed to welcome visitors.

Even if it hadn't given that impression, Mary Rose would have made her visit anyway.

The gate opened with a squeak, and as she walked to the front door, Mary Rose noticed that in at least half of the four upstairs windows, hands pulled back the lace curtains just enough for someone to peer out without being seen.

Undeterred, she marched up the steps to the front door and gave it a sharp rap with the brass knocker.

It took only a moment or two for the door to open. A pretty girl of about seventeen stood in front of Mary Rose and gave her a gracious smile.

"I would like to speak with Sister Emma," Mary Rose said.

The girl blinked. "I'm certain she's not accepting callers right now."

Mary Rose had come prepared for that eventuality. She pulled out a calling card, left over from her days in English society, and handed it to the girl. "If you will kindly inform her that Lady Mary Rose Ashley has come to call, I would be grateful."

The girl read the card and raised her eyebrows. When she spoke again, her voice held greater respect. "Please, do come in. You may wait in the parlor for her answer." The girl stood back to let Mary Rose pass, then hurried up the stairs. As Mary Rose seated herself on a burgundy velvet settee in the parlor, she heard the low murmur of voices. After a moment, she heard light footsteps on the stairs and Emma Smith appeared in the doorway, the girl who'd fetched her standing at her elbow.

Mary Rose stood to greet the Prophet's wife.

Emma waved a hand. "Please, sit down. Would you care for tea?"

Mary Rose glanced at the mantel clock and smiled at her hostess. "'Tis that time."

Emma instructed the girl to bring them tea and scones, cream, and preserves. Sitting back, she settled her gaze on Mary Rose. "I've been expecting you."

Mary Rose tilted her head in surprise.

"Our community is still small enough for word to get around. I knew of your background in England, the great cost you paid emotionally and physically to join us, and lately, how that cost has increased."

"Are you speaking of my husband's second wife?"

She nodded. "And your deep loss. I've lost two babies, and with each I felt I had no reason to go on living. If it hadn't been for my other children . . . for Joseph . . . I don't know what I would have done."

The girl brought a tray and set it on a low Chippendale table between them. She recognized the elegant hand-painted Rockingham English bone china tea set, ivory in color with gold trim.

"Thank you, Melissa, that will be all," Emma said and then poured tea for Mary Rose. "Sugar and cream?"

Mary Rose couldn't help smiling. It was the first time an elegant tea, with exquisite service, had been offered her since leaving the manor house. "Both, thank you."

She handed Mary Rose her teacup and saucer, and as Mary Rose stirred her tea with a silver teaspoon, the Prophet's wife sat back, studying her guest over the rim of her teacup.

"Thank you for seeing me today—and with such gracious warmth." Mary Rose took in the tea service, the elegant surroundings, the woman herself who gave her an encouraging smile.

"I don't know what to do," she said. "I never expected to be drawn into this world . . . I never expected my husband . . ." She hesitated as her pent-up emotions from the night before bubbled to the surface.

Emma leaned forward and when she spoke, her voice was gentle. "I know what you're trying to say. I know, and I understand."

"Because you've lived it?"

Emma gave her an almost imperceptible nod. She reached for the silver basket of scones and handed it to Mary Rose.

"How do you do it? Do you still love your husband?" She spread sweet butter on a scone and bit into it, relishing the taste of home.

"Oh, yes. And I believe in him, I always have." Emma prepared a scone, and then set it on a small plate beside her saucer and teacup.

"But this revelation about taking plural wives . . ." Sounds of women conversing drifted from an upstairs room. The young girl who'd greeted Mary Rose and served tea passed by the parlor doorway with another woman who appeared to be in her forties. Neither paid much notice to Emma or to Mary Rose.

"It's been a practice since before we left Kirtland," Emma said. "I denied it for a long time, not believing it possible." Her smile didn't reach her eyes. "I've also tried to deny that the revelation came years after the practice began. But it's now common knowledge, at least among the leaders of the Church. Some say, because I'm mentioned by name in the revelation God gave to my husband, that he meant to finally settle my mind about it."

"Why did you agree to it?"

"I didn't, not with the first. Or the second, for that matter. Those are the first two I know of, but there may have been others."

"And Joseph took these wives without your permission?"

"Yes. He believed it was God's will. He believes the first part of the Bible proves it's honorable in God's sight—think of David, Solomon, and the many others who thought nothing of taking as many wives and concubines as they liked. Joseph says that God counted these men as righteous. He also asks why God should change his mind about things."

"Is that your belief?"

Emma poured Mary Rose more tea. "My acceptance of the practice comes from my belief in family."

Mary Rose's eyes widened. "That was my conclusion last night. It was the only reason I would agree. I believe with all my heart that we will forever be sealed in heaven. I couldn't bear the thought of being the one to break up our family."

"Or to forgo holding your own child in your arms again." Her eyes grew moist and she reached for a dainty handkerchief.

"Yes," Mary Rose said softly. "I made that final decision because of my baby."

Emma stood and walked to the empty fireplace, touched the mantel clock almost absently, then turned back to Mary Rose. "I am assuming you came here today for advice, not just to talk about the plural marriage, good or bad."

"Yes." She leaned forward earnestly. "What do I do now?"

Emma came over and sat beside Mary Rose on the settee. She reached for her hand and squeezed it for emphasis as she spoke. "Don't ever forget that you are the first wife. Hold on to that position no matter what, no matter the strength of personality exhibited by the other wives to come—and you can be assured, they will come. As sure as the sun rises in the east, your husband will take as many as you allow."

"You said that Joseph took wives without your permission . . ."

"That was before I understood what I needed to do. That was before I turned the tables." The corner of her mouth twitched as if she wanted to laugh, but she didn't. "From now on, you will choose his wives for him."

Mary Rose sat back, astounded. "I've been thinking the only thing I could do was to leave. To return to England."

"Has it occurred to you that should you leave, you could be tried as an apostate?"

"I wouldn't leave my church. Only my husband."

"Then we come back to the issue of eternity. Even if you weren't tried for apostasy and excommunicated—by leaving Gabriel, you risk displeasing him. If you displease him, he will not call you by your holy name into the highest heaven, that place where your family will be—with you, or without you."

"So we come back to the sacrifice for the family, for our babies."

Emma nodded. "Do you love your husband, even after what he's done?"

"Yes, 'tis a miracle, but yes, I love him. I feel betrayed by him, by my dearest friend—but, yes, I love him with all my heart."

"Then you can't leave. You must stay and fight for him. Make him love you above all others. Someday, he may try to bring into your home a wife who's half your age, prettier, livelier, smarter. But you must remain the one he loves most. Consider the others as having been brought in to help you with your chores, to help with the children—and you will have many through the years." She sipped her tea. "Does your Gabriel love you?"

"Until last night I thought so."

"He took his second wife to bed?"

"Yes."

Emma looked away from Mary Rose, letting her gaze drift toward the window. From down the street, the laughter and song of several children could be heard drawing closer.

"That is the most difficult part to accept in a plural marriage." She squeezed Mary Rose's hands again, her gaze almost fierce. "That's why you need to do everything in your power to make him want you, to desire being with you, to converse with you on a level that none of the others know. You are the first wife, the first he fell in love with, which gives you power that none of the other sister wives have."

Mary Rose drew in a shaky breath. "I don't know if I can do that . . . or even if I want to." She pulled a small hanky from her reticule and dabbed at her eyes.

"If you believe that families are eternal, if you believe in your love for your husband and his for you, you will find strength you never thought possible." Emma gave her another rare smile. The children had opened the gate and, from the gleeful sounds, were tumbling up the walkway. Mary Rose recognized the lower voice of the Prophet talking and laughing with them.

"One more thing," Emma said just before the door opened to let the children spill in. "Approach all of this as if you were born to be queen over your own domain"—she looked Mary Rose up and down as if appraising her for the role and seemed pleased with what she saw—"with a glad heart that will gladden the hearts of all those in your household."

Mary Rose gave her an embrace just as Joseph came to the parlor doorway. Emma, facing away from her husband, whispered into Mary Rose's ear, "And if any part of our conversation is repeated and it gets back to me, I will deny everything I've told you."

The Prophet's unblinking gaze rested on Mary Rose's face even as she gathered her parasol and placed the hanky back in her reticule.

"Come back again soon," Emma said as she walked Mary Rose to the door. Her expression told Mary Rose that, in spite of all the children, other women, and even the Prophet himself who occupied the house, Emma was a very lonely woman.

THIRTY-FOUR

Mary Rose pondered Emma Smith's words for several days before she gathered the courage to implement her plan.

One evening after supper three weeks later, she called the family together and surprised them all by asking Gabe, as priest and head of their household, to give them each a blessing each night before bedtime. She explained to the wide-eyed twins and Coal that it was their papa's blessed and precious responsibility and that each bedtime would begin in such a manner. This would follow a time of Scripture reading and prayer in which they would all participate.

"If we are going to be a holy and set-apart people," she said to Gabe and Bronwyn, "if we are following the Prophet's teachings and revelations, I believe we should be committed to taking them all the way."

Gabe blinked and glanced at Bronwyn, who nodded as if in approval. Mary Rose went to a bookshelf to retrieve the Book of Mormon and handed it to Gabe. The children sat at his feet as he read a short passage.

When he was finished, the children lined up to take their turns kneeling before him. One by one, he placed his hand on their heads and blessed them. Bronwyn then knelt before him, holding Little Grace. He took the baby into his arms and laid his cheek on the top of her head for a moment, his expression reflecting the love he felt for the child.

Mary Rose thought of their own child, buried beneath soil and stones, and turned away, unable to bear the look of love he gave the living child and her mother. His voice was low and filled with emotion as he blessed Little Grace.

When Mary Rose turned back, Bronwyn still knelt before him, gazing up into his face with a look of adoration.

Mary Rose forced a pleasant tone into her voice and, standing, said to the other children. "I have an announcement to make," she said, leaning toward them. "I talked to you about returning to England a few weeks ago . . ."

Coal nodded, Ruby said, "I remember," and Pearl's lower lip trembled.

"I've made a decision. We are staying in the place we love the most. We are going to live together as one big family." She smiled at Bronwyn. "Your papa loves us all and has vowed to care for us all through eternity. We are one big family that no one can ever separate."

"What about Mama and Papa in the Thand . . . *Sand*with . . . *Sandwich* Islands?" Ruby said. "Can they be part of our big family too?"

Still seated on the floor, Bronwyn leaned against Gabe's leg while Gabe played peek-a-boo with the baby. Bronwyn looked over at Ruby and gave her a confident smile. "We will pray that they will come to know the only true Church and the testimony of our Prophet."

"Me too," Ruby chimed in.

"I think it's bedtime for all." Gabe stood, still holding Little

Grace, and helped Bronwyn to her feet. A look of understanding passed between them, the same that Mary Rose had seen each night for the past three weeks.

"Gabe," Mary Rose said, stepping between them. "I would like to speak to you privately."

"Of course."

He handed the baby to Bronwyn, and she went upstairs with the children, though she glanced back at him when she reached the top stair.

The evening was warm, and Mary Rose suggested they talk outdoors. Gabe agreed, and they stepped outside. He circled his arm around her as they strolled alongside the garden. Mockingbirds sang and the creek bubbled its way to the river.

"Do you mind if we walk to the creek?" She smiled into his eyes, pale in the starlit night.

He grinned and an eyebrow shot up; she knew he was remembering another night when the air was balmy and the singing creek ran full. A few weeks before their farmhouse was finished, they'd ridden out alone in the buckboard to take a look at the progress of the buildings. Caught up in a moment of passion they'd made love by the creek to the music of the croaking frogs and night birds, and later giggled together as Gabe tried to rid her curly locks of twigs and grass.

Gabe and Mary Rose continued their walk in silence. They passed the barn, the henhouse, and the pasture. Then Gabe pulled back some willows, and they were in the same small clearing beside the creek where they had been that night. Though her eyes had become accustomed to the dim light as she watched his face for signs of love, of passion, even affection, his expression was unreadable.

She remembered Emma's advice to make sure he would always love her best, no matter how many wives he might take in the future.

She closed her eyes and prayed—to whichever god might be listening—that Gabe would think of that night and want to re-create it.

Once inside the privacy of the clearing, she turned to him and touched his cheek, letting her fingertips lightly trace his jaw. He gently took her hand away from his face and kissed her palm.

"Do you remember that night?"

"Aye, my love, and I always will. You know that."

"I don't even know if you love me, Gabe." She turned away from him, facing the creek. "You haven't shown me . . . love . . . since Bronwyn . . . since you and Bronwyn . . ." She stared at the dark, bubbling water, unable to finish.

He came up behind her then and wrapped his arms around her. "I've been waiting for you to tell me it was all right," he said, laying his cheek on her head. "After what you went through with our baby's birth, I didn't know."

Hope kindled in her heart, and she turned to face him. "Truly?"

He smiled into her eyes. "I will come to you tonight, if you're sure you have healed."

"Truly, I am well—body, soul, and spirit," she said, thinking her heart might fly out of her chest.

He kissed her passionately, leaving her breathless. She waited for him to kneel on the soft carpet of twigs and moss, the soft, rich soil, to draw her into his arms so as to lay together again as husband and wife.

But he didn't seem to have a mind for it. Or simply had forgotten the passion they once knew.

He drew her into another embrace and held her close. "Tonight," he said, and then gave her a chaste kiss on the cheek.

"Tonight," she whispered as he walked away from her.

It was after midnight when Gabe opened her bedroom door and stepped in. Mary Rose was drowsy but woke when he slipped into her bed beside her. He reached for her and she let him draw her into his embrace. His lovemaking was as passionate as ever, but Bronwyn's image filled her mind, and as he touched her, she wondered if Bronwyn filled his as well.

She closed her eyes, willing her body to respond just as it always had before. But Bronwyn's beautiful face and perfect body kept returning, bringing to Mary Rose's mind every flaw in her own, real and imagined. And though Gabe breathed Mary Rose's name as he gave her feather-soft kisses along her neck and around the shell of her ears, she strained to hear if he might slip even once and call her by the wrong name.

When he had finished, she turned away from him. "I cannot do this again," she whispered. "It is not right." She swung her legs over the side of the bed and sat there for a moment, holding her face in her hands, weeping. "A man should not have two wives."

Gabe circled his arm around her shoulders, and gently held her while she cried. "I'm so sorry," he said. "Sometimes I wonder myself what we've done, what we've gotten into. I wonder if the Prophet is right . . . or dead wrong." Before she could tell him her thoughts, he stood, kissed her cheek, and left her bedroom, closing the door behind him.

She stared at the closed door, feeling more alone than ever. What could the future hold, if not Gabe's undying love for her, the love she thought would always be hers.

She bowed her head and wept again.

Even Emma's words of plural-wife wisdom brought her no comfort. What good was it to be a strong, even powerful, first wife when she was unsure of the love between Gabe and her?

Mary Rose knew the night she had conceived, because there had been no other. After waiting another month to be certain, she went to Gabe to tell him. She found him at the back of the barn in his workshop, cleaning and oiling his firearms.

As soon as she told him about their baby, his face instantly filled with wonder. He put down his rifle and gathered her into his arms, lifting her from the floor to swing her around. He stopped before he'd made a complete circle and set her down gently, an anguished look on his face.

"Did I hurt you? My joy overcame my good sense. Are you sure you're all right?" He drew her close and wrapped his arms around her protectively.

It felt good to be held in his arms once more, and Mary Rose felt a sting of tears in the back of her throat. "I'm not made of porcelain, dearest. Truly, I'm not. And this time, God is giving us a healthy baby. I can feel it in my very bones."

He pulled back and grinned at her, his eyes reflecting the love she'd so missed.

"Give me a blessing," she said, wanting to prolong this special moment between the two of them.

He took her hands and led her into the sunlight outside the barn. "God is blessing us. 'Tis his gift, telling us we're on the right road after all, Mary Rose."

She knelt before him and, placing his hand on her head, he offered up a blessing to God. When he had finished, he helped Mary Rose to her feet, and then gathered her into his arms. He held her tight, and she heard the beating of his heart. She smiled, remembering how love awakened inside her the first time he held her like this.

"I love you so," he whispered, and captured her mouth with his lips, just as he'd done on that day on the bow of the *Sea Hawk*.

THIRTY-FIVE

Bronwyn watched Mary Rose and Gabe from her upstairs window. She'd noticed her friend's body changing, and knew—perhaps even before Mary Rose did—that she was with child.

Her own heart leapt at Gabe's unabashed joy. If he'd been wearing a hat, she was certain he would have tossed it as high as the clouds. She longed to run out and rejoice and laugh and shout and dance right along with them.

But her own condition prevented her from joining them. That and the sweet knowledge that this was a private moment only they should share. Watching them together, Bronwyn wondered how she could love a friend so deeply and, at the same time, love so deeply the husband they shared.

She watched Mary Rose move toward the garden with a spring in her step, a smile spreading even wider across her face. As she knelt to dig potatoes for dinner, Gabe came up to stand behind her. She glanced up at him, in full view of Bronwyn, who still stood at the window.

He took her hand, helped her stand, and drew her into an impassioned embrace. Bronwyn almost gasped. She blinked and backed away from the window as he led Mary Rose toward the back door.

She saw his face clearly, and she knew the look. Their footsteps would too soon be on the stairs, then down the hall, and through his bedroom door. She grabbed a shawl, lifted the sleeping Little Grace from her cradle, and then hurried down the hall, hoping to be down the stairs and through the front door before they came in the back.

She was too late.

She heard their murmuring voices at the bottom of the stairs, just as she reached the top.

Mary Rose looked up when she saw Bronwyn, and briefly their eyes met as Mary Rose ascended, Gabe's arm wrapped around her. She couldn't be sure, but she thought she saw a glint of triumph. Gabe seemed too interested in nuzzling Mary Rose's temple to notice Bronwyn standing at the top of the stairs, holding Little Grace.

Bronwyn ran to the creek, holding the still sleeping child at her bosom. She had been so sure of Gabe's love for her, his passion, and his praise of her beauty, that she hadn't considered he might turn again to Mary Rose. She dropped her head, ashamed of her jealousy and surprised at its intensity.

Was it the child Mary Rose carried that had turned his head?

Would it turn again when he found out that she too was expecting a wee babe?

She looked down at Little Grace and swallowed hard, a swift and sudden grief, a longing for Griffin overtaking her. Marriages weren't meant to be like this, were they?

She and Griffin had felt the burning of truth inside them when missionaries spoke of the Prophet's new revelation, God's restoration of the only true Church in the world. Together, they had been baptized, rising from the ocean waters as if new beings. Griffin had been so certain that God called them to America, to Nauvoo, to help build his kingdom.

But how would he have felt about Gabe taking Bronwyn as his second wife? Would Griffin have done the same thing should Gabe have been the one to die? How would she have felt if he'd brought Mary Rose into their lives as a second wife? The thought brought with it waves of regret for not understanding how Mary Rose must surely have felt . . . until now.

She rocked Little Grace in her arms, softly singing a lullaby, more to herself than to the child:

Sleep, baby, sleep!
Thy rest shall angels keep,
While on the grass the lamb shall feed,
And never suffer want or need.
Sleep, baby, sleep!

Hot tears filled her eyes as she sang the words *"and never suffer want or need."* She wondered if she would have come so willingly to Gabe if she'd had other choices. Griffin had taken out a loan through a bank in town, owned and run by the Prophet, to have the money to build the farm next to Gabe and Mary Rose.

When Griffin died, Mary Rose's grandfather and his new bride, Sister Cordelia, purchased the property from the bank. Bronwyn neither owed money, nor did she have any of her own.

She was at the mercy of the Church. And, in cold, hard terms, at the mercy of its representative, Gabriel MacKay.

Tears spilled down her cheeks and dripped onto Little Grace's blanket as she wondered about Gabe's rush to marry her. Had it been because of love? Or lust? That thought made her tears fall faster. Or simply because he had been ordered to do so?

She looked up when she heard rustling in the willows and the crunch of children's footsteps approaching on the other side of the creek. Soon, the merry eyes of Coal and the twins peered at her through the foliage, then they tumbled out before her, hopping across the stream's stepping stones and landing on the streambed in front of her.

"You been crying, Auntie Bronwyn?" Pearl said, looking up at her face with concern.

Bronwyn smiled and wiped her eyes. "Just a little."

"Whatth wrong?" Ruby cuddled up beside her on the stone and circled her small arm around Bronwyn's waist.

Coal wrinkled his nose. "Is Little Grace all right?"

She looked down at the baby, who sighed in her sleep. "She's perfect," she assured the children.

"We got to help Grandma Cordelia make andouille sausages," Pearl said, puffed up with pride.

"And I got to thtuff the cathingth . . . casings," Ruby said.

"And Grandpa Earl made me a swing. It's hanging from the big oak tree out back of their house," Coal said.

"Itth for all of uth, thilly," Ruby said.

Bronwyn heard the soft crunch of shoes on gravel, the snaps of twigs, and the rustling of willows. Sister Cordelia appeared next. She gave Bronwyn a wide smile as she teetered precariously on the stepping stones. It didn't help the older woman's balance that she held a basket in one hand.

The children ran into the barn to look for their hoops and sticks, and Bronwyn scooted over to make room for Cordelia to sit beside her.

"You look like you could use a friend," Cordelia said. She placed the covered basket beside the large stone.

Bronwyn started to deny her need and don the mask she too often wore: that of sunny optimism no matter the circumstances.

But her heart was too heavy to attempt it. Besides, she knew Cordelia well enough to recognize that the astute little woman would see right through her deception.

"Aye," she said softly. "I'm feeling lost."

Cordelia reached for her hand. "I wondered how long it would take." Her Cajun lilt seemed almost musical to Bronwyn. She relaxed, just hearing it. Among all the Saints, she knew of no one she admired more—and had ever since the night Cordelia told her how to break a window with the butt of a gun and start shooting at the thugs who surrounded them. A tiny woman with coal black hair and a fiery spirit, she seemed to look upon others with the same grace and acceptance that had been extended to her.

Little Grace stirred and opened her eyes. Cordelia reached for her and bounced her on her lap, cuddled her close, and covered her soft downy head with kisses. "I love how babies smell," she said, smiling at Bronwyn. "You are so blessed to have her, did you know it?"

Bronwyn nodded. "Aye, 'tis true."

Then Cordelia studied Bronwyn's midsection for a moment. "I could be wrong, but there's another on the way, is that true too?"

Bronwyn sighed. "Aye, that too is true."

"And you feel even more like a lost lamb now than before—because, dear, Mary Rose is also having a babe?"

"How did you know?"

"My grandmother was a midwife. Some called her a witch, and had she lived a century earlier she might have been burned at the stake. But she was wise and taught me the signs. I wish I'd listened more carefully when she told me of her herbs and medicines, but her art died with her." She reached into her basket and drew out a fresh biscuit. She broke it in pieces and gave them one by one to Little Grace, who chomped at them with relish.

"You asked if I feel like a lost lamb . . . ?" She laughed lightly. "'Tis true. I just hadn't thought of myself as such."

"Perhaps it's because of our Prophet. I sometimes feel like he's let us down by thinking himself bigger than God. When I first heard his message it was simple and easy to understand. There were no secret temple ceremonies, no revelations of plural marriage, no teachings that said every man can become a god depending on how he follows the 'law' of the Prophet."

Bronwyn caught her breath. She'd heard about outspoken, strong-willed women being tried for blasphemy, excommunicated from the Church, their families shamed. She studied this woman she'd come to love and respect as much as if she were her own dear grandmother, and she feared for her.

Cordelia laughed lightly, and then, as if reading Bronwyn's mind, said, "Don't get me wrong. I love this church with all my heart. I will never forget the love and acceptance I felt after being shunned so long as a fallen woman. Brother Joseph welcomed me with open arms, and when other members whispered behind my back, he called them up short. He wouldn't allow anyone to see me as anything other than one with equal access to God's grace."

"But I've come to realize that our Prophet has feet of clay."

"What do you mean?"

She sighed deeply. "I could be excommunicated for saying this, but I don't care. I think our Joseph lost sight of God's original plan for him."

Bronwyn sat back, astonished. "Does Grandpa Earl know how you feel?"

"Oh laws, yes. And worries himself sick that I'll take over a Sunday meeting and tell the whole congregation."

"Would he ever take another wife—even if commanded to by Brother Brigham or the Prophet himself?"

She laughed, this time louder than before. "He brought it up once, and I simply said it was hogwash and pointed to the rifle over the doorway. Said I'd shoot at any woman who tried to get his pants off and convince him to take her as a second wife. Or any man too big for his britches, ordering others to live their lives in such a way—including the highfalutin so-called apostles. Every one of them takes himself too seriously in my opinion and needs to be taken down a notch or two."

She shook her head slowly and grinned at Bronwyn. "Guess you didn't know you'd inherited such a spitfire of a grandma."

Bronwyn laughed. "I figured it out the night you had me shooting at that mob."

"Well, dear. In my opinion—yet again—you could use some spitfire yourself."

Bronwyn's eyes widened. "Me?"

"Yes, dear. You. We've got some tough times ahead of us. I see all the signs of it in perfect alignment . . . and you, all of us, need to come together as a family if we're going to make it through."

"What signs?" Bronwyn looked down at Little Grace, and her heart skipped a beat.

"The wolves are already nipping at our heels, lying in wait to attack us again, rape our women, kill our children, make old men dance . . ." Cordelia turned to Bronwyn, her face softening. "I'm sorry to go on and on about this." She looked at her evenly. "Are you scandalized, just hearing it?"

Bronwyn didn't answer right away. Gathering her thoughts, she watched the creek for a few moments, the way the water swirled, almost backward from its usual flow, then found its path and gurgled downward once more.

"You've given voice to my thoughts. I haven't dared to say them aloud—not since Mary Rose and I became . . . estranged. We once spoke openly of our feelings about the Church and the Prophet, we laughed at some of the absurdities of his claims." She chuckled at the memories that came to her. "Now our conversations are limited to caring for the children, planning our meals, and, recently, trying to bring a sense of holiness into our house-hold—just as the priesthood teaches."

"You miss her, don't you?"

Bronwyn nodded and blinked back fresh tears. "I betrayed her. I don't know if she can ever forgive me. She smiles and acts as if everything between us is all sunlight and posies, but it isn't."

"They have too much power over us, these men, power that causes more heartache than not," Cordelia said. "We have no voice. Men, supposedly godly men, tell us that we can only be called into glory if we've pleased our husbands enough on earth so they will remember our secret name." She narrowed her eyes. "Do you see the power that gives them over us?"

Bronwyn nodded. "I've known it, but let it happen because I believed the Prophet's revelations." Quick tears rushed to Bron-wyn's eyes. "But what can I do? I have nowhere to go. I have one child, and now another on the way."

"There's another shepherd . . ." Cordelia said, her gaze on the creek again, a slight smile curving the corners of her lips.

"I don't know him."

She turned back to Bronwyn. "Someday you will. You may not recognize his voice right away. But listen with your heart, the deepest, quietest part of your heart. You'll hear his voice." Corde-lia's eyes grew moist. "I promise you. Listen to him; he will tell you which way to go, he will walk with you or carry you if you need him to. Either way, he will never leave you."

"How do you know this?"

Cordelia smiled, gathering up Little Grace, and standing. "Will you bring along the basket, love?" she said to Bronwyn.

Bronwyn stooped to grab hold of the handle.

"Fresh-baked buttermilk biscuits and Cajun sausages, hand-stuffed by Coal, Ruby, and Pearl. Some might find them a bit spicy at first, but I guarantee, your family will love them."

They walked into the opening near the barn, to the shouts

and laughter of the children as they played with their hoops and sticks. Mary Rose and Gabe stepped through the back door, with eyes only for each other.

Bronwyn stopped and caught her breath at the sight. Cordelia touched her hand as she halted. "You asked me how I know about the shepherd," she said, forcing Bronwyn to tear her gaze away from Gabe and Mary Rose. "I know, dearest, because I've heard his voice."

THIRTY-SIX

River Road near Carthage, Illinois

A grizzled, bearded man pushed open the inn's double doors. "Did y'all hear?" Each heavy-booted step and jangle of spurs punctuated his words as he pushed aside a poker game and clambered onto the table. "Old Joe Smith has been arrested! Him and his brother Hyrum. Taken right over to Carthage to be tried for treason. Me'n some others are gettin' together a posse, gonna string 'em up before the trial."

The smoke-clouded room exploded into a cacophony of hoots and whistles. Chairs scooted back as at least a dozen men jumped up to take part.

"It's about time," shouted another man from across the room. "But you can bet yer old boots he won't last out the night. Let's get going. We'll string 'em both up on the spot."

Enid Livingstone's heartbeat increased. She looked across the table at the German immigrants she'd fallen in with on the river road to Nauvoo. She lowered her voice and said to the one sitting next to her, "They talkin' about the Mormon Prophet?"

"Who you talkin' about?" her companion yelled to the grizzled man still standing on the card table. "The one they call the Prophet?"

"Who wants to know?"

"The man sitting next to me."

Everyone in the inn, mostly a motley bunch, turned to look at Enid. She narrowed her eyes in a fixed stare at the man who'd asked the question, lowered her voice, and in an American accent said, "Who cares who wants to know?"

Someone behind him let out a coarse guffaw. "Hey, buddy, no offense. Just thought we might have some Saints among us. Can't be too careful."

Since heading into frontier country, Enid had taken to wearing a disguise: worn and greasy buckskin trousers, homespun shirt, a cloth vest, and a hunter's coat as greasy as the trousers. She wore a wide sash around her waist in the style of a trapper and kept a wide knife, both for protection and show, tucked in the sash, a shooting pouch at her shoulder, and a rifle at her side when riding Sadie. She tucked her flame-colored hair underneath a slouch hat that she kept pulled down to her eyes.

This was one of those times she was glad she'd traded a buckboard for the clothes at a trading post just outside St. Louis. She'd found since leaving the riverboat and heading north on the river road that the West was no place for a lady traveling alone.

Her beloved Foxfire had died before they reached Boston, the voyage proving too arduous. When the horse could no longer stand, Enid had lain down beside her in the small enclosure, cuddling close while she took her last breaths, speaking softly, and even singing, to calm her during the beautiful horse's last hours of life. Enid pulled strings to arrange for a rather unusual burial at sea, with the ship's captain—a man who had known Hosea—officiating at a service that Enid wrote.

She had hitched Sadie to the buckboard she'd brought from Prince Edward Island, but once she reached St. Louis and assessed her options, she traded the buckboard for a saddle, her spinning wheel for the trapper's clothes and a pair of moccasins. In her saddlebag, she'd made room for a woolen skirt and a shawl, which she was saving for the day she'd see Gabe in Nauvoo.

"Who's with us? Who's agin us?" the grizzled man on the table yelled. "You there with all the questions"—Griz pointed to Enid—"you comin' with us?"

Enid swallowed hard and lowered her voice. "Yeah, why not? Nothin' better t' do, I s'pose."

"I got coal outside," someone shouted out. "Yeehaw—let the fun begin."

"I say we tar 'n' feather 'em first off," someone else said.

"Nah, been done to 'em before. I say we string 'em up at the nearest tree, use 'em fer target practice before we slap the hosses out from under 'em."

Enid felt her stomach roil, and swallowed again to keep from losing the jerky she'd eaten the hour before. All she wanted was to get to Nauvoo and the safety of Gabe's arms. She stood, hoping to slip away and get to Sadie at the livery unnoticed, but in their excitement the men seemed to go wild, jostling her as they all tried to get out the inn door at once. Instead of staying at the edge of the mob, she found herself at its center. Her heart thudded harder and she found it difficult to breathe. Not just because she seemed blocked from every direction, but because of the body stench of men who'd gone too long without bathing or taking care of other grooming needs. She grimaced, shuddered, and, holding her breath, stared at the ground for a few moments, trying to get a handle on her fear and her loathing for the mob mentality.

She tried to sidle toward the livery, but a tall man who was missing most of his teeth blocked her way. He grinned as he handed her a chunk of coal. Aware she was being watched, she liberally covered her hands and face, just as the others did.

"Gotta get movin'," Griz said. He'd apparently appointed himself leader, and no one else seemed to mind. "The trial's tomorry. We gotta get to 'em tonight."

Within minutes, Enid had saddled up Sadie, who sensed the tension and nickered nervously. Enid bent low to whisper and calm her.

"Love yer hoss, little boy?" Griz mocked in a high voice, then cursed and laughed as others joined in with the taunt.

Her heart racing for fear of being found out, Enid slouched in her saddle, shrugged, and growled that they ought to get moving before dark.

The posse rode out, at least two dozen strong, and picked up others along the way. Griz goaded the laggers as he rode around the group like a captain of a cattle drive. "We're gonna wipe 'em all from the face of the earth," he said. "This here's just the beginnin'."

"I hear tell we even got the governor on our side this time," someone close to Enid hollered. "First time in history, a governor's thinkin' about ordering the extermination of folks livin' in his state."

It wasn't far to Carthage, but by the time they arrived the mob had grown to some two hundred or more.

Enid sidled Sadie to the back of the group, hoping to take cover in a stand of trees. Her heart beat wildly as the mob chanted outside the jail, below the second-story window where it was said that Joseph Smith and his brother Hyrum were being kept.

"Whatcha doin' way back here, little boy," Griz said, riding up beside her.

Enid's breath caught in her throat.

"I think yer a greenhorn and need to get some experience under that belt. You come on up here now. Once we git the

Smiths and string 'em up, I'm gonna give you the honor of firing the first shot."

He grabbed for Sadie's reins, but the horse reared and kicked.

Griz pulled out a pistol and aimed it at Sadie's head. "I think this here hoss you love so much needs to be taught a lesson in manners."

Enid grabbed her skinning knife, and before the man could take another breath, she moved Sadie close to him with just the pressure of her thighs—and touched the point of the knife to his ribs.

"You so much as cock that weapon, Griz, and you bend over and kiss your horse goodbye," she snarled. "And it won't be yer horse that's headin' to the great beyond, it'll be you." She pressed the knife just deep enough to draw a drop of blood. "Now, I suggest you git up there with yer mob and start doin' yer duty to God and yer country. Ain't that why we're here? To string up the Saints? You better go git started or we'll lose our best opportunity. Go . . . now!" She slapped the rump of Griz's horse, which caused it to leap into the crowd.

Enid sat back in the saddle, stuck the knife back in her sash, and swallowed a smile . . . until she saw what was happening at the front of the mob. The sheriff had come out to try to calm them, but a few surged past him into the jailhouse. She heard their hoots as they raced up the stairs.

"I hope there's more of the vermin in there than just old Joe and Hyrum," someone laughed beside her. "There're likely bodyguards, maybe the top leaders . . ."

"Or," mocked another, "their a-postles. They got twelve of 'em just like in the Bible times."

"Whoever's in there, we'll teach 'em all a lesson they'll not soon ferget," Griz called out from somewhere in the crowd.

"What'd they do?" asked a newcomer.

"Destroyed a printing press that dared write a criticizin' word or two about the Prophet." The speaker drew out the last word with a sneer. "Freedom of the press, that's what all this is about."

Darkness had fallen and, still on horseback, several of the men had lit torches. Their horses whinnied with fear and nervously sidestepped, making the glow from the torches seem alive, moving the men's shadows across the brick jailhouse like they were monsters from a child's fairy-tale book.

Enid's fears grew by the minute. What if Gabe was inside trying to protect his Prophet? What if he was an apostle? She had no way of knowing how far he'd risen within the ranks of Mormonism.

She stared up at the window where the Prophet and his brother were caged. She bit back the urge to cry out that justice should be done, that the trial should be held. Wasn't that the American way?

Shots rang out from inside the building.

"The vermin is shootin' at us," someone within the mob called out. "They got guns. The durn sheriff and his deputies give the Smiths firearms."

The mob roared and moved forward. Sadie danced sideways and nickered, swishing her tail. Enid tried to calm her with pats and whispers, leaning low to avoid being seen, especially by Griz.

More shots rang out.

"Winged 'im," a mobster yelled from inside the jailhouse. "Winged Old Joe hisself."

Another shot. Then another.

Enid imagined the carnage inside and blinked to keep her tears in check.

"Gabe," she breathed. "I hope you're far away from this evil place."

The mob gasped as new movement took place upstairs. More shots. Shattered glass. A body fell backward toward the window.

No, it wasn't a body, she realized. It was someone . . . alive!

Reaching . . . to get out of the window . . . climbing . . . hanging there, facing the mob, as if waiting. To jump? Or to be shot?

"It's Old Joe, sure 'nuff," shouted Griz. "Fancy that, just hangin' there waitin' to be picked off."

The mob jeered. "Let's see how long he lasts," someone called out.

Enid stared. Every fiber inside her wanted to help the man. She was trained to heal the injured, to care for the dying. It didn't matter who he was or what he'd done, whether he was a prophet or an imposter. All she knew was that she had to get to him.

She pressed Sadie gently with her thighs and the horse responded, slowly making her way forward.

But before Sadie had moved more than a few steps, a rifle shot rang out. The man they called the Prophet dropped with a thud to the ground.

"He ain't dead, that son of a gun," someone else yelled. "He's still a-movin'!"

Enid heard the sounds of a body being dragged across the ground. Again, she tried to make her way through the mob, though overcome with a sick feeling that it was too late anyway.

More shots sounded. And still more. Until she thought they would never end.

Finally, silence reigned . . . until one last voice called out: "We ain't stoppin' with these two. We're headin' out to Nauvoo to kill the rest of the vermin. And we won't stop until every last Saint is dead."

She turned Sadie away from the crowd with their bright torches, nudging the horse slowly so they wouldn't be noticed. When they reached the outer edge of the mob and moved into the cover of darkness, she urged Sadie to a trot, almost afraid to breathe until they were a safe distance from the crowd.

They reached a small rise where she halted the mare and

looked back. The torches glowed against the black velvet night. But even from this distance, she heard the triumphant cheers of the mob.

Enid slid from Sadie's saddle and bent low over the ground. She retched until nothing remained in her stomach.

Enid stopped at a creek outside Nauvoo to scrub the coal dust from her face and hands. She quickly pulled off her buckskins and donned the long wool skirt and slipped the shawl over the trapper's homespun shirt. She retied the sash around her waist and tucked in the long-bladed knife for protection, then shook her hair loose from the slouch hat and tossed the hat in the brush. She had no shoes but the beaded moccasins, but gave no thought to the strange apparel. She had one goal: to carry the news of what she'd witnessed to the people of Nauvoo and ask them how to find Gabe.

It was nearly midnight when Gabe woke to the sound of horse hooves pounding the road leading to the farmhouse. Raids had picked up in recent days, and his heartbeat increased as the rider came closer. He swung his legs over the side of the bed, reached for his rifle, and hurried to the window, pulling back the curtain to peer into the moonlit night.

"Is there trouble, Gabe?" Mary Rose whispered as she sat up in bed. She reached for her duster and, slipping it on, came over to stand beside him.

"Looks like a single rider. But more may be approaching from behind."

The figure was closer now, and Gabe could see both rider and horse more clearly. He frowned. "It appears to be a woman."

Mary Rose stepped closer to the window and followed his gaze. "She must be in trouble—out alone at this time of night."

He nodded as the rider halted her horse in front of the house and slid from the saddle. He didn't let go of the rifle. In these days of unrest, he trusted no one.

Mary Rose had picked up a lamp, and he nodded for her to follow. They stepped into the hallway just as a loud pounding sounded at the front door. Lights immediately glowed down the row of bedrooms. Bronwyn stepped out, holding Little Grace.

Coal and the twins tumbled into the hallway, rubbing their eyes. "What's happened, Papa?" Ruby said, running to Gabe.

The pounding at the door grew more frantic.

"I want you children to stay up here until I tell you it's safe to come down. Coal, will you see that they do?"

The boy nodded solemnly. "Yes, Papa."

"Mary Rose, I'll need you to hold the lamp." She nodded.

"I'm coming too," Bronwyn said. "If it's a woman in trouble, it's probably womenfolk she'll need to talk to."

Though he worried about the safety of the two women he loved most in the world, he couldn't argue with Bronwyn's reasoning.

Gabe started down the stairs, Mary Rose directly behind him, Bronwyn to one side. He glanced back at the children at the top of the stairs, their faces white with fear.

Then a voice on the other side of the door cried, "Gabe! Are you there? Please, come. Hurry!"

There was no mistaking the distinctive accent, the lilting timbre of the voice he'd known so well from childhood. His heart quickened.

"Enid," he breathed, and taking the lamp from Mary Rose, made his way to the door.

EPILOGUE

I seek no copy now of life's first half:
Leave here the pages with long musing curled,
And write me new my future's epigraph,
New angel mine, unhoped for in the world!
                              —Elizabeth Barrett Browning

Nauvoo, Illinois
February 1, 1846

Mary Rose waded through ankle-deep snow to the picket gate in front of the two-story mansion that once had been the hub of Prophet Joseph Smith's Church activities. Her heavy woolen gloves made the latch difficult to open, and as she worked it, her breath came out in foggy spurts.

The gate opened at last, and she hurried up the snow-covered walkway to rap on the front door. After a moment, she heard footsteps on the other side. When the door opened, Emma Smith stood before her with a composed smile.

"Thank you for coming—especially in this storm. I didn't know if you'd received my note."

"I had hoped to see you again anyway before we leave—"

Emma waved her fingers as if she didn't have time for the niceties of a social visit and then quickly ushered Mary Rose into the parlor. Dying embers glowed in the fireplace, but Emma made no move to stoke the fire or to add new logs. The furniture was covered as if the family was ready to vacate the house. A stack of small trunks and valises stood by the doorway into the entry hall.

"I'm sorry I can't fix tea—or even invite you to sit for a visit. But Joseph Junior and the other children will be here to fetch me shortly. We're going into hiding until the danger is past."

"I'm so sorry about what's happened . . . that you're not going with us."

"None of that matters now," Emma said as she crossed the room to a small rolltop desk in the corner, opened a drawer, and drew out an envelope. "I found this while going through my husband's papers," she said. "I thought it might be of interest to you."

Mary Rose drew off her gloves, placed them in her cloak pocket, and took the envelope from Emma, flipping it to the back to read the return information, which stated it was from the Office of Land Registry, London, England.

She looked up at Emma with surprise. For years she'd been trying to find out information about the family estate and had been unable to discover any detail about the transfer.

Fingers trembling, Mary Rose opened the envelope and pulled out the letter. She skimmed through the legal descriptions and history of the land, and then her gaze came to a dead halt on a sentence three paragraphs down.

. . . regarding the deed to the properties belonging to the Earl of Salisbury, otherwise known as Langdon Spencer Ashley III, it is our duty to inform you that your organization has no legal claim to legitimate ownership . . .

Mary Rose looked up at Emma. "Did anyone tell my grandfather about this?"

"Joseph didn't discuss such matters with me," Emma said.

Emma gestured toward the desk. "My writing materials are there, should you wish to respond. I can post the missive for you once we've left Nauvoo. I doubt that any mail can get out now that the siege is about to begin." She stepped closer. "You could take your children, leave now . . ."

"You're advising me to leave the Church, leave my husband . . . ?"

"The church that Brigham now leads is not Joseph's, not the true Church. By throwing in with a false prophet, Gabriel is putting your family in grave danger. Brigham is leading thousands of Saints out of Nauvoo—but he doesn't know where he's taking them." She moved her gaze to the window and didn't speak for a moment. Then she said, "And in this weather. I daresay, hundreds will die because of his folly."

Mary Rose clutched the letter close. "You've given me a gift beyond measure in its importance."

"From our previous conversations I thought it might be so."

"I will never forget what you've done for me."

Emma smiled and pulled her into a quick embrace. "God be with you, dear, no matter your choice." Then, releasing Mary Rose, she added, "You must go now, before you're seen with the likes of me. I'm known as a troublemaker—a symbol of dissension among Brigham's Saints." She looked pleased with the distinction.

"'Tis a reputation I enjoy as well," Mary Rose said with a laugh.

"I don't care who sees me here with you. You've been a good friend to me."

"And you to me," Emma said.

With a nod, Mary Rose pulled up her hood and headed into what had now turned into a blizzard.

"Can you find your way home?" Emma called after her when she reached the gate.

Her gloved hand on the latch, Mary Rose turned. "To England?"

Emma laughed. "That too. No, I meant because of the storm—will you find your way back to the farm? Maybe you should stay in town. Liam and Eliza Hale haven't yet left. I know they'd welcome you."

"Gabe drove me here in the wagon—wanted to try out the heavy canvas cover he designed for the exodus. He's waiting in the livery."

"Speaking of design," Emma called after her. "It's a shame he didn't get to complete the temple . . ."

"Aye," Mary Rose said with a small wave of her gloved hand, "'Tis."

Mary Rose stared at the frozen river in front of the oxen team. For three days she'd wrestled with her decision. Even now, she could pull the wagon out of the long train and, in the confusion of the mass exodus, disappear without being noticed until it was too late for anyone to follow or bring her back.

Wrapped in heavy buffalo hide blankets, Mary Rose, Bronwyn, and Grandfather's widow, Cordelia, sat on the wagon bench of the big Conestoga, and all the children were in the back of the wagon, tucked beneath their own buffalo hides. A canopy of stars glittered in the clear midnight sky; the temperatures had been steadily dropping since sundown. It was well below freezing, and had been for days. The Mississippi River was frozen solid—at least that's what the lead scouts claimed. Mary Rose worried that though the ice had held for riders on horseback, it might not support the hundreds of wagons that would make the crossing that night.

One flick of the whip above the beasts' backs, one tug of the reins, and she could climb the embankment and head south on the river road to St. Louis, bypassing the mobs in Nauvoo.

Her heart beat rapidly as she imagined it . . . imagined taking them all home to England with her.

Mary Rose looked back along the long line of wagons and livestock and caught Gabe's glance as he rode up from checking the one hundred wagons under his leadership. He'd become an expert horseman since Enid's arrival. Even now, she rode proudly beside him, her flaming red hair silvered by the starlight.

"Mama," Ruby called from inside the back of the wagon. "What's this little trunk got in it? Is it food? I'm hungry." The sounds of the trunk opening carried toward Mary Rose.

"Uh-oh," Pearl called out. "I thought you said we couldn't bring any books. This little trunk is full of books."

Gabe rode up beside the wagon bench. "Books?"

"Yes, Papa," Ruby said. "Mama's big Bible, and Psalter, some journals and some really big other books. Novels, I think. Maybe some poems. Mama, somebody must have put this trunk in the wagon by mistake."

"No, dear," Mary Rose said, her eyes on Gabe's. "They're mine."

Gabe stared at her for a moment. "Are they more important than a child?" he said. "What if the weight of those books is what pushes the weight of this wagon over its limit?" His horse danced sideways and snorted, its exhaled breath white in the freezing air.

"You know how important my books are to me, Gabe . . . all of them."

"Your last vestiges of English life should be left behind, Mary Rose. Your mother's Bible must weigh five pounds, and you've read the Jane Austen novels enough times to have them memorized. I can understand bringing your journals, but everything else needs to go. Think of it as a sacrifice—one of many that all of us have had to make." He rode to the back of the wagon and asked Coal to hand him the trunk.

"Wait," Ruby said. "I'll get out Mama's journals." Scuffling sounds ensued as the children handed the trunk to Gabe. A moment later, Mary Rose heard the sound of hoofbeats as Gabe rode off to dispose of her treasures.

She tried to hold back her tears, but they came anyway. Bronwyn reached for her gloved hand with her own, giving her a look of understanding. "I'm sorry," she whispered. Cordelia looked as mad as one of the banty roosters in a cage in the wagon in front of them.

"Papa is right," Mary Rose said to the children. "We've all had to make sacrifices, and this is one that may save our lives. You children have had to leave things behind you cared for, and have pleased your papa and me with your willingness to pack as we asked."

Within minutes, Gabe—as captain of the first brigade of wagons to cross—rode to the lead wagon and shouted the order to move out. The first oxen team stepped onto the ice, skittish as their hooves slipped and the big animals tried to find their footing.

There was no time to consider the frightening cracks and pops of breaking ice as the wagon wheels continued to roll, or the even more precarious start of the second wagon as visible rifts in the ice showed near shore.

Mary Rose's turn came next. Gabe had stationed himself beside the river on the eastern shore. He met her eyes as she drove the oxen team to the river's edge. She could still turn the team rapidly to the left, head south . . .

Half standing, she kept her eyes on Gabe's as she lifted the whip, readying it to pop over the team's backs. Her heart seemed to hang in eternity as she searched his face. Then he gave her that crooked half-smile she adored, and his eyes shone with a pure and precious love, just as they had on another starlit night long ago, that night aboard the *Sea Hawk*.

She cracked the whip above the team of oxen and headed straight down the embankment and onto the frozen river. Bronwyn and Cordelia gasped as the hooves slipped and the beasts snorted their nervous displeasure. Mary Rose tried to ignore the cracking sounds beneath the heavy wagon and flicked the whip again, to keep the team moving.

Behind them, Gabe shouted to the next wagon in line, and then the next, and the next. Within minutes, Mary Rose drove the team up the embankment on the far side of the river.

"Whoa-howdy." Coal whistled from behind Mary Rose. "That's some fancy drivin'!" The children had lifted the canvas curtain between the driver's seat and the covered bed, and when Mary Rose looked back, she grinned at the six curious and proud little faces staring back at her. Coal, now twelve, had grown tall and lean and had a bright and curious mind; he said he wanted to be sea captain on a clipper ship someday, just like Captain Hosea Livingstone. The twins were now nine, and loved taking care of their little brothers and sister—Little Grace, now five, and the two latest, Bronwyn's Joseph Gabriel, born exactly a month to the day before Mary Rose's Langdon Spencer Ashley MacKay, a little cherub with a round face and reddish hair.

The scout near the lead wagon gave the signal for the wagons to keep moving. Just before she flicked the reins, Mary Rose looked back, watching the long train winding its way across the frozen river, across the pale ice and starlit snow. Behind the train, Nauvoo was in flames—from the inner city to the outlying farms. The MacKay farm was likely among those either aflame or already a pile of ashes.

I will give you the oil of joy for ashes. The words came back to her . . . perhaps learned long ago at her mother's knee or, perhaps, simply hidden someplace in the depths of her heart.

"Mama, forgive me for I have sinned," came a contrite little voice from behind Mary Rose. The voice belonged to Ruby.

"Me too," said Pearl.

Coal let out a deep sigh. "Me too."

Frowning, Mary Rose handed the reins to Bronwyn and turned in her seat. Instead of looking ready to cry—as she expected—they looked ready to explode with laughter.

"What is it?"

Ruby pulled *Pride and Prejudice* from beneath her blankets and handed it to Mary Rose. Then Pearl did the same with Mary Rose's treasured collection of Elizabeth Barrett Browning poetry, and with a wide grin, Coal handed her two more Jane Austen novels.

Then Ruby reached under her blankets and drew out the Psalter, Pearl did the same with the journals, and Coal, his eyes sparkling, reached under his covers once more and, with great dramatic fanfare, pulled out the treasured Bible.

"Oh, children!" she cried, and then gave each sweet face a kiss. She touched each book with reverence, her eyes filling, especially over the worn journal where she had carefully kept the yellowed newspaper clippings of Elizabeth Barrett Browning's poetry. Then she reached for her mother's Bible and held it close before reluctantly tucking it beneath the buffalo robe. The weight of it on her lap brought her comfort, reminding her of the long-ago and faraway places in her heart.

She gazed up at the starlit sky, thinking about the manor house and the estate grounds. She couldn't remember the exact words, but some Gabe said to her soon after they met came to her:

"Someone with your spirit and gumption and intelligence and heaven-knows-what-else that's inside that beautiful head of yours

doesn't need an ancestral home. It has little, make that nothing, to do with who you are or how you'll make your way in life." Then he'd laughed and added, *"When I saw you climbing over the driver's bench on the landau to save that little ruffian, I knew that nothing, absolutely nothing, would ever stand in your way to get at what you want."*

She chuckled, stood again, and flicked the whip over the backs of the oxen she'd secretly named Brigham and Joseph.

Gabe didn't know how right he'd been.

Prince Edward Island
March 18, 1846

Hosea halted the horse-drawn buggy in front of the small farm that Enid's parents had given them as a wedding gift. Smoke rose from the chimney, and the glow of lamplight filled the windows.

He carefully lifted his legs from the seat, stood to regain his balance, and reached for his walking stick. Then slowly, he limped to the front door and knocked.

After a moment, an older man opened the door and peered at him. It was Enid's father, Jacob.

"Sir," Hosea said, "you probably don't recognize me . . ."

"Who is it?" Enid's mother, Miriam, came to the door to stand next to her husband.

There was no sign of recognition in either of their faces.

"I'm Hosea Livingstone," he said, his voice low and filled with sudden sadness. "Enid's husband."

Jacob scrutinized Hosea's face and then shook his head. "Ye cannot be. He died several years ago. A terrible tragedy, our daughter suffered when it happened."

"I am your daughter's husband," he said.

Miriam stepped closer. "Our daughter is a widow."

"I was captain of the *Sea Hawk* when I was taken overboard by a rogue wave. I don't know how it happened, but I washed ashore on the coast of Maine. It's taken me some time to heal."

"Ye don't look like our son-in-law," Miriam said. "He was taller, a much bigger man."

"Please believe me," Hosea said. "I need to speak to Enid. I want to explain . . ."

"If ye're truly who ye say, why were ye gone so long?" Jacob still blocked the door.

Hosea's weak limbs were about to give out. He clung to the walking stick to stay upright. "I was injured," he said. "I couldn't walk, or even stand, for over a year. A fisherman and his wife found me, nursed me back to health—spiritually and physically." He reached into his jacket pocket for a handkerchief and mopped his face.

"The man needs to sit down," Jacob said to his wife.

She didn't look too keen about letting Hosea into their house, but she stepped aside and he entered. A feeling of warmth invaded him as he glanced about the room, taking in all the familiar furnishings.

"Please, sit down," Jacob said. "I'm still not convinced ye're who you say, but ye look like ye need to rest yer legs."

"Would ye like a cup of tea?" Without awaiting an answer, Miriam bustled into the kitchen.

Jacob sat across from Hosea, still studying his face.

"The scars . . ." he started. "I know my face is disfigured . . . And I've lost weight, a lot of weight."

Jacob held up a hand. "If ye're Hosea, 'tis not the physical that's changed so much, but something else. Something I see in yer eyes."

Hosea laughed. "Aye, 'tis my heart that has changed the most. It needed more healing than all the broken bones, abrasions, and deep wounds put together."

Jacob leaned forward. "Just now, when ye laughed . . ."

Hosea nodded as Miriam came into the room to serve tea. She noticed the expression on her husband's face and quickly set down her tray and went to stand behind him.

"I saw that space between yer teeth. The place for pipe holdin'."

"I haven't smoked a pipe in close to five years." Hosea rubbed the edges of his upper teeth.

Miriam caught her hand to her mouth. "'Tis you, indeed." She stared at him, dumbfounded, for several seconds. Then she went over to Hosea and, not letting him stand, wrapped her arms around his shoulders and kissed him soundly on the cheek. "Ye've come back from the dead."

"Glory be," Jacob said in awe. "Glory be!"

Hosea basked in their wonder, letting their warmth and joy seep into his heart, then he leaned forward. "I must speak with Enid. Is she here?"

Jacob and Miriam exchanged glances, then turned back to him. "She left a long time ago. She went to find Gabriel MacKay."

Hosea closed his eyes and prayed for grace and strength. "Did he send for her?"

"No," Miriam said.

"But she knew he had gone to Nauvoo," Jacob added. "That Mormon settlement on the Mississippi."

"I know of it." Hosea's voice was little more than a whisper. "Have you heard anything from her? Has she written to say how she is?"

"Aye, that she has," Jacob said, lifting an eyebrow. "Apparently, the rumors about plural wives among the Mormons is true. She said Gabe has taken two wives."

"Mary Rose? Did she mention a Mary Rose?"

"Aye, 'tis the name of his first wife," Miriam said. "Did you know her?"

"I married them aboard the *Sea Hawk* just before we reached

Boston." And just before he ordered his dear friend out of his life. He hung his head in shame, remembering his anger.

For a moment only the ticking of the grandfather clock at the end of the hall filled the silence. Then Jacob said, "The last letter she posted said that mobs planned to attack Nauvoo and run them out of the state. She said she was heading west with the group, though no one knew where they might settle."

"We've been so worried," Miriam said. "A traveler from the States visited the island not long ago with word that Nauvoo burned to the ground. All the Mormons have been run out of the state or killed." Her eyes filled. "We don't even know if Enid is alive . . ."

Hosea's weakness set in full force, and for a moment he couldn't move, much less think. The idea that Enid was with Gabe, and was with this group, tore at his insides. He closed his eyes, lifted his heart in prayer, and after a few minutes felt a deep peace settle his thoughts.

"Are ye all right, then?"

He opened his eyes to see that Miriam's worry had deepened the lines in her face. "Ye are welcome to stay and continue your recuperation here." She gave him a gentle smile. "After all this is your farmhouse."

"Thank you," Hosea said. "Perhaps the night to regain my strength. Then I must be on my way."

Jacob leaned forward. "Where will ye be headin' then?"

"I will leave in the morning at first light." Hosea reached for his walking stick, running his fingers over the tau cross that Giovanni had carved near its leather hand-strap. "I will head to the States to search for Enid, and I'll not stop until I find her."

AUTHOR'S NOTE

Dear Reader:

When I began writing *The Sister Wife*, I was immediately drawn into the "what ifs" an author often asks herself as her characters come to life: What if a young woman named Mary Rose Ashley falls in love with a wonderful young man named Gabriel MacKay and, after a romantic whirlwind courtship aboard a clipper ship bound for America, they marry?

A historical romance? Most definitely. But with a twist. What if Mary Rose, who's traveling with her grandfather, has recently become a member of the fledgling frontier church known as the Latter-day Saints? What if, when she marries Gabe, neither knows about the revelation that Joseph Smith will claim just a short time hence: the practice of polygamy, especially the requirement of a Saint in good standing to marry multiple wives in order to make it into the highest level of heaven? What if the other woman Gabe is required to marry is also Mary Rose's best friend?

An interesting bundle of questions, to be sure, and with more than enough intrigue to keep me dying to find out what would happen each morning when I sat down at the computer to write.

In addition, this book allowed me to dig into the history behind this practice that still gets so much attention when it is brought to light in our modern world. My historian husband, whose areas of expertise include American history and the history of the American West, and I have spent years studying this group and its beginnings. My sources include the acclaimed *No Man Knows My History: The Life of Joseph Smith* by Fawn Brodie; *Tell It All*, the original manuscript written by Fanny Stenhouse (married for twenty years to Brigham Young); *The Life and Confessions of John D. Lee* (Brigham Young's adopted son, who was executed for his part in the Mountain Meadows massacre); *Orrin Porter Rockwell* by Harold Schindler; the complete works of Patrick O'Brian (primarily *Master and Commander*); and many others on the history of the American West. The quotes found in Chapter 21 in this book are taken directly from the written document on plural marriage by Joseph Smith.

One of the most fascinating discoveries in my research was a handwritten copy of the Missouri Executive Order 44, also known as the extermination order, issued on October 27, 1838, by Missouri governor Lilburn Boggs. The order was in response to what Boggs termed "open and avowed defiance of the laws, and of having made war upon the people of this State." It declared that "the Mormons must be treated as enemies, and must be exterminated or driven from the State if necessary for the public peace—their outrages are beyond all description." The order was formally rescinded in 1976.

I hadn't gotten far into the story when a much bigger and even more intriguing picture began to surface: a portrait of God's dealings with us, his errant children. I focused especially on his unfailing love for us, the fact that nothing we do (and he knows the worst about us) can ever separate us from his love, his mercy, his forgiveness, his grace.

I began to look up passages in the Bible about God's faithfulness and landed in the Old Testament book of Hosea (which gives us a wonderful story of God's love for his people). I came across the following:

> When Israel was only a child, I loved him. I called out,
>   "My son!". . .
> But when others called him,
>   he ran off and left me.
> He worshiped the popular sex gods,
>   he played at religion with toy gods.
> Still, I stuck with him. . . .
>   I rescued him from human bondage,
> But he never acknowledged my help,
>   never admitted I was the one pulling his wagon,
> That I lifted him, like a baby, to my cheek,
>   that I bent down to feed him.
>
>   Hosea 11:1–4 (*The Message*)

After studying these verses, I realized the story in *The Sister Wife* had broader implications than the complications of my characters. I thought about people today who are caught up in one kind of bondage or another, whether it is within the confines of a cult, a destructive lifestyle, or the worship of "toy gods" such as greed or power.

It hit me that this is the deeper story in the Brides of Gabriel series, that of God's great and tender love for his people, a tenderness akin to that of a mother for her infant.

My characters have a long journey ahead, but their journey will parallel, metaphorically, God's journey with us, his unconditional love for us, and his great and awesome faithfulness. At the heart of the "marriage issue" is this:

I will betroth you to me forever;
   I will betroth you in righteousness and justice,
   in love and compassion.
I will betroth you in faithfulness,
   and you will acknowledge the Lord.
            Hosea 2:19–20 (New International Version)

In the end, that is the truth behind the Brides of Gabriel. It's the truth, the Good News, we all need to hear and tuck in our hearts.

I also want to add a note to sharp-eyed readers, Victorian poetry sleuths, and history buffs: Many of the verses of Elizabeth Barrett Browning's poetry used in this work were not published in book form during the time period of *The Sister Wife*, but it is known that, in 1824, a leading London newspaper, the *Globe and Traveler*, began printing her poetry. She also wrote for several magazines during this period. For the purposes of this work, I choose to believe that Mary Rose could have had access to the *Globe and Traveler* and other periodicals before the more famous poems were published in book form.

I would love to hear from you. Feel free to drop by my web-site—www.dianenoble.com—where you will find more information about the historical research that provided the foundation for this book. You will also find photos and narrative as my historian husband and I follow the same trail taken by my characters in Book Two as they make their way to the Great Salt Lake Valley. Don't forget to sign my guestbook. You can also look me up on Facebook. I read and respond to every e-mail and value your input.

With all joy and peace,

Diane Noble

DISCUSSION QUESTIONS

1. Mary Rose introduces Gabe to the Mormon faith even though she isn't sure of it herself. Why do you think she waits so long to tell Gabe that the "miracle" of Bronwyn's baby's birth was preceded by herbal medications and earnest prayer from someone other than Brigham Young?

2. Do you think God listens and responds to the prayers of those whose beliefs are not in agreement with your own? Why, or why not?

3. Do you agree with Mary Rose's choice to stay with Gabe after his marriage to Bronwyn? Did she have a choice? Did he?

4. What do you think motivates Mary Rose to agree to the consummation of Gabe's marriage to Bronwyn? Is it only because she believes that if she doesn't, she won't spend

eternity with the baby she has lost? Or is there a deeper motivation, perhaps hidden from her awareness? What do you think it might be?

5. Do you see a connection between Mary Rose's acceptance of her circumstances, her seemingly enduring love for Gabe, and a contemporary woman who might remain in a dysfunctional relationship because she thinks she has no other choice? Why, or why not?

6. Mary Rose is a reluctant Saint from the beginning. What do you think most influences her choice to remain with the group and embrace the teachings of the Prophet, even as Joseph Smith's revelation about plural marriage breaks her heart?

7. What in Mary Rose's background could have helped her recognize and stand up against the false teachings? Do you think she has an "inner plumb line" that causes her to question these teachings?

8. As a boy, Joseph Smith asked God to reveal to him the one true church that he had established on earth. Is this a legitimate question for us to ask today? Can a person only know God by belonging to a church? Why, or why not? What are the inherent dangers of a leader proclaiming that his (or her) way is the only way or that his particular brand of religion is the only one?

9. Mormonism teaches that man can become a god in the next life through good works on earth. How does this teaching correlate with Genesis 3:5 in which the serpent says to Eve, "For God knows that when you eat of it [the fruit from the

forbidden tree] your eyes will be opened, and you will be like God . . ."?

10. LDS historians say that Joseph Smith's revelation about plural marriage had to do with taking care of the widows and orphans in a violent society where women had no protection or means of support without a husband or father. Please reread Chapter 21 in this book, which describes Smith's revelation on the subject, keeping in mind that the author used his direct quotes as his dialogue. Do you think today's explanation for polygamy is in agreement with the original revelation?

  Historically, only those men in positions of power and those with the means to support a large household took multiple wives. Why do you think the revelation was made after the practice had already begun? Do you think that rumors of polygamy had anything to do with the persecution of Mormons by outsiders?

11. Ultimately, *The Sister Wife* is a book about relationships. Is it possible, in your opinion, to extend forgiveness, grace, and mercy to a friend who has betrayed you? Is it possible to love this friend again? In your own life—no matter the offense—does it matter if a friend *asks* for forgiveness? Can you forgive anyway?

12. What about a spouse's betrayal with someone outside marriage in today's world? If this happened to you, do you think it would be possible to extend mercy, forgiveness, and grace to the one who betrayed you? Can such a tragic break in the relationship ever be repaired? Do you think it's possible to incorporate this prayer into actual practice:

Forgive us our trespasses, as we forgive those who trespass against us?

Take a few minutes to think of someone you need to forgive . . . or of someone you need to go to for forgiveness. Consider God's mercy, grace, and love toward you and ask him to help you extend that same compassion toward the one he has brought to your mind, or the strength to act if you are the one in need of forgiveness.

ACKNOWLEDGMENTS

I owe a debt of gratitude to the following:

Cynthia DiTiberio, my editor at HarperOne, for catching and holding onto the dream that became Brides of Gabriel and remaining passionate about it from our first conversation through the day I turned in Book One in the series. Thank you, Cindy!

Joel Kneedler, my agent, for your expert direction, astute career guidance, and calm spirit that keep me focused (and sane!). This book wouldn't have happened without you. You're the best, my friend!

Lorin Oberweger, editorial consultant, cheerleader, and friend, for your expert advice and support throughout the writing of *The Sister Wife*. Thank you for being there for me.

Jim and Tori Thomas, for providing this writing gnome a place to write her tome! And to think you decorated C2 just for me. Your Western memorabilia couldn't have been a more appropriate setting in which to write this historical novel. You two are the greatest!

My daughter Amy Martinez, whose daily phone calls never fail to uplift me. Amy, you are a portrait of love in action. It was never more evident than when you and Mark dropped everything to fly across the country to be with me at Mom's passing midway through the writing of this book. Also, a heartfelt thanks to my daughter Melinda Head, whose love and prayers are always with me—and who's always ready to celebrate a book's completion with delightful spa days spent together!

A special thanks to dear friends Linda Udell, Marihelen Goodwin, and Tom and Susan Johnson. Your love never wavered, your prayers never ceased, and your encouragement gave me the strength I needed to continue writing even during my journey through some of life's most difficult emotional places. I love you all!

Big hugs of thanks to my NC family. I'm blessed by their love and their amazing feedback as my first readers—especially my sister-in-law Kathi and my brother Dennis, who also keeps my mind sharp and fingers flying, and Kristin, whose unsinkable spirit always inspires me. Can't wait until *Leap of Faith* publishes and we take our first skydiving "leap" together.

Last, but not least, a heart of gratitude to my husband, Tom, resident historian and chef extraordinaire, whose love and support are without equal. Your historical expertise and literary feedback bring my novels to life, and your knowledge of American history, especially the history of the American West, provides the best possible backdrop detail for my stories. Thank you, especially, for encouraging me to attend the Oregon-California Trails Association meeting with you in Yuma last spring—where the seeds of writing another historical series set in the American West took root.

**Read on
for an exciting preview
of the next book
in the Brides of Gabriel series . . .**

June 28, 1842

Bronwyn twirled in front of the mirror in the brides' room, checking the back of the elegant gown loaned to her by Brigham's wife Mary Ann. Pale blue with ivory lace, it set off her sapphire eyes, her luxurious ebony hair, and skin the color of English clotted cream—though she would never admit to thinking of her physical appearance with such romantic terms.

She almost laughed as she twirled again, enjoying her image in the mirror, skirts and petticoats billowing. She leaned closer to the mirror, pleased to see the sparkle of merriment in her eyes, the glow of anticipation in her expression. After all, it was the day she would be sealed to Gabe for eternity. Why not think of herself with a romantic notion or two?

A twinge of guilt pressed against her heart, but she quickly turned her thoughts to Gabe and the look she hoped to see in his eyes as they knelt, facing each other, and said their vows . . . which made the feelings of guilt return.

Mary Rose. Her dearest friend in the world. How could it be possible that she was about to become Gabe's second wife when she loved his first wife like a sister?

She pinched her cheeks until they were the hue of wild roses, thinking about the plan she and Mary Rose had devised to please the Church leaders, keep Gabe in good standing, and allow her to remain part of the family—just as she and Griffin and Little Grace always had been.

It would work, she told herself, drawing in a deep breath. It had to. For Mary Rose's sake, especially. It worried her that Mary Rose hadn't seemed well earlier that morning, and she planned to pull her aside and reassure her that never would she try to supplant her in Gabe's affections.

She only hoped that Mary Rose would arrive with Gabriel well before the ceremony started so they could spend those few moments alone.

She backed away from the mirror as other brides arrived to ready themselves for the ceremony. As the door opened and closed, the jangle and rattle of horse-drawn carriages and the low bursts of chatter carried toward her.

As the women joined her, it became apparent that the excited voices that had drifted in from outside came from the grooms, not the brides. Most of the women appeared subdued, some of the younger ones even frightened.

As the time neared for all to have arrived, Bronwyn went to the door of the meetinghouse and peered out at the street. Carriages and horses were lined up, empty of their passengers, but there was no sign of Gabe and Mary Rose.

One of the brides, a sad-looking young woman with red-rimmed eyes and trembling hands, spotted Bronwyn and slipped away from a group of three brides.

"I heard you're marrying Brother MacKay," she said.

Bronwyn couldn't help the little smile of pride that tugged the corner of her lips upward. She nodded.

"I've noticed him before. He's a fine-looking man."

"'Tis true." Still standing at the door, Bronwyn let her gaze drift away from the woman's probing scrutiny back to the street, thinking about Gabe, how she'd admired him from the first moment she saw him, long before he and Mary Rose fell in love.

That first moment . . . the day they boarded the *Sea Hawk* in Liverpool and Coal climbed the topmast. He'd perched there, frightening the wits out of every passenger and seaman on deck. Gabe had climbed up after him as if he'd been born with the strength and humor needed to rescue errant boys.

She could never have imagined how their lives would intertwine. Griffin, the man she would love forever, had been at her side, and they were expecting their first child. She didn't imagine then the loss that would soon break her heart. Neither could she have foreseen that one day—this day—she would become Gabriel MacKay's bride, his second. And that his first wife, Mary Rose, would have become the dearest friend she'd ever known. Oh, Mary Rose, hurry . . . ! She couldn't walk down the aisle without her. She hadn't asked, but she wanted Mary Rose to walk with her to Gabriel, their hands clasped in a silent agreement of sisterhood and faithfulness to their plan.

"Where is he?" The woman interrupted Bronwyn's thoughts. "Your Gabriel, I mean," she added, noticing Bronwyn's confused expression. "Shouldn't he be here by now?"

She snapped back to the present. Her Gabriel? "He . . . he should have been here by now. He felt things were getting awkward with Mary Ro— with his first wife and that it might be easier if . . ." Taking a deep breath, she began again. "Brigham came for Little Grace and me, and his wife Mary Ann helped me dress for the wedding at their home. She's keeping Little Grace for me while I—" She stopped to listen as she heard another carriage round the corner.

She flew to the door and stepped outside, just in time to see it rattle by without stopping.

She turned when Brigham came up behind her, his forehead furrowed in a deep frown. He had no need to ask the obvious question. Bronwyn shook her head. "I don't know what's keeping Brother Gabriel."

Brigham pulled out a pocket watch. "It's not like him to be late." He gave Bronwyn a piercing look. "I suggest you return to the brides' room and await your groom. We'll start as soon as Brother Gabriel and Sister Mary Rose arrive."

"I'll need a few minutes to talk to Sister Mary Rose before we begin."

"Unless they arrive soon, there won't be time." He smiled. "There will be plenty of time afterward for sister-wife talk, believe me, Sister Bronwyn."

He took her elbow to guide her back into the meetinghouse, reached for the door, and opened it so she could enter.

Bronwyn stopped just short of entering.

Mary Rose.

It took only a half heartbeat for Bronwyn's mind to whirl with the possibilities. The pregnancy. The swollen, distraught look of Mary Rose that morning. The sounds of weeping in the night.

What if . . . ? She didn't complete the thought, remembering the weariness like unto death itself the morning before Little Grace was born.

Bronwyn took a step backward, almost knocking Brigham off balance; then she turned, gathered her full skirts, and hurried toward the street. "I'm going to find them," she called over her shoulder. "You can start without us."

She didn't bother to stop to ask for approval—or even to see what was surely a look of stunned disapproval on Brigham's face. Instead, she turned her attention to the unattended carriages and wagons lined up in front of the meetinghouse.

She made a beeline toward a lone horse tethered to a hitching post just beyond the last carriage—a gleaming black beast with an arched neck, sleek head, and intelligent eyes. As she placed a foot in the stirrup and swung her leg over the hand-tooled leather and silver saddle, her dress bunching up to her knees, she swallowed a smile. She would have laughed if she hadn't been so worried about Mary Rose. In the old days, she and Mary Rose would have giggled together over such a sight.

She heard a familiar voice shouting from the front of the meetinghouse. Without a glance toward the man, she leaned close to the horse's neck. "Go, boy," she cried, pressing her heels into his flanks. She hoped the beast would respond to the voice of someone other than his master—especially since it was his master doing the shouting, commanding him to halt.

But the horse—the pride of Brigham's stables—appeared to be quite content with Bronwyn on his back. He took off like a fox after prey, and as soon as they were on the open road, she let him take the lead. He seemed to sense the urgency and galloped with hurricane force toward the MacKay farm.

As they raced along, Bronwyn leaning low over the horse's neck, she watched the road ahead, hoping to see the telltale dust of a carriage coming toward her. She had no desire to return to the meetinghouse to go through with the marriage, but she wanted to know her friend was well. Right now, that was all that mattered.

They reached the top of a small knoll, and in the distance lay the farm. She slowed the horse and took in the scene, searching for anything that seemed amiss. The scene was bathed in sunlight, just as it had been earlier that morning. Even with the warmth of the sun on her shoulders, a shiver traveled up her spine.

Something was wrong. The house was too quiet. Where were the children? And Cordelia, who'd offered to watch them during the marriage festivities?

Her mouth went dry, and her heart thudded with fear for her friend as she urged the horse to a gallop once more.

Gabe must have heard the thundering hoofbeats. He ran from the house, and even before she reached him, she could see his pale, disheveled appearance. And the blood on his shirt.

Bile rose in her throat as she drew back hard on the reins. The beast halted and reared. She patted his neck to calm him and then dismounted. Gabe ran to her and grasped her hands. His expression told her more than words ever could.

"Mary Rose?" she whispered.

His voice choked. "How—" His gaze shot to the horse, then back to her. "How did you know to come? She needs you. . . . We need you."

"Is she upstairs?" She didn't want to cry, so she kept her focus on his eyes instead of his blood-stained shirt. "How bad is it?"

"Go to her. Quickly." He squeezed her hands before letting go. When she glanced at the panting horse, he added, "I'll take care of him. Just go to her, please."

Lifting her skirts, Bronwyn raced up the front steps.

Mary Rose's face was the same shade of white as the pillow slip beneath her head. Her closed eyelids didn't flicker, and her soft breathing was almost inaudible.

Bronwyn bent over the bed and gently took Mary Rose's face between both hands. "Dearest one," she whispered, "can you hear me?" There was no response. She embraced her friend, kissed her cheek, and whispered again, "Mary Rose, it's Bronwyn. I'm here for you."

"She fell," Gabe said from the doorway. "She's been unconscious since. I don't think she even knows about the . . ." His voice choked, and he walked across the room. "I did the best I could . . . but the infant was so small, so delicate. He couldn't even take his first breath. I tried . . . I even tried to clear his throat with my fingers. Breathe air into him." He had reached the bed and came around to kneel beside it opposite Bronwyn. He reached for Mary

Rose's hand, kissed it, and, still holding it, dropped his head.

His voice was ragged as he whispered, "Forgive me, my love. I brought this on you . . . on us. Our baby . . . Too much to forgive . . . Oh, Mary Rose . . ."

Behind him, in the cradle he'd spent weeks working on in the barn, lay the baby's body, wrapped in a soft patchwork quilt that Bronwyn had sewn to celebrate the child's birth.

Bronwyn left Mary Rose's side and moved toward the cradle. She sat down beside it, her soiled and wrinkled skirt billowing around her. She gathered the baby into her arms, bringing its still-warm body close to her heart. For a moment, she just knelt there, at first rocking and humming a lullaby from her childhood, and then covering the baby's face with kisses, just as she knew Mary Rose would do.

The sting of tears rose in the back of her throat. Mary Rose had been there for her to help save the life of Little Grace, but while Mary Rose lay suffering, while her baby tried to make its way into the world, Bronwyn was primping in front of the mirror in the brides' room. She dropped her head and wept silently.

She opened the blanket and, holding the wee child in her lap, she touched each finger and toe, gently smoothed the baby's head, and examined his tiny seashell ears.

"I'll need a pan of warm water," she said to Gabe after a few minutes. "And some clean rags. It's time to prepare him."

Still on his knees, Gabe turned to her, his expression raw with grief. "I was so busy, first trying to save him, then so afraid I would lose Mary Rose," he said, "that I didn't get a good look at him."

She swallowed hard. "Would you like . . . to hold him?"

She found the answer in his eyes and laid the child in his arms. Gabe drew in a shuddering breath and drew the child close. He bowed his head, touching his forehead to his son's. His sobs seemed to come from someplace deep within his being, a sound almost unbearable to hear.

Bronwyn moved closer and wrapped her arms around him, her embrace encompassing both father and son. She laid her head against Gabe's heaving chest and found unexpected comfort as he leaned into her arms.

February 1846

Bronwyn laughed with the children when they made their confessions and briefly wondered what Gabe would say when he found out.

Her laughter was short-lived.

Enid rode up just as Mary Rose flicked the reins over the oxen to urge them through the snow.

"I overheard the children," she said, "and I'm surprised that you allowed them to disobey their father."

Mary Rose ignored her, as usual, and popped the whip over the backs of the oxen. They plodded forward, and Enid easily kept pace—and kept talking.

"It's occurred to me lately that some of the same techniques that I use with horses might also work with children."

There was a burst of laughter from the back of the wagon. Cordelia rolled her eyes, and Mary Rose pressed her lips together.

"It's hardly the same thing," Bronwyn said with a sigh. "And as I recall, you have no children of your own and thus no experience with such things."

Enid winced and looked down, obviously hurt by the words. Bronwyn immediately wished she could take them back. But for months, Enid had made no secret of the fact that she wanted Gabe to marry her and that when he did, she planned to take over the household as first wife.

The giggles continued in the back of the wagon, which lessened the seriousness of the moment—and also pointed out the truth of Enid's comment: the children did need a firmer hand. Bronwyn had caught Mary Grace imitating Enid more than once, had corrected her at least a dozen times for that and other offences. Yet from the sound of it, her daughter was at it again, entertaining the others with her newfound ability to mimic everyone from Brigham to Cordelia. It didn't help that Cordelia was delighted and actually gave her pointers.

She sighed and gave Enid a small smile. "Now isn't the time to speak of such things. The Saints have a lot to deal with aside from the errant behavior of children and training them as if they were . . ." A smile tugged at her lips, and she couldn't finish.

The reflection of the spangle of stars on the new-fallen snow gave just enough light for Bronwyn to see Enid's wide smile and the gleam of her wild silver-red mane. She was glad to see the woman wasn't offended until she spoke again . . .

"Have you told the others?" Enid's gaze was fixed on Mary Rose.

Mary Rose glanced at her but didn't answer.

"I suppose it falls to me, then, as many things in the household will in the future." Enid laughed, and the sound wasn't unkind. Rather, it seemed to hold a tone of authority.

Bronwyn leaned forward, tilting her head toward Enid so she wouldn't miss a word.

"We're getting married!" Enid's smile was joyful and triumphant. "Gabe and I are getting married as soon as we reach winter quarters. Mary Rose has finally agreed that it will be the best for us all."

Bronwyn's stomach clenched tight, and for a moment she couldn't breathe. She stared at Mary Rose. "You didn't . . . you couldn't have."

Enid's laughter rang out, and the thud of her high-stepping horse's hooves drummed as if in rhythm with the sound. "She did, bless her, she did." She looked as if nothing could quench her joy.

"Dearest," she said as Gabe rode toward her. "I've just let everyone know our good news."

Gabe's eyes went to Bronwyn first, and then to Mary Rose, who kept her gaze on the backs of the oxen. She popped the whip harder than she had before, frightening the beasts even though the leather tip didn't touch them.

The children had fallen silent as mice in the back of the wagon.

Gabe rode closer, his gaze now on Bronwyn again, searching her face as if looking to her for permission to love another. The look was so fleeting, she thought she had imagined it, but before he could speak, Enid rode up beside him.

"We'll discuss this later," she said to the three women, "and what it will mean to the running of our household." She flashed them another smile before riding off with Gabe.

"The running of our household?" Cordelia laughed heartily. "Methinks if she tries, she'll have quite a time of it, considering the likes of us." The older woman had come to live with them right after Grandfather's death. Though not a wife, she had become the matriarch of their family, full of love and laughter and spunk.

Bronwyn paid little attention to Cordelia's words or even to the rollicking laughter from the back of the wagon as Mary Grace perfectly mimicked Enid's parting words.

She was too busy thinking about Gabe, too filled with wonder at his expression when his eyes met hers, too surprised at the strange stirring of her heart. The look was different than any he'd given her before. It was almost as if he was falling in love with her.

Why now? She fell back against the wagon seat, trying to take in the jumbled emotions.

She'd accepted that he loved Mary Rose and didn't love her— at least not with the same kind of love. The relationship that they'd developed after they married had been based on physical attraction on his part and need on hers.

She craned to look back at Enid and Gabe riding toward the

back of the wagon train, silhouetted against the orange sky of the burning city of Nauvoo.

Never once, during all the times they'd come together, had he said he loved her. She had accepted it as a fact, because in truth, her heart had still belonged to Griffin. And she knew his belonged to Mary Rose.

Now, in that one lingering look, his eyes said he loved her. She was sure of it. She wanted to laugh and cry and have a hissy fit, as Cordelia would say, all at the same time.

Mary Rose looked over at her. "Are you all right?"

"I think so," she said.

"I'm sorry I couldn't tell you," she said.

"Why now? You said you would never give permission for him to marry her."

Mary Rose swallowed hard, and her expression softened. "It had to be now." She handed the reins to Cordelia and turned sideways on the seat. "I couldn't wait."

"You still haven't answered my question."

The wagon wheels creaked in the snow, the oxen snorted, and behind them, the voices of the other travelers could be heard. Finally Mary Rose spoke. "It's because of you."

"Me?"

"Because you are falling in love with Gabe. And he with you." Mary Rose gave her a small smile. "I've seen it in his face long before tonight."

They fell silent again, and then Mary Rose circled her arm around Bronwyn's shoulders. "I gave my permission for him to marry Enid to save you from the heartache of loving Gabriel MacKay."

© Scott Campbell

Diane Noble

Award-winning novelist **DIANE NOBLE** writes stories that tap into the secrets of the heart. Whether her characters live in twelfth-century Wales, nineteenth-century America, or in today's world, Diane explores their secret longings and loves, their heartaches and triumphs, and, ultimately, their redemption. She brings them to life, drawing on her own experiences and observations and digging deep into human emotions common to us all.

Beloved for her heartwarming novellas adapted to stage (*Come, My Little Angel* and *Phoebe*) and acclaimed for her award-winning novels (*The Veil, When the Far Hills Bloom*), Diane's works include romance, mysteries, suspense, and historical novels.

Diane and her historian husband enjoy exploring rugged nineteenth-century immigrant trails in their Jeep and "African safari" tent trailer, and they belong to various organizations that support the exploration and preservation of these trails. Diane is also member of Women Writing the West, an organization dedicated to the celebration of the role of women in the American West, today and yesterday.

Visit Diane's website at www.dianenoble.com and write to her at diane@dianenoble.com. You can also follow her on Facebook and Twitter.